COLOR ME *GREY*

ALSO BY MICHELLE JANINE ROBINSON
More Than Meets the Eye

Dear Reader:

Thanks for picking up a copy of the cutting-edge novel *Color Me Grey* by Michelle Janine Robinson. Michelle is one of my "discovered talents" via my numerous anthologies comprised of erotica from some of the strongest voices in the literary world today. Michelle has participated in many of them, her writing being so strong that I often made her stories the flagship of collections. "The Quiet Room" was the lead-in story for *Succulent: Chocolate Flava 2*, which spent six weeks on the *New York Times* Bestseller List.

I had often wondered when Michelle would write a full-length novel. Ironically, when I asked her about it, she had several ready to roll out for publication. That was a no-brainer for me, since I am one of her biggest fans. *Color Me Grey* has all the trademark signatures of Michelle's writing: vivid imagery, exuberant sexuality, and nail-biting drama. The main characters in this novel have a lot of issues, dating back to their childhood. As I often explore in my own books, what we endure during our youth directly reflects who we become as adults.

Having grown up in foster homes and then the Mannersville Home, Bridget and Jade are byproducts of what happens when children are left parentless; either by death or by neglect, such as drug abuse, prostitution, or lack of common sense and morals. Bridget is determined to make something out of her life, despite the circumstances. But she has one problem: a best friend who is more concerned with using her and, ultimately, destroying her. That is a powerful message. Many lives are ruined, not by known enemies, but by those closest to them; their friends and relatives.

Love is often a complicated thing and when Bridget seeks out the loves that she desires, it is a difficult and long journey.

That is a journey that many women can relate to; unless they are one of the rare ones who find love early on in life and stay married for fifty years. Michelle Robinson is a wonderful writer and I am sure that you will enjoy this novel, as well as her next one: *More Than Meets The Eye*.

Thanks for the support of the Strebor authors. To find me on the web, please go to www.eroticanoir.com or join my online social network, www.planetzane.org.

Blessings,

Zane

Zane
Publisher
Strebor Books International
www.simonandschuster.com/streborbooks

COLOR ME GREY

MICHELLE JANINE ROBINSON

STREBOR BOOKS
NEW YORK LONDON TORONTO SYDNEY

SBI

Strebor Books
P.O. Box 6505
Largo, MD 20792
http://www.streborbooks.com

ISBN 978-1-59309-294-8
ISBN 978-1-4391-8266-6 (e-book)
LCCN 2010925101

First Strebor Books trade paperback edition June 2010

Cover design: www.mariondesigns.com
Cover photograph: © Keith Saunders/Marion Designs

10 9 8 7 6 5 4 3 2 1

Manufactured in the United States of America

For information regarding special discounts for bulk purchases,
please contact Simon & Schuster Special Sales at 1-866-506-1949
or business@simonandschuster.com

The Simon & Schuster Speakers Bureau can bring authors to your
live event. For more information or to book an event, contact the
Simon & Schuster Speakers Bureau at 1-866-248-3049 or visit our
website at www.simonspeakers.com.

ACKNOWLEDGMENTS

For many of us there have been those moments when we have suddenly felt as though we exited from a dark room and suddenly, inexplicably, been bathed in the brightest of lights—those wonderful, eye-opening, *"aha"* moments! The birth of my first novel, *Color Me Grey*, has been one of those moments.

No true journey would ever be complete without re-flection. So, it is no surprise that my voyage through the publishing process has been met with deep contemplation of how I got here; all the hills and valleys that not only run parallel with the completion of this book, but also with my life.

I've regaled readers with tales of the deeply intimate physical and emotional interactions of my characters, only to be reminded that, once stepping outside the pages of a book, so many of us touch without feeling, listen without hearing, speak without caring and look without ever truly seeing. Too often it becomes much too easy to only place value on those relationships to which we feel *"vested."* It has long been my belief that if we considered each and every interaction with another human being a *"relationship,"* then we would truly become a kinder, gentler human race. From the very first moment I was born, my relationships have guided me to where I find myself today; and for that I would like to thank as many people as these pages will hold.

First and foremost, I would like to thank my *amazing* sons, Justin and Stefan. From the very first moment I laid my eyes upon you, you have challenged me to be a better version of myself. And, as you blaze the trail from young boys to young men, I am hopeful that the mistakes I have made with you have not been too plentiful and that the lessons I have taught you afford you a lifetime of rewards. Always know that my confidence in you is boundless and my love for you is unconditional—and will last *forever*.

To my mom, Sylvia Payne, for endowing me with the deepest of appreciation for words and for your unique and beneficial spelling drills. Where would I be without you? You, Mom, deserve an award for *all* that you were able to do.

To my Aunt Dot, Dorothy Tillery; my travel companion, my friend, my confidante and so much more—you were the very first person on this planet to ever call me beautiful. Those few words have helped keep me on track, even when my self-esteem was faltering. I don't say it near as much as I should, but I appreciate you more than you know.

To all my cousins, Linda Tillery, Cynthia Tillery, Bruce Tillery, Bryan Tillery, Nicole Tillery, Tiffany Tillery, Kayla, Kendall, Maya and Chaise—The saying goes that "you can't choose your family," but if I could I wouldn't change a thing. Linda, everyone's rock, what on earth would I do without you? Cindy, you have taught me what it feels like to be true to yourself. I'm not as good at it as you are (yet), but I'm working on it. Bruce and Bryan—I am proud each and every day that my sons are able to have you both as role models. And, for that I am eternally grateful. Nicole—you are all grown up and I can't lose you in FAO Schwarz anymore. But, not only are you a grown-up, but even with the great divide between our ages, *I* have learned so very much from *you*.

To my brothers, Stephen and Oliver—You both are my image of what a man should be; gentle, kind, chivalrous, confident, independent, giving and full of purpose. I could never have come close to picking better brothers than you two, if I tried. And, as if I am not blessed enough to have you both in my life, you each bring with you the most incredible wives! Laura and Ulla, I love you both as sisters. Laura, you are such a wonderful mother! It had to be said. My nephews Depri and Savion are a shining reflection of all that you are. I love you, boys!

To my GIRLS!—The ones who are always there to cry with me, laugh with me and who know where ALL the bones are buried: Christina Williams, Tarra Taylor, Jacqueline Charles, Yvonne Landy and Marciala Remouns, what on earth would I do without you all? I don't know, but I would probably be in a LOAD of trouble. Chris, every time I pick up that phone so you can help "walk me through" life, I think, God, I really need to give more to this relationship—because I get back *so* very much more, I often feel like I'm a bad friend. I know you say that I give to you as well, but from where I'm sitting I feel like my best friend is Jesus or something. You never seem to need near as much as I do. You are the most unselfish person I know. I think maybe in 2010 I'll make it my goal to work on giving back even half of what you give to me each and every day (that'll be a nice start). Tarra, people use that line all the time—you know the one, she's beautiful inside and out. Well, in your case it really is the truth. You are the most positive person I know and your beauty on the outside is evenly matched with that on the inside. Walk that catwalk, GIRL!!!! To Jackie (far away in miles, but never in my heart)—What can I say, for so long you were my teacher. You have been not only a dear friend, but a mentor. You pointed me in the right direction to help me to become not only poised, but learned as well. Yvonne—from the very first moment I met you, I thought, WOW! She is so beautiful. It was so refreshing to learn that the beauty outside was nothing compared to the beauty, humor and kindness, inside. And, to you Marciala—It's hard to believe that we are only a few years apart in age. When we first met, you seemed so much more mature and worldly than me.

You welcomed me into the fold of your family and made me feel protected and accepted.

I have been lucky enough to have a healthy and sound well of support to draw from—mothers, whom I have always considered the *best of the best*, women I have looked to whenever I was in doubt about *how* to best parent. Thank you Michelle Gairy-Tillery, Angela Sanders-Glover, Sharla Callender, Christina Williams, Laura Robinson, Debra Miami and Marciala Remouns for always being the kind of mothers I strive to be. If I am only half the mother each of you are, I will have lived up to the privilege (not the right) granted to me as a mother, and to hopefully be as great at it as you all have always been.

To Jahnelle Moniquette and Maurice Moniquette—Life is often such (as you both will learn as you soon enter adulthood), that often we feel we have fallen short of all we could have been. Often I wish I had been a better stepmother to you both. And, while none of us can truly turn back the hands of time, if I can't be your mother, I would love to be both of your friends—if you let me.

To all of the writers whom I have learned from, laughed with and grown from, Zane (*Total Eclipse of the Heart*), Nane Quartay (*Come Get Some*), Rachel Kramer Bussel (*Tasting Him*), Jasmin L. Harry (*Twisted Gemini*), Keeb Knight (*Swing*) and Amari Yarbrough (*Enigma's Child*)—Thank you all from the bottom of my heart. I still consider myself a newbie, but I am so lucky to have all of you pros to learn from.

To Charmaine Parker—You are an absolute Saint! Thank you! Thank you! Thank you! I know it can't be easy to work with anyone who is learning *everything* for the first time. And, for that, I thank you again for always being so gracious, patient and understanding with me. One down and two to go…But, at least I'm learning. WHEW!!!!

To the people I spend the largest portion of my day with (even more than my family), all those at C&M who have given of their time and encouragement—Rosemary Andress, Alfia McIver, Nicole Welch, Fawn Lloyd, Eleanor Graham, Raffaella Giuliano and Shantay Smith (who helped kick my butt into gear). And, to my *favorite* attorney, Olivier Antoine (and no, Olivier, I'm not just saying that because my review is coming up—hint, hint), thanks for graciously offering to look over my contract for me.

To Clinton Morgan—It's hard to believe we've known each other over 30 years—and after all these years I still feel like that 15-year old girl in awe of her mentor. I am so very proud to have you in my life. You've taught me the meaning of the word perseverance.

To Cecil Moniquette—In all my heart I know there will come a time when we can get past the failings of human emotion and just be friends, be parents to our children, be still. I thank you for always knowing that I had it in me to be all that I want (and need) to be.

To Charles Trovato—Isn't it amazing how relationships

blossom just *exactly* when they're supposed to? You have come to be my greatest calm amidst the raging storm that is so often my life. There's nothing like a good ole rescue to help kick a friendship into gear (but, what about two rescues?) I know you're reading this and don't know what the heck I'm talking about. But you will.

And, to all my readers, I thank you from the bottom of my heart for all your support.

If there is anyone I have forgotten, please know it was not through lack of caring, but most probably, through lack of sleep.

I hope you all enjoy *Color Me Grey*.

Love,

Michelle

Bridget stood high atop the roof of her former luxury high-rise, fully prepared to jump and take the twins with her. Dressed in a black Dolce & Gabbana suit and a black pair of Manolo Blahnik four-inch sling-backs that lent a regal air to her five-foot-eight frame, her attire was little more than remnants of a lifestyle she would inevitably leave behind; dead or alive. Even in despair, Bridget was striking. Her rich, mahogany complexion and flawless skin endowed her with a natural beauty that other women often envied. Bridget had remained slim, even after giving birth to her twins. She was twenty-five years old today and despite the hard life she had endured, she had changed very little. Although Bridget had not had an easy life, somehow, the ugliness she saw was never reflected in her eyes. Bridget's ochre-colored eyes were soft and inviting and her full, sexy lips were what men's dreams were made of. Yet, Bridget had never thought of herself as beautiful, or even pretty for that matter, which was probably the reason she never saw any of this coming. In her wildest dreams she could never have anticipated the havoc unchecked resentment and obsession could yield. That is why she was here today. She had been naïve and trusting. Now she was forced to consider not only her fate, but that of her three-month-old son; Jacob, and daughter, Jasmine.

There was no doubt in Bridget's mind that life was over for her. Her pain was much more than she could stand and, even if she used the logic that she had these beautiful little babies to live for, what did she have to offer them? The answer was nothing—nothing at all. As her grandmother used to say, "She had no pot to piss in, nor window to throw it out of." She had lost everything: her home; her husband; her peace of mind. She had no one and those she trusted the most had betrayed her. She was alone. The only thing left to lose, besides her two beautiful babies, was her freedom, and it was only a matter of time before she lost that as well. She would be going to prison for murder and she knew that, with her history, she would never be able to survive that. There was no statute of limitations on murder. However, the fate of her little boy and girl were still at question. She had to do the right thing for them. But, did she have the right to decide whether they lived or died? The reality was she was all they had and if she were dead, or in prison, what would happen to them? Maybe they might be lucky and get adopted by some nice couple and live happily ever after, or maybe they would be separated; brother and sister who might never even know of the other's existence.

Given the circumstances of their birth, that was more than merely possible; it was very likely. The parents who adopted one baby might not want both; especially given the obvious difference between the two. They were twins, but the degree of separation between them was readily unmistakable. Suppose they were tossed in some horrible foster home somewhere, like she had been, time and time again. Or even worse, what if they ended up with the very people that had brought their mother to this catastrophic crossroad? Bridget was convinced this was the best decision for all concerned. She would send her little angels back to heaven, where they belonged. She would have liked to think that she would be with them in heaven, but given the current state of affairs, she wasn't sure that was where *she* would be going.

Happy Birthday to me, she thought to herself. Bridget stepped closer to the edge of the roof and suddenly the voice of one of her destroyers splintered her thoughts.

"Bridget, don't!"

CHAPTER ONE
MANNERSVILLE

Seventeen-year-old Jade Smith sauntered into the room she shared with her roommate Bridget Grey, who had turned eighteen that day. Jade's frizzy red hair, fair skin, and freckles reminded Bridget of a Raggedy Ann doll she had once owned. Her hourglass figure did not. Her measurements were 38-24-38 and Jade lorded those measurements over men like they were money in the bank. And, as far as Jade was concerned, they were. While Bridget disliked being noticed by men, Jade reveled in it. She fully intended to use her body to get anything and everything that she wanted. Bridget couldn't imagine any woman selling herself that short; especially her best friend. Bridget silently hoped Jade would change. Jade, on the other hand, had every intention of seeing to it that Bridget *did* change.

"Hey, girl. Buster gave me something for you. It's some of that nasty-ass rice pudding you like! I don't know how the hell you can eat that shit," Jade said.

"Jade, I told you not to take anything from Buster; especially not for me. He looks at me like I'm a god-damned steak or something."

Jade and Bridget had both been at Mannersville Group Home for almost six years. They had both been born addicted to heroin and had both been forced to endure the nasty withdrawal symptoms babies like them suffered. It took a special kind of parent to adopt such a baby. Such parents never came along for Jade and Bridget. They were both counting the days until they could strike out on their own. Bridget was a good student and wanted more than anything to go to college someday.

Jade had every intention of going back to her mother when she got out; even though it had been resolved that, as long as she was a minor, she would probably never be allowed to go back to her mother legally. But no one could do anything about where she lived when she turned eighteen. It didn't matter to Jade that her mother was still addicted to heroin and hookin' on Hunts Point. As far as Jade knew, her father could have been any one of the many johns her mother had encountered over the years. Yet, all she talked about was getting out of Mannersville Group Home and getting back to the Bronx. Over the years, she often tried to talk Bridget into escaping with her, assuring her that her mother would take care of both of them. When she was younger, it never even occurred to her that if her mother were truly able to care for her, she wouldn't have ended up here in the first place. But, as time went on, Jade got tougher and stronger and her logic was that she didn't need *anyone* to care for her, including her mother—she could care for herself. Fortunately, Bridget's level head won out. She convinced Jade that running away would be the worst thing they could do. She assured Jade that if they ran, they would be running the rest of their lives and neither of them wanted that. Bridget's mom had died of a drug overdose almost a year after Bridget was born. Her dad, a drug dealer, was killed not long after that by the people he was selling for, when he got caught sampling a little too much of the product. She had a grandmother who had visited her and tried on a couple of occasions to get her out of the numerous foster homes she lived in. But her grandmother had gambling and health problems and could barely maintain a stable home for herself, much less a small child born addicted to heroin. When Bridget was ten years old, the possibility of her grandmother raising her was erased as an option. Her last remaining relative, her mother's mom, Grandma Hilliard, died of complications related to diabetes at the age of 58, young by U.S. standards, but not so young when you've lived a lifetime in the 'hood. Bridget was allowed to attend the funeral and grieved as best she could for a family member that she barely knew.

Bridget and Jade were as different as two people could be. But, Jade was the closest thing to family that Bridget had known, and she wanted more than anything to keep her safe. Bridget was afraid that, without her guidance, Jade was headed down the same road each of their parents had traveled. Bridget made herself a solemn vow that she would never, ever, be her mother, and neither would Jade be hers, if Bridget had anything to say about it. Bridget was eighteen today and, in six months, Jade would be eighteen as well. They would both be free.

"Why you trippin', Bridget?" Jade asked. "Buster ain't so bad. He likes you."

"Buster is a grown-ass man. He's gotta be at least forty. He's old enough to be my father. He fucks around with some of these other girls, but I ain't down with that. My shit is precious and I'm not givin' it up to the first loser that wants it."

"You ain't givin' it up, period," Jade whispered under her breath.

Bridget heard every word she said.

"No, I'm not, until I'm ready. I got plans and they don't include being a pregnant teenage mother or selling myself short. I want more than that."

"Check you out, Miss Thang. I'm only tryin' to help you out. Buster helps a lot of the girls here. I've heard he's even been known to turn his head and allow girls to sneak out on occasion. And, if you're nice to him, I'm sure he'll be nice to *us*."

Bridget had heard through the grapevine that one of the many times Jade had run away, she had been able to do so after giving one of the workers at the home a blow job. She wondered if it was Buster. Not only that, Jade had shared with her countless stories of her sexual encounters with various foster parents and group home workers. She even thought she heard her say once that she worked the streets with her mother the last time she was home. Bridget often hoped they were simply stories that Jade had dreamed up to entertain her, but she suspected that at least some of these stories probably had a ring of truth to them.

"I'll tell you what, if you feel that strongly about it, why don't *you* be nice to Buster for *us*?" Bridget offered.

"One very important reason," Jade answered. "He doesn't like me; he likes you."

"I'm sorry, Jade, but there are some things I won't do; not even for you. Besides," Bridget added, "I've got much more important things to think about; like what kind of cake I want for my birthday."

Each of the children at Mannersville got their choice of birthday cakes every year. Bridget's favorite was chocolate chip cookie dough. It was Sunday, June 15, 1991. The sun was shining, the birds were chirping, and it was her birthday. She was eighteen today! Bridget was especially excited this year, because she would finally leave the numerous "temporary" homes she had lived in and get on with the adventure of living her life. Over the years, she had felt as though she were living in limbo; never truly belonging to anyone, or anything. That is, until she had met Jade. Even though Jade would not be leaving for at least six months, since her birthday was not until December 29, Bridget had no intention of forgetting about her best friend. She had it all planned out.

She had already gotten her diploma last year, thanks to her dedication to her studies, and she was fully prepared to get a job working as a typist or secretary. She had taken typing classes and transcription classes, preparing for her new life. She was going to get a job and a place where they *both* could live, which would be waiting for Jade as soon as she left Mannersville.

Jade, on the other hand, fully expected Bridget to forget about her as soon as she left, and obsessed over it night and day. She had been a horrible student and would be lucky if she could get a job at McDonald's when she got out of there. Bridget was hoping to go to law school one day and she had fine-tuned her researching skills by finding out all that she could about the emancipation laws of New York City. However, Jade had done everything she could to discourage Bridget from attempting to leave at age sixteen. But, there was nothing she could do now that Bridget was eighteen; she was leaving and that was that.

Bridget was looking forward to this birthday more than any other she had ever had. It seemed to her that a world of possibilities was waiting for her, like an open door. She gorged herself on lots of cake and ice-cream and opened her presents. Jade told Bridget there was a present for her in their room, but that she should wait until they got back there before she opened it. Bridget agreed. Lights out was typically at ten, but Mama Dixon, the operator of Mannersville, allowed them to stay up until eleven on birthday nights. Bridget and Jade headed back to their room around ten-thirty. Bridget couldn't wait to open her present.

"Go on, open it," Jade urged.

Bridget ripped open the modestly wrapped, ninety-nine-cent store paper from the package. Inside there was a small, burgundy, velvet jewelry box. When Bridget opened the box, she was surprised to find a beautiful gold, heart-shaped necklace, with what looked like diamonds encircling the heart. Bridget assumed it was gold-plated and that the stones were cubic zircons. After all, there was no way Jade could afford such an expensive necklace, if it were real. She loved the necklace, no matter what it was made of, because it came from Jade, her sister-friend; the only real family she had ever known.

Tears welled up in Bridget's eyes.

"Now don't go startin' that shit," Jade said.

Bridget wrapped her arms around Jade and hugged her with all of her might.

Between the excitement of the birthday party and all the cake and ice-cream, Bridget was asleep in no time. At about three in the morning, Bridget was stirred awake by light filtering through the open doorway. Someone had entered the room. She assumed that it was Jade coming back from the bathroom or something, but she quickly discovered that it was not. The person crossed the room and sat on her bed. It was Buster and he reeked of alcohol.

"Buster, you know if Mama Dixon finds out you're in my room after lights out, you're going to be in big trouble."

He sat there, leering at her. Bridget suddenly became aware of what she was wearing. She was wearing an extremely transparent white T-shirt, no bra, and a pair of sweats. Her blanket was covering her up to her waist, but her upper body was noticeably uncovered.

"Whatcha' talkin' about Mama Dixon for?" Buster slurred. "I came to give you the rest of your birthday present. Three o'clock on the dot; like you told me to." Buster waved in the direction of Jade's empty bed and the clock on the bedside table.

Bridget tried to maneuver herself out of the bed, but Buster had to weigh at least two hundred-sixty pounds and he was sitting on the blanket, almost on top of her. Bridget stared at the door to the room, waiting for Jade. Where on earth could she be? *Maybe she's in the bathroom*, Bridget thought to herself. Yeah, she was probably in the bathroom, which meant she would be back any minute now. She didn't think Buster was dangerous, but she recognized the look; she had been dodging that expression in one foster home or another for most of her life. When you combined that with alcohol, the end result could be unspeakable. Many girls (and boys) she had known through the years had fallen prey.

Bridget tried talking to Buster as calmly as possible; even though she was getting more frightened with each passing second.

"Buster, what are you talking about? Three o'clock? I didn't tell you to meet me here."

"Yeah, you did. You said three, and it's three now." He glanced at the clock. "It's past three; it's three-thirteen, and I got something *real* special for you."

Buster moved the covers out of the way and fell on top of Bridget's body. He was like dead weight. He started pulling at her breasts; pushing his hand between her legs and fumbling with the waistband of her sweat pants, trying to remove them.

"Buster, stop! Just stop it! Please stop, Buster! If you leave now, I won't say a thing to Mama Dixon! Just leave! STOP!!!!"

While he was busy nibbling her breasts through her T-shirt, Bridget tried to scream, to no avail. Buster covered her mouth and no amount of struggling could free her from his grip. His hand against her mouth was like a great big slab of beef, imprisoning her. He forced her sweat pants down to her ankles before he invaded her chaste soul, pounding into her again and again, while he muttered through the horrible stench of his alcohol-induced breath, "Happy birthday, baby. Happy birthday," punctuating every word with violent thrusts that Bridget thought might literally tear her apart. He took from her the one thing she felt separated her from the ugliness of the world she was born into. He stole her most precious gift, one she planned to hold in reserve for someone she loved and who loved her in earnest. Grandma Hilliard always told her she might not have a pot to piss in, but she had her chastity and her dignity. Now, in Bridget's mind, she had lost both. Buster Williams had seen to that. Then, suddenly, it was over. Within a matter of minutes, her life had been irrevocably changed.

He climbed off Bridget and stood up. He reached down and wiped the tears that were streaming down her face, and looked at the blood-stained sheets, remnants of the innocence he had deprived her of. Bridget couldn't understand why he looked so confused, or was it regret at the monstrous thing he had done. Maybe that was the look she had recognized.

"What's wrong, baby? I wanted to give you the rest of your birthday present, like you said. What did I do wrong? Is it because it was your first time? Don't worry; it'll be better the next time."

In that split second, Bridget was like a person sleep-walking through a horrible nightmare. All she heard through her haze were the words "the next time." She leapt out of bed and picked up the desk chair in the corner of the room and began hitting Buster with it over and over again, until he fell to the floor. The element of surprise and the alcohol worked against him. He was powerless. She hit him so hard that the chair leg broke off in her hands, revealing several large rusty nails. She used the protruding nails to beat Buster Williams in the chest until he lay there motionless.

Bridget was soaked in blood, and in shock, when Jade returned to the room. Jade walked in and immediately noticed Buster's prone form. She quickly spun into action.

"Bridget, we need to leave. *Now!* Mama Dixon and the others will be looking for Buster soon. Bridget, you've got to snap out of it. We have to leave *right now!*"

Bridget stared off into space, mumbling, "Never again."

Jade decided Bridget would need a shock to set her "right," so she did what she had always seen people do on TV. She slapped Bridget across the face and, amazingly, it worked. Bridget snapped out of it. She looked around the room, suddenly aware of her predicament.

"Oh my God," she shrieked. "What have I done?"

Jade scrambled around the room, picking up this and that. She grabbed both of their duffel bags from the closet and began throwing things in them at random; her clothes, Bridget's clothes, anything her hand could get a hold of and that would fit into the bags. Then she reached down and started going through Buster's pants pockets.

"What are you doing, Jade? Don't touch him!"

"We have to, Bridget. Otherwise, what are we going to do for money? He obviously doesn't need it anymore."

Bridget stared at Buster's body, dumbfounded. She couldn't believe that she had actually taken another life. She had killed someone; a person she had lived with every single day of her life for the last six years, yet knew so little about. Bridget was suddenly consumed with the thought that if she knew something about him, somehow that would lessen the blow; absolve her of her sin. Maybe he truly was evil.

She looked through his jacket pockets, searching for

evidence of his monstrous existence, and found his wallet, hoping to find something, anything; and that she did. She found a picture of herself. She had given that picture to Jade over a year ago. Jade's mother had cleaned herself up and had petitioned the court to have Jade come and live with her. After much effort, the court was convinced that she was capable of caring for Jade and she went to live with her. Bridget hated being separated from her, but she knew how much Jade wanted to be with her mom, so she had tried to be strong. She gave Jade a picture of her and told her to keep it so she wouldn't forget about her. It lasted all of six months before Child Protective Services brought Jade back to Mannersville. Buster must have stolen the picture from Jade. Also in the wallet was a receipt for $375 from Lazlows Jewelers. Was that all his life amounted to; some unhealthy obsession with her, a lone jewelry receipt and some meager cash? Jade grabbed the cash out of Bridget's hand and counted it.

"Good," Jade said. "Two hundred forty-eight dollars; enough to get us to where we have to go."

Jade took the ring of keys off of Buster's belt and quietly snuck out of the room, with Bridget in tow. Jade had it all figured out. They would quietly exit the building, get to Buster's car, and drive out of there, straight to her mother's place on Westchester Avenue. They were in Middletown. It would only take them about two hours to get there.

The great thing about Mannersville was that there was very little security besides Buster and a few other workers. All they needed was a car; and Jade was sure Buster's brand-new '91 Honda Accord was parked somewhere outside. She seemed to remember him mentioning that it was red. They would have to get outside and find the car before anyone realized they were gone. Otherwise, it would be too late.

Just as Jade predicted, Buster's car was in the parking lot. She took the keys and started the car.

"Jade, I think I should turn myself in. Buster raped me. I could tell the police what happened and nothing would change. I'll be leaving here in a couple of weeks anyway. We could go back to the way things were. And eventually we can put all of this behind us. Just forget."

"First of all, sweetie, you'll never forget what happened tonight. It was your first time. No one forgets their first time. And, second, what makes you think *anyone* is going to believe Buster raped you? He's an employee of Mannersville Group Home and you're just one of its throwaways; a throwaway who killed one of the people in charge of maintaining order at the home. They'll fry you. No, they'll fry *us*. Because, like it or not, I'm now a part of this. I escaped with you; I stole a car. I'm an accessory after the fact. And, if you go down, I go down with you. Are you prepared to take responsibility for that?"

Bridget hadn't thought of it that way. She didn't want Jade to get into trouble because of her. Maybe she was right. No one would believe her. She was what Jade said; a nobody, a throwaway.

"Okay, Jade. I'll do whatever you think is best."

The angle Jade was sitting at didn't allow Bridget to see the smirk on Jade's face when she heard Bridget give in. If she had, she might have run from that car, straight back to Mannersville and given herself up.

It suddenly occurred to Jade that this might be easier than she thought. That's how scared Bridget was.

"We're going to go to my mother's and lay low for a while. They may come looking for us there and they may not. You have no relatives and my mom is my only relative, so if they look at all, that's where they'll look. So, we won't stay long—just long enough to get our shit together."

"What do you mean, if they look at all? Of course they'll look. I killed a man."

"Think about it, Bridget. Buster was a lowly, minimum wage-earning group home worker. He was one step up from a janitor. And, he was black. The New York City Police Department ain't lodging some city-wide manhunt for his killer. After a couple of months, Buster Williams will be a distant memory and his death will join the ranks of other unimportant, unsolved cases."

It was 7:00 a.m. when they arrived at Chantal Smith's run-down Westchester Avenue apartment. Jade knocked on the door. She used to have a key, but she had lost it a long time ago. She knocked hard, in case her mom was in one of her many stupors. She wasn't.

As soon as Jade knocked, she could hear her mother yell. "Who the fuck is knockin' on my door this time of the mornin'; like they ain't got no goddamn sense?"

"It's me, Ma," Jade answered.

Chantal swung the door open. You would think that after at least a year of mother and daughter not seeing each other, there would be some display of affection. But, there was none at all.

"Whatcha doin' here?" Chantal asked. "They let you out?"

"No, Ma, they didn't let us out. You got anything to eat? And, then we can talk about it."

"I ain't got shit to eat. You want somethin' to eat, you betta' go git it yourself. We can *talk* all you want, but you can only stay 'til Friday. I get my best customers on Saturday and I won't have you two tenderonis messing up my shit. You hear me?"

"Yeah, Ma, no problem. We'll be out of here before Saturday."

Bridget could never get used to women like Chantal. She was probably only in her late thirties or so, but, when you looked at her, empty, aged eyes were staring back at you. Chantal Smith had been used up. She was like one of those zombies you saw in late-night horror movies. Her body was still moving, but there was something vacant about her existence. Yet, the johns who frequented her broken-down hovel of an apartment and nearby Hunts Point Market didn't seem to care.

Looking around, Bridget could see that the rats and

roaches were the true tenants here at 1675 Westchester Avenue, and Chantal Smith was a tolerated guest. Bridget wondered where she and Jade would sleep. The walls and ceiling were coated with black mold and appeared to have been white at some time, but now could only be described as gray. There was a brown and yellow plaid couch in the living room with stains all over it. The kitchen housed a rickety farmhouse-style table with four chairs in various degrees of disrepair. Bridget's best guess was that the odors she smelled were probably coming from the bathroom, which she was afraid to see.

It frightened her to think of what was living in the mattresses, or what she might end up sleeping with, if she made a bed on the floor. Not even the worst foster home she had ever lived in had been as bad as this. She wondered why Jade would ever want to come back.

"And what's your name, honey?" Chantal asked.

"Oh…" Bridget stammered. "I'm Bri-Bridget…Bridget Grey."

"Yeah, sorry, Ma. This is Bridget. This is my girl! I don't know what I would've done without her in that place."

"Shit! You say 'that place' like it was so fuckin' bad. I've seen Mannersville. It wasn't that bad. Why'd you leave anyway?"

"We had to, Ma. Bridget got in some trouble and I couldn't leave her out there like that," Jade responded.

"What's up? Now you your brother's keeper an' shit? Bridget betta' wise up and learn how ta' take care of herself. Where you from anyway, honey? Sutton Place or somethin'?" Chantal chuckled.

Jade went into her mother's hall closet and found some bed linens. The couch was one of those sleeper sofas, so Bridget and Jade pulled it out and changed the linens. Despite the scurry of rats running across the floor, Bridget was so tired that she managed to sleep. After Bridget dozed off, Chantal got busy going through Bridget's things to see if there was anything of value. Her heart skipped a beat when she saw that trademark burgundy velvet Lazlows Jewelers box. She could recognize a Lazlows Jewelers box anywhere. Lazlows was one of those upscale jewelers. A few times Chantal had considered trying to stick up one of those jewelry places, but had chickened out. She was a sometimes prostitute, sometimes street corner stick-up kid. Chantal tried not to mess with the big-time. As far as Chantal was concerned, she knew her place; and the big-time wasn't her place.

Meanwhile, Jade was propped up watching her mom, too keyed up to sleep. She wasn't worried about Bridget's things, nor did she really care. Besides, Bridget didn't own anything of any real value. The most expensive thing Bridget owned was that heart-shaped necklace around her neck. If she only knew how much it actually cost or where it came from. Bridget assumed it was from her and therefore, probably thought it was worthless. Jade was amazed at how someone so smart could be so dumb.

Bridget had been at the top of their English class, yet couldn't recognize cunning wording to save her life. Jade played that game with Bridget often, with 100 percent success. She told Jade there was a present for her in their room. She didn't say it was from her. With all the shit Bridget had been through, she was still a bit naïve. Some time in the hood would solve that. They needed money and the best way for poor, teenage girls to get money was with their bodies, that and Jade's own artful twist on "the game." During the last year or so at Mannersville, Jade had worked out the plans in her mind for a hustle that she was confident would net *big* money. She had planned it down to the very last detail. Jade already knew the score, but she would talk to Chantal about how to introduce Bridget to reality.

Although her mother said they could only stay a few days, she knew her mother would be more than willing to help, if it meant her getting a dollar or two thrown in her direction. It would be tough convincing Bridget to work the streets, but work the streets she would. It was the only way her plan could work. And, at least she was no longer a virgin. While at Mannersville, Jade wondered how long Bridget would hold onto that little "treasure" anyway. At least now that wasn't standing in the way. Bridget honestly believed someday her muthafuckin' prince was gonna come along. The girl was seriously deluded. Jade had big plans and none of them involved a prince on a fuckin' white horse. Jade's sleepless nights at Mannersville were spent planning. Her plans involved long-term money. She had no intention of being satisfied with that chump change her mother was getting.

Chantal was the only mother Jade had so she couldn't help being drawn to her. But she couldn't stomach weak women and often felt her mother would be better off if someone put her out of her misery. Bridget reminded Jade of her mother. They were both too easily influenced; her mother by drugs and Bridget by other people. Very often Jade would be in the middle of manipulating Bridget into something or another and she would hold her breath, almost hoping that Bridget might actually wise up and match wits with her. More than anything, Jade longed for a challenging adversary. But, Bridget was too fuckin' trusting; and that would be her eventual downfall.

If there was one thing Jade had learned, both on the streets and off: No one, but no one, was ever to be trusted. The only person you could trust in life was yourself. If it were not for Jade's planning, neither her nor Bridget would be here—exactly where *she* wanted them to be— where fast money could be made. It occurred to her that, in some respects, Bridget was actually lucky she had a friend like her. If it weren't for her, Bridget would be busy preparing for a life that would never, ever, be hers. She was constantly walkin' around with those goddamn law books. People like them didn't grow up and become lawyers. She would try and fail and find herself flipping burgers somewhere. That shit was for suckers.

What she planned involved making real money. After all, that was all it was about; the Benjamins. Besides, she would be helping Bridget, too. It was high time she stopped foolin' herself with ridiculous dreams that would never come true. That kind of life didn't happen for people like them and the sooner Bridget figured that out, the better.

For days Bridget waited for the police to come knocking on Chantal Smith's door and cart her off to prison. The worst Jade would probably get would be aiding and abetting, but Bridget knew she would be going to prison for murder. It wouldn't matter that Buster had raped her. The first question they would ask is: Why didn't you run or scream? And, what would her answer be? She was out of her head? She was scared? In a nutshell, it amounted to no answer at all.

Bridget wondered if the dreams would ever stop. Each night it was like living the experience over and over again. Each night she would drift off to sleep and be awakened by the stench of alcohol and the horrible weight crushing her, depriving her of oxygen; and just when she thought she could no longer breathe, she would wake up, drenched in her own sweat. She thought of that old cliché about time healing all wounds and hoped it was more than a cliché.

Sleep time had always been a time for her to dream; beautiful, incredible dreams of the future, but now her dreams were plagued with horror and the overwhelming sense that she lost so much more than she could ever get back. And it wasn't merely her virginity she was thinking of. She was afraid she lost her ability to trust. Bridget was having a dream in which she was chasing a small piece of paper down the street as huge gusts of wind blew it further and further away from her. She chased the piece of paper and eventually was able to plant one of her feet on top of it to keep it from moving. But as she was about to bend down and pick the piece of paper up, it began to change form, and shift into something else. As she reached for it, it suddenly grew into this ugly, horrible creature bent on her destruction. It chased her as she ran on and on, trying to escape, gasping for breath. Just as she thought it might grab her, she woke up.

Someone was shaking her; *really* shaking her.

"What are you gonna do? Sleep all damn day and night?" Chantal was shouting as she shook Bridget awake.

Bridget slowly awakened and rubbed her eyes. Jade and Chantal were both standing over her. She looked at the clock on the moldy walls. She couldn't believe she slept that long. When she went to sleep this morning, the sun was shining and it was sometime around eight. It was now dark out and close to nine forty-five. She slept for nearly fourteen hours. She focused her eyesight as she slowly became fully awake. That's when she realized how much Jade and her mother resembled one another. Jade was wearing a red pleather micro-mini with zippers on each side, that looked more like a bikini than a skirt.

At the top she wore a black bustier, or was it a bra? Bridget wasn't sure which. She had on red stilettos and was carrying a red fur purse. Jade's mom, Chantal, had on a leopard print lycra dress, which was equally as short as Jade's red skirt, yet somehow it looked even more vulgar on Chantal.

Although Chantal was very slim, probably no more than 135 pounds, her legs were plagued with the ugliest-looking stretch marks she had ever seen. They almost looked like scars, they were so violently etched on her legs. Also, Chantal was a slim woman with a huge gut that reminded Bridget of those starving children you saw on TV. Both Jade and Chantal were wearing Tina Turner-type wigs. Only, their wigs were clearly very, very cheap. Jade's was jet black and Chantal's was burgundy. Under different circumstances Bridget might have found humor in this display, but somehow right here and now, none of this was funny.

"Get your ass up out that bed. It's time to earn your keep," Chantal said.

Chantal was overbearing and more than a little frightening. She was like her daughter, but somehow different. Although Jade was pretty tough, Bridget always thought of her as a kind person. What Bridget didn't know was that Chantal wasn't the person she needed to be worried about.

Bridget looked at Jade and Jade shrugged her shoulders. When she sat up, she saw there were clothes at the foot of the bed and another wig. This wig was long and straight and it was a light brown color. Under the wig, there was a pair of black shiny stretch pants laced on the side and a matching belly shirt, also laced on both sides. Bridget didn't want to believe the truth; that this outfit could only have been placed there for her to wear and, even more devastating, this probably meant they expected her to go out hookin' with them on Hunts Point.

Jade grabbed the clothes and the wig off the bed and sat on the edge next to Bridget.

"Come with me in the bathroom, okay," Jade whispered.

Bridget got out of bed and followed Jade into the bathroom.

"Sweetie, I know this isn't what you want, but this is only temporary. I had to tell my mother what's going on, in case they come looking for us. She ain't gonna let us stay here for free."

"Oh no, Jade, you told your mom! She's going to turn me in! She doesn't like me! I'm going to spend the rest of my life in prison!"

"No, you're not. My mom will protect us; *both* of us. And, what makes you think she doesn't like you? Trust me, Bridget. Chantal Smith's bark is worse than her bite. The only thing we need to worry about is money and keeping a roof over our heads and food in our stomachs. This is what we *have* to do."

"But, Jade, I took typing and dictation classes while we were at Mannersville. I type sixty words per minute. I can get a job as a clerk or a typist or something."

"Bridget, get real. You killed someone. You need identification to get a job and the minute they run your ID, the police will be knocking down the door to cart you off to prison. You may be able to live that life one day when all this shit blows over, but for now, this is it. This is what has to be done. This is what *all* of us have to do. Don't worry. Like I said, it's only temporary. We have other options. We have to do this for now to get some quick money in our pockets."

"But why do I have to wear these clothes? Why can't I just wear my own clothing?" Bridget asked.

"First of all, you'll stand out like a sore thumb if you wear your clothes and, second, these clothes are a sort of *uniform*. They quickly identify you to potential clients while providing easy access."

Bridget reluctantly dressed in the clothing Chantal had provided. However, she was sure she would never be able to go through with it. After all, it wasn't so long ago she promised herself she would never, ever, choose this life. Jade helped her with the wig and applied some makeup to Bridget's face. It was time to go to work.

CHAPTER TWO
HUNTS POINT

Hunts Point and the people that cruised those streets at night reminded Bridget of roaches when you turned the lights on; all that scattering and scurrying here and there, ducking into doorways, all to make paper. One look at Chantal and Jade and you could tell they knew these streets like the back of their hands. They knew where to stand to get maximum exposure, which alleyways to get lost in and the best doorways to "conduct business." There were discarded rubbers everywhere. The whole thing turned Bridget's stomach. She couldn't believe her life had come to this.

Cars came and went looking for quick and easy satisfaction. Girls lowered tops to give potential customers a bird's-eye view. Chantal was attempting to stop cars in the middle of the intersection as they were driving by. She pulled down the front of her lycra dress, leaving her 36-C's swinging free. Chantal had a habit to feed and you couldn't be shy with so much competition. There were girls everywhere, looking for their next trick. A car cruised by checking Chantal out and she stuck her head in the car and spoke to him on the driver's side. She turned to Jade and whispered something in her ear. Bridget wasn't sure what was going to happen next, but she was kind of glad to see Chantal leave. She made her uncomfortable. Chantal got in on the passenger side of the car and the fat white man who was driving drove away. After watching the cars and seeing some of the customers, Bridget was sure she wouldn't be able to do this without throwing up. The thought of these losers touching her, or her them, repulsed her. She didn't drink, but suddenly wished she did; anything at all to help her block all this out. As if Jade were reading her thoughts, she offered Bridget a pill and some bottled water.

"Come on, sweetie. Take this. It'll make it easier."

Bridget took the pill without hesitation. She had never taken any kind of drugs before but, then again, she had never peddled her ass on Hunts Point either. She had also never worn five-inch stilettos and her feet hurt like hell. She couldn't imagine walking for hours in these shoes.

"Chantal thinks you should stay out of cars for now. There are plenty of places on the street where you can conduct business. It'll be safer that way. Most of these guys want to get their rocks off, but every now and then you get a sicko. You're much safer outside of a car than in one; easier to run. Most of the guys that come to Hunts Point want blow jobs. I'm guessing you've never done that before, so I'm going to give you some advice. First, take this." She handed Bridget a string of condoms.

"Don't do anything without using one of these." She ripped one off the end and opened the package. She blew into it and rolled it down over her fingers. Then, she popped it into her mouth and sucked on it by way of demonstration.

"Second, to speed things up, keep repulsion time to a minimum and allow yourself a greater opportunity to make more money in a shorter period of time. When you're suckin' the guy off, play with his balls. Take your finger and trace a line with your fingernail from the back of his balls near his ass to the front of his balls; right down the middle where the line is. When you think he's about to cum, milk his balls, like a cow. And, yeah, make sounds; moaning sounds, sucking sounds. It speeds them up."

"Milk 'em?" Bridget questioned.

"Yeah, milk 'em. Take 'em in your hand and massage them up and down. It'll make him cum much faster that way. Here comes one now," Jade said.

A car pulled up in front of them.

"You can take this one," Jade offered.

Bridget was terrified. But, it wasn't as bad as it could be. At least this guy looked relatively harmless. He was white and skinny and looked like he was probably pretty short; maybe five-four. He reminded her of a science teacher she once had—Mr. Pinchot. Suddenly, the idea of Mr. Pinchot cruising Hunts Point looking for pussy was unbelievably funny. *Wow*, Bridget thought, *since when do I think of it as pussy?*

Suddenly she felt strange, like she was walking through a dream, a good dream. She felt like a hundred hands were pampering her entire body; like she was getting her feet, hands, head, back, front, *everything*, all massaged at once. She hadn't expected to feel this way. She thought she would at least be a little afraid but, surprisingly, she wasn't. Maybe it was the pill Jade had given her.

"Yeah, it probably was the pill," Jade answered. "It's Ecstasy."

"Hey?" Bridget asked. "That was weird. Did you read my mind? I was wondering whether or not the way I'm feeling right now was because of the pill you gave me, and then you answered my question."

"Whew, that was fast!" Jade responded. "You weren't just thinking it; you said it out loud, honey. Now, go to it. That's your first customer. Tell him to park and you can take him over by that loading dock over there. Just watch them hoes over there. Sometimes they try to rip other girls off. And, whatever you do, make sure you get the money up front. Twenty for a blow job, fifty for pussy penetration, seventy-five for anal, and a hundred if he wants to go to a hotel. But, don't go with anyone anywhere yet. You're new at this and I think we should wait on the hotel or car action. If they can't do it somewhere around here, they won't be gettin' none."

"Don't worry, I got your back," Jade assured her.

Leaning into the driver's side of the car, Bridget tried to act like she was tough and experienced, because she figured if she didn't, she would get taken advantage of, or worse.

"It's twenty for a blow job, fifty for penetration and seventy-five for anal. Payment is up front," Bridget demanded.

The guy seemed afraid. He fumbled haphazardly with his wallet, dropping the money.

"No, not in the car. You can park here and follow me."

After he parked, Bridget led him to a dark corner only a few feet away with a doorway that provided a minimal degree of privacy.

"Cou-cou-could I have a blow job?" he stuttered.

It occurred to Bridget that if it were not her standing in front of him right now and it were another of these girls, like Chantal, they would have not only taken the money, but they probably would have given him nothing in return. Bridget hoped she never became that sort of woman. Yet, she recognized the potential for such a thing happening under the circumstances. As much as she hated having to do *anything* with this guy, she was an honest person before she was anything else.

She pulled out the condom, opened it, and instructed "Pinchot-The-Stutterer" to pull down his pants. She rolled the condom over his erect, but tiny penis and sucked him as Jade had instructed. Her only sexual encounter until now had been Buster at the home, and unlike Buster's bravado, this man reminded her of a baby. At one point, Bridget thought she actually heard him whimper; and when Bridget started playing with his balls as Jade had told her to do, he lost complete control immediately. He bellowed so loudly, Bridget was afraid he might summon the police with the noise. When he was done, he thanked her and even gave her an extra twenty. Bridget wasn't sure why, but she hid the second twenty inside of a hole in the lining of her purse. This would become the first in a long line of bills that got shrewdly hidden. She would soon learn that her instincts were more fine-tuned than she thought.

The first night Bridget had three customers. As far as Bridget was concerned, that was more than enough. But, when they got back to the apartment and Chantal demanded her "take" for "living expenses," she was pissed that Bridget only had sixty dollars to contribute.

"What the fuck is this?" Chantal asked. "I can't do shit with sixty dollars!"

"It's twenty dollars for a blow job and I had three customers. I couldn't get any more customers than that," Bridget explained.

"You couldn't get any more customers, huh. Well, honey, you betta' work on getting more customers or you're gonna starve."

Bridget couldn't understand why Jade wouldn't speak up for her. She didn't even try to defend her. Jade told her that Chantal thought she shouldn't get in any cars or go anywhere with any of the customers, and that's what most of them wanted. One guy wanted to have sex with her in his car. In a way, Bridget was glad Jade told her not to go with any of the customers. Although Bridget hated doing any of what she was doing, she imagined that having sex with these strangers had to be far worse than sucking them off.

The days and nights began to blend together and before Bridget knew it, she had been working the streets for over three years. It was hard to imagine. She continued to work the warehouse district of Hunts Point, despite her revulsion about what she was doing. But, at least she had a plan. There was an outreach program for prostitutes and whenever she could, she spoke to the workers; some of whom were ex-prostitutes themselves. She took whatever leaflets and flyers she could get about different training programs, hopefully, without Jade or Chantal knowing. She trusted Jade, but she didn't want to hurt her feelings or make her feel like this life was good enough for them, but not good enough for her. And she was afraid if Chantal found out, she would be out on the streets before she secured herself a job and a place to live. She wanted so much to share the information with Jade, but she couldn't risk it. She wanted Jade to see there were other options; that this didn't have to be their life. Bridget was afraid Jade would become hopeless like Chantal. What she didn't know was that Jade *expected* Bridget to become Chantal and only by doing so could Jade hope to tighten her grip on Bridget.

Jade continued her effort to supply Bridget with drugs,

to no avail. And even when she thought she was successful in getting Bridget to pop a pill here or there, she was
wrong. Bridget was putting the pills under her tongue
and then throwing them away. Bridget was smart enough
to know that if she got hooked on drugs, she would be
trapped forever. Jade was hoping it would help her to
dominate Bridget.

Neither Chantal nor Bridget knew it, but during the
daytime, Jade had been supplementing the income she
made hookin' by boosting in different department stores
downtown and selling the stuff on the streets. She was
also grabbing women's pocketbooks. Jade cased the res-
taurants on the Upper East Side of Manhattan, much
the way a bank robber would case a bank. She discovered
that if you dressed and spoke the part, you could pretty
much blend in and no one would really notice you.
Bridget would have been great at this particular scheme,
because of her ability to "talk-the-talk." Bridget had been
a virtual bookworm when they were at Mannersville,
and she was smart, real smart. But, her dark skin might
elicit too much attention. It was sad, but true, that even
in the nineties, profiling of black folks still existed. Jade,
with her red hair and light skin, got past certain doors
easier than Bridget would have.

Jade discovered that there was this culture of women
living on the Upper East Side that spent their hours
lolling the day away. Most of them were married to rich
men, CEOs of large corporations; and all they wanted

their wives to do was take care of the house and the children. Most of them had cooks and housekeepers and nannies; so they spent the better part of the day sipping tea and coffee with each other, eating lunch and getting manis and pedis.

When they were at Mannersville, every now and then they would take these "field trips" into the city, and Bridget would watch these women forlornly and hope for the same sort of life for herself someday. Jade wondered if after living with her and Chantal, she figured out what the "real deal" was—probably not. Bridget didn't know it, but Jade had seen those brochures she had been hiding concerning employment training programs and housing for "wayward" prostitutes. She was still hoping to grab the brass ring.

Once Bridget got past the initial shock of workin' the streets, she turned out to be quite a little earner. As far as Jade was concerned, if Bridget thought she was going to desert her after she "taught her the ropes," she was dead wrong. No, Bridget couldn't leave until *she* said she could leave, and that wouldn't be for a long, long time yet.

Jade sat in a Starbucks on the corner of Seventy-fifth Street and First Avenue sipping a Grande Iced Americano. Starbucks was one of her best spots. These women were so fuckin' stupid. Most of them would come in with their friends and a baby or two in carriages. They would be so distracted with the rugrats or talking about their latest vacation or their husbands that they wouldn't even notice Jade slipping the pocketbook off the back of their chairs. This was not one of those days.

Typically, Jade would pick up the pocketbook, put it on her shoulder and walk out like it was her bag before anyone even noticed. The key to getting away with it successfully was remaining calm. However, on this particular day, one of the toddlers in the coffeehouse conspired against her. The entire time she had been sitting there, this pain-in-the-ass kid had been getting up from the table where he sat with his mother and her friends and coming over to her table and the other surrounding tables. Even if Jade were not trying to get paid today, she would still have been pissed off because she couldn't understand why everybody in Starbucks had to deal with this lazy bitch's kid. She was sitting there having herself a high old time and everyone else had to contend with his touching things on *their* tables. Yet, if the kid got burned by a cup of coffee or something, the mother would be the first person to scream in outrage. If it were not for the fact that she had come here for a particular purpose, Jade thought she probably would have "accidentally" burned the kid on fuckin' principle. The sequence of events that were to follow, made her wish she had.

She grabbed a beautiful brown, genuine Prada bag and was headed out the door, when the pain in the ass kid began following her out the door onto the street. His mom noticed that her son was leaving the store and screamed at him to come back, causing everyone in

Starbucks to turn around and look toward the door, including the woman whose pocketbook she had stolen.

"Stop her!" the blonde-haired woman with the sensible shoes yelled.

Just before she walked out the door, the counterperson looked her directly in her eyes. Jade thrived on going unnoticed and the key to going unnoticed was never maintaining direct eye contact.

"Shit!" Jade exclaimed, as she hauled ass, running toward Lexington Avenue. She didn't stop until she got to the subway on Lexington and Seventy-seventh Street. She wasn't even sure if anyone was chasing behind her, but she didn't stop running until she was sure she could escape. The subway was a perfect place for that.

Damn! Jade thought to herself.

That was one less Starbucks she would be able to "work" out of. And, that particular Starbucks had been so lucrative for her. Once, she actually retrieved a grand from this woman's pocketbook, not to mention the countless credit cards she had been able to use. She was surprised at how many stores didn't even ask for any form of identification. Not that she was complaining.

Oh well, she thought. *There are plenty of Starbucks to choose from in Manhattan.*

Slightly paranoid, Jade decided to find a bathroom someplace where she could go through the contents of the bag and then dump it. She rode the Number 6 train on Seventy-seventh Street to the next stop uptown to

Eighty-sixth Street where she found a Barnes & Noble bookstore. Often she would keep the pocketbooks, because some of them were worth more than the contents and they were so beautiful and rich-looking.

Jade was starting to get a bit tired of the "strenuous" hustle and thought it time to get her "real" hustle going. She started this whole thing off with a plan and she wasn't going to forget that. The money was okay, but she wanted more than okay. Her months "working" Starbucks had further driven that point home. She wanted the kind of money the "ladies that lunch" were privy to, and she knew where to get it and how. But first, she would need to tie up a couple of loose ends.

"Damn!" Jade said out loud, after dumping out the contents of the purse while sitting inside the bathroom. The bitch didn't even have any money. There was thirty dollars and a wallet full of credit cards; and the woman was sure to report those cards right away, so she wouldn't risk trying to use them. Jade was more pissed that she couldn't keep the beautiful Prada bag. But she wasn't stupid. When you started to get sloppy, that was when you got your ass caught!

When Jade got home, neither Bridget nor Chantal were around. Her mom was usually sleeping off her high before she went out on the Avenue for the night and Bridget would usually be somewhere in the house reading a book. But, for some reason, they weren't there now. That was odd.

"That was such a good movie," she could hear Bridget saying through the door before she walked in. But, she also heard another voice; a woman's voice.

All Jade knew was Bridget better not be tryin' to come up in here with one of them chickenheads from the Avenue or, even worse, one of those fuckin' do-gooders from that outreach program. She was stunned to recognize that the light-hearted voice she heard with Bridget was none other than her own mother. In all the years that she had been alive, she didn't think she had ever heard her mother like this. She actually sounded *happy*. Instead of being thrilled at the sudden change in her mother's usual disposition, Jade was agitated. All she could think of was that she was losing the upper-hand. She had witnessed the subtle changes in her mother's demeanor over the last couple of years and she didn't like it one bit. She had somehow evolved into a kinder, gentler woman. She was becoming something very different than the mother she had known all these years. And all thanks to Bridget. Of all people, Bridget was influencing *her* mother's thoughts more than she was. And, she couldn't have that.

Always equipped with a great poker face, she refused to let on that she was annoyed with their cheerful mood. More than her mother's change in attitude, Jade was even more annoyed with Bridget's "take lemons and make lemonade" way of looking at things. Where once Bridget seemed to be a walking victim, ready to crumble at any moment, she was actually adjusting to what life had handed her and, for some reason, Jade wasn't okay with that. She wanted, no, she needed, to see the people around her suffering. She'd be damned if anyone was walking around having more fun; being happier than she was; especially high-and-mighty Bridget.

"Hey, Jade." Chantal greeted her daughter. "Bridget and I went to see *Blankman*; you know, with Damon Wayans. That shit was so fuckin' funny. I'm glad Bridget talked me into it."

For a moment, Jade was amused with the irony of the choice of films. How perfect, that Bridget would choose a film with a pure-hearted, optimistic, Pollyannish character, someone exactly like herself.

"Oh she did, did she," Jade commented.

It must have been her tone of voice, because both her mom and Bridget looked at her funny. Jade suddenly realized she needed to check herself before Bridget got wise. But, it was too late. Bridget continued on, but Chantal suddenly saw her daughter as she had never seen her before; through wide open eyes.

Bridget was a sweet girl who had been caught up in some unfortunate circumstances. Had things been different, Chantal was sure Bridget could have done incredible things with her life; probably still could. Instead, she was here in this shit hole with her and Jade. Until now, Chantal hadn't truly taken a long, hard look at her daughter. Suddenly it was like turning on a light in a darkened room. She hadn't wanted to admit it, but Jade was a bad seed and Bridget would do well to get as far away from Jade as quickly as possible. Jade was always so busy with whatever it was she was up to that Bridget and Chantal had been left on their own more and more. Not only that, Jade had begun to work the streets less and less. Over time and without Jade's constant influence, Chantal had been given a chance to *really* get to know Bridget, and she liked her; she liked her a lot. And, although Bridget was naïve in some respects, in other respects she was a very wise young woman. Chantal was surprised at Bridget's capability to care for others, when she had been through so much. Bridget had tried over and over again to show Chantal how she could do anything, if she put her mind to it. Chantal was convinced that her life would never be more than what it was right now, but Bridget assured her that life wasn't over until it was over, and as long as she was alive, she had the power to change her own fate. Chantal wasn't sure whether she believed that yet, but she hadn't had any dope today; at least not yet. She couldn't remember the last time she managed to make it through an entire day without drugs.

"What made ya'll go see that, of all the movies you could see?"

"I don't know," Bridget responded. "We were both sitting around talking and feeling a little low-down and figured the best thing to fight depression was a little comedy. So we looked in the newspaper and picked

Blankman. It was playing on Eighty-sixth Street and we're always saying how we'd all like a change of scenery and all. We wanted you to come, but we couldn't find you."

They were all on Eight-sixth Street at the same fuckin' time. What if they had seen her? Then they would've found out about her extracurricular activities, which she definitely did not want to happen; especially given the fact that she was constantly crying broke and trying to get *"everyone"* to work harder getting more johns. Even with her mom, Jade was the leader and Chantal was the follower. If there was one thing Jade figured out from early on, in every relationship, whether it's friends, lovers, husbands, wives, or even parents and kids, there is the leader and there is the follower. And she had no intention of *ever* being the follower in *any* relationship; even one where she was the child.

Jade resolved to stop this shit right now!

"So we workin' tonight or what?" Jade asked

"Of course, we're workin'," Chantal responded. "Just let us get dressed."

Oh, so now it was *us* all of a sudden. Yeah, this shit *had* to be stopped. The two of them together made her odd man out, and she couldn't do her thang if she was odd man out. She knew exactly what to do. Her future success depended upon it. And if there was one thing she learned over the years, she came first, before *anyone* else; and that included her mother. After all, when had she ever put her first? *Never*!

That night was real slow and most of the girls on the Avenue called it a night early. Chantal was stressed out big-time because, although she had abstained from drugs all day, she had a habit and her body wouldn't allow her much more than that. By the time it was two in the morning, she was jonesing for a fix.

Chantal was sitting in the front seat of a Chrysler LeBaron giving a hand job when Jade found her.

"I was thinking we'd call it a night when you're done and go home and watch some DVDs, since I didn't get a chance to go with you guys to the movies. Maybe we could get some smoke, some munchies, and a couple of those wine coolers Bridget likes and kick back a little for a change," Jade said.

"I don't have any money," Chantal told her daughter.

"Don't worry, Ma. Things were slow tonight, but I was able to make a little money. I'll take care of it. You want anything else?" Jade already knew the answer.

She went to Big Rob, a dealer she knew, who had been trying to get in her pants for almost a year now. Hunts Point Avenue was where Big Rob made his best money. But instead of the warehouse district of the Avenue, frequented by johns and prostitutes, he preferred nearby Barretto Point Park on the East River waterfront. Jade knew Big Rob would give her what she wanted, and she probably wouldn't even have to pay for it.

Jade watched Big Rob from across the street before she approached him. He was a big man; about six-five and weighing somewhere around 260. His hair was cut in a nice fade and he was wearing a pair of Tommy jeans and a red and green Tommy sweater with a pair of Timberlands. Homeboy looked good.

"What's up, Freckles?" Big Rob greeted her when she approached, as he soaked in every inch of her body with his eyes.

"What's up, Big Rob? I need something *special*."

"How *special* are we talkin'?"

"I'm talkin' primo and pure as the driven snow; somethin' that will take its rider straight to heaven. You got something like that?"

"You know I do, Freckles, but what you got fa' me?"

"Baby, I got something that'll take your ass beyond heaven. It's sweet and sticky and can ride you sixty-nine ways 'til Sunday. All you gotta do is say the word."

"Word, baby, word. Let me go git you ya' shit. You wait right here; don't you go nowhere."

"Don't worry; I'll be right here waiting for you. Just make sure you bring me what I asked for," Jade responded.

"It's as good as done," Big Rob said.

Big Rob came back with exactly what Jade asked for and more. She was amazed to find that Big Rob was packing more than his Glock 17. He had a dick that would make even a veteran ho salivate. After Jade took what she asked for from Big Rob, she took him in his car and gave him what he asked for. It was difficult to deep throat him because he was so big, but she sucked him so good, his dick grew to even more epic proportions.

"Hold up, lover," Jade said, when she thought Big Rob was about to cum.

She stopped slobbin' his huge member and removed her lips.

"Aren't you going to hook me up with a little somethin'-somethin'?"

"I thought I already did," he said.

"Oh, so it's like that, huh? I thought with all the junk you carryin' you could give a sister a *nice* ride, but I guess you all about gettin' yours."

"Naw, Freckles, it ain't like that. We can *both* get ours. Just hop on, baby.

The veins were protruding from his thick, stiff, throbbing cock and Jade moved from the passenger side to the driver's side of the car. She slid one of the condoms she was carrying down on his dick and then mounted Big Rob, gobbling his cock up with her pussy like it was dinnertime. Jade gripped the back of the seat and slid up and down his cock, slow and easy at first, slowly building the momentum, until Big Rob's breathing was obviously labored. Jade thought she might actually be feeling something. She never enjoyed it with any of the johns she fucked, and she didn't date like young women her age would normally do. She thought she might actually feel herself about to cum and she did. Her body began to tremble and she soaked Big Rob's dick with a flood of her juices.

"Uhm, baby," Big Rob said. "That pussy juice smells good, baby. Damn, baby, you make a nigga feel *right*!"

He met each and every one of Jade's thrusts with a counter-grind, plunging his cock into her as hard and as fast as he could. That is, as hard as he could with his ass pinned to the seat of the car. When he came, it was like a backed-up waterhose had suddenly been cleared. Jade was afraid he might blast the condom up into the deepest recesses of her pussy, never to be seen from again. Jade was too drained to get off of Big Rob right away, so she stayed there for a while; and Big Rob wasn't complaining.

"Dayum, girl, you laid it on me. I knew you had that 24K shit goin' on. So, when can I see you again?"

Jade enjoyed it, but she wasn't in the market for entanglements; and homeboy could definitely become one. She jumped off of Big Rob's now limp dick and made a hasty, but cordial exit.

"I'll catch up wit' ya," she said as she left; knowing full well that she intended to leave that shit alone. As far as Jade was concerned, good dick was like salmonella poisoning; it may taste good goin' in, but by the time it's ready to come out, you realize what a terrible mistake you've made. Jade wasn't prepared to be sick. Besides, she had bigger fish to fry than some dick. Some serious changes had to be made.

CHAPTER THREE
THE HUSTLE

While Bridget and Chantal waited at the house for Jade, Chantal suddenly got an eerie premonition. It was a feeling of impending doom. She wondered if it were the fact that she hadn't had any drugs or whether it was plain old good instincts. Whatever it was, it frightened her; frightened her a lot.

Bridget was in the living room looking for a DVD to watch when Chantal came in the room. They had had such a good day and night, that Bridget was surprised to see the serious look on Chantal's face. She hoped she wasn't going to start acting the way she used to act; all mean and aggressive. But, upon closer inspection, she realized that wasn't the look she recognized it all. This look was one of melancholy; Chantal looked sad.

"Bridget, come here."

Chantal sat down on the couch and patted the seat, so Bridget walked over to the ugly brown and yellow plaid couch and sat down next to Chantal.

"Bridget, I got the strangest feeling, like something is about to happen; something bad."

"No, Chantal, everything is okay. We're fine. You're fine. It's just that you're changing; that's all. It always feels strange when you do things out of character. I felt the same way when I came to live here."

"No, sweetie, it's more than that. Something isn't right, but that's not important. What's important is you. It's finally my turn to be the adult in this house and I need to have a serious talk with you; no interruptions. If anything should happen to me, Bridget,—"

Bridget tried to interrupt Chantal and tell her nothing was going to happen, but Chantal continued.

"If anything should happen to me, you've got to leave here. You're probably not going to believe what I tell you right now, but someday you will. I'm hoping by then it won't be too late."

"What, Chantal? What are you saying?" Bridget asked.

"Jade is bad, Bridget. She's bad to the core. I take responsibility for that because I was no kind of mother. Even her birth was born of the evil of these streets, but, Bridget, she's bad nonetheless. If you stay with her, one of two things will happen; either you will become evil like her or she will eat you alive. I don't want either of those things to happen. You're a good kid, and although I wish it had been under different circumstances, you've come to feel like my own daughter. I feel protective of you and I don't want anything bad to happen to you. Just promise me right here and now, that if anything should happen to me you, will go to one of those people you know at that outreach program and find a way out.

"You're a smart girl and you can do so much better than this. It's too late for me, but it's not too late for you. I can't save my daughter. I'm afraid her evil runs way too deep for any of us to fix. Jade was born bad and she will die bad. But you, Bridget, you have a promising future. You have dreams and a kind heart. Besides, you're so damn young. Life isn't over for you yet. You can still be all the things you want to be. Don't let Jade drain your dreams from you. And, believe you me, she will if you let her. Bridget, walk away. You don't owe her anything. Jade is doing exactly what she's always wanted to do. Jade is one of those people who's got the streets in her blood. She lives and breathes them. She would be lost if she couldn't live this life. She's addicted to the drama of it all.

"But that doesn't mean you have to be a part of that. Let her have what she wants, without you. The thing I've never been able to understand about Jade, though, is I don't consider myself a bad person, just a victim of circumstance. Her father wasn't a bad man either. He was a good, decent human being; a man to be proud of, and our lives would have been very different, if we had gotten a chance to be together. I truly believe he loved me once."

Bridget was suddenly very confused.

"I can see the look on your face. You assumed the same thing everyone has assumed over the years. But, no, Jade's father wasn't one of my johns; at least not technically. It started out that way but we never had sex with each other for money. Jade's father and I loved each other. Or at least, we loved each other as much as two teenagers could love each other who are purposely kept apart. I tried to contact him after I found out that I was pregnant, but between my pimp at the time, J.T., and Jade's father's family, they saw to it that he never knew anything about Jade. That's when I got hooked on drugs. He supplied me with drugs in order to maintain a tight hold on me, and it worked. And, I never saw Jade's father again.

"I even managed to find out where he lived once and I visited his home, but they told me he wasn't there and gave me ten thousand dollars to go away. One of the things I'm most proud of is the fact that I tore that check up. As much as I needed that money, I needed my dignity more. So, whenever I'm ashamed of what I've become, I think of that check and my decision and the fact that I had pride once."

When Chantal was done talking, Bridget sat there dumbfounded. She was surprised at the raw emotion Chantal had displayed in talking about her own daughter and what was probably Chantal's *only* one true love. She was actually crying. She truly believed that Jade was evil. How could a mother think of her own daughter that way? And why on earth hadn't Chantal told Jade who her father really was? Bridget was so confused. Yet, she seemed to be trying to protect her. But why? What could she possibly be afraid of? What could Jade do to hurt her? After all, it wasn't Jade's fault they were here, it was hers.

If she hadn't killed Buster, Jade wouldn't even be living this life. Then it occurred to her that Jade always wanted to come back here anyway. Just as quickly as the thought entered Bridget's mind, it left. Chantal threw her arms around Bridget and hugged her with great force. Bridget was now convinced this was a reaction to drug withdrawal. But, she hugged Chantal anyway, enjoying the closest thing she had to a mother in a very long time. Chantal maintained a tight grip on Bridget, almost like she didn't want to let go; that is, until Jade came back into the house.

"So, what's this?" Jade asked when she entered. "My best girl and my mom all hugged up. Ya'll turning lesbo on me or what?"

"Bridget and I were sharing war stories."

"War stories." Jade grunted. "Miss Bridget has led a charmed life. What war stories could she possibly have to tell?"

At that very second, Bridget was more pissed off with Jade than she had ever been. Come to think of it, she couldn't remember ever truly being pissed off at Jade, but she was now. She felt as though Jade were minimizing her pain. She had been tossed from foster home to foster home her entire life, been born addicted to drugs, never knew her mother or her father, and had been raped by a disgusting security guard at the only place she considered home, the only place she felt safe. Now, she was twenty-one years old and making a living fuckin' strangers in one of the most dilapidated corners of the world imaginable. Her life had earned her the right to call them war stories.

Although Jade, Bridget and Chantal all sat together in the living room and watched *Imitation of Life* together, you could cut the tension in the room like a knife. Everyone was clearly deep in thought. Sometime around six in the morning, when the movie was over, each of them went their separate ways. Chantal went into her room to go to bed, but when she heard Jade leaving the house to go out, Chantal stopped her to ask if she'd picked up her "package." Jade left the house, muttering something about catching up with one of the bitches who owed her money. Bridget settled down for the night to do some reading. So she put on her night clothes and pulled out the couch bed. Bridget read for about half an hour before she drifted off to sleep.

Sometime around nine, nature called and Bridget got up to go to the bathroom. Usually, because of the late hours she kept working the streets, she would sleep well past noon, but the wine coolers she'd had this morning had interrupted her sleep. When she got to the bathroom, the door was closed, but because the door was warped, you could never really close it completely. She could see Chantal through the crack, slumped over onto the floor. First she called to her and then she pushed the door and went in.

She tried to perform CPR, but quickly realized there was no use. Chantal was obviously dead. Bridget remembered Chantal's earlier premonition. She had been right. Something horrible had happened. Chantal had predicted her own death. Bridget wasn't sure what she should do. So, she got a blanket from her bedroom and covered Chantal up. Then, she went into the living room and sat down on the edge of the sofa bed. It seemed as though everyone that loved her or could have loved her had left her. She had only known Chantal a short time, but her absence from her life would be deeply felt. Chantal was the closest thing she had ever had to a mother and she would be greatly missed. Suddenly, she thought of Jade. Poor Jade would be devastated. She adored her mother. As if on cue, Jade was standing in the living room. She seemed in a really good mood. She was smiling. Bridget hated to be the person to wipe that smile from her face.

"What's up, girl? You look like you've seen a ghost."

Bridget started crying. But, when she saw Jade heading toward the back of the apartment, she summoned the courage to speak.

"Jade, don't go in there. It's your mom. Chantal… Chantal is dead."

"What are you talking about?" Jade asked "She's not dead. She's probably just high; that's all."

Jade went into her mother's bedroom, then into the bathroom and that's when she saw her, lying there, with her blanket strewn over her body. She lifted the blanket and stared at her mother's lifeless body. She would no longer be her mother's daughter. She would no longer be anybody's child. The one and only parent she had ever known, was now dead.

Jade's soul was darker than she ever felt it. She realized what she felt wasn't exactly remorse. She didn't know what she was feeling. In some respects, she thought, just maybe, she felt nothing.

Once, when she lived at a foster home with a couple with about three or four other kids, she killed the family cat; slit his throat from ear to ear. The family felt sorry for her and, for a short time, thought all she needed was help. Therefore, they sent her to a psychiatrist. Once, when the overworked, state-appointed psychiatrist was dozing off to sleep, she snuck a peek at his notes on her. She was pissed when she read that he had classified her as a sociopath with homicidal tendencies. Not long after that she left the home of Mr. and Mrs. Sullivan and that's right about the time she ended up at Mannersville Group Home. Jade had been completely offended that she had been classified a sociopath. A sociopath was a fuckin' nut that didn't feel anything. She felt things all the time. How could anyone call her a sociopath? Now homicidal; that was something different. She wasn't offended by that at all. Anyone could be homicidal. There was not a person on this earth that wasn't capable of murder under the right circumstances. Even Miss Polly Purebred, Bridget, had mustered up enough guts to kill someone when she felt she had to.

Standing above her mother's lifeless body, she couldn't get over the fact that she still felt absolutely nothing at all. However, in order to keep up pretenses, she managed to shed a few well-placed tears here and there; enough to satisfy any questions Bridget might have. Jade had to hand it to herself; she was quite the little actress.

When she thought she had cried enough to satisfy Bridget's delicate sensibilities, she got down to business.

"Come on, Bridget. We have to get rid of the body."

"Jade, what are you talking about? We can't do that. We have to give her a proper burial. She deserves at least that."

"Bridget, think about what you're saying. Let's say, for the sake of argument, we do what you're suggesting. We call the police, because in order to give her this 'proper burial' you're talking about, we have to call the police. Otherwise, how will the body get to the morgue? So, we call the police, they classify it an overdose, but they're going to want to know who we are, why we're here and if it truly was an overdose. Whenever there's a death, the police have to investigate, statements have to be taken. Are you really prepared for that kind of attention? Not to mention the fact that *you* are wanted for murder. I don't know about you, but I'm not prepared to take that kind of a chance. Chantal wouldn't have wanted us to sacrifice ourselves like that for the sake of a ceremony for her. My mother lived by the code of the streets and survival *always* comes first."

Bridget remembered Chantal's last words to her: "If

anything should happen to me, you've got to leave here."
She also remembered something else Chantal had said:
"Jade is bad, Bridget. She is bad to the core."

"Come on, Bridget, snap out of it. We've got to do
this *now*!"

Bridget hadn't thought the whole thing out. In some
respects, Jade was right; the last thing either of them
needed was the police sniffing around. But Bridget felt
guilty about getting rid of Chantal like she was garbage
to be thrown in the street.

"Is there someplace we can bury her?" Bridget asked.

"This is fuckin' Hunts Point. Where the hell do you
think we're going to bury a body?"

"I was hoping you might know someplace."

"There are places, but we need a car to get to those
places and the only way we can get a car is to borrow
one. I don't know anyone that's going to lend us a car,
without asking a shit load of questions."

The thought of burying Chantal isn't what shook her
resolve. People died in the streets every day and if you
lived by the streets, you knew there was at least a 50/50
chance that might happen to you; and Chantal was no
different. What concerned Jade was having to deal with
the police. She hated the police and tried her best to
avoid them at all costs. If she and Bridget dumped Chantal in some alleyway somewhere, that might eventually
lead to her; since she *was* Chantal's daughter and was
staying with her. Most of the folks in the 'hood didn't

know all that much about her, Bridget and her mom, but they probably did know that Chantal was her mom and where they all lived. Jade then thought of the person who could help them out, Big Rob. She had turned his ass out last night and, although she had been considering leaving him alone, it occurred to her that Big Rob might be the man to keep around; especially given the fact that she was ready to move on to Phase II of her *"Plan."*

"You know, Bridget, you might be right. I'd like to find someplace dignified to bury my mother. She would've liked that. I think I know who can help us."

"Who?" Bridget asked.

"This brother I know named Big Rob. He's got a car and I'm pretty sure he'll let me borrow it, if I ask nicely."

What Jade really meant was if she fucked him nicely, but she had no intention of telling Bridget her business.

"Sit tight," Jade told Bridget. "I'm going to call him now."

They didn't have a phone in the house, so Jade went downstairs to use the pay phone. She called Big Rob and, sure enough, he couldn't wait to see her again. And, despite a minimal degree of protest, he consented to letting her use the car for a couple of hours.

Jade went back to the house and pulled out a large print suitcase her mother had had since she was a little girl. She could remember her and her mother using it to go down south once when she was very little. She was sure the suitcase would be large enough to fit her mother's body into and she was right. Jade locked the suitcase with the key her mom kept in her empty jewelry box.

"Bridget, I'm going to get the car from Big Rob. Wait here until I come back."

Bridget hated being alone with Chantal's dead body, but she did what Jade said.

Jade rode the subway downtown to pick up the car from Big Rob's place. He must have thought she was stupid or something. He practically spent 24/7 on Hunts Point, but now he wanted her to ride the damn subway all the way into Manhattan to pick up the car. He wanted some more pussy and if he played his cards right, he might actually get some. She had to admit, homeboy was workin' with somethin' there and she hadn't had her shit done up that good since—since *ever*! But first, she was going to square away business. Business *always* came first. She would get the car keys from him and then play it by ear from there.

When she got to the address, she was surprised to see that the building he lived in wasn't half bad. It was a high-rise on Ninety-sixth and Columbus—one of them Mitchell Lama Houses, with a doorman that had to ring you up and everything. You wouldn't have known it to look at Big Rob, that he was living like this. Jade's guess was that he had to thug it up while he was doing business in the hood. When she got upstairs, and looked for apartment 12RW, the apartment door was open. When she walked in, she couldn't believe her eyes. She realized the exterior of the building didn't do the interior of the apartment justice. He had his place hooked up. The living room had red leather furniture that was butter soft when Jade sat on it. The carpet was beige and was so thick and plush it felt as though she were walking on air. There was a huge projection TV in the living room that had to be sixty inches. It was tuned to BET and Salt-N-Pepa's video "Whatta Man." In the corner of one of the rooms, there was a beautiful red Sharper Image massage chair, which she hoped she would have an opportunity to enjoy. The bedroom was toward the back of the apartment and was decorated with varying shades of purple. There was a huge, king-sized, wrought-iron bed in the middle of the room and a purple flokati rug on the parquet floors. Jade had never seen a bed that big in her entire life, much less slept in one. Big Rob was in the kitchen making a sandwich and pouring some Kool-Aid into a large glass. He looked through the opening of the breakfast nook.

"You want me to hook you up?" he asked.

"Naw, I'm alright," Jade answered. "So, how long you been livin' here?"

"Oh, about five years; it was my mom's. I moved in after she passed away. I was livin' with my girl over by Parkchester, but the girl lost her muthafuckin' mind. She started fuckin' wit' my product and shit. I had to cut her loose."

"So, who you livin' wit' now?" Jade asked.

"Me, myself and I. I like it that way. No drama."

"I can relate," Jade agreed. "I been livin' with my mom and my homegirl Bridget for the past five months, but my mom is moving down South and it's just me and Bridget now," she lied.

"So is that why you need the car? To help your mom?"

"Yeah."

"The keys are right over there and the car is in the garage, Level 5, Area E," he said, motioning to the rectangular glass coffee table in the living room. "You remember what it looks like, right? Not that I'm rushing you or anything like that."

He left the kitchen and came into the living room and stood directly behind Jade, cupping her breasts with his huge hands. Her nipples responded immediately. Big Rob was not one to miss a thing. He recognized the effect he was having on her and decided to capitalize on it.

He whispered in her ear, "Did you know that before I met you, you usta' make a nigga's dick hard just passing by me on the street? I been jonesin' for this pussy for a long time, Freckles. Why you gonna go and make a nigga wait for this sweet, sweet punani? And how the fuck you keep that pussy of yours so damn tight, doin' what you do? Girl, you got a muthafuckin' gold mine between them legs."

Jade was never ashamed of what she did but, for some reason, now she didn't like what Big Rob was saying. She wiggled out of his grasp.

Big Rob realized he may have fucked shit up with his big-ass mouth and tried to explain himself.

"Come on, Freckles, don't get the wrong idea. I ain't tryin' to judge you or nothin' like that. You and me, we alike. We know these streets and we know what we gotta do to git paid. You do yours your way and I do mine my way. If I was a female and was workin' wit' what you got, I'd be capitalizing off it myself. So, whatever you do, don't get me wrong; I definitely ain't one to judge. But let me ask you somethin'. You ever thought about steppin' up your game? 'Cause I gotta tell you, Freckles, you sellin' yourself short on Hunts Point. You can do better than that."

Jade relaxed. He was speaking her language and Jade started thinking about a world of possibilities. There was clearly something going on between her and Big Rob. He had lots of connections; connections that might net her bigger rewards.

"You and I need to talk," Jade said. "I got plans, *big* plans that could mean us *both* a big payday. You down?"

"Depends on what you got in mind? Holla' at me."

"I got something I need to take care of tonight with the car, but I can bring it back late tonight, if that's okay. How 'bout we talk when I bring the car back?"

"It's noon now. Meet me back here about midnight and we'll talk," he said.

The entire ride back to the crib, Jade was planning and scheming her next move. One thing she knew for sure was that she had to keep fuckin' Bridget away from Big Rob. She wasn't in-love or nothin' like that, but she was definitely feelin' him and him her. But the thing

about niggas was a hard dick had no muthafuckin' con-
science and, for some reason that she couldn't quite figure
out, Bridget had a strange effect on men. She doubted
Bridget was Big Rob's type, but you could never tell
about these things. If someone had told her two weeks
ago she and Big Rob would be kickin' it, or even thinkin'
about kickin' it, she would have told them that they were
crazy. She used to see him in the neighborhood and she
respected his game, but she never thought of him in a
sexual way. To tell the truth, she hardly ever thought of
any man in a sexual way, unless it had to do with makin'
some money. Somehow, though, Big Rob was different.
He was like the male version of her.

By the time Jade got back to the apartment, Bridget
was pacing the floor like a caged animal; and she was pissed.
Nothing ever seemed to bother Bridget. She always rolled
with it, no matter what. But, now was different. She lit
into Jade as soon as she got into the door.

"Dammit, Jade! Where the hell have you been? Do
you have any idea how long you've been gone?"

Jade glanced at her Timex and realized she had been
gone for about three hours. After leaving Big Rob's place,
she had driven around thinking for a while.

It didn't take Jade long to recover from the shock of
Bridget standing up for herself and to put her in check.

"I had shit to take care of! Did you have any better
ideas? Whenever there's a problem, I'm the one that
comes up with the answers, and you have the nerve to be

questioning how long I took to get the damn car! This brotha' is doing *us* a favor. I couldn't rush him. Besides, have a little fuckin' compassion. This is *my* mother. I got shit on my mind; or hadn't that occurred to you? Damn, Bridget, I didn't know you could be so fuckin' selfish!"

"Oh, Jade, I'm so sorry. You're right; I am being selfish. It's just that this is hard on me, too. Chantal was the closest thing to a mother I've ever had. But, you're right. I forgot that this is *your* mother, not mine, and this has got to be so hard on you. You always seem so invincible, I guess I forget sometimes that you're only human. I'm sorry, Jade. I know how much you loved your mom."

"It's okay," Jade said. "Let's get this over with. I know a place not far from here; Bear Mountain. My mother and I used to go there when I was a little kid. It's in the Hudson Valley and it's a perfect place to bury her. There are plenty of hiking trails. I think she would've liked that."

Jade actually put some real thought into where she would bury her mother. One of the few fond memories she still had of her mother was when she was a little girl and they would go to Bear Mountain for picnics.

Jade and Bridget planned it so that they would get to Bear Mountain late in the evening. It was the middle of the week and Jade was sure it wouldn't be as crowded as on the weekend, allowing them to bury Chantal without being noticed. At sometime around nine, they brought the suitcase with Chantal inside downstairs. It was heavy but, between the two of them, they were able to manage.

They loaded the suitcase in the trunk of the car and left. By the time they got to Bear Mountain, it was dark enough to allow them to bury the body unseen. However, they still had to keep a close lookout. Jade had gotten two shovels from a Home Depot store and they were able to bury the body in no time. Bridget thought it only right that they say a few words and since Jade declined, that left it up to Bridget. Jade begged Bridget to make it short and sweet and she did.

"You leave this earth with much less than you gave. As you stand ready to enter the Pearly Gates, may The Good Lord welcome His daughter back home with open arms. I loved you, Chantal. I only wish I had gotten a chance to tell you that before you left us. I feel far less afraid knowing I have you as a guardian angel to look over us."

Bridget picked up the shovel and walked back to the car crying, while back at the gravesite, Jade stood there staring at her mother's final resting place.

They drove back to the city and both girls decided they would take a night off. Bridget was so exhausted, she went home and got into bed. After she had fallen asleep, Jade left the house, got back in Big Rob's car and drove back to his place. He was half-sleep when she got there. It was after one, but he didn't seem to care.

Jade took off her clothing and climbed into bed with Big Rob. The two of them lay there without speaking. He sensed that whatever it was that she had to take care of tonight was some deep shit, far deeper than just seeing her mother off to a trip down South, and wondered if he knew what the hell he was letting himself in for, dealing with her. But, there was something about her. He had never met a female this young who seemed this strong. It fascinated him and he wanted to find out more. Eventually, the two of them fell asleep. It was the first time in years that Jade had gone to sleep without thinking of twenty things at once.

Big Rob was up bright and early. He had some runs to make and wondered if it would be okay to leave Jade in his crib. He had some expensive shit and, although it was easily replaceable, he wasn't about to be treated like some sucker. He decided he would take a chance and left her a note on the pillow. He told her to make herself at home, fix something to eat and wait for him. He would be back in an hour.

When Jade woke up, she was surprised that he had felt comfortable enough to leave her alone. She was glad he had. It was so nice to slowly wake up in the gigantic bed with all these beautiful things surrounding her. She thought of those women she stole pocketbooks from on the Upper East Side and wondered if this was how they lived. She decided it was even better. The difference between her and them was *she* didn't have to have children to make it happen. One thing Jade decided a long time ago was that she would never bring a child into this world. What the fuck was the point? You live, you die, and it all turns to shit in the end. As far as she was concerned, it wasn't worth the pregnancy and labor and all the other fucked-up shit that followed.

In the bedroom there was another TV, not as big as the one in the living room, but it looked to be at least forty inches. She grabbed the remote on the bedside table and turned it on. She felt like a queen. She lay there watching the news and, for the first time in a long time, she was absolutely famished.

Jade seldom took the time to eat a balanced meal. She went into the kitchen and found a fully stocked kitchen. She made scrambled eggs and bacon and poured herself a heaping glass of orange juice. Remnants of her mother's existence, Jade hated most stimulants and never drank coffee or ingested anything else with caffeine. She took her breakfast back to the bedroom and ate. After she was done, she felt sleepy again and put the plate on the bed-side table and went back to sleep. She awoke to find Big Rob in the bed with her, under the covers, his hard dick poking at her thigh.

"You see what you do to me, girl? You know I don't be bringin' just anybody up in my crib."

"So, I'm special, huh," Jade said sarcastically.

"Yeah, I think you are pretty damn special. 'Cause I don't go around noticing people who ain't special; but if you're asking if you're special to me, no, not yet. For now, we're just kickin' it, but I think you could get to be special to me. But, that depends on you and what you want."

"I want it all, baby. That's what I've always wanted and

I don't need nobody to get it for me. I can do that *all by myself*," Jade said.

"Freckles, that's where you're wrong. I been out on them streets for a long time, and if there's one thing I've figured out is everybody needs somebody. Anybody who thinks otherwise is foolin' themselves."

Jade thought it best to change the subject.

"Right now, I need *you* to fuck *me*," Jade said.

Big Rob was more than happy to oblige. He rolled over on top of Jade and Jade's pussy lips spread open for him. She was wet and waiting. The two of them hesitated. Jade never fucked anybody without a condom and Big Rob was fully aware of what Jade did for a living. However, passion won out and the two of them threw caution to the wind. Big Rob plunged his rigid bone deep into Jade's quivering cavity and fucked her while Jade screamed for mercy. Big Rob knew the psychology of a prostitute; he had known enough of them. He felt like the King of the Muthafuckin' Hill, being good enough to give it to her good enough to make her scream like that. When he thought she might collapse from exhaustion, he turned her over on her stomach and fucked her doggy style. He grabbed her curly red hair and drove his cock into her pussy from behind as Jade's knuckles turned white gripping the bed. He punctuated each thrust with a bite to her shoulder or her neck. Jade had never been fucked like this. She had always been the one in control. Suddenly, she felt like she had a porcelain pussy. As she backed her ass up into his cock to get even more, Big Rob blasted her pussy with a load of hot cum that ignited Jade even more than she already was. Homegirl was hooked.

In her mind though, she cautioned herself not to get sidetracked. Jade knew that when all was said and done, it was all about cash money. But now, she thought maybe she could get her plan movin' much quicker than she had originally anticipated. She was rollin' with the "Master of the Game," and together, the two of them could be unbeatable. But where, in the scheme of things, did Bridget fit in? She still believed she needed Bridget to make the game work, but in order to bring Big Rob on, she would have to keep the two of them away from one another, but how? While she decided the best way to do this, she thought it best to let Big Rob know the reason she had originally come here. She had already tried out her game with one "big fish" she'd encountered while cruisin' Hunts Point, but she soon discovered a glitch in her plan. She had gotten the john talking, hoping he would mention a wife and family. Then she had gotten his address from his driver's license in his wallet. She fucked him every which way and got a crackhead she knew to take pictures. She blackmailed the unsuspecting fool for cash money; five thousand dollars to be exact.

He had been a frightened weasel, who had given her the money rather than have his wife and family find out about his indiscretions. But what could she use against a man with no wife and kids? Thanks to the time spent with Big Rob, she had figured it out. With his help, she could always ply these gullible muthafuckas with drugs; set them up and demand money for silence. If they didn't give her what she wanted, she would threaten them with exposure to their employers, their clients, maybe even the law. Hell, some of these bastards were even judges and politicians. It wouldn't do them any good to be connected to illicit drug use. In fact, it would probably hurt their careers a lot more than a little roll in the hay with a hooker.

Jade explained the entire plan to Big Rob, and he came up with ideas she had never even dreamed of. Much like she thought, he had connections everywhere. And, although he was hesitant at first and wanted each and every detail down to the letter, it seemed as though his interest was definitely piqued. Besides, Big Rob was a pro; she didn't expect anything less from him.

Now, all that was left to do was to school Bridget. She had adapted pretty quickly to sellin' her body, but Jade wasn't sure it would be quite so easy to convince her to sell her soul.

CHAPTER FOUR
DAVID D. McDONNELL, ESQ.

David D. McDonnell was no stranger to Hunts Point. His father, Charles E. McDonnell, Esq., in his infinite wisdom, had deemed it appropriate to introduce David to the seedy world of Hunts Point and sex for hire at the tender age of eighteen. As far as his father was concerned, a teenager overly preoccupied with getting laid couldn't free up his mind for more important pursuits like his all-important eminent career as an attorney. The same career he had enjoyed and his father before him. One might have thought he would have found a much more suitable environment to achieve this goal. But Charles McDonnell had no intention of allowing some college-educated call girl to get any "bright ideas" about his son, such as blackmail or even worse—marriage. No, these hookers on Hunts Point were exactly what the situation called for. Their brand of sexual gratification was akin to a fast-food drive-up window; quick and easy satisfaction, with no messy entanglements. It had been good enough for him, and it would be good enough for his son as well.

Charles knew just the right girl for his son. Her name was Marie and, although she was definitely experienced, (he himself had gotten a "taste" of what she had to offer), she was young enough and appeared innocent enough so as not to frighten his inexperienced son. As David cruised Hunts Point more than twenty years later, he remembered his introduction to this world. It had been winter 1973—January, to be exact. It had been freezing cold with snow on the ground. On that particular day, David could remember being so confused as to why his father had driven them there; away from the warmth and comfort of their Upper East Side condo to what appeared to David to be the "underbelly of the beast."

As they drove through the intersection of Hunts Point Market, David remembered being awestruck and more than a little frightened. During the twelve years he attended prep school in the largely affluent Bronx community of Riverdale, he had never encountered people such as these. He would be graduating in June, yet he suddenly realized just how sheltered his life had been until now. Only a few miles away, life was decidedly different than anything he had ever known.

By the time David understood why they were there, it was too late for him to protest and he wasn't completely sure he wanted to. David was young and handsome and came from a well-to-do family. It was a given that he would follow in his father's and grandfather's footsteps and be an attorney; probably take over as partner at

McDonnell & Simpson when it was his time. The firm was a thriving, successful law practice started by David's grandfather, Phillip McDonnell, over three decades ago. Therefore, it was no surprise that he had no difficulty in attracting the attention of most of the young girls attending The Horace Hanover School. Yet, there was one in particular who caught his eye; Caitlin Gallagher was blonde and beautiful and the ideal choice for an eventual wife and mother of a successful New York City attorney. She was from a family of attorneys as well and it was understood that she, too, would follow in her family's footsteps. Caitlin and David started dating freshman year and were still dating by the time they were seniors and about to graduate. The problem was Caitlin seemed completely disinterested in having sex with David. Like most teenaged boys, David thought about sex night and day and, after four years of everything short of going all the way, he was more than a little frustrated, but Caitlin had no intention of giving it up. Her mother and grandmother had trained her well. As far as Caitlin was concerned, she would not be having sex with David until they were married.

That's where David's dad came in. He understood the pressure his son was under and, in order to avoid the hazards of distractions caused by a constant hard-on, he did what he thought any "good father" should do. He set his son up with a Hunts Point hooker just as young as his son. Marie had been forced to sell her body at the tender age of sixteen. Originally from Memphis, Tennessee, Marie had run away from home after five years of sexual abuse, suffered at the hands of her own father. When she finally mustered the courage to tell her mother, she pretended not to believe her. So Marie decided she had no other alternative but to leave. Still a child, Marie fueled her departure with dreams of one day becoming an actress, and therefore decided to find her fame and fortune in New York City.

Much like other girls her age, that dream quickly turned to dust when she realized she had no place to live and nothing to eat. After a week of sleeping in doorways and looking for food in the garbage, the resident pimp added her to his ever-growing stable of girls who worked for nothing more than a crowded place to lay their heads and a meal here and there. Any small measure of innocence Marie had left after being abused by her father was quickly lost after working the streets of Hunts Point. Marie saw things and did things that no teenage girl should ever have to experience. Her minimal self-esteem dipped to sub-zero as a result of her life on the streets. Therefore, it was no surprise that the attention of any apparently decent human being would leave Marie feeling completely mesmerized.

That was exactly the effect David McDonnell had upon Marie. Marie's pimp, J.T., had certain repeat customers that paid very well (not that Marie saw any of that money), but J.T. made sure all his girls knew that his "special" customers should get *extra* special attention. Charles

McDonnell was one of those customers. Although Marie did exactly as she was told by J.T., she couldn't stand it when Charles McDonnell was one of her customers for the night. Marie knew full well what she did for a living, but certain customers, like Charles McDonnell, had a way of making girls like her feel like less than dirt. Although Marie's self-esteem was understandably faltering, she wasn't stupid. It occurred to her that if she were somehow inferior because of what she did for a living, what did that make customers like high-and-mighty Charles McDonnell who paid for her services? As far as she was concerned, he was no better than she was. So, when he brought his son, David, to Hunts Point, the last thing she wanted to do was take on a younger and equally as arrogant version of Charles McDonnell. However, Marie was surprised to find that David was nothing at all like his father.

The first night that she met David, he was clearly very nervous and, thanks to Marie's encounter with David's egotistical father, she was extremely resistant to making David's first time a memorably pleasant one. In fact, what she wanted more than anything was to make it the complete opposite. However, afraid to incur J.T.'s anger, she did what she was told. Although very young, Marie was wise beyond her years when it came to matters of sex.

"You a virgin?" Marie asked.

David was offended by her remark and tried his best to appear older and more mature in Marie's eyes.

"Of course not!" he responded.

"I'm just asking, because you've been standing over there for five minutes now, and you haven't said one word or even tried to touch me or anything. Oh, I know, are you gay?"

"No, I am most certainly *not* gay! I'm just not in the mood."

"Oh, because if you're gay and you don't want your father or anybody to know, we could hang out for a while and nobody would have to know. I mean, I won't tell anybody."

"Just so you know, I'm not gay, but I would rather kinda hang out. I got a girlfriend and I don't want to cheat on her. I don't know why my father brought me here anyway. He must be crazy. I don't know how he even knew about this place."

Marie sat there, smiling.

"What's so funny?" David asked.

"I was thinking how nice it must be to be so trusting and naïve," Marie responded.

"Trusting and naïve? Are you talking about me?"

"Who do you think I'm talking about? Certainly not myself. I can't believe you actually said that. You don't know how your father could've known about this place. What did you say your name was, honey?"

"David."

"Well, David, think about it. How do you think your father knew about this place? To start, Charles McDonnell is one of my best customers."

It went on like that for two months. At least once a week, David's dad would drive him to Hunts Point. He'd go to a sparsely furnished room somewhere and sit and talk with Marie. After three weeks or so, Marie and David stopped verbally sparring with one another and actually had real conversations. David couldn't understand how a girl as intelligent as Marie could have ended up living this sort of life. Marie was surprised to find that someone who obviously had as much as David had could be so down-to-earth. She was surprised to find that she actually liked him and looked forward to their conversations; and each time David visited Marie, he found he looked forward to their visits more and more. He talked about Caitlin and, on one of their visits, Marie actually felt a slight twinge of jealousy.

"What's wrong?" David asked.

"Nothing," Marie said.

"Marie, come on. There must be something wrong. You sound funny."

"I said *nothing!*"

And suddenly, from out of nowhere, Marie began to cry. This girl that appeared to David to be indestructible was actually crying. He took her in his arms and, despite her feeble attempts to break away from his grasp, David held onto Marie, stroking her back and whispering in her ear.

"Don't cry, Marie. Please don't cry."

Standing there holding Marie in his arms, this was the

closest the two of them had ever been to one another and understandably, David's teenage body responded in the only way an eighteen-year-old boy's body could respond to a beautiful girl. David got so hard there was no mistaking the fact that he was extremely aroused.

David was embarrassed and wished he could control what was happening. He wanted to be a friend to Marie, not treat her like a prostitute. Over the weeks, he had come to like and admire Marie very much. She was one of the nicest, smartest, most courageous people he had ever known and, instead of standing there and comforting her, he was getting a fucking hard-on. He was surprised she hadn't kicked him out. Instead, Marie did the complete opposite. She raised her head and kissed David. David had spent many a night kissing Caitlin for hours on end, but this was different; this kiss made David feel more like a man than a boy. Marie's skilled tongue probed David's mouth, bringing him to new heights of arousal. As Marie's tongue quickly darted in and out of every corner of David's under-explored orifice, David went on an exploration of his own; he sucked at her tongue, eager to taste all of her. Never removing her mouth from his, Marie slowly unbuttoned David's button-down blue shirt, opened his belt buckle, unzipped his pants and removed all of his remaining clothing.

David's four years on the swim team had helped to chisel an impressively strong body, and Marie stood for a moment and admired David's body. She had been so accustomed to her much older clients she didn't think she could remember ever having seen a more beautiful body. She playfully pushed David down onto the bed and began slowly removing her clothing, revealing a body that David could only describe as sweet, rich milk chocolate. David suddenly wanted Marie more than anything or anyone he had ever wanted in his entire life.

Her breasts were swollen mounds of pleasure on top of which sat a deeper, richer shade of chocolate drop, perfectly suited to be licked, sucked and enjoyed by his anxiously anticipating mouth. Beneath her soft, flat belly, a triangular paradise awaited him. Her mound was a thing of beauty and all he could think of was worshipping it with soft, sweet strokes of his tongue. Her body was the canvas on which he would soon paint. But first, there was so much Marie wanted to show him. She started with his feet, sucking each and every toe, enjoying the way his body wriggled and squirmed. From his toes, her tongue mapped out a trail leading directly to his inner thigh, where she suckled for what seemed like hours, feeding on his strong swimmer's legs, enjoying the short gasps that escaped from his mouth each time her teeth nibbled on his pliable flesh. By the time she reached his manhood, David was in danger of shooting his creamy load all over Marie's beautiful face. Marie wanted this night to last forever; or at least as long as was humanly possible.

She slowed things down a bit; slowly tantalizing David

with her tongue, punishing him so sweetly with sporadic sweeps of her tongue across his stiff and anxiously awaiting tool. Just as Marie thought David would succumb to her expert tongue, he grabbed hold of her so powerfully, Marie was completely astonished. He flipped her over onto the bed so that he was on top of her and ravished her body with the adoration she so deserved. He kissed her from head to toe. There wasn't an inch of her body that wasn't showered with affection. He tasted all of her. By the time he reached Eden, Marie was oblivious to anything but the feel of his lips and his tongue exploring her now inflamed button of bliss. Marie inspired in David a level of heightened expertise that allowed him to give Marie great pleasure. Her soft moans were all the encouragement David needed to give her all that she wanted—and needed.

"David, I want you inside me so much. Please, let me feel you. Please."

Both David and Marie made love for the first time that night, exactly two months after they first met. For the two lovers, it would be the last time either of them would be that close ever again. Not long after making love, the tell-tale knock on the door announced the end of their time together. It was David's father returning to take him home. Somehow, Marie knew she would never see David again. The thought of losing what was probably her last chance at a fairy-tale ending was a crushing blow. She sobbed outwardly, unable to hide her deep hurt within.

"Don't cry, Marie. Please don't cry. This isn't an ending; this is the beginning. I'll be back and we'll be together; the two of us. I'll be graduating from high school in a few months and then it's college and law school. I can make a future for us. I'll take care of you. I can. No one will ever hurt you again."

Even as the words flowed from his mouth, they both knew it was a fantasy. Boys like David didn't marry girls like Marie. Yet, Marie knew she had to be strong for both of them; even if she never saw him again. She pressed her finger to his lips to quiet him.

"Even if you and I never see each other again after tonight, I know that, for at least one night, I was loved."

"Marie," was all David could think of to say in a hushed tone. Then, he kissed her. It was the deepest, most soul-stirring kiss either of them had ever shared with anyone. Their lips locked together, sealing the bond they had shared; blocking out all those that would conspire to keep them apart.

As David's father pounded on the door with greater urgency, David's parting words to Marie were, "I love you and I'll be back," as he headed for the door.

Unfortunately, those words were also heard by Charles McDonnell. McDonnell Senior never mentioned David's professions of love, but he resolved, at that very moment, to end any association his son would ever again have with *"that whore"* Marie.

For months, David tried to locate Marie, secretly venturing uptown to Hunts Point, hoping upon hope that he would find her, to no avail. Eventually reality hit; she was gone from his life forever. What followed was an endless flow of one-night stands with upper-crust bimbos and David's equal sampling of every drug he could get his hands on, until he finally hit rock bottom. David was wandering around aimlessly, intent on finding something to fill the void. That's when he met Michael Santangelo.

Michael and David had been classmates at Horace. However, they had never been what anyone would call friends. They played on the basketball team together, but Michael was different than David and most of the boys at Horace. While David and most of the students there had parents that were loaded, Michael was attending the school on scholarship. His parents were blue collar workers who wanted a better life for their son. Most of the students either lived in the finer areas of Manhattan or had homes in Riverdale or New Jersey, while Michael lived in one of the worst sections of Crown Heights, Brooklyn. Not only that, Michael was Italian, unlike his Jewish counterparts at Horace, making him pretty much an outsider. However, he was able to fare better than some of the scholarship students at Horace because he was a star on the basketball team. Michael and David's bond was formed one night when David tried to sneak into a club with a fake ID. Michael was a frequent visitor to the club and, since he could deal with David a lot better than most of the assholes he had met at Horace, he decided to help him out.

"Yo, Vic, that's one of my boys. Let him in," he told the bouncer at the door.

"Michael, I'm tellin' you now, I don't want no trouble outta you tonight," the bouncer responded.

"Me? Trouble? Why would I cause any trouble? Come on, Vic; let him in."

"Go 'head."

From that night on, David and Michael were frequent visitors to Name This Joint, their favorite hangout. Unfortunately, one night the two pissed one of the patrons off by flirting with his girlfriend, and they got into quite a scuffle. The end result: Both boys had to be picked up at the police station by their parents after being arrested. David's mother and father had said nothing until they were in their car on the way home.

"All I want to know, David, is what the hell are you doing hanging out with that Guido in the first place?" David's father had asked. "I didn't raise you to hang out with that element."

"Yeah, right, Dad. You've done nothing but expose me to the upper crust my whole life," David had commented sarcastically.

"David, watch your mouth. Show your father some respect," his mother had said.

As much as David wanted to regale his father with his definition of "*respect*," the last thing he wanted to do was upset his mother; especially since his father did that enough all on his own. Instead, he apologized, more to his mother than to his father.

"I'm sorry. Michael isn't a bad guy. As a matter of fact, it was more my fault than his. This idiot in the club got upset because I was talking to his girlfriend. I didn't even know she was there with anyone."

"That's your answer for everything: I didn't know. Well, quite frankly, I'm sick of it. You just graduated from high school and, God willing, you'll be going to college in a couple of months, and eventually law school. This bull-shit has to stop!"

"Charles, don't use that language," his mother had said. "David, your father and I have tried everything we can think of and we're afraid if we don't do something drastic, things are only going to get worse for you. There-fore, we've decided that the only thing to do is to send you away; someplace where you can get the help you need. Obviously, we can't give you that help."

Nothing his father did could ever surprise him, but the fact that his mother was willing to send him away to some "treatment center" took David completely by surprise.

"Mom, please, I'll stop. I swear I'll stop. It just…It's just been…"

Finally, everything he had been thinking and feeling for the past several months encapsulated itself into one long, heart-wrenching sob.

"I, I, need…"

David knew there was no way he could finish what he really wanted to say. There was no way he could hurt his mother in such a way. She had such high hopes for him. It would devastate her to know the path his life had taken; the choices he had made. Not to mention, what it would do to her to know that her own husband had been a part of it.

"What, David? Talk to me. Please talk to me," his mother implored him.

David looked from his mother to his obviously anxious father and that's when he realized there would be no easy way out of this one. He would have to go away and get himself clean. There was no way in the world he could tell his mother what had been plaguing him all these months.

"I'll go," he stated quietly. "I'll go…"

Between rehab and college shortly thereafter, David managed to keep himself busy enough to try to keep his mind off of Marie and where she might be or what she might be doing. The thought of her sleeping with random men, cruising the streets of Hunts Point and putting herself in harm's way, was often unbearable. But the one thing he was sure of was that drugs, alcohol and an endless flow of random women, wasn't the answer.

Three months after going away to college in Boston, David returned for Christmas break to find an air of change around the house. His mother and father were cooler toward each other than usual, and David got the distinct impression that something was brewing that neither of them wanted him to know anything about. It was David's fervent wish that his mother had finally come to her senses and was contemplating divorcing his father; especially after hearing them arguing one night from their bedroom.

"You're a hypocrite, Charles! You walk around like you're the pillar of the community when nothing could be further from the truth. This is your legacy, this is what you leave to our son; lies and deceit. Well, I won't be a part of it! You can continue doing exactly what you've always done, exactly what you want to do, and everyone else be damned. But I won't. I can't. He deserves to know!"

"And what exactly do you think that will accomplish, Ann? Nothing! We finally got him back on the straight and narrow and your decision is to go and upset the apple cart. What kind of sense does that make?"

"You will not manipulate me like you've done all these years. I'm standing firm on this. He needs to know and I'm going to be the one who tells him!"

"Why don't you do that? Go right ahead, and I will see to it that you leave here with nothing!"

"No court in New York would allow that to happen," Ann said.

"Don't be so sure of that."

"You're only trying to scare me. Unlike you, I have never cheated on you. I've been a good wife to you and a wonderful mother to my son. No court would allow you to take everything away from me."

"I don't know about that, Ann. You've had not one, but two stints in a mental facility."

"That wasn't my fault!" she cried. "I tried to kill myself because of *you*. *You*. You did everything you could to break me and it worked!"

David listened from the hall. He remembered his mother going *"away"* several years ago and everyone being very hush-hush about the specifics. That explained it. It made David even surer about his thoughts surrounding his father. He couldn't understand why she had never left him.

"Yes, Ann, but that, coupled with your ridiculous spending, will prove instability. Not to mention the fact that you signed a pre-nup."

It had been so long ago, she had almost forgotten about the papers he had ensured her were merely a formality.

"But, Ann, I'll make a deal with you. I'll provide you with the life you have become *so* accustomed to and you will keep your goddamn mouth shut. You can do that here or elsewhere. I really don't care. I was done with you a long time ago. But you won't ruin everything I've built all these years."

"Charles, can't we at least ensure that they're not homeless? That's the very least that we can do. We have so much to offer and they have so little."

"You do what you will with your allowance, but rest

assured, if David ever gets wind of what we have discussed this evening, you will have hell to pay."

Any sense of pride David felt in finally bearing witness to his mother standing up to his bully of a father was short-lived. Within moments, there was a crack in her veneer and the frightened, subservient mother he had always known returned. More than anything, David wanted to rescue his mother, but he didn't think it was a good idea to interrupt them now. However, he did wonder what they were talking about. For a moment he thought it might have something to do with the countless charitable organizations his mother contributed to. But why would that have anything to do with him? He snooped around the next day and took a look at his mother's checkbook, hoping to figure out what it was she was talking about when she mentioned someone *being homeless*. But all he found was a check made out to PRIMCO Property Management. For a split second he hoped maybe she might have decided to leave after all. But distracted with the holiday festivities, he never gave it another thought.

The rest of David's Christmas vacation continued as if nothing had ever happened. At the end of the holiday, he returned to Boston. However, within weeks of returning to school, his mother contacted him and let him know that she had moved out—which made perfect sense. The PRIMCO check had most likely been a down-payment for an apartment. David's contact with his father eventually became non-existent. Where before he felt obligated to interact with his father because he and his mother were still together, now he felt no need to. He could talk to his mother whenever he wanted without dealing with his father at all, and the independence he gained by being on his own at school, afforded him the opportunity to pick and choose his level of contact. His relationship with his father went from strained to virtually non-existent.

A little more than a month after that, his mother contacted him, summoning him for his father's funeral. Charles McDonnell had had a heart attack and had died *alone* at their summer home on Long Island. His last will and testament left nothing to Ann, who was still his wife. He left everything he owned to David. With his father gone, David felt free to return to New York and enrolled at New York University and, eventually, NYU Law School. To his mother's great surprise, after passing the bar exam, David took his place exactly where his father had intended, at McDonnell & Simpson, poised and ready to continue the McDonnell legacy.

CHAPTER FIVE
McDONNELL & SIMPSON

Jade noticed the black Mercedes often, yet the driver never stopped to pick up any of the girls, including her. It became a mystery she was hell-bent on solving.

"Hey, baby, you want some chocolate?" Jade beckoned from her favorite corner. "I got whatever you want right here!"

She strutted over to his car, anxious to unveil her mystery man, just in time for him to speed off. Right then Bridget got out of the car of one of her regulars. Undoubtedly, she had given him a blow job. That was what most of their customers wanted; some quick relief and off they went to their homes and families. Bridget often talked of marriage one day and children. Jade couldn't imagine marrying *anybody*. What the fuck was the point; they all screwed anything with a pulse anyway. The only reason Jade saw for getting married was the Benjamins. And if it wasn't in writing and it wasn't *big* money, she still didn't see the point.

It happened every day; some woman *"thinks"* she's got everything her man's got, until he moves on to the next best thing and she's left with nothing. She would never be that kind of sucker and neither would Bridget. Bridget *belonged* to her; she was her cash cow and she would continue to be that, however and whenever she saw fit.

Bridget noticed Jade watching intently as the black Mercedes drove away.

"He drove up right next to me one day and rolled down his window, but Tamika, that junkie that lives over on Boynton, she ran over to the car and he drove off," Bridget mentioned.

"Shit, Bridget! I keep telling you if you act like a punk, these girls are going to take what's yours."

"Jade, what are you talking about? He was just a trick."

"A trick with big money," Jade reminded her. "Did you see those fuckin' seats; all leather. The next time he drives by here, I want you to make your presence known. You hear me?"

"What makes you think he's gonna be back here again? He only comes by once-in-a-blue-moon, and he never picks up any of the girls anyway. Besides, what makes you think he's gonna want me?"

"Because I know my shit, that's why. They always come back. And I'm willing to bet all that I own, you'll be *exactly* what he's looking for."

David *was* looking for Bridget. He found that the more he watched her, the more he wanted her. At first he had fooled himself into believing that eventually his fixation on this young woman would subside. But, nothing could have been further from the truth. If anything, his fascination with her grew. Where once he would visit once a week, he found himself taking a ride into the Bronx twice, sometimes three times a week. He even visited a psychotherapist, convinced that he was losing his mind. One visit to the therapist was all he needed to convince himself that therapy wasn't for him. Instead he threw himself into his work and into watching this woman that reminded him so much of Marie.

Eventually, he worked up enough nerve to approach her, unaware that Jade had given Bridget careful instructions about what she should do if that black Mercedes with the genuine leather seats and the Adonis-looking occupant should ever stop.

Bridget saw the car as soon as it made its way by her.

"Hey, baby, you want some company?"

David couldn't help but think how foreign the words sounded coming out of her mouth. If it were at all possible, she seemed even more out of place here than Marie had seemed all those years ago. There was an obvious innocence about her. He wondered how she survived without being eaten alive by the pariahs circling her, which, under the circumstances, also applied to him.

Here he was, this confident captain of industry, almost forty years old, and this young woman, probably half his age, was making him as nervous as a teenager. It was as if all those women in between Marie and her had never even happened.

"Hi," was all he could muster. "I'm not sure what I feel like doing tonight. Do you have some time? I'll pay you five hundred for the whole night."

Bridget could barely contain her excitement. That was more than she had ever gotten for a trick. Hell, that was more than she had ever gotten in a night; even a week. Often, she was lucky if she got fifty bucks in a night. But, with that excitement, also came a little fear. Once a guy had offered her a hundred, much the same way that this man had, and he had beaten her up pretty bad. She had ended up with a broken arm, and he had punched her so hard in the face that the blood vessels in her eyes had broken. As much as she would have liked to get five hundred and not have to work for the rest of the night, she didn't want to die for it either.

Lured by the prospects of that much money, Bridget couldn't help but take a chance and she got in his car.

"So how does this work?" David asked.

"Depends on what you want."

"Not really sure yet."

"Are you hungry? We could stop and get something to eat."

Now Bridget was sure there was something wrong with him. What did he think this was—a date? Men seldom cruised Hunts Point looking for someone to take to dinner.

"Uhm, I kinda need the money up front."

David retrieved his wallet and handed her five crisp one hundred-dollar bills.

Her heart was beating so wildly in her chest she hoped he wouldn't hear it. She didn't want to let on that this was more money than she had seen at one time in forever.

"So, what would you like to eat?"

He really wanted to take her someplace where they could sit down, eat and talk, but her attire made that a little difficult. He was so fascinated with her, he wanted to know all there was to know about her. She possessed an opposing duality that was unmistakable—girl/woman, sinner/saint, gentle/rough.

"Whatever you want is fine," she answered.

"We could go to a hotel and order room service if you'd like."

"Okay."

Driving into Manhattan, David watched as she passed the sights and sounds of the city. It was as though she were a child seeing everything for the first time. David parked the car and they walked a block or so and checked into the Roosevelt Hotel in Midtown.

Once inside the hotel room, Bridget was surprised to find that he wasn't the nut job she figured he would be. She found out he was a lawyer and told him that she had always wanted to be a lawyer herself, but things hadn't turned out the way she wanted. Even though she knew he probably didn't take her seriously, it appeared as though he was actually listening.

"I think they have a room service menu here. You want to look at it?"

"Yeah!" she said with excitement.

Bridget looked at the menu and was delighted with all the choices. She seldom ate well and it was difficult for her to make a decision. Sensing her dilemma, he told her she could order whatever she wanted, if she couldn't make up her mind. He was surprised to discover that she was actually very conservative in her choices. As far as David was concerned, that spoke volumes about her character.

Sitting with her and talking up close, David's own character surprised him as well. He expected to want to have sex with her as soon as they were in the hotel room. Yet, he was enjoying just sitting and talking with her. It wasn't that he wasn't attracted to her, but he was treating her more like a person and less like a prostitute.

Bridget was full of questions and David found it difficult to figure out whether or not she was more woman or more child. One minute she was cautious to a fault, clearly making decisions to protect herself; the next she was prattling on and on about anything and everything. He got the impression she didn't have many people to talk to.

"You probably wouldn't be able to tell it to look at me, but I can take steno and type."

At first, David thought maybe she might be trying to hustle him for a job. Then he realized her self-esteem was in great need of a boost. Her secretarial skills were obviously something she was very proud of and she wanted to impress him. In many ways, it was very sad.

"Really?" he answered. "You ever think of going to an agency or something and trying to get a job working as a secretary or a clerk?"

"Yeah, I think about it all the time, but Jade always tells me that no one would ever give someone like me a job."

"But, you won't know that until you try, will you? I'll tell you what. I'll meet you at the same place, time and day that I met you tonight in the Bronx, and I'll get you some information that you might be able to use to get started in a new line of work."

Bridget was so excited, she couldn't contain herself.

"Really? Seriously? Thank you so much! I'll be on Hunts Point the same day and time next week, waiting. Thank you so, so much!"

For some reason, it made David feel good that she was so happy. He genuinely liked this girl. He didn't know if it was because he reminded her so much of Marie or because the thought of helping another human being gave him a sense of purpose. He had lived such a narcissistic life; it felt good to know that he could actually have real impact on someone else's life.

David noticed that Bridget's demeanor shifted and the girl/woman suddenly became all woman.

"Now, is there anything I can do for you?" she asked in her sexiest voice.

Although he was attracted to her, for some reason, he felt as though any sense of pride he had in himself at doing a good deed would be lost, if he had sex with Bridget at that moment. He made up an excuse about having to get up early in the morning. Time and time again, after his last encounter with Marie all those years ago, he often wondered if he had waited and continued on the same course with Marie, maybe, just maybe things would have been different. Maybe if he hadn't had sex with her in the first place, he wouldn't have spent all these years unable to let go of a woman he had known only briefly. That was the same feeling he got when he thought of how good it would feel to be with Bridget.

"Maybe the next time," he said.

"Of course," Bridget responded.

She was shocked that he hadn't wanted her to at least give him a blow job. Then it occurred to her that next time he probably wasn't going to give her any money; especially after tonight. But, she suddenly realized that, even if he didn't, she really didn't care.

He told her that he would be staying, so that she could leave before him. She took the hint and prepared to leave but, before she opened the door to leave, he handed her more money.

"Wha…"

Before she could finish, David explained.

"Oh, that's for a taxi."

Once outside, Bridget looked at the cash and it was an additional fifty dollars—just about as much as she sometimes made in one night. Bridget made a mental note not to tell Jade how much money he had given her. The fifty dollars would be sufficient and she would hold the five hundred dollars in reserve. She had been putting money away here and there (without Jade's knowledge). And this money would be a nice addition to the little she now had saved. For a moment she even considered not telling her she met him at all, but she thought better of it.

After riding the subway uptown, Bridget found Jade on Hunts Point, giving one of her regulars head in between two doorways. Bridget decided she would only tell Jade she made fifty dollars off the guy in the Mercedes and another fifty from three other johns; that way she could pocket the other four fifty and she wouldn't feel like she had to work for the rest of the night. If Bridget didn't pull in enough johns, Jade would always try to push her to work more. Jade had pretty much given her a roof over her head since the beginning, so Bridget felt obligated to do what she said. But if Jade felt Bridget had had a busy night, she wouldn't push it.

When Jade was done and her john left, Bridget approached her.

"Guess what?" Bridget said excitedly. "I met Mr. Mercedes tonight and he gave me fifty just for talking!"

"Get the fuck out of here!" Jade said. "I knew that MoFo was *different*. What did I tell you? If he gave you fifty just for talkin', what do you think he's gonna give you to do anything else? Damn! You gonna see him again?"

"Yeah. He said he'll be back the same time next week."

"Good, good. And, did you have a chance to get any of that info I told you to get?"

"Yeah. I got it. It was hard though. It's a good thing

I've got a good memory. I memorized it when he gave his identification and credit card to the hotel clerk. Otherwise, I would've been up shit's creek. I was planning to get it from him after we were done, you know, but we didn't do anything, so I had to rely on what I memorized from the front of his driver's license. I got the name, address and his date of birth."

"Not bad. I've trained you well."

"Jade, what are you going to do with the information? He seems like he's a nice guy. I'd hate to do anything to hurt him."

"You know, Bridget, I don't understand you. You livin' in fuckin' squalor and suckin' dick to stay alive, and you're worried about some rich motherfucka that hasn't got a care in the world. Don't worry about what I'm gonna do with it. I'm gonna improve *our* lives; that's what I'm gonna do with it."

Although Bridget and Jade were friends, she had heard enough stories from other girls on the street about different ways that Jade exacted revenge on people that crossed her. She was ever mindful of the fact that she didn't want to ever get on Jade's bad side, so she left the entire line of discussion alone.

Bridget was surprised to find that one week later, David actually showed up as he had promised.

"You didn't think I was going to come, did you?" he asked.

"No, not really. If there's one thing I've learned about this *business*, nothing is guaranteed."

"Get in," he said, and with that, they drove to the same hotel they had gone to before.

David was sympathetic to her situation, but he also found he was feeling something else. Bridget was right on his heels as he opened the door to the hotel room. He could feel her hot breath on his neck. Once inside the room, the two were standing face to face, and he felt that same old stirring he had felt with Marie, a combination of desire mixed with guilt. Bridget was standing so close to him, there was nothing he could do to conceal his desire.

"You want me to do something about that?" Bridget joked, touching him.

David couldn't figure out why, with her being a hooker and all, but he was suddenly very embarrassed. However, before he could tell her no, Bridget was on her knees, unzipping his pants and relieving him of any thoughts, other than the sweet release being offered by her expert lips. He grew inside of her mouth with each stroke she offered him and, before he knew it, he was shooting what seemed like oceans of cum inside of her mouth. It was unlike anything he had ever felt in his entire life; even with Marie. The fact that Bridget seemed to swallow every ounce with great ease only served to work toward getting him excited once again. But before he could think of that, he wanted to do something for her. They both made their way to the bed and, from his briefcase, David extracted a list of employment agencies that he thought might be helpful for finding Bridget employment.

"I won't be able to see you next week, because I'm going out of town, but if you'd like, until you find other work, we could have a standing appointment with one another. It might even be enough money so that you won't have to work as much on Hunts Point."

"That would be great!"

"As I said, I'm going out of town, but before I leave, I'm going to stop by and drop off something you can wear for your interviews and also for when you and I meet. You'll need clothes that are more conservative. Not that I don't love what you're wearing, but if you're wearing something more conservative, we can also go someplace other than here. If that's okay with you?"

"Okay. That's more than okay. Thanks!"

Fear can be the great equalizer; especially when a person is made to believe they are little more than nothing. In the week since David had left and given her the list of agencies to contact, Bridget had looked at the list over and over again. But, not once did she attempt to contact any of the people on the list. Her first fear was that the moment she used her social security number on any documentation, a red flag would go up and the police would come knocking at her door, ready to arrest her for murdering Buster. But her biggest and most overwhelming fear was that she was incapable of doing anything other than what she was already doing. Although David was disappointed when he returned to find that she hadn't acted on any of the leads he had given her, he understood. The two continued to see one another, at least once a week. Bridget would always give him head and afterward, they would spend some time talking. It went on like that for quite some time. And, eventually Bridget began to speculate as to why he had never penetrated anything other than her mouth. After all, it should have been a natural progression, given the circumstances. Her minimal self-esteem always being a factor, Bridget began to wonder if he was afraid of catching an STD from her. She never asked, but even if she had, David probably wouldn't have been able to tell her anyway— his only fear was how deeply he might fall for her if they did *anything* other than what they were already doing.

When Jade thought she knew enough about David from the things Bridget had told her, and when she had taken enough pictures of him and Bridget in as many compromising positions as she could manage, she knew it was time to spring into action and work on everything she had planned.

"Hey, Freckles."

Jade and Bridget turned around to find Big Rob standing directly behind them. It wasn't often that Bridget had seen Jade come close to anything that could be described as happy, but somehow, when she was around Big Rob, Jade came as close as could be expected from her.

"You can't be sneakin' up on a sista like that in the 'hood, baby. You might get somethin' you hadn't bargained for."

"What you got?" Big Rob teased.

"Bridget, I'm gonna call it quits for tonight; I'll see you at the house."

Bridget didn't particularly care for Big Rob's *type*; the street thug. But, if Jade was happy, she was happy. Not only that, Bridget was doing everything she could to brush up on her office skills and get off the streets. She would feel a lot less guilty about leaving Jade, if she knew there was someone else there for her. Not that she planned on never seeing Jade again. As far as Bridget was concerned, Jade was her sister, in every sense of the word, and she had saved her from prison and God only knew what else. Yet, she knew that Jade would be crushed when she left. They depended on each other. Somehow, though, she thought the blow would be lessened if Jade were otherwise occupied.

"Can I drive tonight?" Jade asked.

"Baby, you can have whatever you want."

"Yeah, right."

Big Rob pulled over in front of the subway station on Elder Avenue and switched places so Jade could drive.

"Damn, girl, you drive like you tryin' to kill somebody out here. We not in a rush. Slow down."

"I'm just anxious to get you home, baby."

"Freckles, you ain't gotta run the hustle on your man. You already got my nose *wide* open."

"What makes you think I'm tryin' to run a hustle? I might be in love."

"As much as that would flatter the hell out of a brotha,

somehow you don't strike me as the love type. No offense, baby."

"Hey, none taken."

Jade slowed down her driving and the two rode the rest of the way to Big Rob's place downtown in silence. Jade's mind was always workin', thinking about the next thing. Big Rob wasn't as easily manipulated as most, but even he had his weaknesses, and Jade had come to learn that she was indeed one of those weaknesses. Yet, even she had to work it right. And, Big Rob opened up a lot better when he was relaxed. So, Jade would drive his car the way he wanted it driven, and fuck him the way he liked it, feed him what he wanted to be fed, and even spend some time cuddlin' up in his crib and flattering him about his accomplishments; then she would go to work.

A few of Big Rob's boys had followed David when he was on Hunts Point and they had been watching him for weeks now. One of his runners even had a cousin that worked at the firm as a long-term temp. In fact, she was very excited that she was soon going to be hired by the firm as a permanent employee. That would give Rob's runner an opportunity to get information. As far as Jade was concerned, David McDonnell was the big score; the sucker that would lead them to even more suckers like him: rich, influential men with fat bank accounts and a whole hell of a lot to lose. Between Bridget and what Big Rob could offer in the way of information, she would be well on her way to knowing everything there was to know about David D. McDonnell.

"His firm is quoted in the *New York Law Journal* and the *National Law Journal* like every fuckin' week. It's one of them firms that was started by his father's father's father and shit. Hell, I'm impressed with the muthafucka myself. Once upon a time, before reality hit and I grew up, I used to wonder what it would be like to go to law school or medical school or some shit like that. Knowing myself as I do, I'm pretty sure my shit would have been on a large scale. Hell, I almost hate to take him down. In another life, I mighta' been rollin' with somebody like him."

"Yeah, I hear you, but take him down we will. I've been hustling and scrapin' since I was fuckin' born. This is my chance to make that big score all the way around, and go legit. That's the only difference between *us* and *them*. Their shit ain't always legit, either, but they got resources to make it legit; like investments and property. If I had all that, I'd never have to trick another day in my life."

"Why you gotta trick now? You got the boostin' thing, and the snatch-and-grab thing, and you got me. Why don't you give that trickin' shit up? You ain't no ten-dollar hooker, baby. I knew that from day one."

"That's what I'm tryin' to do with this, but I need your help," Jade said.

Jade learned early on in life that the best way to divert

a man, or to get him to do what you wanted, was to stroke his ego. In truth, she was thinking that there was no way in hell she was going to depend on any man for her bread and butter, but she wouldn't dare reveal her thoughts to Big Rob. Instead, she made it seem as though she needed him another way.

"So what did your boys get on him anyway? Anything?"

Big Rob was feelin' Jade more and more each day, and he had some shit on this mark that would even shock Jade. She wasn't a sista' that shocked easily, but he wasn't gonna reveal that info yet. Any good game was only as good as its biggest ace-in-the-hole. And, what he had on Mr. David McDonnell was a pretty big fuckin' ace-in-the-hole.

"A few indiscretions with hookers here and there, most recently with your girl, Bridget, an ex-wife with a drug problem. She spent some time in rehab, but nothing major. Just enough to serve our purposes, dangle the threat of a scandal in front of him," he lied. You'd be surprised what embarrasses white folks. Drugs is a fact of life in our world, but in there's even an ex with a drug problem can be considered scandalous if the person in question is high profile enough. And ya boy, David McDonnell, is pretty damned high-profile!"

In truth, Big Rob had learned some things about David, that David himself might not even know yet. All he needed was a little time and he'd have all the pieces of the puzzle.

Jade wasn't stupid. Big Rob was keepin' something from her. He knew something that he wasn't telling her, but why? It occurred to her that she would probably have to do her own discreet investigation. But, in the meantime, she would need someone on the inside. It was only a matter of time before Bridget slipped away and got herself one of those *"honest"* jobs she kept nagging about. What better way to strengthen her hold on both her and Mr. McDonnell than to force him into giving Bridget a job at his firm?

Until now, David had had no contact with Jade. She decided it was about time. David and Bridget had a standing *date* with one another every Wednesday night. Jade ensured that the next time Bridget and David were to meet, she would make sure Bridget was otherwise occupied. When David showed up, instead of Bridget, Jade was there waiting for him.

"You looking for Bridget?" Jade said, as David's black Mercedes kept circling the area where they were supposed to meet.

He had seen Bridget talking to Jade on more than one occasion, but was uncomfortable. There was something about her that didn't sit right with him, and he wanted to avoid any contact with her. But, what if something was wrong with Bridget?

"Yes. Is she okay?" he asked.

"Yeah, she's fine. She had an errand to run. That's cool though, because I think you and I should talk anyway."

"I can't imagine that the two of us have anything to talk about."

"Then, you would be wrong," Jade quickly responded.

"Really?"

"You want to continue this here, with me yelling at you from across the street, or are you going to invite me inside your car, so we can talk like civilized human beings?"

Against his better judgment, David opened the car door so that Jade could get in. She walked toward his car, got in and placed a large manila envelope on his lap. David was smart enough to know that whatever was in it, couldn't be good. He was right. Inside the envelope were numerous pictures of Bridget giving him head. He couldn't figure out who he was more angry with—himself, Bridget or Jade. He decided it was Bridget.

"So, I suppose you want money?" he asked.

"Yeah, I do want money, but that's not all I want. There's something else."

"For the sake of argument, let's say that I do give you money, and whatever else it is you want. What do I get out of this? You have the pictures and God knows how many other copies. What's to prevent you from blackmailing me forever."

"You'll have to trust me. There are only two sets. The originals and these copies. And, if you give me what I want, both sets will be yours."

"What else is it that you want?"

"Give Bridget a job at your firm."

"So, I'm supposed to hire the very person who's blackmailing me to work at my own law firm. I would have to be a complete and utter fool to do something like that."

"You have no choice. Either you give Bridget the job and the fifty grand that I want, or these pictures will be splattered across every newspaper in New York and probably even some national ones. I'm not as stupid as I may look, Mr. McDonnell. I know more about you than how that cute little ass of yours looks. I've read most of those articles you've written, as well as all the speculation about your love life and the very many *"beautiful people"* you've been involved with. You've got a *mighty fine* reputation you've established for yourself. I also know about that whack-job of an ex-wife you have, with her stints in rehab, her questionable taste in men, and her arrests. How would your reputation fare if the media got wind of her, or even your own stay in rehab all those years ago? And how do you think the embarrassment of it all would affect your mother? Do you think she would continue to be oh-so-very proud of her baby boy? David, you *really* don't want to fuck with me!"

She didn't have to convince David that she would do exactly as she said. She was holding all the cards. She had nothing to lose, but he had everything to lose.

"And when do you want this money?"

"Immediately, of course," she answered.

"And the job for Bridget?"

"Immediately. And that's not all. I want intros to some

of your colleagues; the ones that might be interested in having a little fun with me and a few of my girls."

"Okay, now you've lost your mind. I can't exactly go around acting like your...your pimp, or something."

"I didn't ask you to be my pimp. I want a few introductions. You decide who'd be the best people to hook me up with. I'll do the rest."

"Okay. Done," he said. "But could you do something for me?"

"Fire away, baby."

"Just answer me one question: Whose idea was this? Bridget's or yours?"

"Whose idea do you think it was? You and I haven't met until tonight. It sure as hell wasn't my idea," Jade lied.

As far as Jade was concerned, she'd be damned if Bridget was going to have Mr. Moneybags walking around acting all doe-eyed over her. She was going to get all the info she needed about him, his colleagues and his business, and Bridget was going to help. But, she would ensure that neither Bridget nor David would enjoy the time they spent together. Her response guaranteed that David would hate Bridget.

CHAPTER SIX
OBSESSION

When Bridget returned from the wild goose chase that Jade had sent her on, Jade continued on her lying streak. She led Bridget to believe that David had shown up on Hunts Point with such goods new for Bridget that he couldn't wait to see her in person. Instead, he had asked Jade to pass the news on.

"Are you sure, Jade? He wants me to come to work at his firm. Are you sure that's what he said?"

"How many times do I have to tell you? I didn't make this shit up. He told me how disappointed he was that he missed you and that he had some really good news. There's an opening in his company. It's an entry-level position in the word processing department, but there would be an opportunity for advancement."

"I don't believe this! I kept wishing something like this would happen, but I never thought it actually would. A real job! See, I told you he was a nice guy."

"Yeah, real nice," Jade whispered under her breath.

"Huh? Did you say something, Jade?"

"I was agreeing with you. He does seem nice. This is

what you've wanted all along. I didn't think you could pull it off. But, that's my bad; I was wrong. You did it. Congratulations!"

"Did he say when I should start?"

"Monday. Also, he mentioned that you probably wouldn't be meeting once a week like you've been doing, since you're going to be working at the firm now."

Bridget was a little disappointed. She had come to enjoy her weekly meetings with David. He really was very nice to her; nicer than anyone she had ever known. And she was somehow able to get through her obligation to provide sexual satisfaction with him better than any of the other men she had encountered on Hunts Point. She felt he deserved to feel good. It was somehow a reward from her to him, for being so nice to her and treating her like a human being.

"Oh," Bridget said. "But, that's okay; we'll be working with each other every day. We'll still get to see each other."

"I wouldn't count on it. Don't forget how the two of you met. He's probably going to do his best to keep a very low profile. It wouldn't do for his hoity-toity colleagues to know that he spends his nights trolling Hunts Point. Besides, it's his firm and you'll be a part of his staff. So, don't be too surprised if he gives you the cold shoulder."

"Yeah. I guess you're right."

"He gave me the address and everything. The office is at 750 Lexington Avenue, on Fifty-ninth Street. His office is on the sixteenth floor; McDonnell & Simpson. So,

Ms. Corporate Big Wig. You workin' tonight, or you off to swim with the big fish?"

Bridget couldn't believe she had asked her that. The last thing she wanted to do was work. She finally had a real job. As far as she was concerned, she was done with the streets.

"I was thinking I'd go back home, and try to get ready for Monday," Bridget responded meekly.

"Get ready for Monday. It's only Wednesday. How much time do you need to get ready? You can knock off on Friday night or, better yet, Saturday night. You know Friday and Saturday are our biggest nights. Besides, we got bills to pay."

"Okay," Bridget answered. "But Friday is my last day. I'm gonna need the weekend to get my head right for the job. It's been a while since I've done any kind of office work."

Bridget's week was grueling. Jade made sure that every car passing through Hunts Point was pointed in Bridget's direction. By the time she laid her head on her pillow Friday night, she was exhausted. Yet, as she slept, she knew that she would never have to live that life again. For the first time in a long time, she slept soundly, with no dreams of Mannersville, or johns, or even Buster.

Bridget arrived at the offices of McDonnell & Simpson bright and early at 9:00 a.m., even though she was told to get there at 9:30. She was so excited the night before that she could barely sleep. She must have tried on the suit David had bought her ten times on Saturday and Sunday; anxious to look her best.

When she arrived, there was a human resources person waiting to escort her around the offices. When it was time to fill out the legal forms required for employment, she was happy to see that David had made sure that his assistant, Linda, took over. She wasn't sure what had been worked out, but she did read the portion of the application that required a social security card as well as proof of identity. She was sure that she was not going to be able to take the job. However, everything seemed to work itself out. Linda never asked for any of the identification requested on the application. Once again, it appeared, David had come through for her.

It took Bridget a while to figure out where things were and to reacquaint herself with the things she had learned when she was in school. Between the training the company offered on the computer and everything else she already knew, she proved herself to be invaluable by always pitching in when needed, staying late, and working weekends. Despite David's desire to loathe her presence, he couldn't help but notice that she wasn't lying about having some knowledge of working behind a desk. In fact, she had more than a passing knowledge. She was good at what she did and was more than eager to learn anything she didn't already know. Her work ethic was impressive to anyone that witnessed it.

More and more David began to find ways to place himself near and around her. If he needed assistance on the weekends, he requested Bridget. If his assistant couldn't stay after hours to finish something up, he would call the word processing department and ask if Bridget was available. He became so enthralled with her presence, he was unaware of the fact that everyone around them knew he was attracted to her. That is, everyone but Bridget. Despite the circumstances under which they originally met, Bridget didn't treat David like a john, or even a man that might be interested in her sexually. She saw him as her savior, even a father figure, and she would have done anything for him. In her eyes he had done everything for her.

Despite David's desire for her, he always kept his interactions with Bridget purely professional. However, he started to become exceedingly preoccupied with her. He spent every waking hour, thinking about her, what she was doing, where she was going, how she spent her time. And before he knew it, he had taken to following her. At first, he justified it with coincidence and his just happening to leave the office at the same time she was leaving. Then, he became fascinated with the places she went. She seemed so taken with things that he took for granted. On one particular day, he watched her watching children playing in a nearby park. The little things he seldom even noticed seemed to bring her so much joy. It made him want to know even more about her.

From the very first day Bridget started working at

McDonnell, he was angry, very angry. Yet, that anger had minimized the more he watched her work and witnessed her personality. He found it hard to believe that Bridget could have instigated the circumstances of her coming to work at McDonnell. The more he came to know about Bridget, the more he began to believe that Jade was at the helm of all of this. After all, it was Jade who had contacted him on numerous occasions, badgering him to introduce her to his clients and colleagues. More and more David was convinced that he was willing to let Jade do her worst. But whenever he thought of his mother and what a scandal would do to her, he tried his best not to lose his temper. He gave Jade what she wanted, within reason.

David had been so preoccupied with Bridget he hadn't realized that his assistant, Linda, was finding an assortment of ways to rob him blind.

One of Big Rob's runners, Pookie, happened to have a cousin named Brianna who had gone from working as a temp to being hired as a permanent secretary at McDonnell & Simpson. Both Big Rob and Pookie were convinced that with the right incentive, they could encourage Brianna to give them confidential information about the firm. Maybe even find ways to siphon off a bit of cash money. They were wrong. Brianna didn't have a drug problem, so they couldn't ply her with drugs—and she was an honest woman, plain and simple. When they realized that wasn't going to work, Pookie used small bits of information

Brianna shared early on, before she realized what her cousin and Big Rob were up to. Brianna once mentioned that David's assistant, Linda, enjoyed herself a bit of coke every now and again. Once Big Rob and Pookie made Jade aware of Linda, she pounced.

Although her interest was initially purely recreational, after hooking up with Jade, Linda established quite the cocaine habit. Jade needed someone *inside* to get her the information and possibly the money she wanted. Her first choice would have been Bridget, but she knew she didn't have the stomach for it. Linda was just the woman for the job, someone on the edge of desperation. As with any addict, she had to come up with more and more creative ways to feed her habit. And, Jade supplied her with ways to do just that. Ways that, of course, would profit her much more than Linda.

"Linda, could you come in here, please?" David asked Linda one day after she had gotten back from lunch. "The company that's been catering our lunches sent me an email today. It seems they do not *prefer* cash as you have so frequently told me. They've been trying to get the majority of their clients, including us, to pay them with a check or credit card. According to their accounting department, our firm has been resistant to paying by either means.

"Now, with rare exception, they require that all of their clients pay by check or money order, and they felt it necessary to contact me directly. I assumed they were mistaken and they were the ones who had expressed a preference for cash. Therefore, they supplied me with all of the communications you've had with them; along with all of our former invoices.

"Linda, you've been padding these bills. There's no mistake about it. There are bills here that were for five hundred dollars, but you got close to a thousand from our accounting department. There's one here for three hundred and you got six hundred from accounting. Not only that, I checked all of your overtime sheets and some of the weeks when you worked thirty-five hours, I signed overtime sheets for close to seventy. You've done an exemplary job for me, Linda, but there is clearly a problem.

"I'm not going to fire you, but if you don't resign willingly, I will. No one will know why you left. We can tell everyone you went back to Boston if you'd like, which actually might not be a bad idea. I'm not sure what your problem is, but I have a pretty good idea. You need help, Linda, and I hope you go somewhere and get it."

David had seen Jade hanging around the office, often waiting for Linda after work. He knew it was only a matter of time before things went awry. He knew Jade also sold drugs and undoubtedly Linda was one of her best clients.

"I'm so sorry, David," she cried. "I don't know what happened. I've been spending time with some people that I think are bad for me. I'm going to get it together. I promise."

Linda left David's office, happy that he hadn't decided to prosecute her for theft and fraud. She was eager to cop some blow.

She was barely inches away from the building before she beeped him: 9-1-1.

"Rob, you holding?"

"Yeah, Jade will be here. Come on by."

Linda considered taking the subway, but was in too much of a hurry. She had had a horrific day and the only thing she yearned to do was escape. It was tough for her to remember what she had done with her money and her time before she met Jade and Big Rob. At times like this, when everything was going wrong and she hadn't gotten high yet, she wondered how she could've fallen so quickly. But, that feeling wouldn't last for long. She would hook up with Jade, and get herself right. Besides, she had to do something to get it together. She was unemployed now and would have to find the stamina to find another job.

Jade had become Big Rob's connection with a large number of upscale customers; Linda included. Since he had hooked up with Jade, he had everyone coming to him, from secretaries like Linda, to lawyers and doctors alike; not to mention all their rich teenage children and their friends. He was making money hand-over-fist, and he had to admit that he had Jade to thank for that.

Big Rob used to think he was focused when it came to business. But Jade was the only person he had ever met

that was more driven than he was. She always seemed to
be coming up with ways to make more and more money.
Big Rob would watch her manipulate people so well it
was fascinating to witness. He was especially intrigued
by her relationship with Bridget. Often he actually felt
sorry for the girl. Bridget was completely unaware of how
artfully Jade was manipulating her day in and day out.
He wasn't surprised to find out that she had managed to
get her a job at that hot-shot law firm. She had been
playing everyone at that firm like pieces on a chess board;
from the big man to his very own secretary. Jade had a
gift for exploiting a person's weakness. That was why he
made sure he kept Jade at arm's length and on his good
side. Big Rob wasn't afraid of Jade, because he was a
force all on his own, but there was no sense in inviting
undue hassles. As much as he was feeling her, he wasn't
about to be *anybody*'s sucker. Big Rob found himself wondering what was up Jade's sleeve next. For every one of
her actions, there was always a more than equal reaction.
He wondered what would come next.

Jade knew Big Rob didn't like anybody coming to his
apartment, so she made sure she was waiting outside
when Linda got there.

"This is some real good shit I got you today."

"How much?" Linda asked.

"You've hooked me up so much, I'll give this to you
free plus one extra, if you'll do me a favor."

"What?" Linda asked.

"I hear that there's a guy in accounting at McDonnell

that gets high. I think he'll like Big Rob's stuff a lot better than what he's been getting. You gotta admit, Big Rob's stuff is better than most. Don't you think?"

"Yeah. Definitely."

"If you'll make an introduction for me, I'll do the rest."

"That's all you want? An introduction?"

"Yeah, that's it."

"Okay. I'll probably be talking to him some time this week anyway. I got fired today."

"No! You're kidding. How could he fire you with all that you do?"

"He found out about me padding the bills and stuff. So, he let me go."

"That bastard! Considering what that firm probably makes, he could've let you off with a warning or something."

"David's a good guy. I'm lucky he didn't have me arrested. He's right; I need to get it together. I've been getting high too much.

"This is my last," she said, lying to herself. "I won't be calling you anymore."

Jade knew that Linda was full of it but she didn't say a word. Linda was an addict, plain and simple. At some point, all addicts fooled themselves into believing they could "*stop anytime they wanted to.*" Linda was no different.

"Good for you. You don't want this stuff to become a crutch."

"Can I take it now and I'll give Greg a call next week to set things up?"

"I got my cell phone right here," Jade offered.

She wasn't going to let Linda out of her sight without her doing something for her first; especially since it wasn't really *her* product. It was Big Rob's and she would probably have to replace it with her own money. Big Rob wasn't as generous with the cash as he had been before he put her "on staff."

"Oh, okay," Linda agreed. "That makes sense. I can call him now, while it's on both our minds."

By the time Linda was done talking to Greg on the phone, he and Jade made arrangements to meet later on that night.

Although Jade still kept her mother's Westchester Avenue apartment, she had rented a more suitable place to live in the Bronx. She had no intention of sharing her first *real* home with Bridget. And, instead, chose not to tell her that she had even rented a new place. She continued to allow Bridget to believe that the Westchester Avenue apartment was her only residence and excused her frequent absences by telling Bridget that she was with Big Rob. After a while, Bridget stopped asking. Jade would have given the Westchester Avenue apartment up entirely, but at one point when she and Bridget were not making as much money, they had trouble paying the rent. That's when Bridget contacted PRIMCO, the company that owned the building, pretending to be her mother. It was then that she learned the rent had been paid for many years and was still being paid by a corporation called

Swerdly Enterprises. Jade was curious as hell as to why a large corporation would be paying the rent on the run-down Bronx apartment of a junkie and prostitute all these years. But every search led to the same dead-end. She assumed it was probably an obsessed client with money to burn. But, always in the back of her thoughts was the idea that there was more to the story. The new place was on Laconia Avenue. It was still the hood, but it wasn't as bad as Westchester Avenue.

When Greg arrived, she was happy to see that he was a brother, and she had the same effect on him that she had on most men. From the minute she walked across the street on 224th and Laconia, she could see he was feeling her.

"I hope you're Jade," he said as he crossed the street.

"That's me. But, most people call me Red."

"I think I like Jade much better. You know, Jade, I've been at work all day and I'm hungry as hell. Have you eaten anything? There's a great soul food place on 116th Street on the West Side. You feel like breakin' bread with me?"

Jade was thinking it couldn't have gone better, even if she had planned it that way.

"Sure, I'd love to. I haven't had any good soul food in a long time. All they got up here is West Indian food. It's good sometimes, but I gotta tell you, I'm sick to death of curried goat, jerk chicken and oxtails."

"Then, follow me. Once you eat at this place, you won't want soul food from anyplace else."

The restaurant was nothing to brag about. It had un-leveled, cheap wood chairs and tables to match, with plastic tablecloths. But, the food was slammin'. Jade had smothered chicken, macaroni and cheese and collard greens. Greg had barbecued spare ribs, yams and string beans. They both ordered sweet iced tea and had peach cobbler for dessert.

"So, Jade, you married?"

"Why?"

"I'm feelin' you and I figured if you felt the same, may-be we could see where we can take this."

"No. I'm not married."

"You got a man?"

"Not really," she lied.

"I don't know what's wrong with the men in New York. Back in North Carolina, where I'm from, brothas woulda definitely snatched a sista like you up by now."

"Maybe I don't wanna be snatched up. You ever think about that?"

"So, it's like that, huh? Well, I guess I don't blame you. If I was a sista and I looked like you, I wouldn't worry about gettin' snatched up either. Can I get your number? Maybe give you a call sometime. Have dinner again or something else."

"Something else, huh?" Jade joked.

"Nah. Nothing like that. I want to get to know you. That's all."

"So, you just want to get to know me?"

"Don't get me wrong now. I wouldn't kick you outta my bed, but there's no pressure. We can kick it as friends, if you like."

"Okay, Greg. You got a pen or your cell phone? My number is 646-555-3825."

As they left the restaurant, Greg assured her that he would be calling. Jade didn't doubt that for a moment.

Over the coming weeks, Jade saw more and more of Greg. She wanted to have someone inside McDonnell that she was close to, in order to keep an eye on Bridget and David McDonnell. Not only that, she found Bridget was distancing herself more and more from her and she was losing her hold. More than anything she wanted an opportunity to get more involved with McDonnell & Simpson in some capacity. Thanks to David, she had managed to hook up with a number of his clients and colleagues alike.

She now had a *"Bridget-like"* replacement named Divine, who had an addiction to crack, and Jade used that to get her cut of whatever Divine made. For all intents and purposes, Jade was her pimp. And, between the men she blackmailed; the *"introductions"* she made between David's colleagues and other girls; Divine and the money she made and working here and there for Big Rob; she was able to pocket quite a comfortable living. Somehow, though, it still didn't seem to be enough. She wanted more, much more.

"I've got some business to take care of in Atlantic City.

I'm gonna stay the entire weekend. You wanna come along?" Jade asked Greg one day.

Greg was ecstatic. Somehow, despite the fact that they were going out and spending time together, he got the impression that she wasn't feelin' him the way he was feelin' her. On more than one occasion, he had tried to get with her, but she had always found a way to keep from sleeping with him.

Greg had no problem with getting women. He had a creamy caramel complexion, washboard abs, beautiful black wavy hair and deep-set dimples that women always seemed to comment on. He was about six-five tall and talked with a very slight Southern drawl. He wasn't as full of himself as he could have been, but he knew what he was workin' with. The reaction of women walkin' down the street, and the reaction of the female (and some male) staff at McDonnell when he first started working there, also told him that. No, he had no problem getting women, but Jade was another story altogether. He had resigned himself to the fact that he was going to have to work to get her between the sheets. But, somehow, he thought it would be well worth it. Jade had a sensual quality about her that was sexy and dangerous at the same time. Yeah, he had known from the beginning that he would have to be a patient man if he were going to get between her legs. And it seemed as though that patience might soon pay off. He couldn't remember when he had been more excited about screwin' somebody. Then, he realized it was probably exactly what people always said: You always want something (or someone) that much more when there's the possibility that you might not get it.

"Do I wanna come along? Baby, you don't even have to ask that question. Nothing would keep me away. So, what time do we leave?"

"I was thinking Friday night, around seven or eight, after you get off from work. That good for you?"

"Hell yeah. I'm looking forward to it!"

Jade realized weeks ago that she had to step up her game with Greg. Yet, it wasn't the same as with Big Rob. Big Rob was one of the few people she actually had some measure of respect for. And, Jade learned that she couldn't have sex with someone she didn't respect, at least not sex for enjoyment. But, Greg would be just another one of her marks. It wasn't about gettin' off; it was about her runnin' game and achieving the desired effect. She planned to pull out all the stops. If there was one thing Jade knew beyond a shadow of a doubt, it was what men wanted. She could look at a man and, within two minutes, know exactly what got him off. Greg was no different. There had only been one man she hadn't been able to do that with and that was David McDonnell; at least not yet.

"You want me to drive?" Greg asked.

"Sure, why not."

If Big Rob could see this pretty boy sitting behind the wheel of his vehicle, both he and Jade might have been dead. Jade told Big Rob that she was heading down to

A.C. to scout out some new clients. Big Rob had been making so much money since he hooked up with Jade, he had no intention of getting in her way. He let her use the car and anything else that might help her do her thing. The ninety-minute drive was completely devoid of quiet. Greg was more animated and talkative than she had ever seen him. Even though Jade enjoyed sex with Big Rob, she was still in awe of the effect sex, or even the prospect of sex, could have on most people. Greg was a good case in point. His animation was clearly the result of his anticipation of having sex with her.

In order to completely blow his mind and possibly shut him up, Jade decided to give him a brief preview. She unzipped his pants and took his dick out. He was about average size, but she was amazed at how quickly he grew in her hands at the slightest touch. She wrapped her entire hand around his dick and began to slowly slide it up and down, increasing her motions with each moan that escaped his lips. To further intensify the moment, she moved closer to him and began nibbling at his earlobes, darting her tongue in and out of his ear, and licking and sucking his neck.

"Oh, baby," he moaned between breaths.

"You like that?" she asked. "Stay with me, baby. There's more. I wanna taste what you've been savin' for me. I want you to blast my mouth full of my sweet reward. Can you do that for me?"

"You know it, baby," he breathed.

And, with that, Jade lowered her head and slowly and systematically began sliding her glossed lips up and down his dick. She intermittently licked the tip of his dick and the underside of his balls, all while Greg continued to drive. When she thought he couldn't hold it any longer, Jade locked her lips tightly around his dick and slid her lips faster and faster from the very end to the very tip—faster and faster and faster until Greg, gripping the wheel tightly, exploded in her mouth, his leg trembling and battling to maintain a safe driving rhythm. Jade was amazed they hadn't gotten into an accident.

"How about we pull over and change places? I'll drive. You rest."

"Okay," he responded weakly. "Jade, that was unbelievable."

If nothing else, Jade thought, she had shut him the fuck up. Greg slept and she drove the rest of the way to Atlantic City in silence.

They spent the entire weekend in Atlantic City in their hotel room. Jade was surprised to find that he had the stamina to keep up with her. By the end of the weekend he was hers—lock, stock and barrel. He was poised and ready to do whatever she wanted him to do. She had lost Linda, but the hold she'd be able to keep on Greg would be much stronger. He would provide her all the information she needed about McDonnell & Simpson.

Meanwhile, David was knee-deep in work and without an assistant. Everyone at the firm was shocked to learn of Linda's departure. Despite David's efforts to make it clear that Linda had resigned, there were, of course, rumors. Most everyone at the firm, except for David, had noticed that Linda was using something. So, it came as no surprise when she was suddenly gone. And, thanks to the folks in accounting, who were aware of her theft of company money, everyone filled in the blanks. Right up until the time that Linda left the firm, Bridget had noticed that David was cool at best with her, from the moment he hired her. She missed the earlier ease they maintained in talking with one another, before she started working at McDonnell. She was eager to help him when she found that he was at a loss for someone to get his work done. She would pitch in whenever and however necessary. Where some of the girls in the word processing department had rules about what they would and wouldn't do, Bridget filled in, in whatever capacity necessary. So, it followed, that when things got especially overwhelming for David, he enlisted Bridget's aid. And her assistance proved to be well worth her presence at the firm.

"David, I noticed that this letter you're sending to opposing counsel at Baker & Little has the wrong address. They're no longer in Little Falls, New Jersey. They now have an office in Manhattan. They're at 30 Rockefeller Plaza. You want me to go ahead and change that for you?"

"Thanks, Bridget. Thanks a lot for catching that. Could

you send out an email to everyone letting them know that Baker's address has changed?"

"Oh, no problem. I'll do that right now."

"I was going to order something from that Texas Barbecue place that you like so much. You wanna look at the menu before I place my order?"

"Oh, uhm...No, I don't know."

"Bridget. It's just lunch in the office. Did you eat anything yet? I haven't seen you leave your desk to go out in the past two weeks. It's the least I can do."

While she looked over the menu, David couldn't help but take the opportunity to look at her. That's what he did; stole glances at her whenever she wasn't looking. She was so beautiful. He couldn't help it. He had been so angry with her when she'd first started working at the firm, but his façade melted away quickly. It was impossible to be mad at someone like her.

"I know exactly what I want," she said. "I'll have a pulled pork sandwich and fries and one of those slushy drinks."

David couldn't help but smile. One minute she was a woman and the next she was like a child. It made him want her even more. Her innocence was as intoxicating as her maturity.

For the next several weeks, David interviewed secretary after secretary after secretary. None of them seemed to measure up to either Linda or Bridget. Under normal circumstances, he probably would have hired Bridget as his assistant immediately. But, he wasn't sure if he hired her, whether he would be doing it because she was truly the best person for the job, or because of his obsession with her—especially since he now found himself watching her every opportunity he got. He would strategize in his mind around opportunities to *"bump into"* her. In all his years on this earth, he had never been so absolutely enthralled with a woman as he was with Bridget—or at least not since Marie.

CHAPTER SEVEN
THE PROMOTION

"I wonder who's going to get that spot working for Mr. M? I heard his assistant, Linda, moved back to Boston because her mom was sick, or her dad was sick, or something like that. And that leaves the position open. I also heard that they want to fill the position from within the firm," Kimberly, one of the floaters at McDonnell, said.

"Yeah, right, she moved back to Boston to be with a sick relative, my ass! That's just a story Mr. McDonnell created to save face. The last thing he needs is to look like some idiot who doesn't know enough to keep an eye on what's happening with company money. Because, I heard through my sources in the accounting department that the bitch was stealing a shitload of money. Anyway, you and I both know who's going to get that position. She's been stuck up under his ass since she started, and he's loving every minute of it."

Just as they were speaking, Bridget walked by. They both tried to offer a fake smile and hello, but Bridget already knew they didn't like her—and that they were talking about her. She, Kimberly and Tania were the only floaters at the small law firm, and you would have thought that meant they would stick together. Unfortunately, it did not. Somehow, they had decided to penalize Bridget by being nasty toward her; simply because she wanted to get ahead.

Bridget would stay late whenever it was needed and tried to offer up suggestions to Mr. McDonnell, if she thought it would be helpful. All she wanted was to do a good job and ensure that he wasn't sorry that she was working here. She knew that Jade had somehow railroaded him into giving her this job, but she had made up her mind from Day One that she would be a great employee and prove to him that she was more than just an annoying piece of ass. But to Kimberly and Tania, that's exactly what she was. It seemed to Bridget that, no matter what you chose to do in life, there were always going to be people that didn't like it.

She was on her way to Mr. McDonnell's office. He had asked to see her and, instead of thinking about getting the coveted position that Kimberly and Tania were standing and gossiping about, she was afraid that she had done something wrong.

"Come in, Bridget. Have a seat. I wanted to thank you for all the helpful suggestions and all the assistance you've offered since you've been at McDonnell. I've got to admit, when you first came to work here, I was more than a little concerned, but you've proven yourself to be an exemplary employee."

David noticed how noticeably fidgety Bridget became when he mentioned his feelings about her coming to work at the firm. He realized that she probably was uncomfortable talking about how she had gotten the job.

From the moment she started working at McDonnell, watching *her* had become his favorite pastime; first and foremost as a means to ensure that *all* of her dealings within his firm were on the up-and-up.

David was ever-mindful of how this association had been cemented. Although Bridget appeared to be doing a good job from the very first day she started, he was not a stupid man. Therefore, he never *completely* let his guard down.

Under different circumstances, Bridget might have actually been perceived as a *"nice"* girl, naïve even. Yet, he knew where she came from. Even more confusing was her association with Jade. The pair was as different as night and day. David had come to know people like Jade in *all* walks of life; they always had a plan or a scheme, but it never occurred to them that someone might be one up on them. People like Jade always thought they were in control, until they fell from their tower.

As David saw it, Jade was so sure she was manipulating him, that she hadn't even recognized that he might have his own agenda and his own reasons for giving Bridget a job at McDonnell & Simpson. Late one night, he had taken yet another of his weekly drives through Hunts Point, searching for—something. Although, for what he didn't know. For so long, he thought it might have been

Marie. But, it wasn't logical to think that after all these years, she would still be there—waiting. And that's when he saw her. She seemed so out of place—so very much like *his* Marie.

"You want some company?" he had heard her say.

The words didn't seem to fit in her mouth. Her body language wasn't that of someone who was accustomed to this life. He was fascinated by what her story might be, but not yet ready to do anything but watch. He wasn't sure what he wanted or why he wanted to know anything about her. Yet, he watched. For months, that's all he did—watch her. He visited his old haunt much more as a voyeur than he had as a participant. There were nights when she seemed so cold that all he wanted to do was rescue her; wrap his arms around her and keep her warm and safe from harm. There were other times when she would disappear into some car or another. He would feel that telltale ache of jealousy and wouldn't return for at least a week but he would be right back again, enthralled with who this beautiful creature might be and how she had been sucked into such an existence.

For a moment, he thought maybe he might be losing his mind. How on earth could he be jealous of an absolute stranger? When he thought of how many women he had dated and eventually dumped that would have loved for him to be having these very same feelings about them, it almost made him laugh. His ex-wife, Caitlin, was a good case-in-point. Caitlin had been chilly at best when they were dating in high school, but after he had gotten out of rehab, there seemed to be a change in the way Caitlin responded to him. David fully believed it had to do with the bad-boy persona he had established. All those months of sniffing and boozing, flunking and carousing, somehow endeared him so much more to Caitlin than all those years as her boyfriend, the A-student.

However, after Marie and rehab and…everything, David's feelings toward Caitlin had changed as well. There was a time when he would have liked nothing more than to have Caitlin in his bed; yet after Marie and the string of girls/women that followed, somehow David was looking for something more. However, anxious to please his mother after bringing her so much pain, David did what he believed she wanted; he married Caitlin Gallagher. As David fully expected, a happy marriage it wasn't.

Marriage changed Caitlin. Gone was the beautiful, confident young woman he'd met when they were young; in its place was a woman severely lacking in self-esteem and more than just a little clingy. She wanted to know what David was doing every minute of the day. He knew that Caitlin wanted to have children and thought that after she had gotten pregnant, that would be the answer to both their prayers. She would get what she wanted and he would get some breathing room. Unfortunately, instead of a baby, David and Caitlin got something so much worse. Caitlin had a miscarriage in her third month of pregnancy and, because of complications, they were informed by her doctor that she would never be able to become pregnant again. Caitlin was devastated and David felt obligated to be there for her, despite the quick decline of their marriage. Eventually, Caitlin was so depressed and fed-up with the situation that she got hooked on prescription medicine. She graduated from that to coke and eventually, she was a full-blown crack addict. David divorced her with his mother's blessing and Caitlin moved away from New York. The last David heard, she had taken up with some boy toy who was sucking her trust fund dry. He often wanted to call Caitlin, maybe try to talk some sense into her, but he realized he wasn't ready to take on the responsibility of being her savior. Not only that, somehow Caitlin had gotten it into her head that he was to blame for her predicament. And the last time he saw her, she did nothing more than spew words at him like venom. She even blamed him for her losing the baby. David had a lot of high-profile clients, which constantly kept him in the media spotlight. The last thing he needed was a drugged-out ex-wife openly accusing him of being the cause of her miscarriage.

Sitting in his office now with Bridget, on the heels of offering her a position that would probably change her life, David realized he was once again in a position to make a difference. Despite his apprehension, he decided to go full speed ahead with the reason he had asked Bridget to his office. But first, given her body language after he mentioned the circumstances of her being employed at McDonnell, he wanted to put her at ease.

"Bridget, before I continue, let me first apologize for bringing up how you came to work for me. I consider myself a good judge of character. Somehow, I don't believe you were the person that engineered your placement here. I believe it was probably someone else; someone a lot more crafty."

Bridget wasn't sure how she should feel about David's comments about Jade. However, she decided to hear him out before responding. It had taken her a few months, but between David's coolness towards her and comments from her co-worker Brianna, who had found out the real-deal from her cousin Pookie—Big Rob's runner, Bridget eventually figured out how she had *truly* gotten the job at McDonnell.

"That's fine Mr. McDonnell. It's okay. Really."

"No, Bridget, it's not okay. And I'm going to make you a promise today. I will never bring up the circumstances of your employment here, ever again."

David was happy to see that his last comment had elicited a smile from Bridget. It made him happy.

"Well, that's enough of that talk. Okay?"

"Okay," Bridget said.

"Let's get down to the task at hand. As you know, Linda is no longer working here. I've been very impressed with your commitment to this firm and the level of work you've been doing here. I'd like to offer you the position as my assistant. It would be at a significant pay increase from what you're presently making; not to mention an increase in your yearly bonuses, and other benefits. Do you think that's something you might be interested in? It would do me a great service if you say yes. I've been lost without Linda and you seem to be the only person here that even comes close to her abilities."

Bridget was speechless for a brief second. "I... I..." she stuttered. "I...um, yes...of course. I'd love the job. Are you sure? Are you really sure?"

"Yes, I'm sure."

David was so taken with her response, he couldn't think of anything he would rather do right then than take her in his arms, but he knew that would be unacceptable.

"Yes, I'll take the job. Thank you so much, Mr. Mc-Donnell. I promise you won't regret this. I'm going to do a really good job. I promise!"

"I'm sure you will, Bridget. I have every confidence in you. Take the rest of the week off and start fresh on Monday. You've earned a couple of days off. I want you bright-eyed and bushy-tailed on Monday. We've got a *lot* of work to do. Linda's been gone for two months and things have gotten very overwhelming."

Bridget raced out of the office on cloud nine, eager to tell someone. But who would she tell? Jade would surely try to figure out a way for her to do something she probably wouldn't want to do, or she would try to get a job at McDonnell as well. She'd already hinted at that several times. Bridget already told her they only had three floaters and they weren't hiring anymore. If she told her about the promotion, she'd realize that her prior position was vacant. Bridget decided not to share her good news with Jade.

She decided to do what she liked doing best; she would catch an early train to Long Beach and spend the day— maybe even some of the night—enjoying the beach. It was the middle of July and sure to be a great day to spend on the beach.

Bridget also went shopping over the weekend and purchased some clothes with the money she had been religiously saving over the last few years. There was no better time than now to get her own place. Bridget was ready to be on her own. She needed autonomy and, although she knew Jade would be pissed, she had a new-found independent nature. She was quite happy with that and had every intention of exercising it.

Bridget arrived an hour early on Monday morning and decided to spend some time freshening up in the ladies room. It had been so warm that morning, she had opted to commute without pantyhose and put them on when she arrived. She was in one of the bathroom stalls when she heard Kimberly and Tania talking. They obviously didn't know she was there, or they probably wouldn't have been doggin' her out the way that they were.

"He's been checking her out from the minute she walked her skinny ass up in here," Bridget heard Tania say.

"Well, it's his firm and he can do whatever he wants, but the shit is foul. We both started working here long before her. If anybody should've gotten that position, it should have been you or me. That job pays eighty thousand a fuckin' year. My man's out of work and shit, and my kids are startin' Catholic school in the fall. I coulda used that money," Kimberly said. "But no, he gives it to that fuckin' chickenhead. She ain't even got no kids. She's probably gonna end up like the last assistant he had; sniffin' that shit up her nose. God don't like ugly. I woulda felt a little better about him dissin' us, if he'd at least hired somebody from outside the office."

"Yeah. At least that would've made some damn sense. Instead, he hires some young girl with no experience. I asked her where she worked before this and she tried to do a divert. I'm tellin' you, there's somethin' foul about her. I bet you she's fuckin' him."

Bridget heard one of the other stalls open.

Bridget instantly recognized Brianna's voice. She had a high-pitched squeak—particularly when she was excited—and this was definitely one of those moments. Brianna was a sweet girl, but she needed to learn to keep some things to herself. Each and every Monday morning, she'd enthrall everyone with "blow by blow" accounts of her latest sexual encounter. The last two or three weeks, the male *"lead"* in her little sexual melodrama was Kenny; the mail guy or, as Brianna liked to call him, Big Dick. If you could be fired for sexual improprieties,

Brianna definitely had both feet on a banana peel. It wasn't that she didn't like Brianna, or that she wasn't a bit intrigued with her sexual exploits; it wasn't law office conversation. She wasn't the least bit discreet.

Brianna was a Technicolor girl working in a black and white world. She didn't have a clue how to change channels. Not only was she loud, but so were her clothes. Bridget peeked through the opening. Brianna was wearing lime-green vinyl pants and a white button-down shirt. The shirt would've been conservative enough, if it wasn't two sizes too small and the buttons didn't look like they were going to pop off and go flying any minute. Bridget guessed that Brianna wore tight shirts to show off her latest investment—an upgrade from a set of 34B's to a set of 38DD's. She had the audacity to plop them down on Bridget's desk one afternoon, right in front of Mr. McDonnell.

Bridget assumed that the partners and management kept Brianna around as a sexual stimulant to an otherwise ho-hum day. Even ultra-serious Mr. McDonnell seemed to like her. It was rumored that she'd been with other partners in the firm and Bridget wondered if Brianna had been with him, too. Brianna didn't discriminate; she screwed everything from the janitor to the managing partner. It often occurred to Bridget that Brianna's behavior was probably what Mr. McDonnell had expected of her, under the circumstances of which they met.

"You know, ya'll are triflin'," Brianna said.

Bridget had been sitting behind the stall trying to stifle her crying and waiting for Kimberly and Tania to leave. Hearing Brianna stick up for her made her feel better. Despite Brianna's eccentric ways, Bridget always liked her—she was more *real* than most people, more honest. Hearing Brianna defend her made her like her even more.

"Excuse me," Kimberly said.

"You heard me; ya'll are triflin'. The girl came up in here to do a job. She don't bother nobody. She ain't all up in everybody's business, like some people, and she does a good fuckin' job! She ain't takin' coffee and cigarette breaks all damn day and shit. She does her job. And, ya'll tryin' to fault her for that." She paused. "I would've liked to have that eighty grand, but I ain't Bridget. I'm not in here working on weekends and asking other secretaries if they need help when I'm not busy. I don't offer to stay late whenever they're short-staffed, but Bridget does." Brianna sighed. "So, yeah, she deserved that job. More power to her. She's the one who did the research and found that less-costly supplies company. You don't think that went a long way in getting her that job? Well, you're both fools, if you don't think that made a difference. So instead of doggin' her out for doin' her fuckin' job, why don't ya'll spend less time hangin' out in the bathroom talkin' about everybody and go do *your* jobs."

"Since when do you tell us what to do? You don't even work for a partner. You ain't got no right to tell us what we should be doin'," Tania said with spite.

"No, you're right. I ain't got no right to tell you what

to do, but my girl, Bridget, is workin' for the owner of this firm. If he knew you were questioning his choice for an assistant, he might have somethin' to say. In fact, if all the shit you sayin' about her and Mr. McDonnell is true, you know, if he's fuckin' her and all that, I'd be *very* careful about what I say and where I say it."

Both Kimberly and Tania left the bathroom in a huff, fully aware that they were treading on dangerous ground; especially since they both desperately needed their jobs.

"Whatever," Tania said as a parting word.

Kimberly tried to slam the heavy bathroom door and left, fully aware that she had played herself.

"Bridget," Brianna said. "Bring your ass out here. I know damn well you ain't in there cowering because of these tired bitches."

Bridget opened the door and walked out quietly.

"Thanks."

"Thanks for what? We girls and all, but that wasn't only for you. I'm sick of those hoes. They always talkin' about who's screwing who and the two of them are like Grand Central Mother Fuckin' Station. Stupid-ass Kimberly don't know it, but Tania was even screwin' her man behind her back. I can't stand them and they've done their fair share of doggin' me out, too. I don't let these folks ruffle me. I am who I am and I'm not tryin' to live for nobody but me. You need to do the same. You need tougher skin, Bridget. You've got a great opportunity, but you've got to learn to stand up for yourself."

Bridget shrugged. "I don't know why I care so much

about what people say about me. I just do. My best friend, Jade, tells me that all the time."

"The next time you let people's words fuck wit' your head, remember, none of us, and I do mean *none* of us, would like to have our lives on display for the world. So, whoever it is that's tryin' to judge you, has got their own glass house to deal with, with a closet full of skeletons.

"Ignore, ignore, ignore; that's my motto. Kimberly and Tania aren't the only ones you need to watch out for. These other secretaries here ain't your friends either and they're not to be trusted." Brianna stared at Bridget and put her hands on her hips. "This kind of shit burns me up. David's assistant was sniffin' more blow than her nose could hold, but everybody around here is tryin' to act like you pushed her out her job or somethin'. You earned that fuckin' job and don't let nobody tell you otherwise. Pussy is pussy and all that, but Mr. M. is a businessman. I've worked here long enough to know, he's good at what he does, and he ain't tryin' to hire somebody that don't know what she's doin'. That's all I'm gonna say about the matter. Get yours and ignore the haters. At the end of the day, they're not putting clothes on your back or food on your table."

Bridget felt much better.

"Thanks, Brianna. Thanks a lot."

After the two of them left the bathroom, the name Jade kept ringing in Brianna's ears. It wasn't exactly a common name and she knew that Bridget either lived or used to live in the Bronx. She kept wondering if this could be the same Jade that her cousin, Pookie, knew. The same Jade that was Big Rob's woman. Big Rob was Hunts Point's biggest drug dealer and Brianna's cousin was one of his runners. She hoped that wasn't the person Bridget had referred to as her best friend.

She'd met Jade once, a year or so ago and, from what she could remember, Jade's comments about her gullible frien-emy sounded eerily like Bridget. Brianna sincerely hoped she was wrong and that it was a different Jade altogether. If it were the same person, Bridget had bigger problems than the haters at the office. The Jade she'd met was trouble, plain and simple.

For the next several months, Bridget learned all there was to know about expense reports, invoices, HR work, and anything and everything that had to do with running a successful law firm. Her days in the word processing department were over and she was the assistant to one of the most influential lawyers in New York City. She even established some savvy with dealing with the *"haters"* at the firm, as Brianna called them. They were all acutely aware that David considered Bridget invaluable. And they were fearful of losing their jobs, so they didn't dare fuck with her.

"Hi, Bridget," Kimberly said. "David brought this document over to WP. He said you were too busy to work on it. It's all done and ready to go. You want me to bring it in to him?"

"No, thanks. You can give it to me."

Ever since Kimberly and Tania had made her cry behind that bathroom stall with their cruel words, Bridget found herself taking great joy in the level of control she had over them. It wasn't her typical nature, but she enjoyed it nonetheless. The two of them couldn't wait to go switching their asses around David. He was considered quite the catch and was an attractive man. Kimberly's only objective in offering to take his work directly to his office, instead of giving it directly to Bridget, his assistant, as was firm policy, was so that she might have an opportunity to get some attention from David. Just as Bridget was waving Kimberly away, David walked in.

"Bridget, are those the revisions to that brief I took over to WP?"

"Yes. But, I could've worked on this. I wasn't that busy."

"I'd prefer you to continue working on those letters regarding our open invoices. I can't give you that monster Christmas bonus, if our clients don't pay us. Also, we have that first-year associate starting on Monday. Is everything squared away with him? You know, the usual—Human Resources, office set-up, orientation?"

"Everything's pretty much done. I've got his name plate right here, so Office Services can put it on his door. It's Stephen P. Martin, right—Stephen with a 'ph'?"

"Yeah, that's right. I'm sure he'll be here bright and early, but that's not a problem for you, since you're usually here at the crack of dawn anyway. Right?"

"Don't make fun, David. It's all your fault anyway. You keep me so busy I like to have a chance to ease into my day rather than hit the ground running as soon as I arrive. If I get here early, you're not here yet and I can work on whatever is on my desk before I get bombarded with more."

"You know you wouldn't have it any other way. Mc-Donnell & Simpson would crumble without you. I truly don't know how this firm or I ever survived without you."

Bridget was surprised at the ease with which she and David were able to work together. She was full of pride at hearing how valued an employee she was. She often forgot about the circumstances under which she'd come to work at McDonnell & Simpson. It appeared as though he did as well.

"Oh, Bridget, one more thing, I want to pick your brain about the Christmas party and gifts for the staff when you finish sending out those letters. Okay?"

"I'll be done in about fifteen minutes."

"You got any plans for lunch?" David asked.

"No, not at all."

"Tell you what. Why don't we have a working lunch? We'll go to Smith & Wollensky, and have two huge steaks. Oh, and you can also have a steak."

Bridget laughed at David's silliness. He really was a nice guy. To some extent, that made Bridget feel a little guilty. Jade never mentioned anything to her outright, but Bridget knew she had an association with Greg in accounting, that she had tried to forge a relationship with Brianna, and that she had even known Linda for a time. She also knew that nothing Jade did was without purpose. Not only that, Jade had been trying for quite some time to get a job at McDonnell. Bridget didn't know the specifics, but she was sure Jade was planning something. She wondered if Jade would listen, if she talked to her about leaving David and his firm alone.

"That sounds good, but who's going to watch the office while we're gone?"

"You need to lighten up, Bridget. There's something wrong when the employee wants to be at work more than the boss. A long lunch won't hurt. We've earned it. If it makes you feel any better, I'll make sure it's a working lunch. Okay?"

CHAPTER EIGHT
STEPHEN P. MARTIN, ESQ.

Brianna had heard that the associate she would be working with was black and young. She couldn't wait to see what he looked like. It was the first time Bridget had ever gotten to work and found Brianna there before her.

"What are you doing here so early?" Bridget asked, as if she didn't already know the answer.

"My new associate starts today. I wanted to be here early so I could make sure he was comfortable and got settled in okay."

"Now you know you need to stop. The only reason you're here so early is so you can get first crack at a young black attorney."

"Okay, I admit it. But, hell, you gotta be on top of your game around here. You see, the vultures are already circling," Brianna commented as she gestured toward Kimberly.

"Let's forget about Stephen Martin for a minute. How was your weekend?" Brianna asked.

"It was pretty good," Bridget responded. "I took my

road test this weekend, and I passed! I love the beach and now that I have my driver's license, I've been thinking of buying a little hooptie so I can get out of the Bronx on the weekends; maybe drive out to Long Beach. I go every now and then, but it'll be a lot easier with a car than it is riding the Long Island Railroad."

"Ooh, you buyin' a car!" Brianna squealed.

"No, not buying yet; just looking. Between saving for an apartment and hopefully going back to school, I don't have very much left over."

"If you'd listen to me, you wouldn't have to worry about money so much. That Mr. McDonnell's got his nose *wide* open for you. Everybody in the office can see it. That is, everybody except you."

"Brianna, I hope you're not giving into the rumors about Mr. McDonnell and me. We work well together, but our relationship is purely professional."

"Purely professional, huh? I've seen the way that man looks at you and so has everyone else. There's nothing *pure* about it."

Bridget was anxious to change the subject, quickly.

"So—how was *your* weekend, Brianna?"

"It was fabulous! Big Dick and I went to this wild party up in Harlem."

Just as Brianna was about to elaborate, David walked in.

"Good morning, Mr. McDonnell," Brianna gushed.

"Good morning, Brianna. How was your weekend?"

Bridget always dreaded David asking Brianna how her

weekend was. You never could tell with her. Bridget fully expected Brianna to one day regale him with stories of her escapades, if she hadn't already. After all, Brianna had started working at the firm before Bridget. Who knew what went on then, or even now? Bridget didn't get too involved in the social lives of her fellow staff members, or the attorneys, for that matter; partly because she was so very secretive about her *own* past. She lived her life as though she were looking over her shoulder, waiting for someone to cart her off to prison. Yet, she still wanted the house with the white picket fence, the 2.5 children and the minivan. She wanted carpools and soccer games and play dates. She wanted all the things she never had growing up. She wanted a family.

Somehow, though, Bridget had discovered you could run, but you couldn't hide. Her job at McDonnell & Simpson was supposed to be an escape from the world she had known—an opportunity to see, first-hand, how the other half lived. Instead, her first day on the job, she met Brianna, a straight-up sister from the 'hood with edges so rough she needed an economy-sized pumice stone. Despite her rough edges, Bridget liked her. She had a kind heart. It was something you could see right away. So, although Bridget was careful about where and how she spent time with Brianna, she treated her with the utmost respect. After all, everybody couldn't be ultra-conservative. Bridget breathed a sigh of relief at Brianna's response.

"I had a very nice weekend, Mr. McDonnell. How was yours?"

"I worked most of the weekend, but I did manage to get in a little fishing."

"That's nice," Brianna responded.

Before she left, she wished both Bridget and Mr. McDonnell a pleasant day. Even when she was being conservative, a bit of that which was uniquely Brianna shined through. As she turned on her heels to leave, Bridget noticed that Brianna's lime-green pants were sprinkled with a touch of glitter. Bridget hadn't even worn anything that flashy when she was walking the streets. Bridget viewed it as a life lesson; you can't necessarily judge a book by its cover.

Brianna had grown up with a mom and dad who adored her. She went to Catholic schools most of her life, while Bridget's only job before this had been as a prostitute. Yet, if you asked any stranger on the street, most would peg Brianna as the former prostitute and Bridget as the Catholic school girl. It occurred to Bridget that maybe Brianna was doing exactly what she was doing—living out a desire to be exactly the opposite of what she had been growing up.

Bridget discreetly glanced at David to see if there was any reaction. There was none at all. He barely glanced at Brianna.

Stephen P. Martin had been so sheltered from the horrors that many African-American children in the U.S. encounter. He had grown up in a middle-class home in Marietta, Georgia. His father had been a dentist and his mother had been a dental assistant before she went back to school and became a dentist as well. In fact, that was how his mother and father had met. She had applied for a job at his father's dental office and it had pretty much been love at first sight. Both his mother and father were committed to providing Stephen with an exemplary education. Therefore, it was no surprise that they made sure that Stephen stayed on top of his studies, provided him with music lessons; piano, guitar, even the saxophone. They were both committed to community service so they fostered the same in Stephen. However, it was a debate class in high school that first opened Stephen's eyes to what his true calling was. He found he enjoyed expressing his opinion with great zeal and excelled in debate class. That's when he knew that he would be a lawyer. Both Janice and Brian Martin couldn't have been more proud.

After graduating from Marietta High School, Stephen decided to venture North and attended Fordham University. Despite his parents initial misgivings about their only son living in New York City, they gave him their blessings. Initially, Stephen planned to return to Georgia to attend law school, but soon found New York offered him a change in lifestyle that he enjoyed. Where once sheltered by his parents and the Southern lifestyle, he now became enthralled with New York's fast pace and countless possibilities.

After graduating at the top of his class at Fordham, he went on to attend Yale Law School in neighboring New Haven, Connecticut. Before he even acquired his J.D., Stephen was pretty much guaranteed a position at some of New York's top law firms. Despite offers from several firms, Stephen accepted a position as a junior associate at McDonnell & Simpson with little hesitation. He genuinely liked the lead partner, David McDonnell, and felt a kinship to the firm's philosophies.

Bridget was the very first person he met his first day as an associate at McDonnell & Simpson.

"Good morning, Mr. Martin. Mr. McDonnell had a meeting outside of the office this morning, but he will be in around noon today. He asked that I get you settled in and answer any questions you might have. Would you like something to drink; maybe a cup of coffee or some water?"

"No, thank you. I'm fine. But thanks."

Stephen wasn't sure if the feeling in the pit of his stomach was first-day nerves, or due to the beautiful woman standing in front of him. Through his years in college and law school and his recruitment by different law firms, he found that he seldom got nervous about anything. Therefore, he had to presume that this feeling had to have something to do with her.

From early on, Stephen's parents had raised him to be

as colorblind as a black child could be growing up in the South. Yet, the world is not a vacuum, so Stephen, of course, had had his fair share of encounters with racism. In fact, that was one of his criteria for picking a law firm; especially since he had options. He examined the ratios at the firms he interviewed with. Although he didn't obsess over color in his everyday life, he was beyond capable of recognizing the obvious. And, he knew that color was a factor no matter where you lived and worked.

The key was to find a good fit; someplace where it wasn't an overriding presence. He believed he had found that fit with McDonnell & Simpson. Therefore, he was quite happy to see that the person Mr. McDonnell had dubbed his "right hand" was in fact an African-American woman; a beautiful, eloquent, poised, African-American woman. However, he wasn't sure he was prepared for the stirrings he was having upon meeting her. If there was one thing he valued, it was his focus, and this woman definitely could cause an interruption of that focus.

"Mr. Martin?"

That's when Stephen realized he had been daydreaming and hadn't heard what she was saying; a virtual first for him. It would be the first in a series of responses that were so out of character for him. Yet, as time went on, he learned to relish his awareness of Bridget's presence.

"I'm so sorry," he apologized. "I guess it's first-day jitters. I was lost in thought."

"No worries," Bridget responded. "No need for jitters.

We're going to take good care of you. Why don't we head over to your office? I had one of the clerks set your office up, and our IT people have been in to get your computer up and running. I'll let you get settled in and you can let me know if there is anything else you need that will make your office more comfortable. I won't hover. I'll walk you over and you can give me a ring, if there is anything you need. Brianna Ross has been assigned as your assistant. She is really good at her job, and I'm sure she will be willing to offer you a hand in any capacity."

Stephen wanted to say, "please hover, hover all you want," but he was a professional first and foremost. Instead he just mentioned that he was sure everything would be fine.

Stephen was more than fine. Over the months, he adapted well to the fast-paced firm and within a year, he had become invaluable to David and the firm's clients. Bridget, too, took on more and more responsibility, including going to school to cement her ever-growing skills as a paralegal. As far as David was concerned, McDonnell & Simpson couldn't function without both Stephen and Bridget assisting him at the helm, to the dismay of many of the attorneys at the firm. Many of them had tried to ingratiate themselves in David's presence, but David had already decided who his star was: Stephen P. Martin. Unfortunately for David and his growing feelings for Bridget, however, that meant that Stephen and Bridget were spending more and more time together.

"You two up for an all-nighter?" David asked.

"Sure, David. You know I don't have a life," Bridget replied.

David knew all too well that she spoke the truth. McDonnell & Simpson was her life; his as well. David wondered why Bridget didn't date more. She was a beautiful woman. He couldn't imagine most men not wanting her. Every now and then she would meet someone, go out with them once or twice, but nothing ever seemed to last beyond the initial week or so. She was gorgeous, intelligent, strong. In David's fondest wishes, he allowed himself the luxury of believing that he was the reason she was still alone. After all, what did she need with a boyfriend when she had him? They went to dinner and parties together; they even shopped together—often under the guise that it was business-related. But David could tell that she enjoyed his company as much as he enjoyed hers. However, it was clear that their relationship bore little resemblance to what it had been. Things had evolved and at this juncture, David wanted more than just her body, nor did he think she needed saving. He wanted her heart and he believed that one day he would get the balls to make that fact known. Until then, he would be her friend.

"What about you, Stephen? You workin' tonight or you keepin' banker's hours as usual?" David chuckled.

"Naw, David, I'm burnin' the midnight oil with you and Bridget."

"Another one with no life, huh?" Bridget commented.

"No, not really, but I could be persuaded to have one under the proper circumstances."

Stephen's attempt at flirtation had not been missed by either Bridget or David. With each passing month, Stephen had become more and more courageous in his attempts to make his feelings for Bridget known. What Stephen had come to realize was that he had to step up his game and just come right out and ask her out; not some business lunch or dinner, nor these late nights working by her side. He knew he would have to ask her to spend some one-on-one time with him soon or he might lose an opportunity he wanted very much. What was that line his father always used? "If you're slow, you blow." And, Stephen definitely did not want to blow this.

Meanwhile, David silently stewed over Stephen's obvious interest in Bridget. His irritation wasn't at Stephen, however, it was with himself. He couldn't understand why he couldn't cut out the bullshit and tell Bridget how he felt about her. Now, it was pretty obvious, Stephen was probably going to beat him to the punch. David calmed himself with the thought that Bridget would never be interested in Stephen. He was way too inexperienced for her. But then he remembered how naïve Bridget could be. Stephen and Bridget were actually two peas in a pod; bright, knowledgeable, but often very inexperienced when it came to matters of life.

"So what's it gonna be tonight?" David chimed in. "Are

we going with Chinese or pizza as our culinary treat for the evening?"

"Definitely Chinese," Bridget replied.

"That okay with you?" David asked Stephen.

"Whatever Bridget wants is fine with me," Stephen agreed.

The three worked until a little past midnight. Minutes before David was set to offer Bridget and Stephen a ride home in his Mercedes (and, of course drop Stephen off first), Stephen asked Bridget if she wanted to share one of the company cars home.

"Sure, Stephen, it would be nice to have some company on the ride home. You want me to call the car?"

"Thanks, Bridg."

So he is calling her "Bridg" now, David thought to himself when he heard the exchange. *Since when did he start doing that? And why on earth would she say yes to sharing a car home?* They lived in completely opposite directions. David did his damnedest to keep his jealousy at bay, but it was more than a little difficult. He thought of asking Bridget to stay and do some more work, but that would sound ludicrous. They had already worked late and there wasn't one more thing that needed to be done before they returned to the office the next day.

"Good night, David," Bridget called as she left the office.

"Good night. Oh, and Stephen, we've got a really busy day tomorrow."

Somehow David hoped that would influence Stephen to go straight home, to get a good night's sleep. David knew that look on Stephen's face. It was the same look he had each and every time he looked at Bridget. The same look he had from the very first time he laid his eyes on her. Stephen had it as bad as he did, and he didn't even have the knowledge of her checkered past to taint his vision of her. Not that that made a difference to David in the slightest. Yes, David knew exactly where this was going and he was powerless to stop it.

After that night, Bridget and Stephen were inseparable. They had lunch and dinner together, and Bridget did everything she could to make Stephen's day as easy as she possibly could. For every miniscule matter that David laid in her lap to keep her busy and as far away from Stephen as possible, Bridget found a way to get both David's and Stephen's work done. Eventually, when David thought he had run out of ways to keep her pinned to her desk, he started sending her on ridiculous errands; trips to the dry cleaners, meetings with potential vendors. Anyone with any small degree of insight could have seen what he was doing.

Brianna recognized David's vain attempts right away and couldn't help but be amused by his efforts. It was fascinating to watch the way that both Stephen and David fell over themselves trying to get in Bridget's presence. But, Brianna told herself that if she were a betting woman she would put her money on Stephen.

Where Bridget saw David as her boss and a substitute big brother/father figure, she clearly saw Stephen as a bit more than that. The constant stops in the bathroom to check her appearance in the mirror; checking her hair and makeup and readjusting her clothing made it evident that she was in to Stephen. However, it was a chance blackout that blanketed New York City in August that truly brought Stephen and Bridget together.

"I've got a meeting across town, but I'll be back before you both leave. Bridget, if you could cross-check those Bates numbers that would help tremendously. And Stephen, I need you to go over that Gonzalez deposition."

"Okay, David," Bridget responded.

"Okay," Stephen said. "Should I be checking the Manuela deposition as well?"

"No, just Gonzalez for now. If we've got time when I get back, we can go over the Manuela deposition together."

"Okay. We'll see you when you get back."

Heading across town, David couldn't help but notice Stephen's use of the word *"we."* So, when did *they* become *we*, he wondered.

"Get a grip, man," David said to himself aloud. *They're working together. That's all.*

David's meeting went well, however, on his way back to the office, the city was suddenly hit with a blackout. One of the first blackouts in New York since 1977. The city was a mess, traffic was bumper to bumper and everyone was on edge. Yet, it wasn't the blackout or the traffic that David was thinking of. All he kept thinking about was the fact that Bridget and Stephen were alone together in the office. Although they weren't technically alone, there were definitely other staff members there due to the time of day. It was still afternoon. Nonetheless, the city had lost power and it seemed as though it was going to be out for quite some time. He wondered what was happening at McDonnell & Simpson while he was not there.

Back at the office, Bridget and Stephen were doing their very best to figure out a game plan for the staff; especially those members of the staff who had family.

"I've tried our company car service, but it's impossible," Bridget told Stephen and several of the partners, associates and staff members at the firm. "I've also tried reaching David on his cell, but I keep getting a message that all circuits are busy. That may not last forever. It's probably because everyone is trying to get through at the same time. We may have a couple of battery-operated radios around the office and I have a battery-operated television. Maybe we can get an estimate of how long this thing may last from the news. In the meantime, if we have to stay, we've got plenty of food and water. No one wants to be here overnight, but we'll be fine."

Several of the partners got together and carpooled some of the other staff members, since they had driven in. By the end of the evening there were only a handful of people left in the office in addition to Stephen and

Bridget. They had both decided to stick around the office. They were hearing from the few calls they got back from people who'd left that it was impossible to get around— even with cars. One secretary called and said that the car she was in had been stuck on Twenty-second Street for more than a half hour in the same spot.

"I'm going to camp out in the lounge if you want to join me," Bridget offered, after finishing up one of the sandwiches they had gotten out of the fridge.

"Sounds like a plan to me," Stephen agreed.

Sitting in the lounge area, propped up on chairs, hoping to get some sleep, the two talked way into the night, while they listened to whatever reports they could hear about the blackout.

"Bridget, do you mind if I ask you a personal question?"

"I don't know. Whenever someone says they want to ask you a personal question, it's usually a doozy, but I'm game. Sure, go for it. What's the question?"

"You're here pretty much every night working late. How is it a woman as attractive and intelligent as you isn't married, or doesn't at least have a boyfriend?"

"I could ask you the same question," Bridget said.

"Yeah, you could, but I asked first."

They both laughed in unison.

"Well, I haven't found Mr. Right yet."

"So, who is Mr. Right...Or, Mr. Right-for-You?"

"I don't know, someone who is loyal, kind, someone comfortable in their own skin, confident and someone who loves me as much as I love them. When that person comes along, I won't be alone anymore and I'll have to explain to David why I'm not burning the midnight oil at McDonnell & Simpson."

"What about you, Stephen? Who is your Ms. Right?"

"Pretty much the same thing; someone confident, loving, someone who makes me feel good about myself and me about them. My mom is constantly asking me why I don't ever bring anyone home, or why she doesn't have any grandchildren yet, but I've seen so many marriages go bad so quickly. I want what my mother and father have. When I get married, I want it to be forever. I know that sounds a bit unrealistic in this day and age, but that's what I want."

"No, Stephen, that's not unrealistic. Far too many people take marriage for granted. They get married and, when the slightest conflict arises, they're out the door. Like you, I believe that marriage was meant to last, for the long haul, through the good and the bad."

Stephen got up from where he was sitting and walked over to where Bridget was reclining and sat down right next to her.

"We're quite a pair, aren't we? We both spend every waking moment at work and we wonder why we haven't met anyone. The only way either of us would ever meet anyone would be here at McDonnell."

"Yeah, I guess you're right," Bridget agreed.

"You probably would never go for a guy like me, huh? A nerdy bookworm that you work with?"

Bridget wasn't completely surprised. She realized that Stephen liked her, but assumed he would never approach her, given that they worked so closely together. If it had ever occurred to her that he might she might have been better prepared to answer what he had asked.

"I…I…uhm…"

Stephen laughed. "Oh, Bridget, I'm sorry, I've embarrassed you. You don't have to answer that. In fact, I don't know what got into me. From the moment I walked past those doors over a year ago, I haven't been able to think about anything else *but* you. You're one of the most beautiful women I've ever known; both inside and out."

"Stephen, I don't know what to say. Thank you. I never knew you felt that way. I wish I had."

"Why, so you could put me out of my misery a long time ago and tell me I didn't have a chance in hell?" he joked.

"No, Stephen, I wish I'd known because we've been both walking around feeling the same way and wasting so much time being lonely, when we could have been together."

Stephen was shocked. He didn't know what to do or say. He was positively speechless. Bridget knew that she would have to be the one to make the first move and she did. She got up from her makeshift lounger, stood directly in front of Stephen where he was sitting and bent down to kiss him. The feel of his lips pressed against hers was the closest thing to heaven on earth she had ever felt. She had never been this close to him, but she knew right then and there that she loved him. It had taken them over a year to acknowledge their feelings for one another, but their love had grown over time and finally it was out in the open.

"Bridget, this is going to sound crazy, but I love you."

"I know, Stephen. I love you, too."

The last member of the staff had left when her husband picked her up over an hour ago, and Stephen and Bridget were alone. The office was dark and they could barely see what was in front of them, but none of that mattered. It only enhanced the joy of the moment.

Stephen worshipped Bridget's body with kisses, eager to show her all that he had stored up for all these months, thinking of her. They made love to the sounds and the darkness of the city below, oblivious to any of it. As far as they were concerned, they were the only two people who existed in the universe and they each were loved.

CHAPTER NINE
ALL SHE EVER WANTED

Stephen passed by Brianna's desk with such a sly smile on his face that she didn't have the heart to tell either him or Bridget that *everyone* in the office knew about them. But, she couldn't hold it in any longer. She felt like she was gonna burst if she didn't say something.

"So when ya'll gonna start tellin' people?" Brianna asked.

"Tellin' people what?" Bridget replied.

Although she tried to pretend she didn't know what Brianna was talking about, she knew exactly what she meant. Who could help but notice?

"Don't even try it, girlfriend. You and homeboy been walking around here like teenagers in love. I mean, really, do either of your feet ever touch the ground?" Brianna laughed.

"Is it that obvious?"

"*Hell to the yes!* I've seen Stephen smile more in the past few months than I've ever seen him smile. You must have that 24K coochie, huh?"

"You are so nasty, Brianna. Why does it always have to

be a sex thing? Stephen and I could just be right for each other."

"Yeah," Brianna offered. "Right for each other between the damn sheets!"

Bridget couldn't help but laugh at Brianna's comment. The sex *was* good between her and Stephen, really good. She didn't know that sex could be that good, but with Stephen it was. What never dawned on Bridget was that she was, for all intents and purposes, a virgin. Her first sexual encounter had been by rape and after that, they had all been johns. Stephen was the first man Bridget had made love to; he was the first man she had had sex with without any hidden agenda, without any violence. Even her encounters with David, when she was prostituting herself on Hunts Point, had been merely acts— her going down on him because she was giving him something in exchange for what she got, whether it was money, his time...or simply a list of places where she might find work. She was so happy Stephen had opened her eyes to something she might have never known existed. Although she'd had numerous sexual partners, this was all new to her and she loved it. Until now, she had viewed sex as nothing other than a task to be tolerated. But now all that had changed.

"You still didn't answer my question, though. When are you gonna start tellin' people?"

"Tell them what? It sounds so juvenile to go around telling people, 'I've got a new boyfriend, I've got a new boyfriend.' It would be different if we were getting married or something, but we're only dating."

"It's only a matter of time. He's the type. He'll be popping that question before you know it. You'll see."

"You really think so?" Bridget asked excitedly.

"Yes, I do. So be ready. In the meantime, what are you going to do about poor lovesick David McDonnell?"

"Come on, Brianna, you're not back on that again. My relationship with David is...

"I know, I know—strictly professional. Maybe in your mind, but not in his. Haven't you noticed how he's been moping around here? And isn't it a huge coincidence that he started all that moping right around the same time you two started stealing glances in the hallway? Everybody in the office knows, so it follows that David would know as well, especially since all he does is watch your every move."

"Brianna!"

"Don't *Brianna* me. You ain't gonna tell me that, after all these years, you don't see it in his eyes. All I can say is let him down easy. He's not a bad guy, as bosses go. All I wanna know is what the hell you layin' on these men that got them bumpin' into walls the way they do? Whatever it is, I want to duplicate it, because I've been havin' a dry spell lately that rivals the Sahara."

"You? A dry spell? So what do you mean you only had three dates this week instead of your usual five?"

"I'm not kiddin'. Hook a sista up, 'cause you clearly

got somethin'. I haven't seen Stephen as much as look at another woman but you. Believe me, before you two hooked up, I tried. Fine as he is and a lawyer, too. My parents would've thought they'd died and gone to heaven, if I'd brought him home; especially my mother. But, much like his mentor, Mr. Stephen P. Martin only has eyes for you. You go, girl!"

"Brianna, you are so crazy. I guess you're right. I'm not going to make a big production of it or anything, but I think I will mention it to Stephen and maybe we can sort of casually mention it to David."

"Oh, to be a fly on the wall when either or both of you do that."

"It's no big deal. David will be happy. He's been nothing but supportive of both of us. I'm sure he'll be happy the two of us found one another."

"Yeah, he's been supportive of both of you on your own, not together. All I'm sayin' is be prepared. David ain't gonna like anybody, including his protégé, taking you away from him."

"Brianna, you're absolutely, positively delusional," Bridget joked.

"Oh, by the way, Brianna, you're coming to my birthday party tonight, right? Stephen put so much planning into it and, even though I'm not supposed to know about it, I want everybody to come, so all his work won't go to waste. He'd be devastated if everything didn't turn out right. Stephen is so particular about things like this."

"Especially when it comes to his schnookums," Brianna teased.

"So, you coming?"

"I wouldn't miss it for the world. Free food, free drink and you and Stephen acting like lovebirds in front of David. I wouldn't miss it for the world."

"You think maybe I should mention about me and Stephen to David before he comes to the party tonight?"

"Not if you want him to come to the party, I wouldn't."

"My God, Brianna, you're such a drama queen. What do you think he's gonna do? Boycott our party because we've been seeing each other outside the office?"

"*Hell, yeah!*"

"Well, you're wrong. I've said it before and I'll say it again, David is going to be nothing but happy for us."

"Whatever you say," Brianna said sarcastically.

"Oh, by the way, Bridget, how did you find out about the party anyway? Stephen was so careful that you not find out."

Somehow, Brianna already knew the answer to the question. She wanted verbal confirmation.

"Oh, Jade let it slip one night while we were out having dinner. No biggie. She felt real bad about it. But I told her I'd pretend not to know."

"Let me guess," Brianna asked. "She invited you out to dinner that night."

"Yeah, she did. How did you know?"

"A wild guess, that's all."

Brianna had only been around Jade a few times, but she knew a triflin' bitch when she saw one; and Jade was as triflin' as they came. What was even worse was Brianna was convinced that she was a lot more than just a little triflin'. Bridget would do well to keep her handsome new boyfriend away from her girl, Jade. She was one of those women you shouldn't trust around your man as far as you could throw her.

Stephen had told Bridget they would be dining out for the evening alone. Instead, a hundred of their closest friends were waiting at an upscale restaurant in the village called Jasleen's. He had rented the place out, so that they would have it all to themselves for the night. Everyone was waiting to jump out and yell, "surprise".

Because Bridget didn't want to ruin all of Stephen's plans and the joy he would get from surprising her, she had been practicing her best surprised face for days and suddenly felt over rehearsed.

She wore a black silk dress, silver pumps and jewelry and carried a small silver wristlet. The dress clung to her in all the right places and from the look on Stephen's face when she finished dressing at his place, she had made the right selection.

"Oh my God! You're beautiful, absolutely, positively beautiful. How on earth did I ever get so lucky?"

"You're not so bad yourself," Bridget said.

Stephen was wearing a navy blue Hugo Boss suit, which flattered his well-cut physique. His beautiful dark wavy hair was close-cropped, and his shoes were so shiny you could see yourself in them. The two made quite a pair.

"Shall we go?" Stephen asked.

"Sure. What time are our reservations?" Bridget played along.

"Eight o'clock. We should probably get going. It's about a half-hour drive; if we leave now, we won't be late."

When they arrived at the restaurant, it was obviously dark for an Greenwich Village eatery on a Friday night, but Bridget already knew the deal.

As soon as Bridget and Stephen stepped into the restaurant, everyone jumped out of their hiding places and yelled, "*Surprise!!!*"

Bridget was so overwhelmed by all the familiar faces that had come to celebrate with her. She actually pulled off a relatively believable "surprise face." Bridget saw Jade and David. Brianna was there with a great big smile on her face. Even Big Rob was there. Bridget felt honored and couldn't help but marvel at the mixture of types of people that were there to celebrate her birthday. It was yet another example of her multi-dimensional life, and for the first time she wasn't ashamed of it.

Everyone ate, drank and partied way into the night until Stephen got everyone's attention so that he could propose a toast to the guest of honor.

"Someone very beautiful has brought us all together

here tonight. She has touched each of our lives in one way or another. I can remember walking past those doors at McDonnell & Simpson, thinking I had it goin' on and her face being the first one I saw. I was blown away. I couldn't remember having ever seen anyone quite so beautiful before in my life. So I continued to work night and day, all in an effort to spend as much time with her as possible.

"But, I don't want to say that too loud, because David thinks I was an extremely dedicated employee," Stephen jokingly whispered.

Somewhere in the back of the restaurant, Jade was consistently goading David with comments about Stephen and Bridget, as David emptied yet another bottle of champagne.

And, that's when it happened. A collective hush went over the room, when Stephen knelt down in front of Bridget. All of the color rushed from David's face. Brianna was grinning and clapping. Jade's face was etched in her signature sneer. Across the room, Big Rob watched with interest, truly seeing Jade for the first time and not sure he liked what he saw.

Stephen continued, "I say all this by way of saying thank you, Bridget. Thank you for being a constant source of inspiration, thank you for always putting others before yourself, including me; and thank you for reminding me day after day what a gift life is. I also say this by way of asking you to share all that you are and all that you have been to me for the rest of our lives. Bridget, in front of all our friends and loved ones, I'd like to ask you to please be my wife."

Bridget was speechless. She stared at Stephen as if there were no one else in the room; that is until almost everyone started to clap.

"Go on and say yes," Brianna yelled out. "You know you wanna marry that man. Besides, you can't embarrass him here in front of everybody."

Everyone at the party burst into laughter as Bridget nodded her head yes, then finally spoke.

"Yes, Stephen. Yes. I'll marry you."

Stephen took her in his arms and the two kissed for what seemed like eternity, just as the door to the restaurant closed. David left, eager to be as far away from the entire scene as possible. But he wasn't alone; close on his heels was Jade.

"Jade, if I were you, I would get as far away from me right now as possible."

"Why? Do you really want to be alone at a time like this? I know how you feel about our girl."

"There it is again, that thinly veiled note of sarcasm in your voice. Why on earth would I want you anywhere near me; making fun of me with every word you speak?"

"David, I'm not making fun of you. I've never understood why everyone always chooses her. Why? She and I were both on Hunts Point. Why, out of all those girls, me included, did you choose her to be the one?"

"Don't you get it, Jade? You don't choose love. It chooses you."

Standing there in the dark, with Jade's questioning gaze, her hazel eyes boring right through him, David was suddenly reminded of oh, so long ago when he and Bridget had first met. Jade's presence only served to further remind him. He suddenly took Jade in his arms, backed her up against the concrete wall of the restaurant and kissed her with such urgency, Jade wasn't sure whether he wanted to love her or to kill her. His mouth smothering hers took her breath away, yet Jade still saw this as a golden opportunity. He was vulnerable and she would swoop down and attack. Just when she thought she had him exactly where she wanted him, Big Rob opened the door to the restaurant, witnessed the scene that had just played itself out and went back inside. But it wasn't before making both Jade and David aware of his presence. Jade should have been the person startled by Big Rob's presence, under the circumstances. But, it wasn't her that was startled back into reality; it was David.

"I can't do this. I don't know what the hell got into me."

He walked the half a block to his car, got in and quickly drove away, as Jade whispered under her breath.

"Gotcha!"

By the time Jade went back into the restaurant, everyone was preparing to leave and Bridget, Stephen and Brianna were gathering up Bridget's birthday presents.

Walking by Big Rob, barely acknowledging his presence

and heading straight toward Bridget, Big Rob grabbed Jade's arm before she could get away.

"Don't you ever disrespect me that way again. These other folks may not see you, but I do. I know who you are. Don't you ever, ever disrespect me again, or I promise you, you will have hell to pay in more ways than one."

Even Jade knew when to back down. She didn't give him as much as a sideways glance. All she did was nod her head in agreement; a silent acknowledgment of Big Rob's power.

"The gift I got you is for both you *and* Stephen," Brianna offered.

"I can imagine," was all Bridget could say.

"Don't you know our girl here ain't into that slutty, trashy look," Jade commented as she approached the pair.

Brianna wasn't stupid; she knew girls like Jade quite well. Her comment was merely an indirect diss of her. It might have worked with some, but Brianna wasn't an insecure woman. Every time she got up out of her bed in the morning, took her shower and brushed and flossed her teeth, she knew her choice of attire would garner any measure of glares, stares and negativity. But she didn't dress to please anyone but herself.

"I don't recall mentioning what was wrapped up inside of the box I gave her, but yes, I will agree with you, Bridget is not into that slutty, trashy look. She's a class act. In fact, I believe there are those that could learn a thing or two from Bridget about dignity."

"Ain't that the truth," Jade agreed.

Bridget always made sure that Brianna and Jade were far away from each other. Because from the very first time they ever met, it was clear they were like fire and gasoline. It was a little surprising given the fact that Bridget thought they were so very similar to one another—that daring, fearless nature was so characteristic of both of them.

"Brianna, do you need a ride home?" Bridget asked.

"No, hon. I'm fine. David told everybody at the firm to call a car service, if they didn't drive."

"He never ceases to amaze me. Just when I start to think he is going to drive me out of my mind with his constant demands at work, he goes and does something like that. I have to thank him. Do you know where he is?"

"I saw him leave a few minutes ago. I was outside having a smoke and he drove off in a hurry," Brianna said.

Right after mentioning to Bridget that David had left, Brianna shot Jade a look. More than anything, she wanted Jade to know that she had been there, and that she had witnessed the entire scene between her and David. All Jade did was smirk, but there was hell in her eyes. That was when Brianna knew beyond a shadow of a doubt that she was trouble. More than anything, she hoped that Bridget would figure that out before it was too late.

Driving home alone, David wondered why he had stopped with Jade. The last thing in the world he needed tonight was to be alone. It would have been so easy to take her home with him, if for no other reason than to ease his pain. Yet, David recognized the fact that such a decision was wrought with trouble. Jade could obviously be extremely manipulative and she was Bridget's closest friend. Not only that, she was there with some thug that would probably want to break him into pieces for as much as looking at Jade. No, he had done the right thing. But, above and beyond all of the obvious reasons not to have sex with her, there was something nagging at him that just didn't feel right. Yes, he had definitely done the right thing. No point in creating more problems than he already had to deal with. He was already trying to figure out how he was going to contend with Bridget and Stephen being a couple, out in the open for all to see; especially him, not to mention them getting married. The best he could hope for was a ridiculously long engagement.

"You make me so happy," Stephen said as they were leaving the party. "In my wildest dreams, I could never have imagined being this happy."

"Oh, Stephen, I love you, too."

"Not that I didn't say I loved you or anything, because I do, but I want you to *really* understand what I said and that I truly mean it. I'm a firm believer in the possibility of love without functionality. Just because two people love one another doesn't necessarily mean that they make one another happy. But you, Bridget Grey, you make me very, *very* happy. I hope I do the same for you."

"Stephen, of course you do. I'm happier than I've ever been in my life. And, that is because of you. And, I intend to make it up to you for the rest of your life."

By the time Stephen and Bridget got to his place, they

were so hungry for one another, they could barely wait
to get inside of his apartment. Bridget was more voracious
in her desire for him than she had ever been; grappling
with his clothing, eager to remove every stitch, sucking
and nibbling at his nipples, quickly opening his pants to
extract his burgeoning hard-on. She pushed him into his
desk chair in the living room and straddled him, gasping
as he entered her. Bridget was so tight and so wet, Stephen
could barely contain himself. The feel of Bridget rising
and falling, contracting with each stroke, didn't afford him
the opportunity to hold on very long before exploding
inside of her with great intensity.

"Oh, baby, oh, Bridget, oh, God. That was so, so good."
Bridget had made good on her promise. More than
anything she wanted to make Stephen as happy as he
had made her and she believed tonight she had. Yet, she
couldn't help but shake the feeling that while some measure of what she had done tonight had been in the spirit
of love, to a degree some of it was a form of acting, a
playing out of the ways she had been taught to please a
man from her experiences on the street. But, was what
they had just shared as real for her as it was for Stephen?

CHAPTER TEN
THE WEDDING/BUSTER SIGHTING

"So where are you two bourgeois gonna live anyway?" Jade asked while she feigned helping Bridget get ready to walk down the aisle.

"Stephen found a beautiful condo on East Seventy-third Street. It's perfect; two bedrooms, eat-in kitchen, a den, and a huge living room. He's already talking about turning one of the rooms into a nursery."

"Damn, homeboy's tryin' to keep you barefoot and pregnant with a swiftness."

"No, that's not it. It's just that he knows how much I want children. I've always wanted a big family; a family of my own. When we were at Mannersville, it was all I ever thought about."

"That's not how I remember it. From what I remember, *all* you talked about at Mannersville was law school."

"I know, I want both. I want the whole package; a career, family, a home. All the things I never had."

"Hmph. I also remember that when we were at Mannersville, you said *we* were family."

"We are Jade. It's just, it would be nice to start a family

of my own. To feel that life growing inside of me. I want an opportunity to do things right, different than my parents."

"I ain't never havin' no rugrats. Children bleed the life out of a person. I'll never let anyone do that to me."

"Jade, that's an awful thing to say."

"Yeah, awful, but true."

"So if you're so ready to be a house frau, what is your problem? You are marrying a handsome, rich lawyer. You better walk your ass down that aisle with a quickness, before I take your fuckin' place."

"I love Stephen and I know he loves me, but I feel like I'm living a lie. Would he still love me as much and want to marry me as much if he knew about my past? I feel like this marriage hasn't got a chance in hell, unless I tell him everything there is to know about me."

"Have you lost your damn mind? What is to be gained by tellin' Stephen all those sordid details? You tell him and you're a fool. Haven't you had enough drama in your life? Sometimes in relationships a secret or two is necessary. Trust me, the last thing you want to do is open up your mouth."

"Jade, can I ask you something?"

"What now?"

"Do you ever miss having a father?"

"How the hell can you miss something you never had?"

"This is supposed to be the happiest day of my life and all I keep thinking is, I don't even have a father to walk me down the aisle."

"Shit! Is that all you're vexing over? I can get Big Rob

to walk you down the aisle. He's been there for us more than either of our fathers ever could have been."

"No, that's okay. Big Rob is cool and all, but it would be nice if it were someone special; someone who really cares about me. I asked David, but he got so weird with me that I left it alone."

Jade grinned to herself while Bridget was preoccupied with her thoughts. It amazed her that after all Bridget had been through, she could still be so fuckin' naïve. Ever since she had come to work at McDonnell & Simpson, that man had been walkin' around feenin' for her ass. Somehow she had managed not to notice a thing. Why the fuck would he want to walk a woman down the aisle that he was consumed with?

"Bridget, you know how David is; Mr. Low Key."

"Yeah, I know. Still, I think this would have felt more like a wedding, if I had someone like David to walk me down the aisle."

"Well, Bridget, I hate to break it to you, but that ain't gonna happen, at least not this go-round."

"God, Jade, why do you say things like that? It's my wedding day and this will be my *only* go-round."

"All I'm saying is you got two hundred-plus guests waitin' for you to make your grand entrance. In other words, get your ass in gear. Speakin' of which, who the fuck are all those people anyway?"

"I have no idea. Clients, friends of Stephen's and his parents. But I think mostly clients. You know Stephen, always trying to cement his business relationship with his clients. David hit the jackpot when he hired that man. I hope he knows how lucky he is to have an associate like Stephen at his firm. Speaking of guests, has David gotten here yet? I thought he would at least stop by and wish me well."

"He's probably already taken his seat, *like everybody else waiting for you!*"

"Okay, okay, I get the hint. I'm ready."

Jade knew exactly where David was—exactly where she had left him, in his office, doing what most lovesick men would be doing at a time like this—getting drunk. Jade made sure he was well supplied with his signature Dalwhinnie, so he could sufficiently lick his wounds, ultimately fuckin' up Bridget's day.

Uhm, Jade thought to herself, *I wonder if Bridget might like another male figure in her life to walk her down the aisle; one she hadn't seen in a long, long time.*

"Jade, Jade, I'm ready."

"Where were you?" Bridget asked. "It's my wedding day and you're more preoccupied than I am."

"Just thinking about how far we've both come, that's all. So, you ready to do this or what?"

"Yeah, I'm ready."

As Bridget approached the opulent doors to where she was about to marry the man of her dreams, she marveled at what her life had become. As she approached the beautiful red carpet which adorned the ash wood floors of the Altman Building, an elegant landmark building owned by none other than David McDonnell, she looked for

David's face among the crowd of guests, eager to flash him a smile, a meager means of thanking him for all that he had done for her and Stephen. Instead, the face she saw drained all the life from her body and she collapsed right where she stood.

As Bridget lay at the entrance to the wedding hall, overcome by the sight of her greatest nightmare sitting among all the well-wishers, David stood directly behind her, a bit disheveled, but there nonetheless. He had sat in his office, in the dark for hours, when he realized there was no way in hell he could sit there and not see her. Even though she wasn't marrying him, nothing on earth could keep him from seeing her in all her beauty, on her wedding day. And, of course, as with most people in love, who can't have the one they want, he was ever hopeful that he still had a chance of her changing her mind. A minimal chance, given he had never shared his feelings with her, but a chance nonetheless.

"Shit!" Jade muttered under her breath. "That fuckin' girl must have her own damn guardian angel."

Once again Bridget was going to get exactly what she wanted and ruin all of her fun. Jade still believed Bridget lived way too charmed a life. It never occurred to the envious Jade that all her attempts to fuck with Bridget were met with the opposite effect. In Jade's case, karma truly was a bitch.

Bridget slowly awakened to find all of her loved ones at her side; Jade, Stephen—and David.

David, who was standing directly behind her when she

had fallen, was holding on to her tightly so as to ensure she wouldn't take another tumble.

In a vain attempt at levity, coupled with a desire to get as close to her as possible, his lips brushed her ear lightly touching the pearl earrings he had given her for her birthday a year earlier, whispering, "You didn't have to pass out in order to get me to escort you down the aisle. I'm here. I'm just a little late—as usual."

The wedding reception was abuzz with speculation at what might have caused Bridget's sudden collapse: the excitement of her nuptials; illness; and, of course, pregnancy. But only Bridget and Jade knew the true reason she had passed out.

Jade had always made it a sport toying with Bridget— but tonight was too good to be true.

"What was that all about?" Jade asked.

"It must be all the excitement of the wedding. I thought I saw *him*."

"Him, who?" Jade asked with exasperation.

"Buster."

"Now I know you're coming unglued. Buster? Is that wishful thinking on your part or are you just more stressed than I thought?"

"It might be a little bit of both. I guess somewhere in my mind I can't help but wonder how different things might be, if I hadn't left Mannersville the way that I did. I mean, don't get me wrong, I love my life. But there's always that lingering worry that one day everyone will find out. I don't think I could stand that."

"No one's going to find out. But, don't get it twisted; Buster is definitely not popping up at your wedding. Honey, you removed the chances of Buster popping up anywhere a long, long time ago."

"I know. I guess it's just wishful thinking."

"Why the hell would you wish some shit like that?"

"No matter what he did, no one deserves to die. I took someone's life into my own hands, and I didn't have that right. I just wish I had it to do over again."

"This is life, sweetie; you don't get do-overs. The sooner you recognize that, the better off you'll be."

Bridget thought of what Jade said. But, hadn't they both gotten *do-overs*? Look at their lives. Look at her wedding. If someone had told her the day she ran from Mannersville that this would be her life one day, she would have laughed in their face. But here she was in an impressive wedding hall marrying one of New York's most coveted bachelors. And, the entire wedding had been paid for by her boss. Life had been kind to her, indeed. And, although Jade had chosen a different path than she had, gone were the days of either of them going to bed hungry. After their life-altering escape from Mannersville, she felt as though she had most certainly gotten one hell of a do-over. Bridget was grateful for whatever force allowed her life to unfold as it had. She was committed to seeing to it that she lived an exemplary life so that she would always feel worthy.

Bridget watched Stephen from across the room mingling with their guests and she felt overwhelmed with pride. Unfortunately, nagging somewhere in the pit of her stomach was her concern at being "found out." How would Stephen, or his family, for that matter, react if they knew who she really was?

"Jade, I hate to interrupt this whole maid of honor, bride moment, but may I dance with my beautiful bride?"

"I don't know, Stephen," Jade responded. "I'm starting to think you don't like me. Everyone in the wedding party has danced with you except for me."

For a moment, Stephen looked from Jade to Bridget, eager for Bridget to rescue him. For some time he had a developing level of discomfort around Jade. He couldn't put his finger on it, but there was something about her that aroused an undercurrent of unease.

However, this was his wedding day and he didn't want either Jade or Bridget to believe he took any sort of issue with Jade, so he obliged her.

"Bridget, do you mind?" he asked.

"Of course not, sweetie. The night wouldn't be complete if you didn't dance with my girl."

Gliding across the floor, the soulful melody of Toni Braxton's "Un-Break My Heart" playing, Jade's body pressed against his, Stephen was more than a bit uncomfortable. He wouldn't have guessed that he would be attracted to Jade, but his body in such close proximity to her seemed to cause a reaction. He could feel his nature rising in response to the closeness of her. Eager to break free, he was just about to make an excuse in order to get away, when Brianna tapped Jade on the shoulder.

"May I cut in? I haven't had a dance with my boss yet. You don't mind, do you, Jade?"

Jade's stare was like daggers through Brianna and she made no attempts to conceal it. Neither did Brianna make any attempts to camouflage the fact that she was completely aware of what Jade was up to.

"Of course I don't mind," Jade responded. "I've got plenty of time to dance with my sister's new husband. Don't I, Stephen?"

Until now Brianna hadn't realized how perfect Bridget and Stephen were for one another. They were so very much alike. Standing there with Jade, a wolf in sheep's clothing, Stephen had so easily become Jade's prey. Brianna had been watching her all night. She was a complete and utter bitch, and the minute she saw her swoop down on Stephen, she had given Jade a moment—only a moment to dance with him—before she came to Stephen's rescue.

"Thank you," Stephen whispered as he took Brianna's hand and danced.

"You're quite welcome, boss man. You looked like you needed rescuing."

"We're gonna have to talk to the *real* boss man about getting you a raise." He chuckled.

"You better! Keeping that she-beast in check is a full-time job. I don't know why Bridget doesn't cut her loose."

"They're really good friends. Why do you say that? Don't you trust her either? She makes me very uncomfortable. There's something about her that doesn't ring true. I don't know. There always seems to be a double meaning in everything she does and says. There always seems to be some sort of game plan; a goal. She's so unlike Bridget. I can't understand how they have managed to stay such close friends for so long."

"Stephen, you just answered your own question. Jade is as manipulative as they come and, for whatever reason, Bridget doesn't see it. It may be that Bridget doesn't want to see it. That would mean having to let go of someone that's been a big part of her life for a really long time. Keep an eye on her. I don't trust Jade as far as I can throw her. My cousin knows her really well and, I'm telling you, she's bad news. Don't get sucked in by her, whatever you do."

"I won't. What would make you think I could?"

"You forget, Stephen, I watched the two of you on the dance floor before I made a beeline over here to free you from her grasp. You were seconds from getting caught up."

Stephen could feel a heated blush rising to his cheeks at the thought of how he felt between his legs while he had Jade in his arms. He was suddenly very embarrassed.

"Don't worry about it. I'm the only one that noticed," Brianna said.

"Noticed what?" Bridget asked as she walked over and joined them both.

"Your new husband here was stepping on my feet. We really must get him some dance lessons," Brianna quickly responded.

"Stephen is a fantastic dancer," Bridget offered. "But then again, I didn't marry you for your dancing, did I, baby?"

"Ooh, sookie, sookie now!" Brianna screamed. "Somebody's gonna be in trouble on their honeymoon!"

"No, you definitely didn't marry me for my dancing skills. Did you, baby?"

Stephen looked at Brianna as she walked away and whispered *thank you* once again, for saving him.

"I'm going to throw the bouquet now," Bridget announced as Brianna retreated.

"Alright!"

All of the single women gathered as Bridget stood poised and ready to throw the coveted bouquet. Just as Brianna was about to catch the bouquet, Jade reached her foot out, tripping Brianna and grabbed the bouquet for herself. It was subtle enough that most of the guests missed the deliberate maneuver; but not so subtle it didn't go unnoticed by either Bridget or Brianna, or any of the other women attempting to catch the bouquet. Jade, in true sociopath fashion, raised the bouquet in triumph. Despite Brianna's initial instinct to slap her across the face, she didn't want to ruin Bridget's day; so instead, she walked away quietly without saying a word.

Now it was time for the garter.

"You ready to toss the garter, honey?" Bridget asked Stephen.

"Most definitely."

As all the single men in attendance gathered together, David sat watching and drinking.

"David, come on," Bridget coaxed, attempting to pull David to his feet.

David stood up and wobbled over to where all the men were standing. Stephen aimed right for him and David couldn't help but catch the lacy garter between his fingers. Jade couldn't have been more ecstatic, if she had planned it herself.

She sat in the chair, eager for David to roll the lacy undergarment the full length of her leg. David, more than just a little tipsy, could barely focus on where her leg actually was, but he did manage to wrap it around her foot and roll it up. Jade was so happy she had worn a dress. As he got closer and closer to her thigh, she wondered if such proximity to her was having any effect on him. Just when she thought it might, David fell flat on his ass on the floor. All the champagne he had been drinking proved to be too much. Stephen and a couple of the other attorneys at McDonnell helped David to a back room to rest.

CHAPTER ELEVEN
RESIGNATION

"Good morning, David."

"Where the hell have you been?" David bellowed.

"Excuse me?"

"I've got a business to run here. This isn't a fuckin' charity. I can't run my business sufficiently, if I don't have an assistant...here...on time to do her goddamned job!"

"David, I told you I would be a little late this morning. Stephen and I had an appointment with that fertility specialist."

The mere mention of Stephen and fertility specialist in the same sentence only served to agitate David even more. Yet, Bridget was even more oblivious of David's feelings, now that she and Stephen had gotten married. She was helplessly in love and enjoying her new life.

A few feet away, Brianna listened from her desk, wondering what Stephen would say if he heard the way David was talking to his wife. Stephen was intensely loyal to David and despite his obsession with Bridget, somehow David never took his jealousy out on Stephen. For whatever reasons, he reserved that for Bridget alone. And, over the past several months, their once content working relationship had gone from bad to worse. The whole situation was extremely uncomfortable for all concerned.

"David, I'm sorry if my appointment this morning somehow put you in a bind, but I will not have you disrespect me. I told you about this appointment weeks ago, and I will not apologize for taking personal time that I am entitled to."

"Entitled to?" David chuckled. "Entitled to? If that isn't the funniest thing I've ever heard."

"What the hell is that supposed to mean?" Bridget asked.

"Why don't you save the naïve role for Stephen? You know *exactly* what I mean."

"I'm warning you, David! Don't push me!"

Brianna had never seen Bridget so angry, and clearly, her warning didn't fall on deaf ears. David did back down—slightly. However, Brianna wondered what that heated exchange was all about. There was clearly something hidden beneath each of their words that only the two of them were privy to.

Bridget stormed off into the bathroom and Brianna followed quickly thereafter. When Brianna entered the bathroom, Bridget was there pacing.

"What the fuck was all that about?" Brianna asked.

"I don't know what's gotten into him. Ever since Stephen and I got married, he's been acting like a fuckin' asshole. He's miserable and he wants everyone else around him to be miserable. Between him and Jade, it's like I owe them my life or something. I finally have some measure of independence and they both want to feed off me. My relationship with both of them is fuckin' symbiotic and I can't take it anymore. I want to live my own life for a change. I've earned it!"

"Of course you've earned it, but you first have to face facts. Number one, Jade is jealous of you. She wants to be you, she wants to live your life and if you let her, she will take everything that belongs to you. I've known women like her my whole life. She walks around acting like she's the best thing to happen to you since sliced bread, when in reality, it's the other way around. You are the best thing to ever happen to her. Now, I don't claim to know all that much about your relationship with Jade, but I've seen her enough times to know exactly what Miss Jade is all about. I know a lot of people look at me with my tight clothes and big boobs and think *I'm* a boob, but I'm smarter than I look…"

"No, Brianna…"

"It's okay, Bridget. You don't have to say anything. You're my girl and you've always treated me with the utmost respect, but I recognize how I come across to people. I'm me and I have no intention of changing for *anyone*. But getting back to what I was saying, I see more, and am aware of more, than most people realize. And that girl Jade, she ain't nothin' but trouble. If you keep her around, you and yours are headed for trouble. And I would definitely keep her away from your husband, if I were you. I know people here at McDonnell were whispering and shit when I got the position working for Stephen and then some more after the two of you got married, but I don't roll like that. Just because I like to show off my body, don't mean I don't have principles. And I don't mess around with other women's husbands, especially not women whom I call friends...and Bridget, I do consider you a friend."

"I do, too," Bridget whispered.

"Now on to point two—Bridget, David McDonnell is in love with you, obsessed with you, whatever the case may be, but he's got it bad and the longer you fool yourself into believing otherwise, the more difficult things will be. Now, as I see it, you have a couple of alternatives. You can recognize that he has these intense feelings and stick around and deal with it, or you can leave. But, whatever you do, don't sleep on the fact that this man wants you in a bad way."

"I'm probably going to have to leave soon anyway. That is, if everything works out as planned. Stephen and I saw the fertility specialist this morning. We've been trying to get pregnant and so far nothing, but I just think both of us are too stressed, what with the job and all. I might be better off, if I just resign now and try getting pregnant without the responsibilities of this job to weigh me down. I was going to wait until I got pregnant to leave, but I'm getting really sick of David's shit, and truth be told, I don't really have to work. Stephen has already told me I can quit anytime I like. Although he did mention how lost David is going to be."

"David will survive. He will get over his feelings for you and he will find himself another assistant. That is what people do. You're not an indentured servant girl. You've got to live your own life."

"You know, Brianna, you're right. I'm not sure what I'm going to do yet, but whatever my decision, it's going to be *my* decision— not everyone else's. Thank you so much for the ear. I needed someone to bounce all of this off of."

"No problem, girl. What are friends for anyway?"

"You're always coming through for me. I'd like to reciprocate one of these days."

"Your time will come. I'm gonna need and I'm going straight to you when I do." Brianna chuckled.

"And I'll be there," came Bridget's response.

"Well, let me get back to that asshole. I swear he's trying my patience. I almost quit on the spot."

"Don't let him take you out of your groove. You and Stephen are fuckin' newlyweds, for Christ's sake. Enjoy it."

"We are. Believe me, we are. I'm not taking this home with me. It's just when either David or Jade call us at home, I feel like I have no haven. When I leave here at the end of the day, as far as I'm concerned, it's over, but lately home is not the sanctuary it started out as. Jade and David both call constantly. I know what David's problem is; he has no life. But Jade has a man. I don't understand how she has so much time on her hands to keep bugging me."

"And I thought David was obsessed. You got two stalkers in your midst, girl," Jade said.

"I don't know if I would call them stalkers, but they are both very annoying, especially lately."

"You can dub it whatever you want. But anytime you're paying that much attention to any one person to such a strong degree, there's some obsessive shit goin' on."

Bridget knew she was right, but didn't want to believe it.

Despite her best efforts to hang in and give David a chance to clean up his act one day, he eventually pushed her much too far.

"Bridget!"

"Yes, David," Bridget managed to reply calmly.

"Could you get in here? I don't want to sit here, screaming back and forth."

"You could have fooled me," she whispered under her breath.

"Did you say something?" David asked.

Although Bridget thought she had whispered her comment, the look on David's face told her that he might have actually heard her.

"Didn't I ask you to remove these files from my office? I'm gonna trip over them. They're in the way and they're a hazard."

"I know, David. I called the records department several times but they are so bogged down with that project you have them doing; revamping the file room. It's taking up most of their time."

"Well, then why don't you remove them?"

Bridget realized he was purposely pushing her buttons and she was pissed.

"Can't you push them to the side until they can come pick them up? Those boxes are heavy."

"Oh, now, all of a sudden, you're a snowflake," he said sarcastically.

"No, I'm not a snowflake, but I'm also not going to move those boxes. That is not my job."

"Not your job! Not your job," he bellowed. "Your fucking job is to do whatever I tell you to do and I told you to move the goddamn files and move them now."

"You know what, David? Why don't *you* move them? Because, if you're waiting for me to do it, it'll be a cold day in hell!"

Bridget stomped out of his office and went back to her desk. Angry that she was standing up to him, and in his eyes usurping his authority, David began removing the files from the boxes. One by one he went over to her desk and tossed them directly in front of her, spilling her coffee all over the desk after which he demanded she clean up *her* mess.

"Fuck you!" Bridget yelled. "I quit!"

By the time Bridget left her desk in a huff, everyone in the office had witnessed the display, including Stephen. He left his office and rushed to Bridget to find out what could have possibly happened. Bridget had only touched on a few of the disagreements she and David had had over the past few months. She knew that Stephen liked David and she didn't want to drag him into their issues with one another.

"Bridget," Stephen asked, "what the heck is going on? I could hear you all the way in my office."

"I'm sick of this, Stephen. He treats me like crap and I've had enough of it. I won't work for *anyone* who treats me like that, including David."

"You're having a bad day; that's all. Why don't you go home and cool off and come back tomorrow?"

"I won't be coming back. I've had enough of this. I've tried to make allowances for his miserable life and his loneliness, or whatever it is that's going on with him. But he's not the only person in the world with problems. None of it gives him the right to treat people like shit."

"Don't forget, baby; it takes two for an argument to continue."

Bridget was outraged. It almost seemed as though he were taking David's side, sight unseen.

"You didn't hear the way he was talking to me a few minutes ago. Cursing and yelling."

"You mean like you were just doing?"

"Yeah, but I didn't start it. He did."

"Bridget, listen to yourself. You sound like a two-year-old. He started it."

"Well, he did. And, it's not the first time. Ever since we got married, he's been behaving this way and quite frankly, I've had enough."

"Maybe you're distracted, honey. We've been trying so hard to get pregnant. Maybe you're missing some things because of it."

"No, Stephen. I'm not missing anything. I'm doing the same job I've always done. He's just jealous because his life is so fucking miserable. That's all. And, why are you taking his side?"

"I'm not taking anyone's side. I'm just trying to give an impartial perspective."

"It doesn't sound impartial to me. It sounds like you're taking the side of the asshole who just cursed at your wife. You know what…I'm not even going to discuss this anymore. I'm going home. Did you mean what you said about me staying at home and being a mom or not? I can't think of a better time than now. Maybe, without all the stress of this place, I'll finally be able to get pregnant."

"You know I meant it, Bridget. I don't want you leaving for the wrong reasons. You and David are more than just employer and employee. You are, and have been, friends for years. I would hate to see you spoil that."

"I didn't spoil a thing. He did. I will not be a doormat. I won't. I've tried to be understanding. I've tried to reason with him, but enough is enough."

"Are you going to be okay?" Stephen asked as Bridget stormed from the office.

"I'll be fine. I'll be just fine."

David suddenly realized how completely unglued he had become. But, it was too late.

CHAPTER TWELVE
A NEW EMPLOYEE

Sitting by his mother's hospital bed at Sloan Kettering Hospital, the shell of a woman that lay there reminded him little of the stunning woman he remembered as a child. His mother had always been beautiful. At eight-two pounds and in such obvious pain, even the morphine drip the hospital had provided wasn't quite enough. He prayed for an end to her existence. After so many years of unhappiness with his father, she had finally achieved some level of contentment. Despite the fact that his father had left her nothing when he died, David had seen to it that his mother wanted for nothing. He had also ensured that she maintained her dignity. He hadn't provided her with an "allowance" as his father had done.

As soon as his father's wishes were made known, David had taken everything and split it all right down the middle. The money, the stocks, insurance, shares in the firm; all of it was just as much hers as it was his. In fact, at the outset, David had pleaded with his mother to take it all. He wanted to sign everything over to her. He felt she deserved it so much more than he did. But, his mother wouldn't hear of it and finally settled on fifty percent of everything, which suited David just fine.

"David, David," she gasped.

Lately all his mother seemed to do was sleep. She had so little strength, she seldom did much talking. And, even when she did speak, her words were seldom lucid. Even today when she spoke, David wasn't completely sure how much of it made any sense. However, he listened anyway—all too happy to soak in whatever words she had for him. He was fully aware that anything she said to him might well be the last words she ever spoke.

"David, come closer."

David moved his chair closer to her and leaned in so that he could hear her more clearly.

"No, come sit down next to me on the bed...like you used to when you were little. Remember how you used to come and get in the bed with me on those nights when your father didn't come home?"

"Yes, mother. I remember. I always hated sleeping in that big room all by myself and I was so afraid of the dark. I knew if Dad wasn't home, you would let me come and sleep with you."

"You were so little. Often you would hear me crying, and you would come in and tell me you would protect me. You were only six or seven years old, but you were trying to protect me, even back then."

"Yeah." David laughed. "I think I had read too many books about boys slaying dragons."

"You know I'm proud of you, don't you, son? I feel like you're the only thing I did right with my life."

"Mother, no. You…I'm so proud of *you*. You sacrificed everything for me; for the life that you thought I should have."

"There's something I have to tell you, David. I've kept it from you all these years. I promised your father I'd never tell you. But now, it seems so unfair and so pointless. I should've never kept that kind of a secret. You deserved to know. It was your right to know. She came to see me and she was so young and so afraid. We should've helped her, David. We shouldn't have made her go away. We should've helped her. Sometimes I think this cancer is my penance for being so selfish."

Then she started to cry. She coughed and it took so much out of her. As much as David enjoyed the opportunity to hear her speaking again, he realized how much it took out of her and all he wanted her to do now was to rest. He knew she was dying, but like most children, even adult children, he wanted her alive for as long as she could be.

"Mother. You need your rest. Sleep. Sleep now. We can talk again tomorrow."

"No, David, I have to tell you. There's no time. I have to tell you now…you would've been a good father, David. If only we'd given you a chance. You would've been a good father."

Before she could say anything else, the machines she

was hooked to began to go off, ringing, and making noises that could only mean one thing. David McDonnell would never have an opportunity to speak to his mother again. His only wish was that her last words hadn't been ravings of dementia, or maybe they hadn't been. Maybe they were her hopes for what might have been.

On the day of his mother's funeral, David couldn't help but notice that there was no one there that truly loved her, besides him. No best friend, no husband, or companion, for that matter. Were it not for his presence, Ann Swerdly McDonnell would have been laid to rest without anyone who truly cared for her present to mourn her passing. Sure, her funeral was a packed house. Many of the firm's clients had shown up and most of the staff, but no one besides him, who truly loved her. David didn't just mourn his mother's death that day. He mourned her life. He mourned a life that had been so dependent upon another person for so many years, that she had never truly learned how to have a life of her own. And, just when he thought the pain in his heart had become unbearable, Bridget walked in. He had been such a bastard toward her, he truly had not expected her to be there. But she was. It occurred to him that she probably only came out of duty to her husband. Stephen was an associate at the firm. He, like everyone else from the firm that showed up, knew their presence there would go a long way.

Bridget and Stephen approached David at the end of the services.

"I'm so sorry, David. If there's anything at all that I can do, please don't hesitate to call on me," Stephen offered.

Bridget said, "David, I'm so very sorry."

Bridget hugged David and, for a moment, he thought his heart actually stopped. Suddenly, nothing at all but this moment mattered; not his mother's death, his practice, not even the fact that Bridget's husband was standing right there with them. At that very moment, David would have traded every single thing that he owned in the world and even the next, just to be able to hold on to her for even five minutes longer.

Not long after his mother's death, David threw himself into his work. When he wasn't working, he was sleeping with anyone and everyone who would have him. He mourned both the loss of his mother and the loss of Bridget with work and sex. Most of the women he encountered, he dropped quickly. One in particular, however, was relentless and endeared herself to David, if only as a means to occupy his sleepless nights. Then he realized she could serve another purpose.

"I was thinking maybe we would invite one of my associates, Stephen Martin, and his wife Bridget, over for dinner."

"Bridget. Oh, yeah. Isn't she your former secretary? She's the one that married your mentee, right?"

Gwen knew full well who Bridget was. She saw the look on his face whenever her name was mentioned. Even if she missed that, she could never have missed that it was her name that he often called out in the middle of the night—right before he woke up drenched in sweat.

"I'll do all the cooking myself," Gwen offered.

"You sure about that? We can always cater it."

"No, David. Catering at home is so impersonal. I'll cook. I haven't cooked in so long, I think I might actually enjoy it."

"Okay. Go for it."

David invited both Stephen and Bridget over for dinner. He told Stephen it was a way of thanking him for all of the extra work he had been putting in at the office. It was also to apologize for being so difficult with Bridget right before she resigned. He knew that would smooth the way for Bridget to accept, since he was sure the last thing she wanted to do was to spend an evening with him. But, he had to do something. If he thought he spent too much time thinking about her when they worked together, it had gotten even worse since she had resigned.

Bridget and Stephen arrived promptly at eight.

"They're here, David! They're here!"

Gwen had been more excited than even he'd been all week. David presumed it was because she was excited about demonstrating her culinary talents. He couldn't have been more wrong. In fact, Gwen was chomping at the bit to see Bridget, up close and personal. He knew she had David by the balls, and how. She wanted to see what it was Bridget had that she didn't. David was the catch of the century in their circle of friends. Gwen had been introduced to David by his mother before she passed away. She knew that he'd had a string of women before her; news traveled fast. But for whatever reason, he had stuck with her for a while now. As she saw it, she had gotten closer to him than anyone—that is, except for Bridget. And, she wanted to eyeball her competition.

David answered the door, since Gwen was putting the finishing touches on the meal she had prepared.

"Gwen, this is Stephen and his wife, Bridget."

Even now, the word *wife* got stuck in his throat when he said it in reference to Bridget and Stephen. Still, he genuinely liked and respected Stephen. But, his feelings for Bridget far outweighed his association with Stephen.

"Hi, Bridget; Stephen. It's so nice to meet you. I hope you're both hungry. We've got baby greens with balsamic dressing, roasted leg of lamb, Provençal sauce and tapenade. And I made tiramisu for dessert."

"Wow," Bridget said. "You made all of this? I'm impressed. I have to admit I'm a terrible cook."

"Don't believe her," Stephen said. "She's greatly exaggerating."

"I have no doubt that she probably is," David offered.

As much as Gwen wanted to dislike Bridget, she couldn't help but like her. She was honest; that was the only way to describe her. There seemed to be no pretense with her. She was beautiful and probably could have gotten any man she wanted, but Gwen could tell there wasn't a narcissistic bone in her body. Under better circumstances, Gwen thought that she might actually have liked her. However, considering that the man she wanted to eventually marry was in love with this woman, she couldn't let her guard down long enough to like her. She tried to tolerate her at best.

"So Bridget, what are you doing now that you're not at McDonnell?" Gwen asked.

Bridget stifled a giggle, looking at Stephen.

"Actually, Stephen and I have been trying to get pregnant, so that's been occupying a lot of my thoughts and time."

Bridget couldn't help but think of what she and Stephen had done before they had arrived at David's house. Bridget had taken her temperature. Since she was ovulating and they were due at David's and hadn't gotten a chance to at home, the two of them had had a quickie in their car on the way there.

"You're such newlyweds," Gwen commented with a smile.

The smile was actually joy at knowing that sometime soon Bridget would be pregnant.

"You guys are trying to have a baby already?" David questioned. "Isn't that a little quick? Don't you want to spend some time getting to know each other before you add a baby to the mix?"

Stephen and Bridget presumed that David was guarding the level of commitment of his best associate. Gwen, on the other hand, could see inside David's mind; a baby would further seal the commitment the two had made to one another.

"Don't worry, I'll still be on top of our cases," Stephen assured him.

"Yeah, David. I plan on having lots of babies, so Stephen will need to stay *real* committed to take care of his barefoot and pregnant wife." Bridget laughed.

Everyone at the table was laughing, except David.

Stephen was a doting husband, but if a stranger had walked into the house that night, they would have been hard-pressed to point out who indeed was Bridget's actual husband. David spent so much time paying attention to Bridget, it was as though Gwen didn't even exist.

"So Gwen, do you live here in the city?"

"Actually... I guess, it's okay, huh, David? Actually, I'm moving in with David this weekend. I spend so much time over here anyway, David and I just decided last week to make the situation more permanent."

"Wow! Congratulations," Bridget said with a little bit too much bravado.

Bridget wasn't sure why, but for just a second, she thought she felt...jealous. She couldn't figure out for the life of her where that had come from. If anything, she should be happy that David had found someone, finally. She often wondered why he was alone and now he had someone in his life. Maybe, he would loosen up now; start enjoying life.

"Good for you two," she said. "David needs someone to keep him on his toes."

"Yeah. I knew something was up when he stopped doing all those all-nighters. Although, I guess now that may mean that *I'll* be doing those all-nighters. Sorry, honey," Stephen said.

Gwen wondered if Stephen noticed David stealing glances at Bridget throughout dinner. Though usually annoyed when David and his colleagues took to David's office to discuss business, she was actually relieved when he and Stephen finished dessert and decided to go there. They needed to discuss a brief they were in the midst of working on. Gwen reasoned that she would much rather he shift his focus to anything other than Bridget.

"Gwen, did you have anything to do with the pretty new touches I've noticed in David's apartment? This apartment has always been very nice, but it now has that little bit extra…a woman's touch."

"Oh, I didn't realize you had been here before."

"Only a couple of times when I was working with David at McDonnell. But, it's much nicer now. Some fine textures and colors to go with all that leather, stainless steel and glass."

"It was David's idea. He thought I should make it feel more like home for myself. So, I took the ball and ran with it. Sometimes, though, I don't think he likes it all that much."

"Are you kidding? I love flowered curtains in my office. That was the only thing missing," David shouted sarcastically from his office.

"I thought you and Stephen were discussing business. Why are you listening to what Bridget and I are discussing? Nosy. Don't worry, we're not talking about you two."

David got up from his seat in the office and went to the bar and retrieved a bottle of Scotch. Gwen enjoyed David's company, but she absolutely hated it when he drank. When she'd first met him, he drank quite a bit, but she hadn't seen him drink more than a glass of wine at dinner for the past several months. Once she saw him grab that bottle of Scotch, she knew this was not going to be a one-cocktail night.

David returned to his office with the bottle and offered Stephen a glass. The two sat discussing their newest client, when Stephen suddenly realized the latest version of the brief he was supposed to bring with him was on a disc in his office.

"I'll go get it," Stephen offered.

Gwen and Bridget were in the kitchen discussing the apartment and Stephen and David's colleagues when they heard the front door open.

"Stephen, where on earth are you going?" Gwen asked.

"I left the disc that I was supposed to bring tonight in my office. I'll be right back."

"No, Stephen," Bridget said. "Go sit down with David. I'll go get it.

"Do you need my card key?" Stephen asked.

"No, I still have mine. That is if *somebody* didn't have it deactivated."

"No, it's not deactivated," David lied.

In truth, he had had the card deactivated the moment she resigned. He didn't tell her that now because they were having such a good time together, and he didn't want her to start hating him again. He was only twenty blocks away from the office. He decided, instead, to jump in a cab and zoom over to the office—under the pretense that she didn't have the key to his inner office; or at least that was what he was going to tell Bridget. He would tell Gwen and Stephen something else entirely different.

"We're out of Scotch. I'm going to go to the liquor store on Broadway and get a bottle. Okay?"

"At this hour?" Gwen asked.

"Yeah. It's eleven o'clock on a Friday in Manhattan. There should most definitely be a liquor store open. I'll be right back."

"Okay."

For a split second it crossed Gwen's mind that Bridget's and David's exits could have been a ploy so that they could be alone together. But, she reasoned that her intuition was pretty good and nothing she had seen tonight indicated that David's feelings for Bridget were anything other than one-sided.

"Oh my God. David, you scared the life out of me!"

Bridget practically jumped out of her skin when David tapped her on the shoulder outside the office building, announcing his presence. He had hoped to get to the office before she tried her card key, but he had been too late.

"So, I see you *did* deactivate my key. You could have told me that. I wouldn't have taken it personally."

"No, it's not that. I think the new person deactivated it, just because it's procedure and all."

Bridget didn't believe a word he said, especially considering how she left the firm.

"Yeah. Okay," was all she said. "I guess I might as well leave since you're here and all."

"No, we can go back to my house together. Stephen will be there waiting for you. Just give me a second to get that disc."

David opened the outer doors to the building and pressed the button for the elevator. Enclosed in the elevator with Bridget, the scent of her perfume filled the small space, invading his nostrils and leaving him higher than the drinks he'd had earlier. Watching her walk down the hall after they exited the elevator, her hips swaying thanks to the height of her four-inch pumps, David was more aroused than he could ever remember himself feeling. He had a raging hard-on, and the Scotch, despite the night air which had diminished the effect of the alcohol, only served to increase his desire for her. Once inside, Bridget made her way to Stephen's office to get the disc.

"I'll go get the disc and meet you in the lobby. Okay?"

"Okay. I just need to look for a hard copy in my office, real quick."

Bridget quickly found the disc and was about to return to the lobby when she heard noises coming from David's office. She walked in, and saw the look of what appeared to be agony on his face. For a moment she thought that he might be having a heart attack or something. By the time she got close enough to him, she realized his pants were undone and he was holding his penis in his hand and jerking off. As she turned to quickly leave the office, David grabbed her from behind. He initially just wanted to explain, but holding her close to him, his penis gently rubbing against her, he was even more aroused.

"Oh God, Bridget! I miss you so much. I don't think I can live without you!"

"David, stop it! What are you talking about? I'm married to Stephen. You can't do this. What about Gwen?"

"What about her! She means nothing to me! It's always been you that I want! Always!"

"David, stop it!"

Bridget's struggles and her words were all in vain. David was bigger, stronger and he was overcome with desire for her. He turned her around, pulling at her dress, ripping open the buttons. The sight of her naked before him was more than he could stand. He lifted her body in his arms like a rag doll, sucking at her breasts, licking her nipples. Bridget was powerless to stop him.

He gripped her body tightly to him and entered her. So enraptured with being inside of her, Bridget's protests fell on deaf ears. When he was done, he held Bridget's motionless body to him. Neither of them said a word, before she finally crumpled to the floor in a heap and just lay there. Looking at the scene before him from a distance, and with a clearer head, David could not believe what he had done. He attempted to console Bridget but each time he reached for her, she cried out or whimpered. He decided it was best to keep his distance. Instead, he mentioned that they should probably get going as Stephen and Gwen would be waiting for them. That was the first time she spoke.

"Oh my God! What am I going to tell Stephen?"

"I'll take you home," was all he could say.

While Bridget tried her best to put her dress back on, despite the buttons that had been ripped away, David handed her his suit jacket. He called a company car and rode with her first to her apartment to make sure that she got inside safely. He had the driver stop at a liquor store, so he could have an explainable decoy, then he had the driver drop him home. When he walked in, Gwen was sitting in the kitchen, pissed as hell. Stephen, thanks to the Scotch, the heavy food, and his long hours of work throughout the week, was asleep in David's office. He woke up looking for Bridget, surprised to see she hadn't returned.

"Where is Bridget, didn't she come back yet?" he asked.

"She called. She got sick coming out of the office and decided to get in a cab and go straight home. I told her not to worry about the disc. We'll deal with the brief on Monday. Why don't you go home to your wife?"

"Is she okay?" Stephen asked.

"I'm sure she's fine," David lied. "But she's probably waiting for you."

Gwen looked from David to Stephen and for a moment she considered saying something to Stephen. After all, what did she have to lose. She clearly didn't have a chance with David. She was no fool; she knew exactly what had gone on tonight. Instead, she sat in silence. She truly felt sorry for Stephen. He seemed like a nice guy; a nice guy that was going to get his heart broken.

David watched Gwen's eyes, well tuned in to what she was thinking and prepared to stop her from opening her mouth if need be. As soon as Stephen had left and the door was closed, David spoke.

"You know what, Gwendolyn, you and I both know this is going nowhere. Don't you think it's best to just end it right here and now and not drag this out endlessly, until we both hate each other? Because, I gotta tell you, I think I'm close to being there."

"You have the nerve to turn this around on me and act like *you're* angry at *me*. Then again, I guess you *are* angry. You're angry at anyone that's not her. You know what, David, fuck you! You're nothing, less than nothing, and you use that firm and your wealth as a means to qualify yourself. You're a small, sad little man and that attractive exterior you have now will soon be gone. I mean, do you really think your looks are gonna last forever? You're going to end up old, sad and alone. I just hope I get to see it so I can tell you I told you so."

"Don't worry, you won't be. You'll be somewhere, sucking somebody's dick to 'qualify' *yourself*, honey."

"Don't kid yourself into believing she could ever love you. She loves that nice young, successful husband she's got."

And, with that, she stormed out of David's apartment, but not before tossing a vase to the floor and breaking it.

Despite his best efforts, David couldn't sleep all night. He considered calling both Bridget and Gwen and thought better of both. Instead, he did something he seldom did anymore—he got up early and went into the office on a weekend.

"Did someone call for a temp?" Jade asked sarcastically.

David was startled to find Jade standing in the doorway to his office.

"How the fuck did you get in here?"

"I have my ways."

"Jade, I'm *really* not in the mood for your shit today. Get the fuck out of my office and don't come back. Your hold on me is gone, so go find some other mark. What you've never been able to understand is none of this has ever been about me and my embarrassment. I don't embarrass that easily. I would have taken my lumps and, in a year or so, everyone would have forgotten all about my indiscretions. I only allowed you to manipulate me for fear of what exposure would do to my mother; now she's dead, so do your worst. Someone like you could never understand this, but my mother sacrificed her entire life for me; staying married to my father far longer than she should have, a man who treated her like shit. And in the end, I couldn't even live up to her expectations for me. I ended up following in my father's footsteps and making the same mistakes he made. My father never respected women and I have demonstrated the same character he possessed. I loved someone very much once and I left her to those same streets you seem to love so much. When Bridget came along, I think I became so consumed with having a second chance that I just repeated all my old habits. And now I've ruined my chances with her as well.

"Let me ask you a question, Jade…Have you ever been in love?"

Jade stared at David as though he had truly lost his mind.

"If you're ever lucky enough to fall in love, take my advice, don't blow it. Some people never find love even once in their lives; and I was lucky enough to find it twice and blew it both times. So, Jade, whatever it is you have in mind, go on and shout it from the rooftops— my sexual indiscretions, the insider trading, my artful accounting with my clients. Because, quite frankly, I don't give a shit; I've lost everything I've ever wanted."

David noticed the look of surprise on Jade's face.

"What's wrong?" he asked. "Didn't it occur to you that while you were watching me, that I might be watching you as well? I know all the dirty little secrets you've learned about me. And, quite frankly, I don't care."

It was the first time David had ever seen Jade speechless. But that only lasted a moment.

"David, I do believe there is still something, or should I say *someone* you do care about. Haven't you ever wondered how your naïve, sweet-tempered Lady Love ended up my life-long friend; or how she ended up selling her goodies in the Bronx warehouse district?"

David wasn't anxious to play any more of Jade's games, but his fascination with Bridget won out.

"What are you talking about?"

"You're a lawyer. Tell me, what's the statute of limitations on murder?"

"So, that's it. You've been blackmailing her, too. What do you have on her? What murder?"

Despite his concern about the hold Jade had on Bridget, he was somehow relieved. It all made sense now. It just made him love her all the more. It meant everything he believed in his heart to be true about Bridget indeed was. She truly was the beautiful, courageous, honest human being he perceived her to be; which meant by translation, he was, in fact, the monster. He had justified what he had done to her by telling himself that she was nothing more than some hooker he had picked up off the street;

that she somehow didn't rate being treated like a decent human being; that she had to have some sort of ulterior motive for *all* of her actions. He couldn't have been more wrong.

"Jade, I can't talk to you now. I'll call you. We'll work something out. But, I can't do this now."

Jade was careful not to push too hard. No use in pushing the cash cow too far over the edge.

"Yeah, we'll talk. But keep in mind I want in. I want a job here; at your firm—something with a title maybe. Maybe even your assistant—something that lends credibility, but not too far-fetched. I want to go legit."

David was too smart a man to fall for that. He knew Jade's kind. She was up to something. But, he needed time to think it all through.

"I said I'll call you."

Jade sauntered out of David's office with a wave of her hand, quite pleased with her latest accomplishment.

"Just make sure you don't wait too long to call. I'm not a patient woman."

For at least a week Jade called, sent emails and generally harassed David, until he realized he had no other choice but to hire her in some capacity or another. He decided the place she would do the least damage would be as a general clerk. It would be her responsibility to copy documents, perform a minimal degree of one-handed typing of forms on a typewriter, and act as a general inter-office runner between floors. She hated it.

But, it afforded her the opportunity to get her foot in the door.

Greg was beyond shocked when he first saw her in and around the office. He hadn't helped to get her the job and she hadn't mentioned applying for one, but he had to admit, he was excited to know she was there. Besides the customary calls she made to him for information regarding the firm, Jade had slowly limited her contact with him, until it was virtually non-existent. While she was on her orientation tour, the manager brought her over to the accounting department. Jade looked through him as if he weren't even there. Instead of choosing to question her lack of recognition, Greg chose to believe that she didn't want anyone to know that they knew each other; for fear that it would affect both of their positions.

CHAPTER THIRTEEN
AND BABIES MAKE...FOUR?

Lately, Bridget had found it even more difficult to concentrate than usual. If her raging pregnancy-induced hormones were not enough, she had been walking around with a secret too overwhelming to keep to herself, but too earth-shattering to share. After all, who on earth could she tell? As if the guilt of keeping yet another secret from Stephen were not enough, not being able to *truly* share with her husband in the excitement of her pregnancy was almost more than she could bear; especially since learning from her doctor that she was carrying twins. Stephen was beyond ecstatic while she managed to play the part of the delighted wife and mother-to-be.

She thought of talking to Brianna. Through the years she and Brianna had come to be good friends. But, Brianna had gotten married and picked up with her husband and moved to Georgia. She was so happy and so far away. The last thing Bridget wanted to do was contact Brianna with more of her drama. Especially, since she had warned her about David. For years Brianna had advised Bridget to recognize that David was not only in love with her, but in fact, that love might be bordering on obsession. But Bridget hadn't listened. She had gone on believing that Brianna's comments were merely the ravings of a woman obsessed with sex. Despite their friendship and Bridget's desire to be as good a friend to Brianna as she had been to her, she had to admit that she, too, judged Brianna as much as everyone else in the office.

Now, in hindsight, she realized it was quite ironic. She had spent the first few years of her adult life as a prostitute while Brianna had grown up with a preacher for a father and a nurse for a mother. She had grown up in a close family with brothers and sisters who loved her and parents who took good care of her. She had gone to Christian schools, but somehow Bridget judged Brianna for her number of sexual partners. Instead of allowing Brianna the same respect she wanted for herself, she had done what many people do. She had tried to label Brianna with one of the many labels society as a whole had deemed appropriate. Bridget had decided that Brianna was promiscuous. But what she had learned, was that promiscuity was in the eye of the beholder and that typically people only labeled someone promiscuous because they were probably having more sex than they were having. And, if she labeled Brianna promiscuous, wouldn't those same labels apply to her as well?

Bridget must have picked up the phone three or four times before she finally decided she hadn't the nerve to tell Brianna what had happened. Instead, she decided to try and take a nap. Sleeping at night had become so fitful for her lately. She was fully aware of the fact that now that she was pregnant, she needed her sleep.

"No, Stephen, what have you done? No, you couldn't have. Oh my God! David, David, wake up. Oh God! Please don't be dead. Please, please, don't be dead! Stephen, what have you done?"

She awakened drenched in her own sweat. The dreams had increased in severity over the months and were more vivid than any she had ever experienced. Often Bridget woke up believing the dreams were real, her bed soaked; remnants of her either running from or after someone. Usually she could only remember portions of the dream. The most she could remember from this dream was that David had been killed, possibly by Stephen; and that somewhere in the distance, a phone was ringing, quite loudly. Bridget knew that dreams were nothing more than manifestations of events and encounters that took place while a person was awake. So, there was no secret why many of Bridget's dreams ended with David's death.

"Brrrring, brrrring." It took Bridget a moment to figure out it was actually the phone and she wasn't dreaming. She got out of bed, stood up and answered the phone.

"Hello?"

There was clearly someone on the other end of the line. She could hear whoever it was breathing, yet they hadn't answered her.

"Hello," she said again.

That's when she heard his voice. The voice she hadn't heard for several months now. The voice of the person that had haunted her dreams night after night, ever since the last time she had seen him.

"Hello Bridget. It's me, David."

Suddenly it was as though she had been sucked into a dark hole. The room started to spin quickly and she fell, hitting her head against the bedside table.

"Bridget, Bridget! Are you there?"

David heard the loud thud on the other end of the line and knew that Bridget was at least six or seven months pregnant, maybe even more. He raced over to her apartment and convinced the building superintendent to open the front door. She was lying on the floor, the phone dangling from the bedside table, and her head was bleeding. Concerned that an ambulance or the police would take far too long, David picked Bridget up in his arms and took her downstairs to the street level where the super got him a cab.

"New York Presbyterian Hospital," he instructed the cab driver. "Quickly."

David took out his cell phone and dialed Stephen.

"There's been an accident. I'm on my way to the hospital with Bridget. She's unconscious. Meet me at New York Presbyterian. Yeah. It's on Seventieth and York Avenue. And Stephen, hurry."

"She's at about thirty-three weeks gestation, with a possible concussion. Her former employer brought her in. He's in the waiting room."

"I'm Dr. Aryanni. Do you have any idea what happened to Mrs. Martin?"

"I don't know. I telephoned her, she picked up the phone and then I heard this loud noise. When she didn't answer, I rushed over to her house. I knew she was pregnant and I thought something might have been wrong."

"It seems as though she may have fallen and hit her head. It doesn't appear to be too serious, probably just a mild concussion. We're attaching a fetal heart monitor to keep a watch on the babies. Luckily, you got to her quickly. I understand her husband is on the way."

"Yes, I called him. He should be here soon."

David couldn't help but feel guilty about the entire incident. Maybe if he hadn't called Bridget in the first place, this would never have happened. But, he had to know. He had to ask her directly whether or not there was any chance that she might be pregnant with his babies and not Stephen's. It was selfish of him. But, he could think of nothing else, ever since he had heard Stephen talking to one of the secretaries about Bridget's due date. He had counted back from there and could only come up with one conclusion.

Stephen entered the lobby wild eyed and full of questions.

"What were you doing at the house?" Stephen asked.

"I wasn't...I mean... I hadn't...not yet. I called the house. There was an address I was looking for and I knew Bridget would know where to find it," David lied. "One minute we were talking and the next minute, I heard this loud sound and she was gone...off the phone."

"Is she okay?"

"I'm sure she's fine, Stephen. The doctor thinks she might have tripped and fallen and hit her head on something. She might have a mild concussion from the fall, but otherwise they think she's fine. They're monitoring the babies' heartbeats though, as a precaution."

"She kept telling me how tired she was and I wouldn't listen. Maybe if I had, she wouldn't be here now."

"Stephen, it was probably just a freak accident. She probably tripped on something and fell."

The doctor joined Stephen and David in the waiting area.

"Mr. Martin?"

"Yes, I'm Stephen Martin. Can I see my wife?"

"Bridget is fine, but she does have a mild concussion. It appears as though she may have fallen and hit her head. About a half hour ago Bridget began having contractions. We want to avert her pre-term labor, so we have given her something to delay delivery for a few days. She is only roughly at thirty-three weeks; a tricky time. Bridget is healthy and neither of the babies appear to be in any distress or immediate danger. We are going to do an amnio today to determine the maturity of the baby's lungs and then we will most likely proceed with administering corticosteroids, which will aid in the advancement of the babies' lungs."

"Could Bridget or the babies die?" Stephen asked.

"Her chances—and the babies' chances—are very good, especially once we administer the steroids. Our biggest concern is whether or not their lungs are developed enough. Otherwise, there have been countless babies that did fine at thirty-three weeks gestation."

Meanwhile, David stood nearby listening and quite frankly, everything the doctor had just shared with Stephen was more than a little overwhelming. He wanted to run to her, protect her, apologize for any part he had played in any of this. Instead, he had to stand by waiting in the wings.

"You can see Bridget for a few minutes, but we want her to get as much rest as possible. We would like to go ahead with the amnio and the first round of steroids."

"That's fine, doctor."

David realized that even if he could come up with an excuse for seeing Bridget, it probably wasn't in her best interest or the interest of the babies to see her now. He would only upset her further and right now that was the last thing she needed. However, lingering somewhere in his thoughts was the possibility that those could be his babies that were in possible danger. He might not be able to see Bridget, but nothing on earth could have made him leave that hospital waiting room.

"Stephen, I think I'm gonna stick around the hospital. I'm going to see if I can get some coffee, maybe something to eat. You want anything?"

"No, David. I'm fine. In fact, you can go home. There's really nothing you can do here."

"What's wrong? You afraid I'm gonna try to put you to work or something? Maybe chase some ambulances," David joked. "You can't get rid of me that easily. I'm staying put. Besides, did you see all the beautiful nurses in this place? I'm staying!"

"Suit yourself. I'm going to check in on Bridget. I guess you'll be here when I get out."

"Yeah. I'll be here."

Even during trying times, David would have done anything to switch places with Stephen. He realized he would rather spend days, weeks, even months in a hospital with Bridget than do anything else in the world. Unfortunately, he would have to satiate himself with acting as moral support to Stephen. Not only that, he still genuinely liked and appreciated Stephen, even though he was married to the woman he loved.

From the moment Stephen entered Bridget's hospital room, it struck him how small she appeared to be. He had always thought of Bridget as being bigger than life. But, lying there in that hospital bed in her blue-and-white-striped hospital gown, her eyes shut and a bandage wrapped around her head, she didn't seem quite so big. She seemed vulnerable and all he wanted to do was to protect her. He crossed the room, stood over her and gently smoothed back her hair. When she woke up, he was happy to see she still had that unmistakable glint in her eyes that was uniquely Bridget.

"Hi, baby. I was so worried about you. You okay?"

Bridget slowly nodded her head yes.

"You don't have to talk. The doctor wants you to preserve your strength. Has he been in to speak with you?"

That's when Bridget tried to speak.

"Why? What's wrong. Is something wrong with the babies?"

"Shh. Everything is fine, Bridget. You have a mild concussion but that should heal in a few days. And, the twins are fine, too. The doctor just needs to give you some steroids. He doesn't want you to go into labor yet, before their lungs are developed, so they need to give you an amnio to test the babies' lung development. I believe he said you were having contractions earlier. From what he said, it's a pretty simple thing. They do it all the time. He also said that babies are born at thirty-three weeks all the time, too. So, you shouldn't worry."

But, Bridget was worried. She was worried and she was feeling guilty. She somehow thought she had brought all of this upon herself and in turn upon her babies. She kept thinking that somehow she had led David on, that is why he had done what he had done and that's why she was here.

"How did I get here?" Bridget asked.

"Mr. Johnny-On-The-Spot."

"Huh?"

"It was David. He heard you fall while he was talking to you on the phone and raced right over to the house. If he wasn't there, I don't know what would have happened."

Yeah, Bridget thought, *if David wasn't there, what would have happened? If David weren't there, maybe I wouldn't be here in the first place.*

"Where is he now?" she asked.

"Somewhere in the hospital, chasing nurses or something. I think that was just an excuse to stick around and make sure you were okay. I told him to go on home, but he wouldn't hear of it."

Bridget was surprised to hear the words herself as they came out of her mouth.

"Could you ask David to stop by before they do the amnio? I wanted to thank him."

"Okay, baby. I'm sure he'll be happy to see you're doing okay. Maybe it'll put his mind at rest and he'll go home. There's really nothing he can do."

"You should go home, too, baby. You must be exhausted after the week you had at work and now this."

"I'm not going anywhere. The hospital is going to have to kick me out and even then they're going to have a fight on their hands."

"I love you, Stephen."

. "Baby, I love you, too—so very much. I already knew

that but I didn't know how much until David called me and told me you were hurt. I don't know what I would do without you."

Stephen kissed her lightly on the forehead, then on her lips.

"Go get David and then I want you to get something to eat. Knowing you, you probably haven't eaten a thing all day. I'm gonna have to call Jade and have her check in on you—make sure you're taking care of yourself. By the time I leave here, there are going to be two more additions to our family, and they need their daddy in optimum condition, too."

"Yeah. So I can do diaper duty, huh?"

"Absolutely." Bridget chuckled.

"I'll be back in a few, okay, baby? I'll let David know you want to see him."

David was in the waiting room when Stephen returned, pacing like a caged lion.

"You're worse than me," Stephen said.

"She's fine; consummate Bridget, a pillar of strength, pretending like she's not scared to death and talking about whether or not I've eaten today."

"I thought of that. There's a hamburger and fries in there," David said as he handed Stephen a bag.

"I don't think I could eat a thing. Oh, by the way, Bridget wants to see you. I think they're going to do that amnio soon, so you should probably go see her now."

As much as David wanted to see Bridget, he was afraid.

He couldn't remember when he had been so afraid of anything or anyone. This would be the first time he had spoken to Bridget since their encounter at his office all those months ago. He knew she would be more than justified if she spit in his face.

"Hi, Bridget."

"Hi, David. I wanted to thank you for saving my babies' lives. I don't know what would have happened if you weren't there. So, thank you. I also wanted to say that I never want to speak of that night again. Stephen considers you a friend and it would crush him to know what happened. I would never want him hurt that way. I'm not sure why you called me, but whatever the reason, I would much rather you keep it to yourself. I think it's for the best."

"But, Bridg…," David began before Bridget interrupted him.

"No, David. I don't want to talk about any of it. I want to pretend that it never happened. Okay. Please, just do that for me. Do that for Stephen. Don't I deserve even that?"

"Bridget, you deserve that and more, but that wasn't why I called you. I…"

Just as David was about to clarify things, the doctor and a technician walked in to give Bridget her amniocentesis.

"We'll talk later," David said.

"Okay."

And with that, David left, still convinced that the babies Bridget was carrying might be his. He knew that the most humane thing to do would have been to forget about all of it, just as Bridget had asked. But he wasn't sure he could simply forget if those babies were indeed his. There were some things that just couldn't be forgotten.

Six days later, and after two rounds of steroids, Bridget was scheduled to give birth on St. Patrick's Day, March 17th. The doctor thought it best that she have a Caesarian section, given the fact that she was having twins and that she would inevitably be having them prematurely. Stephen called everyone he could think of that was important to both him and Bridget; his father and mother, Jade, Brianna and David. Everyone was on their best behavior, including Jade, and Brianna told Stephen she would try her very best to catch the next available flight from Georgia to New York. Stephen held her hand during her epidural and "suited up" and joined Bridget in the delivery room. They knew they were having a boy and a girl and had picked out the names Jasmine and Jacob. Bridget wanted Jade (her original family) to know that she was still very much a part of *their* new family, so with Stephen's agreement, they decided to give both the babies names that started with a "J." Bridget hadn't told Jade yet, but hoped she would like it.

Bridget had hoped that her own doctor would be there for the delivery. She hadn't anticipated Bridget's delivery being so early and therefore her doctor was out of the country. So, Dr. Aryanni would be delivering little Jasmine and Jacob into the world.

Less than fifteen minutes into the delivery, Bridget

(numb from the waist down due to the epidural, but awake), heard the first cry. It was baby Jasmine. She was absolutely beautiful. Bridget cried, but was alarmed when her baby was taken quickly to the back.

"Stephen! What's wrong? Where are they going with her?"

Stephen followed. He knew Bridget would want to know that Jasmine was okay and she was more than a bit occupied. Jacob had yet to be born. Jacob was about to arrive when Stephen came from the back where they had Jasmine. Just as his sister had done minutes earlier, Jacob let out a hearty cry, amidst a look of great surprise on everyone's faces. From where Bridget lay, everyone appeared stunned. Her first thoughts were of Jasmine.

"Where is she? Where is my daughter? What has happened to her?" Bridget screamed.

Then, she saw little Jacob. His hair was obviously light as was his skin, which was practically white. And when she finally did see him up close, she realized his eyes were not brown at all. If anything, they appeared to be almost blue. For a moment, she allowed herself to believe that all babies, including black babies, were lighter when they were born. After all, even from what little she had seen of Jasmine, she was light as well. But, Jacob was obviously lighter than his sister and how could she explain the light hair and the eyes? The eyes were the most telling. The looks on the faces of everyone in the delivery room were even more telling than Jacob's light-colored eyes. And, the look on Stephen's face spoke volumes.

After both Jasmine and Jacob had been sufficiently cared for, they brought them both over so that Bridget could see them. One of the nurses held Jacob and Stephen was holding Jasmine. Bridget wondered if that was Stephen's choice. Bridget wasn't sure whether the tears spilling from her eyes were tears of joy or fear. Both Jasmine and Jacob were beautiful, but lingering in the back of her mind was the realization that David could very well be their father.

Because they were premature and therefore small babies, each at a little less than four pounds, they were kept in the neonatal unit for over a month. Bridget understood the benefits of breastfeeding, but the twins' premature status and her stress level made it very difficult. The more tense she became about breastfeeding, the less able she was to feed them, further frustrating matters. And, the obvious tension between her and Stephen just compounded matters, especially when she told Stephen that she didn't want the babies to have any visitors other than the two of them.

"Bridget, you're not making any sense. I spoke to the doctor and he ensured me that there is no reason why our family cannot visit Jasmine and Jacob. They are both in good health and beside the heat lamp that Jacob is under for jaundice, they're normal. In fact, the doctor said we could probably take Jasmine home if we'd like."

"Why would we take her home, without her brother?"

Everything had become a conspiracy with Bridget. She thought Stephen wanted to take Jasmine home before

Jacob because she wasn't a reminder of the "500-pound elephant in the room" that no one wanted to talk about.

"I know, Bridget. I already told the doctor that we would probably want to wait. In the meantime, why can't my parents, Jade and David come and see the babies?"

"Because they are still so small. They've only gained an ounce or two. I don't want all those outside germs around them until they're stronger. Besides which, David is not family. I thought you talked about family coming to see them."

"Bridget, you and the twins might not even be here, if it wasn't for David. And, he's just like family. I mean, the man paid for our wedding, for Christ's sake. How many employers do that? He *is* a member of our family."

"I guess I have no say in this! Just lay open the doors to the unit and let anyone who wants to come and gawk at them!"

"Bridget, it may be the hormones or whatever, but you are not acting rationally."

"Oh, so now I'm crazy, too. I offer one opinion about my own babies and now I'm crazy. Great!"

"You know what, Bridget? I've missed a lot of work and it seems as though you need some time alone. So, I'm going to leave, okay, and try to catch up on some of my backlog."

"You might as well. The hospital was nice enough to provide us with someplace to room in even though I'm not a patient. They even provided you with a bed here as well and you haven't stayed once, not once. I haven't been home since Jasmine and Jacob were born, but you, you come for a couple of hours and go home."

And with that, Bridget was awash in tears.

"Bridget, I really can't do this right now. I'm sorry but I can't."

He walked out of the unit and left, feeling somewhat guilty about not consoling her, but also plagued with thoughts of why his *"son"* looked nothing at all like either of them.

Finally, after a month and two days, Bridget and Stephen were given the okay to take Jasmine and Jacob home. Bridget continued her objections to anyone being around the twins and eventually it began to anger Stephen more and more.

"My mother and father haven't seen Jasmine and Jacob yet. You are not making any sense. What are your intentions? Are you going to keep everyone from seeing them—forever?"

"Stop being so dramatic, Stephen. I just want them to have a chance to build up their immunity before exposing them to all sorts of germs."

"Bridget, be honest with yourself. It would suit you just fine if no one ever laid eyes on them, especially Jacob."

"What are you trying to say, that I'm ashamed of my son? Why don't you just spit it out? Say what's been on your mind. Go ahead and say it."

"Under the circumstances, I don't think much needs to be said. The reality of the situation is staring us in our faces each and every day; and not just our faces, but the faces of the hospital staff, the doctor, even your private doctor, or didn't you see her reaction when she first saw Jacob? I've been trying to avoid having this conversation for long enough. For a month now I've been dodging requests from Jade, my parents, everyone, to see Jasmine and Jacob. Given the fact that I don't understand why you wouldn't want anyone to see them other than the obvious, it's been difficult to say the least. I was at such a loss, two weeks ago, I even went over to Jade's to try to garner some understanding of why. Needless to say, it was quite enlightening. All I have to ask you is why have you been lying to me, Bridget?"

Bridget wasn't sure how to respond. There had been so many lies. Truth be told, she wasn't sure which particular lie he was referring to. The lie about her family, the lie about her and Jade, the lie about what she had done for a living before McDonnell & Simpson. Or maybe he was talking about the lie surrounding why Jacob looked so different than any of them, including his sister, Jasmine.

"How did you and Jade *really* meet?"

That's when Bridget realized Jade must have told him the entire story of how they met. But why would she have done that? She had made it clear to Jade a long time ago that she hadn't shared with Stephen who her parents really were. Or, maybe, she had been backed up against a wall and revealed more than she had intended. Somehow, though, that didn't sound like Jade. She never got *backed up against a wall*. She was always in such control.

"Why don't you tell me, Stephen, since you seem to have all the answers?" Bridget replied sarcastically.

"You know what, you don't have to answer that question. Why don't you answer the most important question of all? Who is Jasmine and Jacob's father?"

"What are you trying to say? So now you believe I was cheating on you! Is that all you think of me, just because I lied about my parents?"

"No, Bridget, I'm just stating the obvious. Jacob is clearly white, or hadn't you noticed that?"

"Of course I noticed it, but for obvious reasons, I don't know what I could be mixed with, and for that matter, neither do you. I saw your family at the wedding. That Uncle Clifford of yours was damned near white."

"Bridget, come on, first of all, Uncle Clifford is not my uncle by blood. He married my Aunt Lillie and you're talking about very distant relatives here. It seems to me you're grasping at straws."

"What is that supposed to mean? You sound like you don't trust me. I don't know what I could be mixed with. I barely knew my mother or my father, and my mother was addicted to heroin. Who knows what she was doing to get her drugs."

"Speaking of which, Bridget, since *you* brought up the issue of trust, when we first met you told me your mom was a nurse and your dad was a cook and that you were this close-knit family. It wasn't until just recently that I learned the true story. And, I wouldn't have found out about that if it weren't for Jade. Not that she wanted to reveal your little secret, since you two are thick as thieves. I think she just let it slip. But she's the one who told me when and how you two met and who your parents really were. Every time I would ask either of you about how you met, you would change the subject. You've told so many lies, how am I supposed to trust you? How do I separate fact from fantasy?"

"My life was very different before you and I met. It's not so much I lied as I just put that part of my life behind me and started fresh. I didn't want people to judge me for things I had no control over. After all, I was just a child. I had no control over my birth."

"The thing is, Bridget, I'm not 'people.' We made vows to one another and I believe honesty and trust were part of those vows. Did you have so little trust in me that you couldn't be honest? Then, as far as I'm concerned, our marriage was based on a lie."

"You and I both know, if you and your family had known the truth about my birth and my life, we would never even be having this discussion, because you would never have looked at me twice."

"That's your opinion. But, I should have at least been given a chance to know the real you, not this persona you created for the world to see. Can't you see, Bridget, that is the reason you have never really opened up to anyone, including me? You can't live a life based on lies and expect to be free. It's no secret that your friend Jade and I have never gotten along, but the one thing I can say about Jade is that she is upfront with who she is. There's no surprises with her. But you walk around acting as though you're the poster child for integrity, when nothing could be further from the truth."

"I'm trying my best to tell you the truth now, but you won't listen…you won't give me a chance to explain."

"Bridget, it's just that I've altered my life for you—for us. My relationship with David is so strained now that the two of you don't seem to get along, but I've not interfered with that, even though you've been tight-lipped about that as well. That's the problem Bridget, everything, and I do mean everything, is a tightly guarded secret with you. But, this can't be one of those things. I want to know what is going on with Jasmine and Jacob and under the circumstances, I think you owe me that much. I want a DNA test done and quite frankly, it doesn't matter whether you agree or not. You knew who and what I was when you married me. I'm a lawyer; I deal in the facts, and the fact is two black parents made one black child and one white child and that just doesn't add up."

Bridget had convinced herself to tell Stephen everything, but the mere mention of David's name caused an automatic shutdown. She raced from the bedroom and ran into the bathroom slamming the door. She already knew what the DNA test would reveal, because as Stephen had put it, two black parents, one black child and one white, just didn't add up. David had to be the twins' father.

CHAPTER FOURTEEN
THE TEST

"**D**r. McKenzie, this is Bridget Martin. I need to see you regarding...a personal matter...related to the birth of my twins."

Dr. McKenzie was surprised it had taken her this long to call. You would have to be blind not to see that a black couple had given birth to a white child. Bridget and the twins had visited Dr. McKenzie's office shortly after both babies came home from the hospital and it was obvious that something was amiss. There was no doubt about the fact that little five-pound two-ounce Jacob Martin was white, right down to the blond hair. Yes, Jacob had clearly been conceived with the assistance of a white father. And, judging from the looks of mocha-complexioned Stephen Martin, he wasn't that father.

"Of course, Bridget, I can see you today at two p.m. Is that too early?"

"No, it's eleven now. I'll be there; two on the dot. Thank you."

Bridget wasn't sure what she would say to Dr. McKenzie when she got to her office, but she had to have some of her questions answered.

Bridget was so anxious to meet with Dr. McKenzie she actually got there fifteen minutes early. The doctor, fully aware of how dire Bridget's circumstances were, had cleared her calendar for the day.

"Hi, I'm here to see Dr. McKenzie. I'm a little early. I had a two o'clock appointment."

"That's fine. I'll let Dr. McKenzie know that you're here."

"Dr. McKenzie, Mrs. Martin is here to see you."

"Show her right in."

Bridget didn't disrobe and go to her usual examination room since she wasn't technically here for medical reasons. Instead, she met with Dr. McKenzie in her office.

"Hi, Bridget. How nice to see you. I was hoping you would bring the babies. I would love to see them."

"I'm fine physically. It's just that everybody is so surprised at Jacob's appearance…including Stephen. So surprised, in fact, that he has pretty much demanded that I have a DNA test done on the babies. I have a few questions for you. I probably could have spoken to Jasmine and Jacob's pediatrician, but I feel so much more comfortable with you. I just hate to take up your time."

"Don't worry about that at all. It's no problem. What can I help you with?"

"I'm sure you're maintaining your professionalism by not mentioning it, but I'm guessing it's just as obvious to you as it is to everyone else that has seen both myself and Stephen and our twins, that Jacob looks nothing at all like either of us. So, I give you permission to speak freely with me about the...difference between Jacob and his sister. My first question, I guess, is whether a DNA test is safe for Jasmine and Jacob at this point?"

"It is absolutely safe. It used to be done with needles, but now it's as simple as a cotton swab in the mouth. I can give you the address for a DNA testing center, and they'll test both you, your husband, the two babies and anyone else you would like tested."

"Anyone else?" Bridget asked.

"Excuse my candor, Bridget, but do you have any reason to believe that anyone other than Stephen could be the father?"

Bridget couldn't hold it in any longer. She broke down. She told her about her and Stephen, how they met, and that David (the man that raped her) had been her boss and still was her husband's boss. Dr. McKenzie was the only person she had ever told about that night. It had been the first time she had forced herself to even think about it. Until now she had tried her best to block it out, to no avail.

Dr. McKenzie got up from behind her desk and did her best to console Bridget.

"Although, I must be honest, it's been several months and there is no evidence of the rape, my opinion is that you should report this man; no matter who he is. But, I can't make that decision for you. You have to decide whether or not you're going to take this to the police or not."

"No," Bridget balked, still afraid of the police. "I don't want to go to the police. Him and I don't even see each other anymore and I just want to put it behind me, but what if he is the father of my babies? What will I do? Stephen will probably leave me."

"You may not want to go to the police, but you may need to consider telling your husband about this. Otherwise, and this may sound harsh, you may lose your husband."

Bridget just sat there shaking her head back and forth and muttering, "I can't, I just can't tell him."

"I tell you what, I'll set up the appointment for you at the DNA testing center for a week from now. That will give you an opportunity to think about this before you make any decisions. And, if you like, I can have the testing center forward the results to my office. Both you and Stephen can come here when the results are in. Okay?"

"Okay."

Bridget left Dr. McKenzie's office, dazed and confused, unsure of what she should do next, but sure she would have to do something.

She and Stephen barely spoke to each other the entire week before the test date. The two operated on autopilot, going through the motions of life, but doing nothing more than was absolutely necessary. Bridget couldn't help but love Jasmine and Jacob, no matter what, however, Stephen seemed withdrawn and unable to interact with either of the babies. It was torturing Bridget to watch him ignore them both. She consoled herself with the thought that no matter what, she would soon know the truth. In the meantime, she had decided that with or without Stephen, she was going to be a good mother to her son and daughter.

It had been exactly one week and three days when Dr. McKenzie called to say that the results of the DNA tests were in. She refused to give the results over the phone and instead told Bridget that they would have to come to her office to get the results. As far as Bridget was concerned, that couldn't be good.

"Dr. McKenzie called today. The testing center forwarded her the results of the DNA tests and she would like to see us both tomorrow at three o'clock."

"Tomorrow at three it is, but I can't imagine that she would be summoning us to her office to tell her that these are *both* our babies."

"Stephen, you don't know that."

The next day Stephen left his office and met Bridget at Dr. McKenzie's office. When he got to the doctor's office, Bridget was already there.

"Is she ready to see us?" he asked.

It was hard to believe that this was once the kind, playful, loving man that she had fallen in love with, and he with her. Bridget couldn't help but think that it seemed as though he hated her.

Dr. McKenzie walked out of her office and into the waiting area.

"Come on in."

Stephen and Bridget both sat down and waited to hear the worst.

"As you know the testing center did DNA tests on both you, Bridget; you, Stephen; and both Jasmine and Jacob. Normally the results only take a day or two and I had even asked the center to put a rush on it and to send me the results immediately. However, when I got the results back, it was so surprising I asked them to run the results again, just to make sure. They ran the tests again and the results were conclusive."

"I don't understand," Bridget queried.

"Yes, Dr. McKenzie, what were the results?" Stephen asked.

"What has taken place here is so rare that it actually has changed the protocol for the testing of fraternal twins in paternity tests, especially as it relates to child support and child custody decisions. I need you to listen carefully until I'm done explaining it, and then both of you can ask whatever questions you need to ask. Is that acceptable to you both?"

"Yes," they both answered in unison.

"There is a phenomenon in medical literature that is known as heteropaternal superfecundation. In essence, fraternal twins are formed when two separate eggs are fertilized by two sperm. There is a small window of time when eggs are able to be fertilized during ovulation. Sperm cells can live inside a woman's body for four to five days and once ovulation occurs, the egg is viable for twelve to forty-eight hours before it starts to fragment, which means the fertile period can stretch anywhere between five to seven days. Until recently, the incidences of such a medical phenomenon while in existence was much rarer. However, with the rate of the number of twins being born each year increasing and the accuracy of DNA testing increasing, more and more incidences are being detected."

"What is it that you're trying to tell us doctor?" Stephen asked.

"Jacob and Jasmine were formed by two separate eggs that were fertilized by two sperm," Dr. McKenzie supplied. "Contact with the sperm of more than one individual during Bridget's fertile time period has produced fraternal twins with...two different fathers."

"Are you saying what I think you're saying?" Stephen asked.

"Yes, Mr. Martin."

"Oh, my God," Bridget cried.

"So, I was right. Jacob isn't my son."

"But, Jasmine is your daughter. Stephen, she is yours. Right, doctor?"

"Yes, Bridget, the DNA test revealed that Jasmine is indeed both you and Stephen's daughter. However, Jacob is your son, Bridget, but not yours, Stephen."

"So that means you've been fucking around behind my back; making you the liar I said you were. Nothing has changed here. You obviously had an affair and this is the end result."

"No, Stephen. That's not it, at all. Please just let me explain!"

"There is nothing to fucking explain. You're nothing more than a two-bit whore!"

And with that, Stephen bolted from Dr. McKenzie's office. As Bridget rose to leave, prepared to run after him, Dr. McKenzie assessed the situation and gave the best advice she could give under the obviously volatile situation.

"Bridget, give him some time to think this all through. It's a lot to take in. Although, I still think you should tell him. You've done nothing wrong here. You are the victim and the sooner you tell your husband the truth, the sooner the two of you can get past this."

Bridget was barely listening. Between the news the doctor had given her and Stephen's response, she was dumbfounded. It was as though she were sleepwalking.

"Oh...okay, doctor, I'll think about it. I will. I need to get home to Jasmine and Jacob."

"Are you sure you're okay?" Dr. McKenzie asked. "You didn't drive here, did you?"

"No...no, I took a cab. I'll take a cab back home. Thank you, doctor."

"Bridget, please keep in touch. If there is anything you need, don't hesitate to contact me. Okay?"

"Okay."

Bridget was anxious to get home, unsure of what her fate was, not to mention the fate of her two babies. All the way home in the cab, she kept going over possible scenarios; all of them with the worst possible conclusions. What if Stephen left her? What if David found out about Jacob? It was altogether possible. After all, he and Stephen did work very closely together and over the years, David had become more than just a mentor to Stephen; he had become his friend. For a moment Bridget thought about what might happen if she did tell Stephen what really had happened. As many times as she had gone over this possibility, she already knew what she was going to do. She couldn't do that to Stephen. He had worked so hard to get where he was. If she told him, his career would be so dramatically altered, she didn't think he could handle it. Her other thought was, there was the possibility that Stephen wouldn't even believe her, then where would she be; right back where she started.

By the time Bridget got home, it was readily apparent that Stephen had already been there. He had packed up some of his things and he had left. Suddenly, the thought that Stephen might have taken Jasmine occurred to her and she raced to the twins' room. She was relieved to find that the sitter was still there with both babies. The look on the babysitter's face told her that she was aware that something was going on. Bridget had hired Consuelo even before the twins were born. She was wonderful with the twins and came with great credentials. However, her English wasn't the best.

"Mrs.," she said to Bridget. "Do not worry, the Mr., he will come back. You will see. Everything will be good."

Bridget managed the best forced smile she could muster, knowing full well that if Consuelo, or anyone for that matter, knew the truth, they too would know that chances were pretty good Stephen would *not* be coming back.

How would any man forgive a woman in such a situation?

"I am fine," was all Bridget could say. "Thank you so much for watching Jasmine and Jacob today. I don't think I will need you for the rest of the week. I'll call you on Friday and let you know what my schedule is for next week. Is that okay?"

"Yes, Mrs., that is okay."

Consuelo left, patting Bridget on the back as she left Jasmine and Jacob's bedroom. As she left, she wondered if Bridget's "friend" Jade had anything to do with this. On more than one occasion, Consuelo had seen Jade trying to cozy up to Bridget's husband, saying things about Bridget that might cause problems for the couple. A few times she had considered saying something to Bridget, but she had learned over the years that it was never a good idea to get involved in a couple's relationship, especially when you were employed by that couple.

The twins were sleeping soundly, so Bridget decided to lie down and take a nap herself. She learned how important it was in the hospital to get enough rest and drink enough fluids in order for her milk production to be adequate. Over the last few days, she noticed that she wasn't producing as much milk and it was very difficult for her to feed Jasmine and Jacob. She figured it also probably had a lot to do with the stress she was under. So she slept, as much for herself as for Jasmine and Jacob. Because she knew, now more than ever, they needed a healthy mother; not one that was near complete and utter collapse.

Bridget awakened to noises coming from the babies' room. When she walked in, she found both Jade and Stephen there. Barely awake, she assumed that Stephen had come back home and was ready to talk about their situation. She couldn't have been more wrong.

"Hi, Stephen. I'm so glad you came back home. Now we can sit down and talk. I want to explain—everything."

"What could we possibly have to talk about? I don't want to hear any more of your lies. The only reason I came back here was to get my daughter. I'll be damned if I leave her here with a whore like you. She's coming with me!"

"Stephen, what are you saying? No. No. Don't say that. Just let me explain! Once I explain everything to you, you'll see it wasn't my fault. Please, Stephen. Don't do this to me. Don't do this to us."

Jade observed her handiwork from her comfortable place in the middle anxiously awaiting her opportunity to manipulate the situation.

"Jade, please help me explain it to him. You know. You know what happened. Please, Jade!"

Like most aspects of her life, Bridget had shared with Jade what happened to her that night in David's office.

"Bridget, you have to calm down. Just take a deep breath and calm down. I'll talk to Stephen, but you have to calm down, okay?"

"Stephen, I know I'm your least favorite person, but as I see it, both of you need to take a step back and figure out what is best for Jasmine and Jacob. So, why don't you and I go into the kitchen? You can have a seat and we can talk or not talk, but maybe if you sit down for a few minutes and think about what you're going to do next, you can gain some perspective," Jade offered.

"Okay, but I'm taking Jasmine with me. I don't trust her."

Stephen's words cut through Bridget like a knife. She had to wonder how they got to this place where he could actually have so little trust in her. The basic truth was, she really hadn't done anything wrong. For so long now she had been blaming herself for what had happened with David. But the reality was, David had raped her; and her husband, the man who should have trusted her, had abandoned her when she needed him the most. She couldn't think of anything that could be more painful.

Jade did sit with Stephen in the kitchen and "*talk.*" However, nothing she said to Stephen could be construed as anything that might help Bridget's situation.

"I know Bridget much better than you do, Stephen. Despite what you may think, the only thing to do when she gets like this is to humor her. I agree with you; you do need to put plans in place to protect your daughter, but you also need to tread very softly with Bridget. She can be very volatile. She makes bad decisions—she's been doing that as long as I've known her. And, right now she has your daughter."

"That's the whole point. I need to get Jasmine away from her."

Jade needed time to work through what her next move was going to be and she didn't want Stephen saddled down with a baby while she was doing that. So she did what she did best.

"I tell you what. You can come stay with me. That would put Bridget at ease and calm her down, and I will be there to help with the baby when need be. And, you can figure out what your next move is. Doesn't that make sense? I mean, think about it, Stephen. You're a busy New York City attorney. Do you really have the time to care for a brand-new baby? You need to be logical about this. I know you don't particularly care for me, but what other options do you have?"

Stephen was wary of Jade, but she was right. Jade knew Bridget better than anyone, and if she said he needed to be careful of Bridget right now, then she was probably right. And, it would be good to have someone there to take care of Jasmine. He wanted to spend as much time with his daughter away from Jacob and Bridget as possible. He would stay with Jade until he found his own place and a nanny. Until then he would put things into place that would ensure he got custody of his daughter. The other upside to staying with Jade was that he could find out things about Bridget that she would never tell him herself; things that only Jade would know. Then, he could really fight her in court for custody of his daughter.

"Okay. You're right. But, are you sure you have enough room?"

"More than enough."

"I'll pack some things and meet you at your place in an hour or so."

"In the meantime, Stephen, I'll go talk to Bridget and try to calm her down."

Jade left the kitchen feeling very proud of herself. The divide between the "happy" couple was widening by leaps and bounds.

"Bridget, I've spoken to Stephen and he has agreed to stay with me for a while until he can sort this whole thing out. My advice to you is don't tell him a thing about what happened between you and David. That is not going to help things one bit."

"Jade, what are you talking about? I have to tell him. You heard him. He thinks I was having an affair. If I don't tell him David raped me, he will go on believing that I cheated on him. Besides, I'm sick of keeping this secret. It's eating me up inside."

Suddenly, all the conversations she and Stephen had had about Jade dawned on her. Stephen had made no secret that he didn't like Jade, so why would he now decide to go and stay with her?

"Why is he staying with you? I would expect him to go to David, or even his parents in Georgia, before staying with you."

"Yeah, I know he doesn't like me."

"No, no, that's not what I mean."

"You don't have to spare my feelings, Bridget. I've

known all along that Stephen doesn't care for me very much. But, he wants to know all there is to know about you, and that's probably why he is going to come to my house. He's probably hoping that he can pump me for information about you. Not that I ever would. But he doesn't know that. Also, he wants to start spending some time with Jasmine. I guess he figures I'm Jasmine's godmother and there would be no one better than me to watch her when he brings her to spend time with him."

"How long does he plan on staying that he feels he will need help?"

"However long it is, he's got to work for a living and I guess he figures help from someone he's not particularly fond of is better than no help at all. But, what are you worried about? This is a good thing. I'll be there with him, working on getting him back into your arms and your bed. And, before you know it, he'll be back home with you, Jasmine and Jacob."

"He's never going to accept Jacob. Especially if I don't tell him how Jacob came to be."

"You'd be surprised what a man in love will do," Jade commented.

"I just hope he still loves me."

While Stephen packed his things, Jade went outside and got into the car she had borrowed from Big Rob.

Stephen left the apartment without so much as a sideways glance in Bridget's direction, leaving Jasmine in her room. He wasn't even sure he could stand to be in

Bridget's presence. That's how disgusted he was with the turn of events.

While Stephen and Bridget parted ways, David was sitting in his office, contemplating things he already knew the answers to. After all, he had been there in the hospital along with everyone else. It was abundantly clear that Stephen was not the father of Bridget's twins; and David knew Bridget well enough to know that there was only one other person that could be.

"Bridget, we need to talk. I…"

Before David could finish the rest of his sentence, Bridget had hung up the phone. She had been through enough of a ringer lately. The last thing she needed was to have any association with the very person who had caused it all.

David called and left messages all day. He was relentless. Finally, Bridget took the phone off the hook, hoping that would mean the end to his calls. Unfortunately, that just made it worse. Just a half hour after she took the phone off the hook, there was a knock at the door.

"Bridget, I know you're in there. Open up the door right now. We have to talk."

She was so embarrassed that he might say something that her neighbors would hear, she decided to open the door.

"David, haven't you done enough? What do you want from me, now?"

"Nothing. I want to see my son and daughter."

"What? What are you saying? Have you lost your mind? What the hell are you talking about?"

"Bridget, you and I both know you're a terrible liar. It's written all over your face. Jasmine and Jacob are mine, aren't they? They're my son and daughter."

"No, they are not."

"You're lying!"

"I am not. And, what if they were? You have no right to them. You know what you did. You have no right to be here. No right to come anywhere near my babies. And, if you don't get out, I'm going to call the police."

Suddenly a smile crossed David's lips. It was the most disturbing look she had ever seen on David's face. It frightened her so, it sent chills through her.

"David, you must be drunk or high or something. I'm not going to tell you again, just get out. Get out of my apartment right now!"

"Or else what?" he said.

This was a side of David Bridget had never seen and she didn't like it one bit.

"You don't belong here. I can make you leave."

"And then what, Bridget? I'll petition for a paternity test to prove those are my babies, then I'll tell the court how we met. And I'll not only get to see Jasmine and Jacob, I will have complete custody of them. Is that what you want? All I'm asking you is that I see them. I'm not trying to make trouble for you. I just want to see my son and daughter. Stephen doesn't even have to know. I just want an opportunity to spend some time with them."

"What makes you think they're yours? After all, I'm just a whore, right? Their father could be any number of men, right?"

"Bridget, I never, ever treated you like a whore and you know that."

"The sad thing is, David, you're treating me like one right now and you don't even know it. The truth is, David, Stephen already knows."

All of the color drained from David's face.

"Don't worry, though. Your reputation with him is completely intact. He doesn't know you are the father. He just thinks, like you, that I'm a whore that was fucking around on the side."

"Bridget, I'm so sorry."

"It's too late for sorry, David. I'm going to lose him. The only man I've ever loved and I'm going to lose him, thanks to you."

Despite that he and Bridget were never more than friends and he had never made his feelings for her known, he was somehow wounded by Bridget mentioning that Stephen was the only man that she had ever loved. Somewhere in his mind he had hoped that Bridget had some small measure of feeling for him that went beyond mere friendship. But, her comment dashed all hopes for him and just made him all the more intent on securing his rights to his offspring.

"Be that as it may, Bridget, I will see my son and daughter, whether it's with your permission or without. I don't really care what Stephen knows or doesn't know. I want an opportunity to be a father and Stephen has nothing to do with that."

"That's where you're wrong, David. Stephen has everything to do with that. You see, I wasn't lying to you completely. Jasmine and Jacob are not your children; only Jacob is, and that does affect Stephen, because he is Jasmine's father. No matter how this situation plays itself out, it will affect all three of us; you, me *and* Stephen. But, I won't let you see him, David. I won't let you turn Jacob into what you have become. I want more for Jacob than that."

"Look who's sitting up on their high horse! Have you forgotten where you came from? When I met you, you were so far down in the gutter you could barely reach up; now you're judging me. Well, you can play that card if you want to, but I will see my son, with or without your permission!"

"I may have been working the streets and I may not have had much money, but David I never hurt anyone, not like you."

"So we're back to that again. How can I take something from you that you were willingly giving away?"

The moment he said it, he saw the hurt it inflicted.

"Get out," she yelled. "Get out right now. You may try to take Jacob from me, but for now you're in my home and I want you out!"

"I'll see you in court," David said as he left.

CHAPTER FIFTEEN
THE INVESTIGATION

"Michael, it's me, David. I've got some work for you."

"Is it a new client?" Michael asked.

"No, it's personal. But, first, you and I need to talk. A lot's been going on and I haven't told anyone about any of it. We've got to tread very softly on this one. It could mean my reputation, the reputation of the firm and my livelihood, but more to the point it could irreversibly affect my son. So, you've got to be impartial on this one and just bring me the facts. Then I can proceed with whatever it is I have to do."

"First, I want you to contact this place called the DNA Diagnostics Center. It's somewhere in Ohio. I believe the director's name is something like Bard or Baird, something like that. Normally, if this were client-related I would have one of my paralegals research this, but I can't risk anyone asking questions about why. Okay?"

"You know I got your back. But, what's this all about? Your son? What the fuck is goin' on?"

"Get that information for me first and I promise you I'll fill you in on all the rest. Okay?"

"Okay. I'll take care of it right away."

"Say, David," Michael said before they hung up. "You gonna be okay?"

"Man, I hope so. I really hope so."

It took Michael less than twenty-four hours for him to gather the information David requested. He contacted the director, a Dr. Michael Baird, directly. With his credentials as an investigator he was able to get a quick meeting and get more extensive info on the very unusual subject David had asked him to research. He called David the next day, anxious to share with him what he had found.

"I got that information you wanted. But, I'm gonna tell you right now, I'm not givin' you shit until you tell me what the fuck is goin' on."

"Okay, okay. But just listen. Don't tell me how badly I fucked up, or anything like that, because I've already done that myself ad nauseum. I've gotten myself into a little trouble and I'm trying to figure out what my next step needs to be. The research you compiled for me, I think it involves a kid of mine, but it's much more involved than even that."

"Meet me at Fitzpatrick's, okay? I'll bring you the report. We'll have a coupla cold ones and discuss what trouble you've gotten yourself into this time. Okay? But, you're buyin'!"

"No shit," David responded. "Don't I always?"

David sat at the bar at Fitzpatrick's, a pub on the Upper

East Side, waiting for the "always late" Michael to arrive. He finally got there about forty-five minutes late.

"Damn, man. Can't you ever get anywhere on time?"

"I'm a busy man. A mover and shaker, I can't be confined by anything as mediocre as a clock. By the way, here's your report. I must say, I've seen a lot of shit in my day, but this has got to be by far the craziest shit I've *ever* seen. Leave it to you to get yourself wrapped up in something like this. Anyway, here's the report."

David took the report from Michael and read it from beginning to end:

DNA Paternity Test Reveals Twins With Different Fathers Cincinnati, OH U.S.A. December 13, 2005 — DNA Diagnostics Center (DDC), a leading DNA testing company, reports several cases of twins that DNA paternity testing proved to have different fathers. Such occurrences, although rare, are being more frequently revealed via DNA testing.

These cases underline the necessity for testing both fraternal twins in a paternity test, if any doubt at all exists about the circumstances surrounding the twins' conception," says Dr. Michael Baird, DDC's laboratory director. Paternity test results are often used as a basis for child support and child custody decisions. Further, the biological father's medical history, such as information about hereditary diseases, could be important for a child's overall health maintenance.

"Fraternal twins are formed when two separate eggs are fertilized by two sperm. If a woman has contact with different

partners within her fertile time period and has multiple ovu-
lations, it is possible for her to have fraternal twins or even
triplets with different fathers. This phenomenon has been dubbed
in medical literature as heteropaternal superfecundation.

There is a small time window when eggs are able to be fertil-
ized," says Dr. Baird. Sperm cells can live inside a woman's body
for four to five days. Once ovulation occurs, the egg remains
viable for twelve to forty-eight hours before it begins to disin-
tegrate. Thus, the fertile period can span five to seven days."

In her article Multiple Births, *Dr. Terence Zach of Creighton*
University states that the average birth rate of fraternal twins
in the United States is about 8 per 1000 births (identical twins
are 4 per 1,000 births), although the rate varies by race.

The rate of fraternal twinning and other multiple births
has been increasing since the 1970s, with the advent of assisted
fertility methods, such as in vitro fertilization (IVF). DDC
has had a paternity test case in which the donated sperm for
the IVF proved to be a mixture from two males, according to
laboratory staff.

"The frequency of twinning is quite low, and so such cases
[of twins with different fathers] are even rarer," says Dr. Baird.
"Previous DNA testing methods, based on blood antigens, were
able to detect some of these cases, but DNA testing is much
more powerful and now we can begin to get more accurate
statistics. More accurate paternity testing might prove it to be
a long-standing but little known phenomenon."

"Jeez," David said to no one in particular.

"What the hell am I going to do?"

"So David, you're telling me that you got some chick knocked up and she got pregnant with twins, and one is yours and the other twin is someone else's. Is that what you're telling me?"

Then, suddenly, it dawned on him.

"Holy shit. I fuckin' knew it." he yelled.

"Why don't you tell the whole fuckin' bar," David said.

"I fuckin' knew it. All that time you've been tellin' me there was nothing between you and that hot-ass secretary of yours, the two of you were doin' the nasty. I fuckin' knew it."

"We were not. You are wrong; as usual. There is nothing between me and Bridget. Nothing at all."

"So you're telling me you know another woman that has twins and one of them is yours. Get real!"

"No, that's not what I'm telling you. The twins in question are Bridget's babies; Jasmine and Jacob. But, we didn't have a relationship. I mean...we..."

"Spit it out, man. So, you didn't have a relationship with her. So what happened, you had like a one-night stand or something?"

Then Michael realized why David wanted all of this to be hush-hush and why he initially mentioned the possibility of his reputation being ruined.

"Oh, David. Nah, man. You didn't?"

Somehow Michael had always been the consummate fuck-up in their friendship. David was suddenly aware of the shift in their roles and he wasn't sure he liked it.

"See, that's what I told you about holding all that shit

inside. That's what happens when you try too fuckin' hard to be perfect. If you had just told that girl a long time ago how you felt about her, this shit would never have happened. And, isn't she married to one of your associates, that one you initially mentored as a first year? Oh shit, that black guy, Stephen. Oh David, no. Does he know yet?"

"He knows that the babies have two different fathers, but he doesn't know the other father is me, and he doesn't know the circumstances surrounding my becoming Jacob's father. You would think he would. I mean, he's married to a woman who spent the better part of the last few years with only two men; me and her husband, but somehow he's clueless. He knows that Jacob is not his, but somehow he hasn't figured out, or even questioned, that it might be mine. Although, I'm sure that's subject to change."

"You do know when he does find out he's gonna want to kick your ass, right?"

"I've got much more important things than that to worry about. She doesn't want me to have anything to do with my son and that's just not going to happen."

"What are you trying to say? You're going to try to fight her for custody of her own child? Come on, David. Under the circumstances, don't you think you better just cut your losses and let her take the lead and maybe, just maybe, she'll eventually come around? I mean, if I'm hearing you right, you did rape the girl, didn't you?"

"Yeah. I know and I'm so sorry. I feel guilty as hell

about that, but that doesn't negate the fact that I have a son. Shouldn't my son know who his father is? It's his birthright."

"David, you know you're my boy and all, but really. Listen to yourself. You do know who you sound like right now, trying to justify what you've done?"

"I don't sound anything at all like him. I can't believe you just said that."

"Ask yourself one question, David. If you truly believe you don't sound anything like your father, why was that the first person you thought of? And it was, wasn't it? Your father was the first person that came to mind."

"Touché," David said. "Nevertheless, I really do want to do the right thing here. There are things that I've never told you about how Bridget and I met, and if I have to, I will get sole custody of my son with that information. But, I need all of it. I want you to dig up everything you know about Bridget Grey and Jade Smith. Those may be aliases, but I want you to start from there. Put everything together and then let me know what you find. Okay, Michael? If your moral fiber doesn't permit you to help me, then I completely understand."

"Naw, man, didn't I tell you I got your back? I meant that. Who the hell am I to judge anyway. I'll get right on it. Now, let's get our drink on. Something tells me you could use more than just a beer."

"Barkeep," Michael said jokingly. "Bring us a bottle of your best Scotch!"

Michael was very good at what he did and with as little

information as two names, he was able to uncover much more than even David probably could have anticipated. If there was one thing Michael had learned being an investigator, it was that most ordinary people had secrets; those things they didn't want their neighbors or their spouses or even their families to know about. Usually it was things like clandestine affairs, questionable paternity or petty thefts, but he found he hit the jackpot with Bridget Grey and Jade Smith. He wasn't sure if it were one or both of them. But clearly, either or both of them was very dangerous. Before he went to David with what he had found, Michael decided to dig a little deeper.

"Didn't it seem a little strange that these girls would attack one of the security guards and they were going to be leaving the home soon anyway?"

"According to the report in both of their files, the girls both shared a room. One night the director of the home was looking for one of the security guards, a Buster Williams, and she found him in Jade and Bridget's room. Someone had beaten him with a chair leg. The police and the social worker assigned to the home tried to locate the girls for a while but eventually they stopped. If I were going to make a guess, I would say that one or both of the girls was raped by Mr. Buster Williams. In fact, according to this, there was vaginal blood and semen found in one of the beds."

"Did either of the girls have any family?" Michael asked the representative at the Bureau of Family and Children's Services.

"Bridget Grey had no family; both of her parents died when she was a baby and her grandmother died not long after. However, Jade had a mother, Chantal Smith. She was a junkie and a prostitute. Her last known address was somewhere on Westchester Avenue."

"Any record on what happened to her mother?"

"Not on anything we would have kept. Once they leave the system, they're no longer our problem. But, I bet the police would know. People like Chantal Smith always eventually find their way to the police one way or another. I would check with them."

"Oh, by the way," Michael asked as he left. "Who was listed as Jade Smith's father?"

"According to this, her father was listed as unknown. Although in such cases that is not uncommon."

Michael knew he couldn't get the information he needed through usual channels so he decided to call an old friend.

"Yo, Santucci, I need your help on something. I got a woman, disappeared maybe twenty years ago, without a trace. She may be difficult to locate, frequented Hunts Point; a junkie. You know the type."

"What's in it for me?" Michael's old contact at the police station asked.

"I'll owe you."

"Yeah. That and a metro card will get me to Brooklyn."

"I see we've forgotten the numerous times I've saved your ass. Haven't we, Santucci?"

"I'm just pulling your chain. What info have you got on her? I'll see what I can do."

Within forty-eight hours Michael had more than enough info on Ms. Chantal M. Smith, including the fact that for several years someone had continued to pay the rent on her rundown Westchester Avenue apartment. Michael was sure the information he had collected was much more than David was ready to hear. Chantal had been killed, buried and eventually unearthed. But, her true identity might be more than even David could handle. Based on the report, Michael had a pretty good idea who had killed Chantal. Michael knew that the facts contained in this report would be earth-shattering for all those concerned. He also knew he would have to get every bit of information he could gather before presenting any of this to David. Unless he could back everything up with cold hard facts, it would be difficult for even his best friend to believe. He had bits and pieces but he needed more.

"He's lost without you," Jade assured Bridget. "You just wait and see; he'll be home before you know it," she lied.

Nothing could be further from the truth. When Stephen initially left Bridget two weeks earlier, he had gone from angry to depressed and back again. But Jade had seen to it that the tide changed in exactly the direction she wanted—toward her.

"I don't know why she doesn't just tell you the truth and end this farce here and now," Jade told Stephen.

"What farce? What are you talking about? What did she tell you?" Stephen asked.

"It's not for me to say. Bridget and I are more than just friends; we are sisters. What would I look like telling you things that she clearly doesn't want you to know? No, I won't betray her confidence, just as I would not betray yours. But, you have to be smart about this whole thing, Stephen. You and I both know Bridget is not equipped to care for either of those babies. She can barely take care of herself. If I were you, I would do everything I can to make sure your daughter is protected as well as Jacob's father is ensuring that he is protected."

"Who is he, Jade? I know you *must* know who he is. Who is Jacob's father? You are the only person Bridget would ever tell. Was he just some random guy she picked up somewhere? But, that doesn't sound like Bridget," he said more to himself than to Jade.

"Stephen, how do you really know what is or isn't like Bridget? The two of you worked together, yeah. But, you dated for such a short time before you got married. You really don't know much of anything about her."

That's when Stephen realized that everything Jade said was absolutely true. He really didn't know Bridget as well as he initially believed himself to. That was one of the things his parents had tried to point out when he first announced to them that he would be proposing to Bridget. His mother, especially, thought that Bridget was very vague about her life before meeting Stephen. But, Stephen had allayed his mothers fears by explaining to her how much she missed her parents and how she had tried to forget the painful memories of their death by blocking that part of her life out. However, now he realized there was much more to it than that. He also realized the only hope for finding out all he needed to know, both for himself and for Jasmine's well-being, was to enlist Jade's aid. Yet, he wasn't sure he trusted her either. He had at least loved Bridget, once, but Jade he had never trusted. She had always struck him as a calculating, manipulative woman that should be avoided at all costs. Now, here he was living in her home, spending time with her. Something about this situation just didn't seem right.

"It's not for me to say who it is, Stephen. That's a matter for you and Bridget to discuss. I won't get in the middle."

Jade left the room—left to allow Stephen to stew over what she had said. He was an even easier piece to move around her virtual chess board than Bridget was. Over the years, Bridget had become less and less vulnerable to her influence, to Jade's dismay. Jade always knew that was a danger when she started working at McDonnell. She had made a mistake in allowing that to happen, but since that time she had made up for that mistake in countless ways. She had learned of ways to manipulate Bridget without even dealing with Bridget directly. Now, she was going to take the last thing that Bridget had left.

Stephen's emotional exhaustion was affecting him physically as well. Where he once worked long hours and spent time in the gym, he was now constantly tired. He went into the living room and laid on Jade's pullout couch. Stephen's dreams were always the same, with little to no variations in theme. They would start out with him and Bridget making love. He would be close to ejaculation and just as he was about to let go, there would be a faceless white body standing behind him, naked and waiting for him to finish so that he could have his turn; and that's when Stephen would inevitably awaken.

Jade, better than anyone, knew the tell-tale sound of passion, even in someone's sleep. She watched Stephen having his "dreams" night after night, carefully planning her next move. She decided that tonight would be the night. She approached Stephen where he was sleeping, wearing nothing more than a sheer T-shirt and her panties under the guise of waking him from his "nightmare." She stood above him, the scent of Bridget's signature Mont Blanc cologne filling his lungs. Semi-awake, Stephen reached for her in the night, pulled him to her and already erect from the dream he had just had, he embraced her, sought out her mouth with his, kissed her, plunging his tongue deep inside of her mouth. Jade met his tongue with an equal level of voracity. By the time he was fully awake, his hardness was already poking at Jade, eager to enter her. For just a moment he tried to resist, attempted to pull away, rise from beneath her, but Jade held fast. Stephen flipped her over and entered her, pounding away at her with a mixture of anger and lust. When he was done, he could barely look at her, yet he was still mildly aroused and fighting an inner battle to go for round two. Guilt was not enough to make him walk away. Round two would be just one of many times the two had sex over the coming months. And, eventually, with the help of Jade, Stephen had convinced himself that he had done nothing wrong. *After all*, he thought to himself, *hadn't Bridget herself slept with another man long before I ever even thought about cheating on her?*

"Hi, Jade. Can I speak to Stephen?"

"He's sleeping, Bridget."

"It seems like every time I call, he's sleeping."

"Well, Bridget, just like you, he's been through a lot. It's affecting him just as much as it is affecting you. You have to be able to understand that, or there is no hope for the two of you working things out."

"Yeah, but how can we work things out, if we don't communicate with one another? Every time he's supposed to come and get Jasmine, you come and get her. We don't even get a chance to talk to one another then."

"What are you trying to say? I didn't sign on for this. I've been trying to help *both* of you. I didn't ask to be put in the middle of this."

She knew just what buttons to push, as she played the role of the victim.

"I know that, Jade, but I think now is the time for you to step out of the middle nonetheless. If you keep allowing Stephen the opportunity to avoid me, we will never have a chance to mend our marriage."

"I tell you what. Why don't I just kick him out of my place and you two can have all the time you want together? Although, that will just afford him the opportunity to consider getting his *own* place and then where will both of you be? Things will be much more permanent then."

Jade was pushing the right buttons indeed. She knew that was Bridget's greatest fear. She knew that Bridget somehow felt better about him staying with Jade because that meant he wasn't making a more permanent decision about their marriage. What she didn't know was that was the furthest thing from Stephen's thoughts. Over the past couple of months, he had in fact made lots of decisions, none of which Bridget was going to like.

CHAPTER SEVENTEEN
BRIDGET'S BREAKDOWN

For months Bridget waited and hoped for Stephen to come around. He was still staying with Jade, so she hoped that meant that he hadn't made any drastic decisions. After all, if he hadn't gotten his own place, didn't that mean he was still on the fence as to whether or not he would be returning home? So, it was no surprise when one afternoon Stephen called her and asked to meet with her at their favorite restaurant for dinner. She asked Consuelo to watch the twins and spent the better part of the day dressing for her night with Stephen. She wanted everything to be perfect. Jade kept her abreast of Stephen's mood, his thoughts on the separation, and his general feelings on the situation. She was hopeful. According to Jade's interpretation, Stephen was heartsick and that hadn't changed during the three months that they had been apart. What Bridget kept wondering was why he hadn't come home. Then it occurred to her that that was probably why he wanted to have dinner with her tonight at her favorite restaurant. He was probably going to come home.

Bridget spent the better part of the afternoon making sure absolutely everything was just so and left the house to head downtown a little early. She had been so preoccupied with the breakup and caring for the babies that she hadn't been taking care of herself as well as she could have. Her hands and nails looked awful and she decided to treat herself and get a manicure.

Bridget was slightly disappointed when she walked into the restaurant and realized Stephen wasn't alone. He had brought Jade along. Over the past couple of months, Jade had been a godsend—allowing Stephen to stay at her place, and in Bridget's mind, preventing him from seeking a more permanent residence. She kept Bridget abreast of Stephen's ever-changing state of mind and acted as her own private cheering squad. Or, so she thought. Therefore, despite Bridget's initial disappointment at not being able to have this time alone with Stephen, she understood why Jade might be there. Bridget presumed she was acting as a buffer between the two.

As Bridget crossed the room and made her way to the table where Stephen and Jade were sitting, she had a smile on her face that was unmistakable; the look of a woman in love that was soon to be reunited with the object of her affection. That smile was quickly diffused when she reached Stephen and attempted to greet him with a kiss. Stephen's first reaction was to pull away. When he saw the wounded look on Bridget's face, however, he made a vain attempt to recover and planted a dry, half-hearted kiss on her cheek. Sitting at the table, Bridget glanced at Jade and took note of the fact that she would not maintain direct eye contact with her.

"Hi, Jade," Bridget initiated. "Are you okay?"

"Oh, yeah. I'm fine. Everything is good."

As Bridget prattled on and on about the twins and anything else she could think of in between, Stephen realized how pointless this all was and decided the best thing to do was to get straight to the point.

"Bridget, I want a divorce."

Bridget's face went ashen.

"Stephen, you…you don't mean that."

"Jade, I thought…," she started.

"There is really nothing else to say. I am in love with someone else and I want a divorce. I didn't go out looking for someone to fall in love with. It just happened. She's been there for me."

When Stephen reached for Jade's hand and held it, everything became crystal clear. Stephen and Jade were having an affair behind her back. And, not only that, it was more than just an affair. He said he was in love with her. The usually calm Bridget, did something so uncustomary for her. She lost control. She jumped up from her seat and pushed everything on the table onto the floor and ran out. For Stephen it was an embarrassing scene that would mark the end of all the drama he had experienced since they'd first said, "I do." But, for Jade, it was only the beginning of her carefully planned handiwork.

"All I'm saying, Stephen, is if you keep giving her money and paying all of her bills, she has no reason to give you custody of Jasmine. You know I would never do anything to hurt Bridget. She's been my best friend my entire life. I'm just thinking of what's best for my god-daughter; and for you. I know how much you love that little girl. I love you and I just want you to have an opportunity to have a relationship with your daughter. I didn't know my father, so I understand better than anyone how important it is. Most people think it's so much more important for a boy to have a relationship with his father, but I think it's even more important for a girl. The relationship a daughter has with her father and the kind of man he is shapes what sort of men she chooses in the future. I think you're a great father and I can't imagine a better father for Jasmine. I want that for her. If not, I'm afraid to imagine the alternative. I know Bridget well enough to know that she doesn't always make the best choices. And, I hate to see Jasmine suffer for *her* decisions."

"You might be right," Stephen agreed.

The next day Stephen canceled all of Bridget's credit cards and barred her from accessing their checking account.

"Mrs., your check. It bounce," Consuelo informed Bridget.

"Are you sure, Consuelo? There's no way that check could bounce…unless. No! Wait right here. Stay with Jasmine and Jacob. I'm going to the bank."

First, she used her bank card and tried to get cash at the ATM. She got a message telling her to see her financial institution and when she did, she was told by one of the people at the bank that there was a hold on her account. Bridget was devastated. She stood in the middle of the bank, unsure of what to do. She had nothing. She didn't even have all of the money she had saved all those years. For the longest time Bridget had been so cautious about everything, she hadn't even kept a bank account. She kept all of her money at home. But, when she met Stephen, she realized she was living in the Dark Ages. When they got married, she thought that meant they were one and therefore they shared everything. So, every dime she had went into their joint bank account.

Now, what was she going to do? Stephen had served divorce papers and he was seeking full custody of Jasmine. Normally, she would have turned to Jade or David for help, but they, too, had abandoned her. For the first time since her childhood, she was truly alone. Then she realized, she wasn't alone. She had two defenseless little babies to care for. Two babies, no income and no money. She stood there in the bank overwhelmed with the veracity of it all.

"Miss, is everything okay? Is there something I can help you with?" one of the bank representatives was asking her.

"It's Mrs., Mrs. Bridget Martin."

She ran from the bank leaving behind a virtual sea of onlookers, curious about what was wrong with her. The bank rep who had informed her of the status of her bank account turned to her office mate and said: "There goes another woman who should have had her own bank account. These women need to learn that you never put all of your money in an account with a man, husband or no husband. Men have their pre-nups, and all women should have their own bank account. I've seen women leave banks with that same look on their faces more times than I care to remember."

Bridget wandered the streets, unsure of what she should do next. She thought of riding the subway down to Penn Station and getting a train to Long Beach, but she wasn't alone anymore. She had two very small babies at home. She couldn't just go traipsing off to the beach when things got rough. Yet, she couldn't bring herself to go home yet. She had to have time to think. Consuelo was at home with Jasmine and Jacob and they would be fine for now. Bridget wandered the streets, unsure of what she should do next and full of desperation. She finally had to admit it to herself, that all of her dreams of a fairy-tale happy ending probably weren't going to happen. After all these years, Jade had been right. Ever since meeting Stephen for dinner and learning that he and Jade were together, Bridget tried her best not to think of Jade. Jade, the woman she once considered her sister. How could she have betrayed her in such a way? Bridget could somehow justify Stephen's betrayal a whole lot easier than Jade's. Bridget, like so many other women, reconciled herself long ago that relationships between men and women didn't always last, but somehow she couldn't reconcile herself to the fact that her relationship with Jade was over. She had been the force that had sustained her all these years when things got *really* bad. What was she going to do now? Who would she turn to? That's when she thought of Brianna.

Bridget decided it was time to call Brianna. The last time she had spoken to her, she had told Bridget that she wouldn't be able to come to New York to see Jasmine and Jacob, because she and her husband, Trevor, were having some mild financial difficulties. However, that she would travel to New York as soon as things improved. She also had told Bridget that she and Trevor were going to try to have a baby. They had bought a house and Brianna sounded ecstatic about her life, even with the added pressure of a mortgage and planning a family. That's why Bridget was so surprised to find that Brianna no longer lived there when she called.

"I'm surprised Brianna didn't mention it or get in touch with you, but she moved back to New York. We split up," Brianna's husband, Trevor, said.

"It's really important. Do you have a number where I can reach her?"

"Yeah. Her home number is 718-555-2889 and her work number is 212-555-3200. She's probably at work now."

"Are you okay?

That's when Bridget realized what a bad friend she had been. Brianna had been there for her so often and she had gotten so caught up in her own life, once again, that she hadn't been there for Brianna when she needed her. Now, here she was reaching out again because she was in need. At first she considered not calling at all. Now, like so often, she had wanted to call Brianna, but decided against it because she was feeling so needy and didn't want to burden Brianna with her troubles. Instead, she decided she *would* call, if nothing else, but to say hello.

Bridget was half-way through dialing the number when she realized it was McDonnell & Simpson she was calling. She really had no desire to speak to anyone at McDonnell and make small talk about what she had been doing since she left, so she hoped the receptionist didn't recognize her voice.

"Good afternoon. Could you connect me with Brianna Taylor's line, please?"

"One moment, please, I'll connect you."

Bridget thought she heard a note of recognition in the receptionist's voice but if she did recognize her, she didn't bother to say anything.

"Brianna Taylor, can I help you?"

"Hi, Brianna, it's Bridget. Sorry it's been..."

Just as Bridget was about to speak to her long-time friend, she saw Consuelo coming down the block with Jasmine and Jacob in their double stroller. She had a bag with her and seemed out of breath.

"Mrs., Mrs., Miss Jade, she come to the house with the Mr. and they want to take Jasmine and Jacob. I tell them no, no. I work for the Mrs. but they no listen. They have papers, Mrs., with all kinds of bad stuff written on it about you. They say you bad lady and they have right to take the little ones. I know you want me to find you. Did I do the right thing, Mrs.?"

"Yes, Consuelo, yes! Of course, you did."

"Bridget, Bridget!" Brianna screamed into the phone.

But, it fell on deaf ears. Bridget hung up.

Brianna had heard the entire exchange between Consuelo and Bridget, and although she didn't have a clue as to what was going on, she knew it didn't sound good.

Over at Bridget's apartment, Stephen and Jade were trying to figure out where Consuelo might have gone with Jasmine and Jacob.

Not being an attorney, Consuelo didn't realize that the papers she was looking at were not official legal documents. Jade had called the house earlier and knew that Bridget was not at home and therefore, only Consuelo and the babies would be there. Her time at McDonnell & Simpson had trained her well. She had taken one of the documents on the company's computer system, duped it and made it appear to be papers that indicated her and Stephen's right to take the babies with them. Knowing that Stephen would not have agreed to be a part of anything like that, she waited until he was not paying attention and had handed the papers to Consuelo. The document mentioned that Bridget was unfit and wanted for murder, that she had cheated on Stephen, and that she was not caring for either of the twins. Instead, she had sunk into a deep depression and was allowing the two babies to be cared for by an illegal alien. Consuelo looked over the papers, and afraid to turn the babies over to Jade, had quickly gone out of the apartment's back door.

"Why do you think she bolted like that?" Stephen asked.

"I don't know. Bridget probably warned her to do that if we ever came by. I told you before, we're not dealing with a rational person. That is exactly why you need to get legal custody of your daughter."

"I wanted to see Jasmine. I hadn't even planned on taking her anywhere. I wanted an opportunity to see her. That's all."

"Again, you keep acting like this is a rational human being. She's not."

"I guess maybe you're right," Stephen conceded.

As much as Consuelo wanted to help Bridget, her immigration status *was* an issue and the last thing she wanted to do was get caught in the radar. Bridget was well aware of that fact and had no desire to make things difficult for Consuelo because of her mess.

"Thank you so much, Consuelo…for everything. I appreciate it more than you know."

"Thank you, Mrs. You've always been very kind to me. I'm sorry I never tell you about Miss Jade. I think maybe, if I tell you, things wouldn't have gotten so bad."

"Tell me what, Consuelo? What about Miss Jade?"

"Many, many times I hear her say very bad things about you. She try to touch the Mr. and she try to kiss him, but he say no. One time she tell him you stole her family from her. She tell him that she not have a family because of you; that you very selfish and only care about you self."

Bridget didn't have a clue what any of this meant. She didn't know whether Consuelo was confused or whether Bridget was out-and-out lying. She decided it was the latter.

"It's okay, Consuelo. I probably wouldn't have listened then anyway. I thought she was my friend."

"She no friend, Mrs. Miss Jade *muy malo*…very bad."

"I know, Consuelo. I know. I'm so sorry about the check, Consuelo, but I promise I'll find a way to get your money to you."

"No worry, Mrs. It is okay."

And with that Consuelo hugged Bridget and kissed each of the twins on their foreheads and said good bye. Bridget realized how sorry she would be to see her go. She really liked her.

In her hurry to return to New York after things didn't work out between her and Trevor, Brianna had left many of her things behind, including her phone book. There were no hard feelings between her and her ex, so she decided to call Trevor and see if he could locate her phone book so she could get a number for Bridget. She thought of asking someone at McDonnell but thought against it. No, she would try her phone book first, and then if she had no luck, she would try to see if she could get the number from someone at work.

"Hey, babe," Trevor answered the phone.

"How did you know it was me?" Brianna asked.

"Caller ID. Ain't technology grand?" he quipped.

Brianna got that same old feeling she always got when he called her "babe." She had hoped that after the two of them split up and she moved to New York, that would have changed. She was wrong. She decided to ignore her inner voice and concentrate on the issue at hand.

"How you been, Trevor?"

"Oh, I been okay. How 'bout you?"

"Okay, I guess. A friend of mine is in trouble, though. I realized I don't have my phone book. I may have left it in Georgia. You haven't seen it, have you?"

"As a matter of fact, yes, I have. Do you need a number out of it? Let me guess, Bridget."

"How did you know?"

"She called earlier today and I told her you'd gone back to New York. I don't believe you didn't tell her we split up."

"It's been a while since I've spoken to Bridget. How did she sound when you spoke to her?"

"Well, I don't know her and all, but if I were going to guess, I'd say she didn't sound great. She clearly had something on her mind. Is everything okay?"

"I don't know yet. She called me and I caught the tail end of a conversation that concerns me. But, I'm going to do my damnedest to find out what's going on. You got that number?"

"Here it is. 212-555-6875."

"Thanks, Trevor. I really appreciate it."

"Anytime, babe; anytime."

Just as Brianna was about to hang up, Trevor spoke. "Brianna, I know you got a lot on your mind right now, but when you're done helping your friend out, I was thinking maybe I'd come up to New York, maybe you and I could talk."

"We'll talk. I'll call you. Okay?"

"I'll be waiting for you to call, Brianna. Bye, babe."

After hanging up the phone with Trevor, Brianna saw David's friend, Michael, rush through the office on his way to David with a special level of urgency. Brianna wondered what was up and whether or not it had anything to do with Bridget and her phone call earlier. The first and last thing she heard Michael say before David shut his office door was, "Man, we've really got to talk."

Behind closed doors, David was still so agitated about the situation with Bridget and the call he had left with her earlier in the day. He was so convinced that she was actually at home and refusing to answer the phone because of him that it angered him even more. He barely heard a word Michael said.

"Michael, man, I'm at the end of my fuckin' rope. Bridget won't budge an inch. She won't take my calls, and refuses to let me see my son. Please tell me you've got something that's going to make all of this a lot easier for me."

"David, that's what I'm trying to tell you. But, you

need to calm down and just *listen*. What I'm about to tell you is going to be a big shock. And I'm pretty sure that once I do tell you, you will get your son back. However, I don't think it's Bridget you need to be worried about. There's a lot more going on here than meets the eye. And believe me, Bridget is not the enemy. If anything, you and Bridget would *both* be best served as allies."

By the time Michael was done recounting all that he had learned during his investigation, David was speechless, beyond speechless; and he was afraid. But, not for himself; he was afraid for Bridget and the twins. Clearly, all of their lives were in immediate danger. That is, unless he acted fast.

"There is one more piece of this puzzle that is missing in action. I'm going to go follow up that lead now. Make sure you leave your cell phone on and I'll let you know when I've located him. In the meantime, you need to get to Bridget."

"I'm going to do that now. She's not going to be all that willing to listen to what I have to say, though. I don't believe what a fool I've been. It was all right there in front of my face and I ignored all my best instincts. When I think of the message I left on her voicemail today, I'm the last person she's going to want to talk to. She must be feeling so alone right now."

"Tell her everything I've told you. Make her listen, David."

As David and Michael were leaving his office, Brianna caught the tail end of what they were saying.

"Are you talking about Bridget?" she interrupted.

David was cautious about telling Brianna too much, but he remembered that Brianna and Bridget were friends when Bridget worked at the firm.

"Yes, we were," he said. "Do you have any idea where Bridget might be?"

"I don't know. She called me today and I heard a conversation between her and a Hispanic woman; I think it might have been her sitter. From what I could gather, Bridget seemed to be in some sort of trouble. Is she? Is Bridget in some sort of trouble?"

"Yes, Brianna, I believe she is. If we put our heads together, we can probably find her. Maybe we should split up. I'm going to go to her apartment. Do you have any ideas?"

"I might have one idea."

"Okay, you follow up there and make sure you call me on my cell if you find anything. I'll do the same." David turned to Michael. "The same with you. Once you find the guy mentioned in that report, call me right away. I think it'll help if Bridget knows she has nothing to worry about in that department."

"Even if I don't find him, make sure you tell her she's not in any trouble, one way or another. It's also probably a good idea to start looking for Jade."

Brianna remembered her cousin, Pookie, and she instantly knew how they could find Jade.

"I know someone that's sure to know how to find Jade. My cousin's a runner for Jade's boyfriend, Big Rob. In fact, Jade works for Big Rob; they all keep very close tabs on one another. Yeah. Pookie will definitely know how to find Jade, or at least he'll be able to point us in the right direction. And, if he doesn't know where she is, Greg might."

"You don't mean Greg in my accounting department?"

"Yeah. That Greg. He and Jade are pretty tight."

"Shit! I've been completely clueless. That would explain a lot of things. I'll take care of that right now."

David picked up the telephone at Brianna's desk.

"Greg, could you come over to Brianna's desk, now?"

Greg was shaking in his boots. He wondered if Mr. McDonnell figured out what he and Jade had been doing with the books. But, he relaxed a little when he thought it out. If he had figured it out, what would that have to do with Brianna? Why would he be calling him from her desk? It was probably a project of some sort that he needed him to assist Brianna with.

"Where's Jade?" David asked as soon as Greg arrived.

"Jade. I don't know. She didn't come to work today."

David suddenly grabbed Greg's shirt and slammed him against the nearest wall. "Don't fuck with me. Where the fuck is she?"

"I told you. I don't know. The last time I saw Jade was a week ago. She doesn't come to work half the time anyway, so I didn't make much of it. I tried calling her a few times and the last time I spoke to her, which was last Thursday, I believe, she acted like she barely knew me, like she didn't want anything to do with me. You don't have to tell me twice. I figured she had moved on to bigger and better and left it alone."

"So you have no idea where she might be?" Michael asked.

"No. I have no idea. We went out a couple of times, but Jade wasn't exactly the kind of person who told you her life story. You know what I mean? What's this all about?" Greg asked as he attempted to adjust his disheveled clothing.

"None of your business," Michael answered. "In fact, you can leave. You're fired."

"You can't fire me. You don't even work here. Who are you to fire me?" Greg protested.

"You're right," David agreed. "But, I can fire you. Get the fuck out of my office."

Gone was Greg's initial fear. He was suddenly full of bravado. "I'm gonna sue your ass. This whole fucking firm. I'm gonna sue all of you."

"Yeah, yeah, yeah. Just make sure you tell them how you and Jade have been robbing this company blind."

Defeated, Greg left the office quietly, hoping that he wouldn't have to do time in prison.

Bridget figured Jade and Stephen had probably left the apartment by now and decided the only thing she could do would be to leave town. But, where would she go? She had five hundred dollars in cash in the apartment and she would need to pack some sort of bag. As soon as she entered the apartment, she could see the flashing red light indicating she had messages:

"Bridget, I don't know what is going on in either of your heads, but I came by to see Jasmine and Consuelo bolted from the apartment like she had lost her mind. What the hell is going on with you? You're clearly going over the deep end and I won't let you take Jasmine with you. Call me as soon as you get this message. Don't make me come back over there. If I have to do that I will go get a court order and prove that you're unfit."

The next message was from David:

"Bridget, I have begun taking steps to get permanent custody of Jacob. I tried to work with you. We could have worked this out among ourselves but you have pushed me too far. I have to do what is best to protect both mine and Jacob's interests. If you don't call me back, I will have no other choice but to proceed. Bridget, you don't want to lose one, or even both, of your children due to stubbornness. Once an investigation is started that is exactly what may happen."

Bridget had worked with David long enough to know that there was no place that she could go that he wouldn't be able to find her; especially not with little more than five hundred dollars cash in her pocket. She realized she was trapped. Stephen, Jade and David were going to take her babies from her. The same people she had trusted, the same people who had claimed to love her; and they were trying their damnedest to take her children from her. If she truly believed she was unfit as a parent, she would have given Jasmine and Jacob to them willingly, but as far as she was concerned, they were the ones that were unfit. She was afraid for her babies. She couldn't let them be raised by people like this. But, what was the alternative? As far as she could see it, she had none.

If Bridget had listened to the rest of her messages, she would have known that Brianna had located her phone number and called her at home. She didn't. Instead, she quickly got dressed, packed a bag for Jasmine and Jacob, and prepared to leave. She stood in the middle of the apartment and remembered the day she and Stephen had first moved in. It was hard to believe how much her life had changed since that day. For the first time in a long time, Bridget truly felt broken beyond repair and she was suddenly more tired than she had ever been.

When Bridget first moved to 320 East Seventy-third Street, she was awestruck by the opulence that some people were afforded. Although by others' standards, the apartment might not have been considered lavish, it had been by Bridget's standards. She remembered thinking, on the day she'd first moved in, that she had come from nothing and that she now had all of this: the prestigious Upper East Side address, the well-appointed furnishings, and the man of her dreams. Amazing how quickly life can come crashing back down to earth. Bridget opened the door and said good bye to the luxurious life she had known; if only for a short time. But, before she left, she wanted to once more take in her beautiful view from the rooftop. After all, this would be the last opportunity she would get to take in all that had once been hers.

Bridget sat on one of the chairs on the roof and thought

of what her next move should be. She didn't have a clue. She was truly lost and so, therefore, were her babies. For so long she had promised herself that she would never be her parents. No, she hadn't become an addict, but she had brought her children into a world where she was incapable of caring for them. She had been selfish. She wanted so much to have someone to love that she hadn't anticipated what would happen to them if she fell short. And, for that, Jasmine and Jacob would have to pay the price.

Bridget gathered up both Jasmine and Jacob and walked with them to the edge of the roof. She looked out over the city and found she couldn't make them the same promise she had made them on this exact same rooftop when they were born. She couldn't promise to give them everything, because she had nothing. She couldn't promise to protect them until they were capable of caring for themselves; she had no idea what her fate would be. After all, she couldn't care for two babies from a prison cell. That's when Bridget realized that not only her life, but Jasmine's and Jacob's lives as well, were doomed. She had no intention of allowing people like Jade, Stephen or David to crush her little angels, as they had crushed her. And she definitely didn't want either of them to be sentenced to life in some God-awful group home.

Bridget had come here to say good-bye and as her tears gently fell from her tired eyes, she suddenly realized that was exactly what she had to do.

CHAPTER EIGHTEEN
BRIDGET'S RESCUE

"Get away from me, David. I won't let you have him, I won't. I'd rather he die than end up with you!"

"Bridget, please, step away from the edge of the roof. I'm not here to hurt you, or Jacob. There are some things you need to know about Jade."

"I already know all about Jade. She and Stephen, they want to take Jasmine from me. They want my daughter. I deserve this, but Jasmine doesn't. She's only a baby; innocent baby with the misfortune to end up with me as a mother."

"Don't say that, Bridget. You're a wonderful, loving mother, and you don't deserve any of this; none of it. I'm so, so sorry for what I've done to you. But, please, please, don't take it out on our son."

"Is that what you think I'm doing? Taking it out on Jacob? I'm trying to protect him. I won't be here to protect him and this is the only way I can think of to save him from all of you."

"But that's just it, Bridget, you…"

"You raped me, David. I trusted you and you raped

me. Without me here, is that what my son is going to become? A rapist like his father? Every time you look at him, are you going to see his mother, the whore? Admit it, that's what you see when you look at me. So how am I to know you won't treat Jacob any different? I'd rather see him dead than have him continue the McDonnell legacy."

David was crushed. He had never heard the words said out loud, but that is exactly what he had done. He was no better than some of the scum he and his colleagues had defended through the years. He was little more than a rapist; he knew it and Bridget knew it.

"Bridget, I made a mistake, which I'll spend the remainder of my life paying for. I realize that this is too little, too late, but I loved you so much. Seeing you in love with someone else was killing me. And like always, I exercised my non-existent control. Please forgive me. I know you will probably hate me for the rest of my pitiful life, but please listen to what it is I have to say. After you've heard me out, you can make your own decision as to what your next steps should be."

He told her everything the investigator had told him, including the information he had learned on his own. After getting the investigator's report, he and Michael went about following up on all the leads, contacting as many concerned parties as they could, whether they had to strong-arm or in David's case, pay them to tell them all they knew. He revealed to Bridget how all these years she believed she'd killed Buster Douglas, when in reality he was anything but dead. He told her about Jade's attempts to rattle her by making Buster *"appear"* at optimum times, like her wedding to Stephen. And, even though no one had conclusive proof, David was pretty sure it had been Jade who had given Chantal *Marie* Smith the lethal dose of heroin that eventually killed her. Marie's body had been found where Bridget and Jade buried it all those years ago. There had been an autopsy and it was determined that pure, uncut heroin had been injected into Marie's veins, something that seldom occurred by accident.

Bridget remembered that day; how could she ever forget it? It had been Jade who had gotten Chantal the drugs that fateful day.

"You mean she killed her own mother?" Bridget queried to no one in particular. She already knew the answer.

Suddenly, all the pieces began to fall together in a rush. That night that Buster raped her, he kept mentioning how she had asked him to come to her room that night. She thought it was his confused alcoholic state that made him believe that to be true, but it wasn't. As far as he was concerned, he had been summoned there by Bridget, with Jade speaking as her proxy. She had always wanted Bridget to follow her to Hunts Point and that was the only way to see to it that the two of them left together. Jade knew Bridget would be leaving before her and she wanted to make sure that she was tied to her...for life. All of the bumps and scrapes that Bridget had encountered for the past few years of her life had been systematically engineered by none other than Jade.

"But how could she have known that things would turn out exactly the way she planned them? How was she to know that I would strike out at Buster the way that I had? How could she have known that I wouldn't have killed him?"

"Bridget, Jade is a textbook-case sociopath. She didn't care one way or another. She knew *something* would happen that would achieve her desired goal, and whatever that thing was, she would work from there."

Bridget was so dumbfounded by all that David shared with her, she hadn't even realized she had spoken those words out loud.

"But her own mother?" Bridget asked. "How could she have killed her own mother?"

"Right after you resigned as my assistant, Jade wanted your job, or any other job that would put her close to the 'action.' I asked her if she had ever been in love. I was so caught up in my own pain that I didn't really pay close attention to her response. But I've had some time over the last couple of months to look back, and I now realize there was no response. Her reaction was vacant, completely devoid of any emotion—at all. I truly believe Jade is incapable of love; or even hate, for that matter. Jade is all about outcome. She wants whatever it is she wants for the moment and it's not about love or hate; it's about instant gratification. And once her need is satisfied, it's on to the next thing. That's why you and the twins have to get out of here. I hired a private investigator when I thought I was going to try and take Jacob from you, and there's a lot more to what he found out. The investigator also learned that Jade has hired her own investigator and eventually will learn many of the things that my investigator has shared with me; some of which even Jade isn't aware of. I'm afraid that when she finds out, she's going to be ten times more dangerous than she's ever been. That's why you've got to come with me."

Bridget wasn't sure who she should trust or what David could be talking about. Only weeks earlier, he had threatened to take her son from her or worse. Now, here he was proclaiming his love for her and acting as her savior. She hesitated, unsure if she should go with him, or take her chances on her own.

David was hurt by the fear he saw in Bridget's eyes and his heart ached to know that he had inspired that look through his own acts and deeds. He had to believe that he had her trust once. He also had to believe that he could win that trust back once again. In the meantime, he would have to appeal to Bridget's common sense.

"I understand why you wouldn't trust me, Bridget, but you were there; not me. Doesn't everything I've told you add up? And, if my word isn't enough, I have the investigator's written report in my car. Believe me, all I want to do is save you and the babies. I want to do something right for once."

The look on Bridget's face visibly softened. For a moment, he saw a glimmer of the younger, less tainted Bridget he had been so taken by for so long now.

Bridget couldn't help but remember how things were with her and David when things were good. He had been her teacher, her father, her employer. He had been the personification of all the things she had so desperately wanted and longed for all those years, growing up at Mannersville Group Home. In fact, hadn't he been the person who paid for her and Stephen's wedding? Whatever his feelings for her; obsession, love, it had to be difficult for him to pay for the very wedding he hoped upon hope would never take place. For so long her heart had ruled her decision-making. This time, she was going to do exactly what David suggested; she was going to deal with cold hard facts and work from there.

"Okay, David, but where are we going? Jade knows everything there is to know about *both* of us. She made sure of that. There's no place we can go to hide from her."

"Don't be so sure about that. Even Jade doesn't know everything."

"David, you've got to be careful. If she's capable of killing her own mother, what's to prevent her from hurting you in the worst way? After all, you've got the most to lose here. She could ruin you, and your business."

"She's already started that. She's stolen so much money from my clients and made it appear as if it were me that, at this point, she's truly in the driver's seat. What we need to figure out is how to turn this around so that it's in our favor."

"Just be careful, David. I'd hate to see you lose everything you've worked so hard for."

"I wish I could say I've worked hard for everything I have. But, the truth is, I never wanted any of this. This is the life my parents wanted for me; especially my father. I have a son now and I want the very best for him. Therefore, I'm not going to throw his birthright away, but this was never the life that I wanted. Besides, being here with you and the twins is more than I could've ever hoped for. Anything more than that is a godsend."

"David, I'm only doing this to keep Jasmine and Jacob safe. There's a lot we need to discuss. I'm not ready for anything more than that."

"Oh, no, I understand that. It's just here and now is more than I could've ever hoped for. Even when I was married to Caitlin and she yearned for children so much, I was never truly sure that was what I wanted. I was such a terrible husband, I owed her something. But, when I found out that Jacob was my son, I can't even begin to put into words the joy that I felt. That's why I was so terrible to you. It was bad enough that you didn't seem to share the same feelings, but the thought of you taking him away from me was more than I could bear. That's why I threatened to take him away."

"But, David, if you love me the way that you say you do, doesn't that mean you know me for who I truly am? What kind of person would I be if I kept Jacob from knowing his father and you from knowing your son? You had no faith in me being a person with a decent heart and soul."

"I was an idiot. But, if you'll let me, I will do my damnedest to make up for it."

After they had driven for over an hour, Bridget began to wonder where they were going. She looked at the signs indicating they were in Long Beach. For a long time this had been her private little retreat. Whenever she felt overwhelmed or afraid she would ride the subway down to Penn Station and board the railroad to Long Beach. She would spend the entire day there, dreaming of what her life would have been like if she had been born into another life. When she was on the streets, she had a john that was lonely and he would meet with her more to talk than have sex. He talked about Long Beach and how he had grown up there. It always sounded like such a fun place to grow up. One day she got information on how to get to Long Beach and rode the train there; spending the entire day lying on the beach and wiggling her toes in the ocean. That first day there had been the first time she had experienced such joy and freedom. She watched the families with their children and the carefree ways they seemed to live and again, she wished and hoped. Then when she started working for David, she would ride the train there on the weekends to get away from her guilt and her nightmares and her hopes. At Long Beach she could just *be*. Once she had gone exploring and saw a sign indicating a house for sale, right near the beach. To some it probably wouldn't have been considered anything special, but to Bridget, it was a mansion. To Bridget's surprise, David pulled up in front of that very same house. She looked at David, unable to speak, yet her eyes were full of questions.

"How?" she managed to muster.

"I'm old enough to be your father. But, right now I feel like a four-year-old that's been caught with his hand in the cookie jar. I want to be honest with you, Bridget, but I'm afraid that if I tell you the whole truth, you'll run away from me."

Bridget already knew the truth. All those times she could've sworn she was being followed. She finally understood that old line: "Just because you're paranoid, doesn't mean they're not after you." For the longest time she had believed paranoia and guilt were at the root of her fears of being followed, but now she understood completely.

"I'm ashamed to admit it, but I've been watching you since I saw you in the warehouse district of Hunts Point. From the very first moment I saw you, I've been drawn to you. At first I thought it was because you reminded me of someone I once loved very much, but now, now that I know everything, I realize that my meeting you was predestined. I sound like some woman-stalking nut, but once you know everything, you'll see why I feel the way that I do. Bridget, you and I were meant to meet for reasons far bigger than us."

On one of those many days when he had followed Bridget under the guise of making sure that she wasn't doing something that might hurt his business affairs, he had seen her looking at the house and he had been hoping, just as she had been hoping, that one day that house could be hers; if she wanted it. However, he wanted more than anything to share it with her. Despite that he had never shared with Bridget his feelings for her, he had always been hopeful. Therefore, he had bought her that house, untouched, with everything exactly as it had been.

He had watched her through the open window, picking up the various trinkets in the home, gazing at them with hope in her eyes. He knew the only thing he could do was buy that house for her. He had purchased it from the owner; along with all of its furnishings. However, he had to be careful that Bridget never found out about it, or she probably would've figured out that he had been following her, just as she had today. Therefore, this was the only piece of property that Bridget had never been made aware of when she paid his various bills, etc. He had taken care of anything related to this house.

Bridget was absolutely speechless. And, when it seemed as though she might speak, David put his finger to her lips.

"Wait, Bridget, before you say anything, let's go inside first; see the house."

David was afraid of her reaction to all of this and hopeful that once she saw the inside, she might be willing to at least listen to what David had to say.

Walking in, Bridget was surprised to see the foyer had not been changed a bit, neither had the living room, nor the kitchen.

"David, it's exactly as it was when I first saw it. I don't understand."

"I thought you would prefer it this way. When I saw you that day, the look on your face. I knew it had to be left as is, exactly the way you saw it, exactly the way you remembered it. In my heart, I knew one day you would get a chance to see it again."

In truth, David had made sure that the house was left to Bridget in his will. In his greatest wishes he hoped that it could be a home they would enjoy together, but he wanted it to be hers, no matter what.

"There's something I want you to see," he said.

As he took Bridget by the hand, her first reaction was to flinch and draw back and it pained David to realize why.

Recognizing the hurt in his eyes, Bridget tried to gloss over her response.

"I'm sorry, David, I, I'm just thinking too much about Jade and her finding us. That's all."

David knew it was a lie, but it gave him hope that she cared enough to lie.

"I want you to see the upstairs. One of the upstairs rooms has been changed. It's the only room in the house that's been touched."

Bridget had never even seen the upstairs rooms. She had been content to see the downstairs the last time she had been here. It had been more than enough to satisfy her longing for a better life.

"I can't wait to see it. I don't think I saw the upstairs

rooms when I came here the first time. I'll let you lead the way."

David showed her each of the rooms in turn. The house was bigger than she originally thought. There were three bedrooms upstairs and a smaller room, which appeared to be an office.

"The room at the end of the hall is the one I would like you to see. If you'd like to change anything, feel free to—"

"But David, I—"

"I know, Bridget. I'll explain everything in a minute. Okay?"

David was relatively sure about what Bridget was about to say and he would have been right. Bridget wasn't quite ready to accept anything from David, including a house; even the house of her dreams, just yet. She didn't want to give David false hope about the prospects of the two of them having a relationship; at least anything beyond mother and father to their son, Jacob.

"I'm sorry, I didn't get a chance to come here and air the room out before I brought you and the twins here."

Bridget couldn't believe how nervous David was. It made her more than a little curious about what was behind the door.

As David opened the door, for the first time since David had shared with her all of the information about Jade, Buster and himself, she cried. So overwhelmed by what was an obvious gesture of love, not only for his son, but for her as well, Bridget finally let go of all the pain and fear she felt and just cried.

"David, it's, it's...so very beautiful."

It was a brilliantly decorated nursery for the twins. In one area of the room, there was a beautiful antique-white curved top, three-in-one crib, which could be set up as a four-poster bed crib or a canopy crib, decorated with a white eyelet canopy with an eyelet double ruffle. Sitting near the crib was an adult-size rocking chair and matching stool, with spindle-style legs, a wide headrest, and a gently curved back and armrests. Bridget imagined herself rocking baby Jasmine and Jacob to sleep in that rocker or reading them a bedtime story, or even drifting off to sleep herself in it. Above the crib was a black-and-white mobile with various shapes and designs. The room was positively full of every imaginable stuffed animal and toy. In one corner, there were two teddy bears; one brown and one white, which seemed to be bigger and taller than even she was. But that wasn't all. Somehow, whomever had decorated the room had designed it in such a way that despite being housed between four walls, it almost doubled as a second room. Another area of the room was what Bridget was sure was Jacob's crib and living area. There were balls for every sport, a baseball glove, a red wagon and oodles and oodles of age-friendly toys. And the crib was royal blue in color with a crib bedding set complete with comforter, bumper, dust ruffle and fitted sheet, with every sport from baseball to hockey in its design. To top it all off, there was a blue adult-sized rocker with sports appliqués all over the chair.

Bridget couldn't help but love this room, no matter what her little voice was saying. Despite some small reservations, she realized it couldn't hurt to allow both Jasmine and Jacob a comfortable place to sleep; at least for now. They hadn't been in their own cribs for hours now. She decided to get them comfortable and allow them an opportunity to relax. Bridget was a good mom and she knew that even though Jasmine and Jacob were only three months old, babies, too, were capable of feeling the stress of those around them; especially that of their mother.

"I think I'll put them to bed," Bridget said.

"Oh, of course, they must be exhausted."

In fact, both Jasmine and Jacob had slept the entire trip to Long Beach in their car seats, with only slight stirs in their sleep once or twice.

"I'll leave you to get comfortable. I'll be downstairs. There are baby monitors throughout the house, so if you need anything, just let me know and I'll hear you."

Looking around the room, Bridget realized David had thought of everything. Nothing had been left out. There was a breast pump, two dressers full of every item any baby could need. He had even bought nursing bras of various sizes (probably because he wasn't sure what size she wore). There were pacifiers, baby grooming kits… everything, including the monitors he had installed throughout the house.

"Who did all of this for you?" she asked.

"No one. I did it."

"Yeah, right," Bridget joked.

Bridget suddenly remembered the easy-going relationship they had shared when they worked together and enjoyed each other's company. The late nights working and gorging themselves on Chinese dumplings and lo mein. She missed that more than she cared to admit. Right now, at this very moment, all of the drama that had secretly filled their lives was forgotten.

"No, really. I picked out every single item with my own little hands. In fact, it was kind of fun."

"David, would you mind staying to help me with the babies?"

David was elated. Finally there was a chink in her armor, a glimmer of hope for the future. He would be sure not to get his hopes up. But, it was something.

Bridget was amazed at the ease with which David handled Jacob. He actually changed his diaper! Watching him with his son, Bridget felt brighter about the future as well, yet she, too, realized now was not the time to build up false hope, either for herself or for David. She would have to take a wait-and-see approach; a little bit at a time.

When he was done rocking Jacob to sleep in the sports rocker, he laid him peacefully in his crib. Jasmine was a little cranky and despite getting her diaper changed and Bridget breastfeeding her, she wouldn't calm down.

"You mind if I try?" David asked.

Bridget was surprised. Jacob was David's son but he had nothing vested with Jasmine. It was even reasonable to expect David to harbor some resentment toward Jasmine under the circumstances, but he seemed sincere about wanting to help comfort her.

"O-kay, I guess," Bridget stammered.

She handed Jasmine over to David with only a slight bit of trepidation, yet as soon as he saw her beautiful daughter lying contentedly in David's arms, all of her uncertainties melted away. He was really good with her. He sat in front of the window, rocking in the white rocking chair and talking to her. For the first time since she had known David, she felt stirrings she had never felt before. For the first time, she saw him as someone other than a really good friend and employer. Something about the ease with which they settled into this temporary domesticity warmed her in ways she could never have anticipated. She felt a physical attraction to David right now unlike anything she ever felt for any man.

"Are you hungry?" Bridget asked.

David was so engulfed in his banter with Jasmine, he hadn't even heard her.

"I'm Uncle David and I think you and I are going to be really good friends," he said in his baby voice. "If there's one thing you've gotta know about Uncle David it's I am a die-hard Mets fan. And, I'm not one of those fair-weather Mets fans either. I'm a fan, no matter what, and that's exactly the kind of friend I am. So when you and your brother are big enough, I'll teach you both how to throw the knuckleball that made me the envy of all the Little Leaguers at the Horace Hanover School. Speaking of which, Horace Hanover is a *really* great school, no pressure or anything."

"*David*, she's only three months old!" Bridget laughed.

David had been enjoying his talk with Jasmine so much he had almost forgotten Bridget was still in the room.

"Now that I have your attention…Uncle David…are you hungry?"

"Yeah, come to think of it, I don't think I've had anything to eat all day. Yeah. I bought some groceries, or we could order some Chinese. I'm sure there's a Chinese restaurant around here somewhere."

Jasmine had finally fallen off to sleep in David's arms. He tucked her into her crib and followed Bridget downstairs to the dining room. Bridget found a menu for a local Chinese restaurant in one of the drawers in the kitchen.

"Wanna give Peking Duck House a shot?" she asked, waving the menu at David.

"Kung Pao shrimp," they both said on cue, laughing.

The Chinese food arrived quickly and Bridget made a place on the coffee table and sprawled out on the floor with David. The revelations of the day had left Bridget exhausted and she didn't think she could muster the energy to sit at the dining table. The pair sat on the floor eating Kung Pao shrimp, egg rolls and lo mein—eager for the events of the day to melt away. For the most part, they had. Anyone from the outside looking in would have been hard pressed to see them as anything other than a couple relaxing in their home after having eaten dinner. The ease with which they had just shared dinner together brought back to Bridget the feelings she experienced earlier in the nursery and she couldn't help but notice the way David looked at her; especially when he thought she wasn't looking.

All that time Brianna had been right. David McDonnell loved her. He had loved her all these years and she had been too blind to see it. That was when it occurred to Bridget that she might actually love him, too. She hadn't planned on loving him or expected the possibility of loving him, but maybe that was the reason she had been so short-sighted. Bridget had spent her entire life feeling unworthy of love. So, of course, when rich, handsome, accomplished David McDonnell came along, she couldn't see the forest for the trees. But, if that were the case, why was she able to see the possibility of Stephen loving her? Bridget understood that as well. Stephen had come to McDonnell & Simpson inexperienced and needing guidance. Bridget felt that was something she could give him. She had been his champion. Bridget had always thought of herself as a victim who constantly needed saving, but in reality, she was the strong one always willing to stand up for the underdog: Jade, Stephen, even David, had all leaned on Bridget in one way or another.

"David?"

"Yes, Bridget?"

"It was never my plan to get *anything* from you. I wanted an honest job and, if I had known that Jade railroaded you into giving me one, I would've never taken it. I didn't find out how I got this job until after I'd worked with you for quite some time. And, as usual, Jade tried to justify it and I went along with it. What I'm trying to say is, I'm sorry. I'm so sorry that we never got a chance to meet each other the way normal people do. Maybe we could've bumped into one another at a museum or something, and you could've asked for my phone number and I would've sat at home, waiting for the phone to ring, hoping you would call me.

"I don't want you to ever think that I've spent all this time trying to take advantage of you. Nothing could be farther from the truth. Sometimes, I even think I quit working for you partly because you had become such a little shit," she joked. "But, mostly because I felt guilty every single day when I realized what Jade was trying to do and what part I played in it. I never meant to hurt you. Really, I didn't."

"Bridget, shouldn't *I* be telling *you* that? You have no reason *at all* to apologize to me. If it were up to me, I would spend my entire life trying to make it up to you for all the pain I've caused you."

"No, David—"

"Let me finish, Bridget. I did a horrible, horrible thing to you, something I never even thought myself capable of. For the longest time, I blamed my raping you on Jade, on you, on alcohol, but when it really comes down to it, I am the *only* person to blame. Alcohol didn't make me rape you, Jade didn't make me rape you and you certainly didn't ask for it. I made that decision, a conscious decision that I'll regret for the rest of my life. For that I'm more ashamed than I'll ever be able to put into words. For the longest time, I made myself believe that I was nothing at all like my father; a man who had no respect for women and treated them terribly, including my own mother. The truth is that I'm no different than he was. I may actually be worse. Despite my father's various shortcomings, I don't believe he ever raped anyone."

"David, you've been there for me in so many ways, I probably should hate you, but I don't. I had all these preconceived notions about who you were and I'm guessing that you did, too, about me. When it comes down to it, we're both just people; fallible human beings with our strengths and our weaknesses. I saw something good in you, or I wouldn't have enjoyed working with you so much, and I wouldn't have enjoyed the time we spent together as friends. We *were* friends once?" she questioned.

"Of course we were, sweetheart. The problem was the whole time we were friends, I kept wishing we were so much more. That's what got me into trouble. You're precious, Bridget; a rare and beautiful jewel, to have survived all that you survived. And, I guess I wanted more than anything to be a part of that; a part of you."

David wanted to stroke Bridget's face, to kiss her lips and to let her know that everything was going to be alright, but he'd made that mistake before. His longing for her was so intense that he didn't trust himself to stop. Luckily, for him, he didn't have to labor long over his thoughts; Bridget made that decision for him. Before he could say another word, Bridget held his face in her hands, stroked his hair and kissed him with such intensity, David was sure the world, as they knew it, had rotated on its axis in the mere seconds it took for her to press her lips to his. Bridget left no doubt in either of their minds that her kiss had little to do with friendship and everything to do with raw, unbridled passion that had been smoldering for David for several years now, unbeknownst, even to her.

David was hungry for her, yet careful not to frighten her away. So often he had thought of a night much like this, he was afraid of how so many years of unrequited love would demonstrate itself, if he made love to her now. As if reading his thoughts, Bridget spoke to him, with such love, it took his breath away.

"David, don't hold back. I want all of you. Show me what you've been thinking. I want to feel everything you've been feeling. David, I want you to love me."

Although he had already seen Bridget's naked body, it was as though he were seeing her for the very first time.

"I want to look at you," he said.

David undressed Bridget, very slowly and methodically, anxious to savor the moment, unsure of what tomorrow would bring. He removed her clothing, piece by piece, first her skirt, then her tank top, then her bra and panties. He was content to merely gaze at her. There was a part of him that was afraid that if he touched her, she would disappear. That's how convinced he was that it had to be a dream, but it wasn't.

"David, I want you as much as you want me. Take me. I'm here. I'm here."

"You're so beautiful," he said. "So very beautiful."

Gone was the savage passion of the first time he had penetrated her. This time David made *love* to Bridget, kissing every inch of her, inhaling the sweet scent of her signature Mont Blanc cologne, which he had bought her for the very first Christmas they worked together. He remembered how thankful she was when he'd bought it for her, and since that time she had never worn anything else. The combination of cologne intermingled with the scent of baby powder, just made him want her even more. This woman he had craved since the first time he had ever laid eyes on her was the mother of his child, his best friend, and soon to be his lover. His mouth hungered for her lips, her breasts. He wanted to nibble at the base of her spine and taste places on her and inside of her that he had never had the luxury of experiencing. He suckled at her breasts, and experienced a hunger unlike any he had ever felt. The taste of mother's milk and Bridget's moans was enough to drive him completely insane. If ever there were a soul mate, a woman that was his one true destiny, she was his. Bridget's eyes were closed, so enraptured with the feel of his mouth on her, but he wanted to gaze into those ochre-colored eyes of hers, and he wanted her to look into his as they made love; he wanted to know that this was what they both wanted—more than anything else in the world.

"Baby, please open your eyes," David implored her. "I want to see all of you and I don't want you to miss a thing. I want you to see the sweet joy and agony I feel as you capture me within you. So, please, Bridget, open your eyes."

And as Bridget's eyes slowly opened to look into David's, he entered her slowly. He had waited for this for so long; the moment when she gave herself to him—*willingly*. He would make sure to savor each and every tantalizing moment... Unfortunately, for Bridget and David, however, they were so oblivious to anything but their lovemaking, that they didn't hear the sounds on the baby monitor of what was happening upstairs in the nursery.

While Bridget and David lay sleeping on the living room floor, Jade had slipped into the house through an open window, along with a crackhead she ran on Hunts Point.

"What the fuck?" Divine said. "They got black and white parents or something? This one's white and blond and the other one's as black as can be. That's the craziest set of twins I ever saw. You did say they was twins, right?"

"Divine, would you shut the fuck up! I ain't never in my entire life seen a ho flap her gums as much as you."

"It's kinda crazy; that's all. Why you gotta' be so mean, Jade?"

"Shut up. No talking until we get on up out of here. Okay?" Jade would have had harsher words for Divine if she didn't need her. "Just take the little girl."

"Which one is the girl? The white one or the black one?" Divine asked.

"Geez. The black one is the girl. Take her and I'll take the boy."

Jade took Jacob and Divine took Jasmine. Jade found

a baby carrier and strapped it on and handed one to Divine
as well.

Divine looked at Jade like she had two heads.

"What do I look like? Mary Fuckin' Poppins? I don't
know how to put that thing on," Divine said.

Jade exhaled loudly and, after attaching the baby carrier
she was wearing and depositing baby Jacob inside, she
attached Divine's and put Jasmine in that one. The pair
then laboriously exited through the same window they
had come through, but not before Jade left a note for
David and Bridget. It had taken her hours to put that note
together and she couldn't wait until they both read it.

Bridget was the first to awaken. She hadn't slept much
since Jasmine and Jacob had been born, but she had
gotten accustomed to waking to feed them both. Yet,
somehow she hadn't heard a peep out of them since she
had gotten here. David was sleeping so soundly and she
didn't have the heart to wake him, so she got up from
the floor quietly and went upstairs to check on Jasmine
and Jacob. Nagging at Bridget was the eerie quiet of the
entire house. Taking the steps two by two, her mother's
intuition was working overtime and, although shocked
when she walked over to Jasmine's crib, she wasn't completely surprised. Her crib was empty and so was Jacob's.
Someone had taken her babies. For a split second, it
occurred to her that maybe this was some sort of scheme
on David's part to get his son. Bridget quickly trashed
that idea. That was love she had felt and she knew David
well enough, both before and now, to know that he would

never have done this. No, this was someone else. Then it dawned on her. *Jade*!

Before Bridget could scream out to David, he was standing in the doorway of Jasmine and Jacob's room, as white as a ghost.

"David," Bridget cried. "She's taken the babies. She's taken them."

David's astonishment didn't last long before he recovered and sprang into action. Picking up the telephone, he dialed a number and spoke.

"It's too late, I think she knows, and she's taken Jasmine and Jacob. We may have had our differences, but we need to do something and do something now. You don't know Jade the way that we do. She will not hesitate to hurt both Jasmine and Jacob, if she feels as though she's backed up against a corner. And given what I know, I don't think it will even take that. Up 'til now this has been little more than a game for her. An entertaining way to shuffle people around as though they were pieces on a chess board. Now, it's about more than that. In her own sick little mind, this is about justifiable vengeance. And, if you don't want Jasmine to end up on the receiving end of that vengeance, I would suggest you put your feelings for Bridget and I aside and we all work together. I'm not sure what she has in mind, but as I see it, Jacob and I are more of a focal point for her anger than any of you, but we all know Jade. She doesn't care who gets caught in the crossfire. So, are you with us or not?"

On the other end of the line, Stephen was explaining

to David that he wasn't for anyone *but* Jasmine, but that he would do whatever it took to keep her safe, even if it meant joining forces with David and Bridget.

Bridget stared on, dazed and confused, unsure of the meaning of the conversation David had just had and afraid of what David was sure to tell her next.

"David, who was that and what did you mean about Jade wanting vengeance. Vengeance for what?"

"One of the reasons I brought you here was to tell you the rest of what my investigator learned when he was trying to find out about you and Jade. How much did Jade's mom tell you about Jade's father?"

"Nothing really. Jade never knew her father. Oh, except, Chantal did tell me once that he was a good, decent man. I remember being surprised because Jade and everyone else who knew Chantal assumed Jade's father was one of many johns she had known through the years and that even she didn't know who Jade's father was. But once, right before she died, she told me how much she loved Jade's dad. I'll never forget that night because it was one of the best talks I had ever had with Chantal. It was the only time I had gotten to see the soft side of her, and just as quickly as I saw that part of her, she was dead. In fact, she died that next morning, I think."

"I hope what I'm about to tell you doesn't change what *we've* just shared. But, you need to know *everything*. The fact that I only recently learned of this doesn't excuse my part in it. But I must mention, that I didn't know anything about this until I hired that investigator. When I was a teenager, my father, in his infinite wisdom, decided to take me to a prostitute, hoping it would keep me from getting my girlfriend pregnant, or being too preoccupied with sex to concentrate on my studies, or for whatever reason his warped mind came up with. Anyway, he took me to Hunts Point. I was terrified. I felt like I was trapped in some bad vampire movie or something. There were girls everywhere, some of them half naked and walking the streets as if it were commonplace. Well, my father set me up with this prostitute who was about my age. Her name was Marie. She was eighteen or so, black, pretty, and I later found out, very nice. At first, I wouldn't touch her and I really thought she hated me and what I represented, but after a few visits we became friends and eventually, as would be the case with any healthy teens, she and I had sex; in fact, she was my first, but our encounter was fleeting. As soon as my father learned that I considered Marie more than just a prostitute, he made sure that she and I never saw one another again. Remember, when we first met and I mentioned that you reminded me of someone I once loved very much; that was Marie. And although I've never considered myself a religious man, now that I know something of what happened to Marie, I believe wholeheartedly that she brought the two of us together. I believe that she loved us both and she wanted us to be happy. And somewhere from beyond, or whatever you want to call it, she made sure that our destinies were intertwined."

"David, what are you talking about? I don't understand

any of this. And, what does it have to do with Jasmine and Jacob, and what you were talking to Stephen about on the phone?"

"Bridget, Jade's mom, Chantal; her middle name was Marie."

"So. What does that have to do with...?"

Then it dawned on her, but not before David explained.

"Bridget, Chantal Marie Smith was the woman I knew as Marie. I loved her, Bridget, and she loved me, and that is why I believe she decided to have our child. She was a good, loving, kind person, who got the dirty end of the stick in life and in death—and she loved both of us. Bridget, I am that man that Chantal talked about, the one that she told you she loved. Bridget, Jade is my daughter."

Bridget was dumbfounded, she didn't know what to say or think. Her first thought, however, was that her children were in *unbelievable* danger. For whatever reason, Jade envied her beyond reason. She was an evil, calculating human being. If Jade were aware that she and Jacob were indeed brother and sister, it would not sit well with her. She would be harboring enormous jealousy for Jacob, and it wouldn't matter that he was just a baby. David was right—it was bad, and even though Jasmine probably didn't matter in the least to Jade, it was not improbable that Jasmine would get caught in Jade's crossfire.

"David, I've got to speak to Stephen."

At first David was hurt, but he quickly realized this wasn't about him and Bridget, or Stephen and Bridget. This was about their children, and Stephen and Bridget shared the same bond that he and Bridget shared; they had a child together. And, obviously, Stephen loved his daughter no less than he loved his son. Clearly, Stephen had made his choice when he chose to be with Jade.

David handed Bridget the phone, but Bridget hesitated.

"David, do you think it's a mistake trusting him? After all, he was just with Jade only weeks earlier. What has changed?"

"Don't worry, Bridget. Before we came here, I made sure that Stephen got a copy of the investigator's report. I figured we would need him and I knew he wouldn't believe a thing I said unless it was in black and white. I even gave the investigator permission to speak with Stephen about his findings, in case Stephen decided to call him. He knows everything."

"But, Jade can be very manipulative. She has a way of twisting a person's thoughts, making them believe what she wants them to believe."

"Believe me, I understand what you're saying. I've been on the receiving end of Jade's manipulations more times than I care to mention. But I have enough faith in Stephen to know that this time out, he won't be so easily maneuvered. He has so much more at stake."

"Where do you think she is?" Bridget asked.

"I know it sounds cliché, but she's probably done what

every criminal does. She's returned to the scene of the crime."

"Hunts Point," they both said in unison.

All of their questions were answered as they read the note Jade left behind:

Daddy Dearest,

As you probably already know, you're the piece of shit that knocked up my mother and left us both to the wolves. I can't wait to sit down and tell you all about what my life has been like since you left us. But, I'm sure you can already figure all that out. I bet you're so happy you decided not to fuck me when you were cruising Hunts Point looking for pussy, huh? Well, anyway, I'm sure it doesn't take a rocket scientist to figure out what it is I want. I want money, and lots of it. In fact, I want $100,000 for every single year that you should have taken care of me + $200,000 thrown in for good measure (you know, college, incidentals and the like) and I want it today. You see I'm thinking of starting a new life, far away from the hustle and bustle of New York. Now, I can make this change, with or without my baby brother. That's your decision. I can leave the black baby (you know, the one you don't care two shits about) here to be picked apart by the degenerates or they both can come home with you and your clueless Lady Love. You hold the key to their fate, Daddy Dearest. For their sake, you better not fuck up!

Leaving Long Beach, Bridget didn't know what she was more afraid of; Jade or her two angels being exposed to the very same Hunts Point element she had sworn they would never be exposed to.

"David, we have to find them. We just have to!"

"We will. I promise you, we will—if I have to move heaven and earth in the process."

Driving through Hunts Point was like a none-too-pleasant walk through memory lane for both Bridget and David. Not much had changed and they both felt as though their lives were flashing before their eyes. He went over and over it in his mind, thinking about both Marie and Jade and how things had turned out. He wished he had it to do all over again. Things probably wouldn't have turned out the way that they had. Bridget couldn't help but think about the relationship she thought she had with Jade. Once upon a time, she considered her a sister, but she now knew that had all been a lie. How could she have been so blind? Then, Bridget's thoughts shifted to Chantal. She and Jade had buried Chantal's body in a grave in the park like an old piece of garbage. She now understood Jade's mindset, but why had *she* done it? Didn't that make her no better than Jade? She pacified her guilt with the thought that she was young and afraid and promised herself that somehow, someway, she would make it up to Chantal.

"David, did that report mention where Chantal's body is now? I would really like to ensure that she finally has a proper burial."

"Yes, of course. The strange thing is Marie's body was somehow unearthed maybe a year or so after you and Jade buried her. It could have been an animal, the rain, any number of things. But, once her body was discovered, she was so decomposed and with so little to go on, she was classified as yet another Jane Doe. She was buried in a gravesite the State designates for unclaimed bodies, usually for the indigent, or unloved. Fortunately, between what Michael and the investigator were able to learn about you and Jade and your connection with Marie, they were able to canvass the area of the apartment where you all lived, ask questions and connect the timeline of Marie's disappearance with several Jane Does. Don't worry, Bridget, I know exactly what you're thinking. We found her."

"She wasn't indigent or unloved. Chantal was greatly loved by me. She was the closest thing to a mother I ever had. When all of this is over, can we make sure she has a proper funeral? At the very least, she deserves that."

"I agree. She deserves that and so much more. I wish there was something I could do for Jade. I can't help thinking that there's got to be some part of Jade that is good. Her mother was a kind and giving person, and I know I'm not perfect, and I've made a *lot* of mistakes along the way, but I've never intentionally hurt anyone. I can't believe that the two of us could have made a daughter with absolutely no redeeming qualities. I have to believe that I can get through to her in some way."

"I understand what you're saying, David, but our first priority should be Jasmine and Jacob, and I have to be honest with you. I have every intention of doing everything and anything I need to do to save them. I know that's your daughter and all, but if saving Jasmine and

Jacob means having to hurt Jade in the process, that is exactly what *I* will *have* to do."

"I know."

"I wish it didn't have to be this way. My father left me well-fixed and despite Jade's attempts to rob me blind, McDonnell has consistently made money since its inception. There has always been enough of everything; enough money, enough of everything, to go around. She really doesn't have to do this. I actually believe her. She is entitled to everything she wants, with the exception of hurting Jasmine and Jacob. I would have no reservations about giving her all of my money, if that's what it takes. But, I don't think that is really what she wants. I think she wants to make all of us pay for the life she had or didn't have. I just don't understand why she wants you to pay. I mean, weren't you right there living the identical life?"

"That's something I've never been able to understand either. Jade has always behaved as though my life was somehow better than hers. When in reality, in some respects, she had so much more than I had. Even as damaged as Chantal was, I often envied the fact that Jade had a mother because I never did."

By the time they arrived at their rundown former Westchester Avenue apartment, Stephen was outside waiting for them and eager to see both David and Bridget. In all his life, Stephen had never seen such squalor. He felt such empathy for Bridget, now more than ever before.

He didn't know if they would ever be able to put this behind them and be friends, but he no longer felt any measure of hate for her. In some respects, he believed Bridget was to be commended for surviving and triumphing over this life.

He wondered if he would have been able to do the same under similar circumstances. He suddenly saw her for the courageous woman that she was.

"Have you been here long, Stephen?" Bridget asked.

"No. I only got here ten or fifteen minutes ago. I haven't even gone in the building yet."

"That's probably a good idea. There's safety in numbers," David chimed in.

"Our apartment was on the third floor. The one furthest to the back."

"Okay, Bridget. Why don't you wait here in the car and Stephen and I will go up."

"I'm not waiting here. My babies are up there. I'm not going to just sit in the car. I've played the victim long enough. It's about time I took control over my life."

Stephen looked at Bridget with great sincerity and warmth; a gesture which immediately got Bridget's attention, since she believed he felt nothing for her but contempt.

"Bridget, you have done nothing but take control of your life from the very beginning. I can't imagine what it must have been like for you—here—and with Jade as your only friend. It makes me so angry with her and even angrier with myself for not being able to open up my eyes and see what was directly in front of me. I still can't believe that I actually allowed myself to be taken in by her. You are one of the most courageous people I have ever known and you have nothing to prove. Let someone protect you for a change. I believe David, and I know I, will feel much better, if we know you're safely out of reach from Jade's clutches."

"I want to see and know that Jasmine and Jacob are alright. I finally believe what Chantal told me all those years ago; Jade is evil and now she has my babies. I can't sit here and wonder what is happening up there. I need to be wherever they are."

"I understand," David said.

"Yes," Stephen agreed.

"But Bridget, if Jade is up there, do not get too close to her. She's probably capable of anything," David cautioned.

"Why don't we call the police in the meantime?" Stephen asked.

"She's my daughter and I'm going to do my best to protect Jasmine and Jacob, but I don't want Jade hurt either. After all, this is my fault as much as anyone else's. I'm going to do my best to get Jade the help she needs. I wasn't there for her her entire life. The least I can do now is try to save her. I don't want her locked away in some prison somewhere. I have to believe that even Jade is not beyond saving."

Until now Bridget had always been Jade's greatest

champion. Now, however, she was only concerned with saving her son and daughter.

"David, you know I love you and once upon a time, I loved Jade very much, but you know where I stand. If it comes down to saving Jasmine and Jacob or saving Jade, Jade is expendable. I can't allow her to hurt them. I can't."

"I gotta tell you, David. I'm with Bridget on that one."

David took great pride in his legal expertise. He realized that ability would have to be the force that guided him in not only rescuing Jasmine and Jacob, but Jade as well. He would have to present the most riveting and convincing opening argument he had ever put together, if or when it came to that.

David, Stephen and Bridget took the stairs leading to Bridget's former apartment; all unsure of what they would find waiting for them behind those doors. All three of them stopped at the entrance. Then, David produced a key.

"Where did you get that from?" Bridget asked.

"Didn't you ever wonder who was paying the rent all those years?" David said.

"David, you were paying the rent on this place?"

"No, not me. My mom was. It seems, all those years ago when Marie got pregnant, she tried to contact me, but instead got in touch with my parents; my mom and my dad. She probably would have been ignored and given a few thousand dollars to keep quiet, if left up to my father, but my mom was a good woman. Knowing my mother, she probably even wanted to get to know her granddaughter, maybe even raise her. But my father would never have heard of anything even close to that. So, I guess my mother did the only thing she could do. She created a dummy corporation called Swerdly Enterprises and paid the rent on this place under that corporation's name. I'm not sure how she ended up with this key. Maybe, somehow, she was able to get a copy from the management company before Marie first moved in. I really don't know, but for whatever reason, she kept a copy among her things. I thought I knew all there was to know about my mother, but when she died, this key was one of the mysteries I was unable to solve. As soon as I found out about her paying the rent on this place, I knew that's what that key was for. My mother ensured that living or dead, Marie and Jade would have a place to live, no matter what. I didn't know anything about any of this until my investigator starting digging around. In my mother's wildest imagination, I'm sure she would never have envisioned the sort of place her money was paying for. I believe if she had known where Marie and Jade were living, she would have probably bought them a house or something. It's just that she was so damned afraid of my father and so...controlled by him. I guess, in many ways, I'm just like him."

"David, you're nothing at all like your father. He went to his grave the same person. You've done more to become a better person in the last few months than some people have done in their entire lives. You made mistakes, that's all. That thing that defines us is not our mistakes but how we handle them and grow from them. You've done that."

When David first told Stephen the story of how Jacob came to be, he was so angry with David he punched him square in the jaw. But now he realized that David truly did love Bridget. He loved her as well and was sorry he hadn't had it in him to love her beyond their obstacles. But David loved her beyond everything. He had stuck it out for the long haul, despite all that he knew—and didn't know—about Bridget. He, unfortunately, had not, and he would probably regret that for years to come.

David used the key he held and slowly opened the door. It was readily apparent that no one was there and that no one had probably been there for quite some time. Bridget looked around. Everything seemed to be exactly as they had left it. It was more than a little disturbing to Bridget's memories. Despite the fact that the apartment appeared to be empty, they decided to check each room, just in case. That's when Bridget saw it—little Jasmine's Dora the Explorer pacifier, lying on the floor of the bathroom. That's when Bridget knew where Jade had taken Jasmine and Jacob.

"Let's go! I know where they are."

"David, why don't you let me drive? You're going to get us all killed! You must be driving a hundred miles per hour. Not to mention the fact that we're screwed, if we get pulled over by the police."

David realized that Stephen was right and slowed down.

"Okay, okay. I'll slow it down. We're almost there anyway. Aren't we, Bridget?"

"Yes. And, I'm pretty sure I know where she'll be. I just hope I can remember the *exact* location."

"Oh," David said, suddenly realizing the area Bridget was referring to.

"What?" Stephen asked.

"I'm guessing that she'll be where we took her mother, or at least somewhere in the vicinity. The area may have changed a little since then."

"Well, if that is where she's gone, I have the exact location in the investigator's report. It was all documented by the police after Marie's body was found."

"Maybe we should find somewhere to park the car and search for them on foot," David suggested.

"Yeah, if the area is the way I remember it, I think you're probably right."

It didn't take long for them to find Jade. She was exactly where Bridget expected, sitting on a rock, just waiting. But, where were Jasmine and Jacob?

"Jade! Where are Jasmine and Jacob? Where are my babies?!"

"You mean my brother and his sister? Ain't this a fucked-up situation. Not at all what you expected, huh, Bridget? Your perfect little family, your perfect little life is still just as imperfect as it's always been."

"Yeah, it is, Jade. Thanks to you!"

"There you go again, playing the poor little victim. I'm so sick of hearing that song I could puke. You never take responsibility for your own fucking life. That's what makes you a target. I had you pegged from the moment I first met you. You were a whining bitch back then and you still are."

"Jade, what the hell are you talking about? When we met we were just little girls."

"Yeah. We were and you took my family away from me; the first and last family that ever wanted me. I could have had a life. A *real* life—the life I deserved. But no, you waltzed in your first day at Mannersville, sat your skinny ass down at that old-ass piano in the waiting room, and started to play. The Bennetts were hooked instantly. They were all set to take me home with them. I was going to be their daughter and then you came in and showed off. And instead of me, they wanted you. And the fucked-up thing about it is, you stayed with them for all of a week and you were right back here, whining and crying about some 'traumatic incident' that happened while you were there. You were so fucking stupid and pathetic!"

"Jade, Mr. Bennett was a fucking pedophile. He tried to rape me! We were *both* better off not living there. If anything, I saved you from the Bennetts!"

"See, that's one of the *many* ways in which you and I are so different. I wouldn't have cared. I would have given Mr. Bennett whatever he wanted in exchange for the life he and his wife were offering. Once you came back, I kept hoping that the Bennetts would realize they had made a mistake when they chose you and do what they had originally intended—come back to Mannersville and take me home with them. That never happened. You ruined it for me, the way you ruin everything. You ruined that, you ruined my chances with Buster. Buster liked me best when he came to work at Mannersville. He even let me leave once. We had an understanding. I took care of him and he took care of me. It made my days at Mannersville livable. Then, you started developing—finally, and all of a sudden his attention shifted from me to you. Giving you extra food, asking where you were, what you were doing. I wanted to kill him myself for betraying me, but I figured what better way to get the fuck out of that hell hole and to keep your dumb ass under my thumb than to let you kill him. I didn't know that old, fat drunk bastard would live."

"Jade, I would have done anything for you..."

"And you did, didn't you?" Jade chuckled.

"We could have had a better life a lot sooner, without all that ugly stuff that we had to do."

"There you go with those pipe dreams of yours. Who do you think would have hired an eighteen-year-old secretary who had never had a job and just got out of a family group home?"

"Jade, people do it all the time. If I had been living with my family and just graduated from school, it would have been feasible. It's not like I had a prison record, nor you. We were in a home—a home for children with no parents.

"And look, the proof is in our lives. Look at how far we've come. It didn't have to be like this. David told me what he found out—I mean, about him and your mom. Just think of the life you could have had, could *still* have."

"Yes, Jade," David spoke up. "Whatever is mine is yours. Just tell us where Jasmine and Jacob are."

"You could care two shits about me; you just want that little half-breed boy of yours. I wonder if we flashed back to the day I was born, would you be quite so willing to pay for my life. Huh, would you, Daddy Dearest?"

"Jade, I would have given anything to just know that you existed. I never knew. No one ever told me. I swear to you. I would never have abandoned you, if I'd known."

"Yeah, that's what you say, but I guess we'll never know, will we?"

"Jade, you'll just have to trust me."

"Yeah, right." Jade laughed. "Me trust the likes of you. My name is not Bridget."

"Why are we playing cat and mouse with this crazy bitch?" Stephen asked.

David turned to Stephen to silently caution him to take it easy. However, Jade was way ahead of him.

"If it isn't Mr. Bourgeoise. What do you want, your nappy-headed baby? What would you do if I told you one of my crackhead friends was up in a crackhouse selling her to the highest bidder as we speak?"

Stephen lunged for her, but David was able to stop him before he could cause any damage. Realizing David had his hands full with Stephen, Bridget attempted to reason with Jade once again.

"Jade, what is it that you want? Whatever it is, I'm sure David will give it to you. Just tell him what you want."

"I want my life back. I want to live the life that your two precious babies are going to live. That's what I want! Can he give me that? Well, can he?"

"Yes, Jade, as a matter of fact, he can. He can give you that and more. And I do believe he is more than willing to do that; was willing to do that even without you kidnapping his son—if you had just given him a chance."

"You still don't get it, do you? Nothing will ever be enough to make up for what was stolen from me. All that he has, all that Jasmine and Jacob will have, that was my birthright just as much as it was theirs. But instead, what did I have? Nothing, less than nothing. Did you know I can't have children? Every time I would hear you talk about a family and all that shit, I would tell you how I was never having children. Damn right, I wasn't having any! I couldn't have any—can't have any, because one of my mother's johns raped me when I was two years old— two *fucking* years old! Fucked me up so bad there isn't a chance in hell that I'll ever have a baby. Bet you didn't know that, huh?"

Bridget kept thinking that this was the point in movies when the person telling the story would start crying, but

Jade's eyes were dry as a bone. Then it dawned on her that the only time she had ever seen Jade shed anything even close to a tear was when she killed her mother. Bridget was convinced those tears had been fake. The thought chilled Bridget to the bone. As she stood there, she was hoping for a glimmer of a tear from her eyes, hoping that somehow that would free Jade from the evil that had kept her bound all these years. In the shadows Bridget could see someone sneaking up behind Jade. Just as Bridget was about to yell at the person, whoever they were, to stop, Jade was wrestled to the ground. Sitting on the rock next to Jade was a duffel bag. She and Brianna, the person who was engaging Jade in the fierce struggle, were battling over ownership of the duffel bag. That's when Bridget, and then Stephen and David, all heard the faint sound of a baby crying.

"Oh my God, they're in the bag! Somebody, help! Jasmine and Jacob are in that duffel bag! No! Somebody do something!" As Bridget rushed over to save her babies who were now sitting dangerously close to the edge of a ravine, Brianna and Jade were fighting tooth and nail for possession of the bag. David and Stephen both rushed over, unsure of what they should do. The fall was sure to kill both babies. And under the right circumstances, David's daughter, Jade, might also die, not to mention Brianna. David watched the situation and decided the only thing they could do, would be to try and grab both Jade and Brianna and pull them from over the edge.

Someone would have to carefully grab the bag, especially since Jade was trying to throw it over the edge with every turn. Watching the bag bump against the rocks, Bridget feared that even if the bag didn't go over the edge, the twins might still perish. The constant assault on their tiny little bodies coupled with the lack of air could prove to be fatal. That's when she decided the only thing she could do would be to dive for the bag and grab it as quickly as humanly possible. It would take split-second timing, but she would use every bit of energy she had to get that bag out of Jade's hands. As Bridget leaped for the bag, David pulled at Jade's hand, attempting to pull her up just enough to grab her by the waist. It would afford him more leverage, while Stephen tried grabbing Brianna. Amidst the mayhem, Bridget was able to wrestle the bag from Jade's hand, but not before both she and Jade tumbled head first into the ravine.

CHAPTER TWENTY
CONCLUSION/JASMINE AND JACOB

Bridget was amazed at her babies' resilience. They spent a couple of nights in the hospital, but had gotten a clean bill of health. There had been no injuries to either of their bodies and the hospital had ruled out the biggest concern, lack of oxygen.

Stephen and David were also both very happy to learn that their children would be fine. However, David was mourning a great loss; at least to him. No one involved could believe that the twins had survived while an adult, Jade, had suffered such a crushing blow. After both Bridget and Jade had fallen, Jade's chest was impaled by a tree branch, piercing her lungs. At first, David thought she might survive—she appeared as feisty as ever, spitting, spewing and cursing until the end. But, she succumbed to complications in the hospital and died. David was devastated. For years he had a daughter he had never known about, yet somehow she had been brought to him—literally placed on his doorstep—but he hadn't found out she was his daughter until it was too late. He would never have the opportunity to make it up to her. She was gone.

He still remembered her last words; the words that would haunt him until his dying day: "We'll be waiting for you."

If no one else knew what she meant, he sure did. She was talking about hell. She meant she and her mother would be waiting for him. He couldn't help but think that her comment, while saddening, was more that just a little fitting. He couldn't help but feel overwhelming guilt for the legacy (albeit handed down to him), that he had in turn handed down to his own offspring. But, Jade was wrong about Marie. If there *was* a heaven and a hell, Marie was surely watching over them *all*—as an angel.

"How are you doing?" Bridget asked her matron of honor, Brianna, as she fussed over Bridget's makeup.

"Girl, shouldn't I be asking you that? You're the one jumpin' the broom today."

"But to answer your question, my boo is back. We've been fuckin' like minks since we got back together. We decided to compromise and stay here in New York because quite frankly I *hate* Georgia and I'm so glad I'm home! Not only that, little Jacob and Jasmine are going to have a playmate soon."

"Oh my God. No!"

"Yes!"

"No! You're pregnant. Oh, Brianna. You're gonna make such a good mom and I'll have someone to talk about mommy stuff with. Does Trevor know yet?"

"Yeah. He knows. He was right there holding the pee stick for me. I adore him."

"I know you do, honey."

"And you know, if it wasn't for you and your *drama*, we might never have gotten back together."

"I don't know about that," Bridget said.

"No, we wouldn't have. He and I are both so stubborn. We both missed each other, but we were both too damn stubborn to make the first move. You brought us together. So, thank you."

"I should be thanking you, over and over and over again. Speaking of which, how is your arm doing? Are you in any pain? I really hate that you got hurt because of me. And, there's something I've been meaning to ask you for quite some time. How did you end up on that rock in the first place? How did you know we were there?"

"When I couldn't get in touch with David, I called the only person that was sure to know exactly where David was and how to reach him—Michael. Michael, who is usually in so much control, seemed a bit frazzled, so I badgered him into telling me what was going on. At first I tried to convince Michael that you all needed us, and when he told me to stay out of it, I considered calling the police. I thought better of that and decided to show up on my own."

Bridget couldn't help but feel responsible for all the events leading up to this blessed day. After all, it had been her association with Jade that had brought about the chain of events.

One look at Bridget's face and the usually jovial Brianna was suddenly reflective.

"How many times do I have to tell you that you don't have to feel any guilt for any of this? Jade's mother was right. Jade was evil. And, she had no one to blame for that but herself. You hear stories all the time of people who have gone through horrific circumstances and come out on the other end of hell as people deserving of respect and honor. Jade had a tough life, but so do so many other people, including you. She chose her adult circumstances. You, nor her mother, nor Mannersville Group Home had anything to do with the choices she made in life. So, don't waste a moment of guilt thinking about Jade, or the part *she* played in her own death or my broken arm. *You* had nothing to do with any of those things. You have a good and kind heart. You just happened to believe in the wrong person and she took advantage of that at every turn. Even until the bitter end, Bridget, you still maintained that compassion. It was Jade who remained true to the evil inside of her and she paid for that choice with her life. Now, it's time for you to move on. You have found love, honey, despite every pitfall that was placed in both you and David's path; the two of you found one another above all else. Let that be the force that guides you, not guilt. Guilt will only hold you back. Besides, you've got those two beautiful little babies to think about and they deserve to have a mother who is free of unwarranted guilt. Don't you agree?"

Bridget nodded her head in agreement.

"Brianna, if I tell you something, will you promise not to laugh at me or think I'm a damn fool?"

"I'll try. But, I'm not making any promises."

"This is one of the happiest days of my life, but there's a part of me, even with all that happened, that thinks, somehow..."

"That Jade should be here," Brianna finished her thoughts.

"Yeah, does that make me an utter and complete glutton for punishment, or what?"

"No, it doesn't. It makes you human. It makes you a kind, loving person who doesn't stop loving a person just because they're a psycho maniac. And, I'm sorry to dog your girl like that but she was. She was a *serious* psycho. But, no, I don't think you're a fool. We've all been fools for love at one time or another. It's usually for a man. But who says it can't be for a friend?"

In some ways Brianna reminded Bridget of Jade, but in so many countless other ways, she did not. Despite her often coarse exterior, Brianna had a heart of gold. She had proven herself to be a loyal friend who was willing to lay down her life for her, if need be.

"So, you ready to get married or what? Because, that man is about to wear a hole in that ugly green carpet if you don't leave this room right this second."

"Yes, I'm ready. And what do you mean ugly? This is my dream house, down to the very last knick-knack. Someone who loved me very much bought me this house before I even loved myself."

Bridget had never mentioned how the house had come to be and all the events leading up to it. She never told anyone. The story behind it was something special that only she and David shared, and she wanted to keep it that way. However, Brianna could easily guess who had bought the house.

Making her descent down the stairs of her Long Beach home; the home that had been hers for years yet she hadn't even been aware of, she couldn't help wonder what the future held for her and her new family. Stephen had come to terms with the circumstances of Jasmine's birth and he, Bridget and David had sat down and come up with a reasonable way for all of them to share custody of Jasmine. She doubted that she and Stephen would ever be great friends, but she did know that they both would try their damnedest to be great parents and that was enough. She didn't know what she would tell Jasmine and Jacob of the events surrounding their birth, but she had plenty of time to figure that out. When she did, she was confident that everything would work itself out. Although she, David and Stephen had made their fair share of mistakes, they were essentially good people—each of them—and that was the most important thing.

Bridget and David both decided together that the traditional wedding song just wouldn't do. Instead, they had chosen the only song that seemed fit for the occasion. Brianna gave the cue for someone to start the music. They had not shared with anyone what the song would be. All everyone knew was that it was the first song on the blank CD that was already in the player.

At last, my love has come along,
My lonely days are over,
And life is like a song,

Ohhh at last
The stars above are blue
My heart was wrapped up in clover,
The night I looked at you

I found a dream that I could speak to,
A dream that I, can call my own,
I found a thrill, to press my cheek to,
A thrill that I, have never known,

Ohhh you smile, you smile
And then the spell was cast
And here we are in heaven,
For you are mine, at last!

Standing at the foot of the stairs, Bridget stopped and took in her surroundings. Her wedding to Stephen had been grandiose with hundreds of guests and opulence beyond her belief. Yet she had not felt whole. Her marriage to Stephen had been a lie because she was living a lie. Standing there about to marry David, she felt as if she were living life for the very first time. She had been granted an opportunity others seldom get. She had been given a second chance at life. David knew exactly who she was, "warts and all," and she wouldn't have it any other way. For the first time in her life she could just be; no lies, no hiding, no pretense. She could experience the joy of being Bridget.

David's breath literally caught in his throat as he watched Bridget stop before making her way toward him. He wasn't sure if it was his realization of just how beautiful she was or fear that she might be having reservations about their nuptials. One thing he was sure of was how grateful he was that some power greater than both of them had brought the two of them together, despite countless adversities. And, that is when he thought of her—Marie. This time, however, his thoughts were different. So often, through the years, his thoughts had been that of longing and regret. Now, however, he thought of her with thanks. David didn't consider himself a religious man. Yet, he couldn't help but believe that Marie had somehow brought him and Bridget together. Waiting for the love of his life to agree to be his wife, he silently whispered, *thank you*.

"You are going to give that man a heart attack," Brianna whispered in Bridget's ear from her place behind her.

Bridget smiled and looked at David with loving eyes that told him everything was alright. She continued her way over to the man who had loved her long before she even knew she was loved.

Before the minister could start the ceremony, David took Bridget in his arms, eager to hold her, not wanting to let her go.

"Hey," the minister interjected. "You'll both have plenty of time for that—after."

The small gathering of well-wishers, which included a handful of David's relatives, Stephen, Trevor and, surprisingly—Big Rob, all chuckled. Rob, as he now liked to be called, since forming a reputable business with David, was no longer a drug dealer and had chosen to try life straight for a change. He had been very helpful to David and Michael when they were first trying to sort out the history behind Chantal, Jade and Bridget. And, while discussing the circumstances surrounding Jade's death, David was surprised to learn that among other things, Rob was quite a savvy businessman.

"Dearly Beloved," the minister began. "We are gathered together here in the sight of God—and in the face of this company—to join together this man and this woman in holy matrimony, which is commended to be honorable among all men; and therefore—is not by any—to be entered into unadvisedly or lightly—but reverently, discreetly, advisedly and solemnly. Into this holy estate these two persons present now come to be joined. If any person can show just cause why they may not be joined together—let them speak now or forever hold their peace.

"Marriage is the union of husband and wife in heart, body and mind. It is intended for their mutual joy—and for the help and comfort given one another in prosperity and adversity. But more importantly—it is a means through which a stable and loving environment may be attained.

"Through marriage, David and Bridget make a commitment together to face their disappointments—embrace their dreams—realize their hopes—and accept each other's failures. David and Bridget will promise one another to aspire to these ideals throughout their lives together—through mutual understanding—openness—and sensitivity to each other.

"We are here today—before God—because marriage is one of His most sacred wishes—to witness the joining in marriage of David and Bridget. This occasion marks the celebration of love and commitment with which this man and this woman begin their life together. And now—through me—He joins you together in one of the holiest bonds.

"Who gives this woman in marriage to this man?"

Big Rob stood and spoke.

"Her family and friends gathered here today do."

"This is a beginning and a continuation of their growth as individuals," the minister continued. "With mutual care, respect, responsibility and knowledge comes the affirmation of each one's own life happiness, growth and freedom. With respect for individual boundaries comes the freedom to love unconditionally. Within the emotional safety of a loving relationship—the knowledge self-offered one another becomes the fertile soil for continued growth. With care and responsibility toward self and one another comes the potential for full and happy lives.

"By gathering together all the wishes of happiness and our fondest hopes for David and Bridget from all present here, we assure them that our hearts are in tune with theirs. These moments are so meaningful to all of us, for what greater thing is there for two human souls than to feel that they are joined together—to strengthen each other in all labor—to minister to each other in all sorrow—to share with each other in all gladness.

"This relationship stands for love, loyalty, honesty and trust but, most of all, for friendship. Before they knew love, they were friends, and it was from this seed of friendship that their destiny flourished. Do not think that you can direct the course of love, for love, if it finds you worthy, shall direct you.

"Marriage is an act of faith and a personal commitment, as well as a moral and physical union between two people. Marriage has been described as the best and most important relationship that can exist between them. It is the construction of their love and trust into a single growing energy of spiritual life. It is a moral commitment that requires and deserves daily attention. Marriage should be a lifelong consecration of the ideal of loving kindness; backed with the will to make it last."

The minister directed his attention toward David, who was more than a little anxious to continue.

"Do you, David D. McDonnell, take Bridget Grey to be your wife, to live together after God's ordinance, in the holy estate of matrimony? Will you love her, comfort her, honor and keep her, in sickness and in health, for richer, for poorer, for better, for worse, in sadness and in joy, to cherish and continually bestow upon her your heart's deepest devotion, forsaking all others, keeping yourself only unto her for so long as you both shall live?"

"I will."

Then it was Bridget's turn to take her vows.

"Do you, Bridget Grey, take David D. McDonnell to be your husband, to live together after God's ordinance, in the holy estate of matrimony? Will you love him, comfort him, honor and keep him, in sickness and in health, for richer, for poorer, for better, for worse, in sadness and in joy, to cherish and continually bestow upon him your heart's deepest devotion, forsaking all others, keeping yourself only unto him for so long as you both shall live?"

"I will."

By the time Bridget and David got to the exchange of the wedding rings, Bridget was on the brink of completely ruining Brianna's very carefully applied makeup job.

"What token of your love do you offer? Would you place the rings in my hand?"

David turned to Michael, who fumbled for the rings in his pants pocket.

"Don't worry. Don't worry, man. Worst comes to worst, we'll use some beer tabs until we locate the rings."

Noting the look of exasperation on David's face, Michael figured this wasn't the best time to joke.

"Damn, man, can't you take a joke? Here they are. I've got the rings right here."

Michael then handed the rings to the minister, while David rolled his eyes in mock annoyance.

"May these rings be blessed as the symbol of this affectionate unity. These two lives are now joined in one unbroken circle. Wherever they go, may they always return to one another. May these two find in each other the love for which all men and women bear. May they grow in understanding and in compassion. May the home that they establish together be such a place that many will find there a friend. May these rings on their fingers symbolize the touch of the spirit of love in their hearts."

The minister handed one of the rings to David.

"David, in placing this ring on Bridget's finger, repeat after me: Bridget, you are now consecrated to me as my wife, from this day forward. I give you this ring as the pledge of my love and as the symbol of our unity. With this ring, I thee wed."

David gazed into Bridget's eyes. He had waited so long for this day and it was hard for him to believe that he wasn't dreaming. He couldn't remember ever being this happy.

"Bridget, you are now consecrated to me as my wife, from this day forward. I give you this ring as the pledge of my love and as the symbol of our unity. With this ring, I thee wed."

The minister then handed the other ring to Bridget.

"Bridget, in placing this ring on David's finger, repeat after me: David, you are now consecrated to me as my husband, from this day forward. I give you this ring as the pledge of my love and as the symbol of our unity. With this ring, I thee wed."

Bridget thought of the words the minister had spoken, grasping the meaning. Suddenly, for the first time in her life, she was part of someone and someone was a part of her. She had her very own family.

"David, you are now consecrated to me as my husband, from this day forward. I give you this ring as the pledge of my love and as the symbol of our unity. With this ring, I thee wed."

"May you always share with each other the gifts of love, be one in heart and in mind, and may you always create a home together that puts love, generosity, and kindness in your hearts."

"In as much as David and Bridget have consented together in marriage before this company of friends and family, and have pledged their faith, and declared their unity by giving and receiving a ring, they are now joined."

"You've pronounced yourselves husband and wife but remember to always be each other's best friend."

"What therefore…God has joined together…let no man put asunder."

"And so, by the power vested in me, by the State of New York and Almighty God, I now pronounce you man and wife. May your days be good and long upon the earth."

"You may *now* kiss the bride!"

ABOUT THE AUTHOR

Michelle Janine Robinson's short story "Mi Destino" was included in Zane's *New York Times* bestseller *Caramel Flava* and her short story contribution "The Quiet Room" was the first featured story in the *Times* bestseller *Succulent: Chocolate Flava II*. Michelle has contributed to other anthologies, such as *Purple Panties*, with the story she wrote titled "Hailey's Orgasmic Splendor" and *Honey Flava* with the story "The Flow of Qi." Michelle is also a contributor to the oral sex-themed anthology, *Tasting Him*, with her story "A Tongue Is Just A Tongue," edited by Rachel Kramer Bussel. She is the author of the novel *More Than Meets the Eye*, published by Strebor Books in 2011. Michelle is a native New Yorker and the mother of identical twin boys. She is currently working on her next novel, *Serial Typical*. You can find Michelle at www.myspace.com/justef, www.facebook.com/michelle.j. robinson or follow her at www.twitter.com MJanineRobinson.

SERIAL TYPICAL

COMING SUMMER 2012 FROM STREBOR BOOKS

"What are you doing here?" he whispered to his wife, through clenched teeth. "Haven't I told you to *never, ever* bring that thing to my place of business?"

"But Samuel, it won't stop crying. I don't know what to do. I've tried everything."

Her husband forbade her to call the child by name. Therefore, Marie did not. She did *exactly* as she was told, always. The only order she didn't follow was to kill the child.

"I don't care what you do. Just get it out of here! That is your cross to bear, not mine. In fact, if it were up to me, I would sacrifice that evil to the heavens and gain favor with the Lord. Surely, we would be granted entry through the gates of heaven if we did."

"This abomination has been visited upon us because of the evil we have committed. You must atone for your sins, Marie. You must repent for luring me with your wicked and wanton ways. Maybe God will forgive you and free us from this hell. The sins of the flesh, Marie, the sins of the flesh."

Marie often wondered what the people of Lobeco would think of her and Samuel if they could see them now. All the girls back at the South Carolina church she once attended had vied for the attention of the handsome and articulate

Samuel Richardson. His crisp, cocoa-brown complexion and granite pecs, coupled with his extensive knowledge of the Bible, and his quick wit and intelligence, made him quite the catch. He was the complete package, handsome, articulate, intelligent, financially stable and God-fearing, to boot. But Marie had been the one who caught his eye. Most people would have described Marie as a Plain Jane. She wasn't an ugly girl, but she was stick thin, without so much as a bump or a curve. Even her breasts were little more than a molehill, with her 32A bra size. Her wheat-colored complexion, while flawless and free of even the hint of a blemish, was sallow at best. Her clothes consisted mostly of items recovered from Goodwill. She had large feet, at least by female standards, and wore a size twelve shoe, which made it close to impossible to ever find anything even bordering on attractive. Marie and her family were quite poor. She had three brothers and one sister, and their single mother just barely survived, caring for them all on public assistance. Their father had abandoned them long ago and her mother made it clear to her eldest daughter, Marie, that her only escape from poverty would be to marry well.

Samuel's father, on the other hand, was Lobeco's town pastor and everyone assumed Samuel would eventually follow in his father's footsteps. Samuel's mother had been the child of affluent parents, and when she died of cancer, she left both Samuel and his father well-fixed in the way of money.

Therefore, most of the people in their hometown, especially the young women, were quite surprised when Samuel chose to spend most of his time with the poor, plain and painfully shy Marie.

Samuel's father could not forgive him when he discovered that Marie had gotten pregnant. He had always had high hopes for his only son and assumed that Marie was a temporary dalliance that he would eventually tire of. The pair married quickly and left South Carolina, at the pastor's insistence. It was his fear that their dirty little family secret would be revealed and his reputation would be ruined.

Marie was crestfallen. For the longest time, she believed that Sam's father accepted her. At first she thought his father's reaction was purely because they were having a child out of wedlock. After accidentally overhearing a conversation between Sam and his father, she knew it was more than that. That conversation was one of the most difficult things she had ever had to come to terms with, and the most difficult conversation to ever forget.

"How could you choose her, of all people? You could have had your pick of girls. Why her? A girl like her belongs with her own kind."

"Dad, what are you saying? You're a preacher. You've built this entire family and your parishioners' lives on loving our fellow man. Now I see what you really meant. Fellow man to you only includes the more affluent among us. I love Marie. She's got a heart of gold and she's got courage. She supports her family and gives me unconditional love, and she does all of this without having any money at all. Our child is going to be lucky to have her as a mother."

"You have brought shame to this family. I spent my life building our place in this community, and I will not have you and that urchin ruin the reputation I spent so much time creating."

"What are you saying?"

"I'm saying, if you must be with this woman, it needs to be someplace other than here."

"So, you would drive us out of our own community in order to preserve an image?"

"What we have is more than just an image. We have a responsibility. I have a responsibility to set a good example, and what kind of example would I be, if my own son was irresponsible enough to bring a bastard child into the world."

"Thanks, Dad. Thanks a lot. You have made this so much easier for me. This has been the only home I've ever known but now I think I *can* leave. I *want* to leave. I know now better than ever why I chose her. She's more real than any of you in this *community* will ever be. You think I could have done better just because she doesn't have any money, and because her home and clothing doesn't fit some sort of misguided image you have. There's one thing I know for sure, though. None of those girls you handpicked for me would have wanted a thing to do with me without my family name or without my money. None of them would have had the sheer will to survive what Marie has survived. She's got something none of them will ever have. Hell, she's got something you and I will probably never even have. She's got strength. Her life has been so damn tough, but she's still here, still standing. She hasn't given up."

Marie remembered standing there as her pain melted away into overwhelming love for Samuel. She was afraid of leaving the only home she had ever known, but she knew with Samuel by her side, she would be fine.

Samuel never knew Marie had heard the entire conversation and was not eager to share it with Marie, so he convinced her that moving away would be best for all of them. He explained to her that he knew he would never be able to fulfill his father's dream of becoming a preacher, and had decided that more than anything, he wanted to create another life, someplace far away. Samuel had always been very creative and he decided he would try his hand at being an artist of some sort. He was talented and loved sculpting and painting and convinced Marie that New York was the place for them.

In order to ease the fear and tension of Marie leaving her entire family behind, he assured her that once the baby was born, they would return to South Carolina so everyone could get to know their new addition. He had no real desire to return but had every intention of keeping his promise for Marie's sake, in the hope that once they settled in New York, she would love it so much that their return to South

Carolina would be nothing more than a brief visit. All of that changed once the baby was born.

Marie's pregnancy was a difficult one. She suffered through morning sickness from the very beginning until the very end. And from five months until the time she gave birth, she was constantly being rushed to the hospital with false contractions, which she had to be medicated for, since it was too early in her pregnancy to have a safe birth. For months, Samuel reasoned that it was little more than the stress of being in a large new city and being away from her family. He told himself that as long as she and the baby got through the pregnancy safely, everything would be fine—that is until after Marie gave birth and it was readily apparent that their baby was not exactly *normal*.

It didn't take long for Marie to witness the change in Samuel. Within minutes after she gave birth, he left her in the delivery room and didn't return until the next day. When he did return, Marie was surprised to find him holding something she never expected to see. In his hand was a Bible. Although Samuel had never voiced with anyone else how torn he was about his father's expectations for him, he and Marie had often discussed how disinterested he was in becoming a preacher and how conflicted he was about religion in general.

Eventually, the baby was released from the hospital. However, the doctors made it very clear that there were certain hard decisions that would have to be made by both her and Samuel, as the parents. With each passing day, Marie watched as Samuel sank deeper and deeper into despair. Whenever she mentioned all that had been discussed with her regarding their baby's care, he became angry and then sullen. He would lock himself in the basement of their home and she would hear all sorts of banging. She assumed he was working on some sort of artwork and was happy that he had found an outlet for his pain. She decided she wouldn't bother him and would take on all the responsibility of caring for their baby alone, for as long as she had to. It went on that way for several months. By the time Samuel resurfaced, he was a mere shell of the handsome, vibrant suitor she had once known. Not only that, where he had once been doubtful as to whether or not he wanted to follow in his father's footsteps, he had now become obsessed with religion; so much so, that Marie became more than just a bit concerned. Not a word was spoken nor a deed carried out that didn't revolve around the words of the Bible. Although Marie had been raised in the church, she could clearly see the difference between a healthy reverence of God and an unhealthy obsession.

While she loved her baby, she was devoted to Samuel. Any thoughts she had, any desires she held, took a back seat to his. When he first voiced his wish that they abandon their baby, Marie was shocked, but knew that she would never give in to what he wanted. She hoped that eventually, he would snap out of it and see things for what they were. They were a family with a child that wasn't born like most children, but it was nothing that couldn't be dealt with. As time moved on, Samuel was even more vocal about his wishes. However, he had gone from putting the baby up for adoption, to abandoning it at a church somewhere, to eventually insinuating that there were ways they could ensure as if the child never even existed. That's when Marie started to get frightened and decided she could never leave Samuel alone with their baby. That was also when she decided she would do anything and everything else he wanted. She believed if she cared for him well enough, and made him happy enough, everything would be okay. She never contradicted any of his other wishes. As time passed, she considered it a miracle that the child was even still alive, given Samuel's thoughts on the matter. From the moment she left the hospital, and Samuel demanded they leave the hospital without the baby, the only times she ever shirked his authority was when it involved the baby. Marie had wanted a baby more than anything and it didn't matter what their child looked like. All she cared about was that it was created by her and Samuel. He, on the other hand, considered their child a spawn of the devil, and frequently referred to their baby as an abomination. According to Samuel, their *situation* was just punishment, because they had *lain together in sin*. After multiple conversations and constant coaxing from Marie, Samuel made it quite clear that he would never acknowledge the child as his own.

One day, in particular, the baby had been crying more than usual. Marie was all alone in a big city with no friends or family to help her. And the perfect marriage she always thought she would have with Samuel, was little more than a shambles. However, he was all that she had, so she decided to visit him at work, hoping that he would, once and for all, help her or at the very least, feel empathy for their small baby's discomfort. From the moment she arrived at his office and saw the look on his face, she knew she had made a terrible mistake.

"Woman, why are you standing there looking like a damn fool? I have work to do. Why on earth are you here?"

"I'm sorry, Samuel. I just didn't know what to do. The baby's been crying since you left. I've tried everything."

"You know what you need to do. I've told you time and time again what needs to be done. Just go home, now, and do it! And, tonight, we will pray together for redemption."

As she left, Samuel knew that she had no intention of following through with the instructions he had so often given her; to put a stop to the baby's endless wails. Therefore, he would have no other alternative but to handle its discipline himself.

Eventually, the baby wasn't a baby anymore, and Samuel began working longer hours. Marie welcomed the ten to fourteen hours a day he spent at work. Trying to run interference between him and a toddler was exhausting for her, especially when she began to realize that when she wasn't quick enough, it was their child who paid the price.

The bruises were the first thing she noticed. At first, she tried to convince herself they were normal bumps and bruises that every child got. Eventually, she realized it was so much more. Samuel was angry one day and locked the child in the basement. When Marie first heard the cries and the pounding on the door, she did everything she could do to make it right. It was the first time Marie was truly afraid. She was afraid for both of them and not sure what Samuel would do, so she didn't open the door. She did everything she could to make the basement a comfortable place for the child, and it eventually became a permanent bedroom. For a while, she thought that would ease the tension, until she realized Samuel made it a point to visit the basement often and antagonize the child as frequently as possible. It wasn't until Marie was in a minor car accident and had to go to the hospital that she realized how fragile the situation was. She had only been at the hospital for a few hours, but by the time she returned home, she found blood on the walls. And what she found in the basement was the most frightening thing she had ever seen. Samuel had never lied about anything he did. However, this time, he swore to God that he had nothing to do with what happened, and Marie couldn't help but believe him. She did her very best to make everything right again. This time, she had to be more than a mother and protector. She had to use what little skill she possessed to nurse her child back to health.

DAD

It had been a long hard ride, but Marie had done everything in her power to make this day possible. Despite the pain endured, it was hard to believe that eighteen years had passed and her *baby* was now going off to college.

"Thank you, Mom."

It was three small words, spoken in a whisper in passing, that Marie never expected to hear. She considered herself no better than Samuel. She was sure the guilt she felt would never leave her, but knowing that her child appreciated what little she had done, was enough to ease her guilt a small bit.

Freedom had finally arrived. There would be no more weekends that stretched into endless darkness, never knowing the difference between night and day; no more dull aches of hunger, the withdrawal of food imposed at the simplest infraction. There would be no more beatings, or any of the other atrocities, perpetuated from the confines of the dank basement that had become a prison. Freedom had arrived in the form of education. College awaited; college and the greatest gift anyone could ever imagine: sweet freedom.

Marie sat in the living room, listening as her only child packed, knowing it would probably be the last time they ever saw each other. She had tried to be a good mother but knew she had failed. Her last redeeming act had been to ensure that her child went to college. She had been very secretive in her efforts, hiding books anywhere and everywhere, so that Samuel would never find them. As soon as Samuel went off to work, she would spring into action; first, researching how best to home-school her child, then ensuring that her educational efforts met the standards that allowed this day to come to pass. Her self-esteem had always been so low, but somehow her teaching efforts allowed her to feel some level of self-pride. If not for her efforts, this day would never have happened. She had done it. In her mind, it was the very least that she could do. That is, until today. Her work wasn't finished. There was one last self-sacrificing act that only she could carry out. It would be the only way to ensure some semblance of a life for her child. She hoped that the departure would be uneventful, and there would be no need to carry out her plans. Somehow, though, she knew it would not, and she would be forced to take a stand, once and for all. She knew Samuel would never allow their child to leave quietly.

Over the years, his descent into madness had been progressive, but great. He was now little more than a vicious wielder of punishment, doling out his form of justice; first, to their baby and eventually, to Marie as well. Sex with him had become some twisted form of worship, release and punishment that Marie was sure she would never understand. After all, how could a sane person understand the actions of the insane? While she often considered leaving, her love of Samuel, albeit illogical, had not abated. She still adored him as much as she ever had. In fact, her adoration had been replaced with a certain protectiveness, since she fully knew that he was stark raving mad—and subject to confinement at any time—that is, if anyone ever discovered what went on behind closed doors.

Downstairs, in the basement, Samuel stood in the doorway, smiling, silently taunting the only child he had ever known; the same child he never acknowledged as his own. His words spewed forth like venom.

"The world knows what you are, you know," Samuel said. "You are, and will always be, an abomination, and college and moving away will never change that. Even the doctors can't fix what you are. God knows, I tried. I know exactly what you are, and soon the world will know. You will never know peace. There is no peace for those created in the demon's image."

"You might just be right. But, you know what, if the world knows what I am, then it knows what you are as well. After all, didn't you help to create me? I don't just mean your rancid seed. I'm referring to the hell you have subjected me to all these years. Everything that I am, I owe to you, you and my poor, disillusioned mother. You are a sick and evil man, who shrouds his evil in the name of The Lord. You can keep your *Lord*. I don't need Him *or* you. You have made life for me here hell on earth, so how much worse could it get for me? Yes, you can keep Your Lord. I don't need him and I definitely don't need you! My only regret is that my mother will die here, never having known what life could have been like if she hadn't been married to a sick fucking bastard like you!"

Samuel's face contorted into a shape and had taken on a hue reminiscent of complete and utter evil. Suddenly, he realized he no longer had any power. For years, he had waited for the constant reminder of his inadequacies to meet with some obvious and ill-fated destiny, yet it had never come to pass. Here it stood, taunting him, ridiculing him, and taking the name of the Lord in vain, all the while standing triumphantly, in his own home. He would not stand for it!

Upstairs in the living room, Marie sat biting at her last remaining fingernail, the others now painfully gnawed to the quick. The silence was more deafening to her ears than the eighteen years of screams and wails she had been forced to helplessly listen to. The threat of impending doom reverberated throughout her entire being. It occurred to Marie that she had never been a champion to her only child, but today, God-willing, she would be. The basement door slamming was the last sound she heard, after what seemed like endlessly agonizing moments of silence. Marie raced downstairs, taking the steps two at a time.

Throughout the years, Marie had proven to be artful at turning a deaf ear to all she heard. But, somehow, she had always avoided *seeing* anything altogether. The moment she entered the basement, she was mortified. The full realization of how her child had probably been tortured by her husband time and time again, became a far too tangible reality. Memories swirled around her, dizzying her, crippling her, until she saw what he held in his hand. It was a crude object, of twisted metal, carefully hand-crafted by an evil man with evil intentions, for the sole purpose of inflicting pain, the same object that had probably harmed her child so many years ago. Marie felt as though she had risen from some invisible tomb, stronger than she had ever been, maybe even invincible.

"You bastard!" she yelled. "There never was an accident! How could you? How could you mutilate your own child? I always knew! I always knew it was you!"

From the moment Marie rose from her bed early that morning, her actions had been set on autopilot. She went about her usual day, preparing breakfast, making the beds. Everything had been all so commonplace, that is, until she took her place in the living room, while her child prepared to leave. Marie settled in and waited. As she sat, she maintained a firm grasp on the Glock she had purchased from a neighborhood thug just a few days earlier.

"Marie? What are you doing? Where did you get that? Now, now calm down. I was just... I was... Now, hold on a damn minute! You mean to tell me, you're holding a gun on me in my own home! This is *me*, Marie. What are you doing? It's *me*, me! There is no reason..."

While Samuel pleaded with his typically dutiful wife to lower the gun she was holding, Marie considered the implications and watched and listened as Samuel alternated between being apologetic, angry and confused. As he approached her, fully prepared to pounce, Marie Richardson aimed the gun and fired.